Her Scandalous Intentions

Everything about James seemed to set him apart from the ordinary. Perhaps it was the champagne, but searing insight suddenly pierced her awareness; her whole life had been more poignant, more affecting, more . . . colorful since her association with him. Instinctively she knew that his touches and kisses belied a more powerful encounter that awaited them. Her body clamored for it and she desperately wanted to know.

"Is it possible, James, to . . . explore the attraction between us?"

He sucked in his breath, his arms tightening around her. "You do not understand what you are proposing."

"I think I do." She was coming to the awful conclusion that her life would never be the same after James, that once the season ended, she could never fall into the insipid arms of a less magnificent man.

"Bloody hell, Charlotte!"

His mouth claimed hers with a ravishing fervor . . .

Other AVON ROMANCES

ALL MY DESIRE by *Margaret Moore*
A CHANCE AT LOVE by *Beverly Jenkins*
CHEROKEE WARRIORS: THE LOVER by *Genell Dellin*
HIGHLAND ROGUES: THE WARRIOR BRIDE
by *Lois Greiman*
HIS BRIDE by *Gayle Callen*
THE MACKENZIES: COLE by *Ana Leigh*
THE ROSE AND THE SHIELD by *Sara Bennett*

Coming Soon

ONCE A DREAMER by *Candice Hern*
THE WARRIOR'S GAME by *Denise Hampton*

And Don't Miss These
ROMANTIC TREASURES
from Avon Books

THE BRIDE BED by *Linda Needham*
THE IRRESISTIBLE MACRAE: BOOK THREE OF
THE HIGHLAND LORDS by *Karen Ranney*
WHEN IT'S PERFECT by *Adele Ashworth*

SARI ROBINS

Her Scandalous Intentions

AVON BOOKS
An Imprint of HarperCollinsPublishers

This is a work of fiction. Names, characters, places, and incidents are products of the author's imagination or are used fictitiously and are not to be construed as real. Any resemblance to actual events, locales, organizations, or persons, living or dead, is entirely coincidental.

AVON BOOKS
An Imprint of HarperCollins*Publishers*
10 East 53rd Street
New York, New York 10022-5299

Copyright © 2002 by Sari Earl
ISBN: 0-06-050353-X
www.avonromance.com

First Avon Books paperback printing: December 2002

Avon Trademark Reg. U.S. Pat. Off. and in Other Countries, Marca Registrada, Hecho en U.S.A.
HarperCollins ® is a registered trademark of HarperCollins Publishers Inc.

Printed in the U.S.A.

10 9 8 7 6 5 4 3 2 1

To Olen, always

Acknowledgments

I am forever indebted to my #1 sister, premiere writer and best friend, Nanci.

Special thanks to Mom and Dad and Lenny and Amy and our family and friends for their constant support.

My gratitude to Lyssa Keusch and the rest of the exemplary Avon Books/HarperCollins staff.

Thanks to The Beau Monde, GRW and RWA.

Prologue

Southbridge, England
May 9, 1814

"I will take that package or I will take your life. Your choice entirely."

The young man stared up the barrel of the thief's pistol into the steeliest blue-black eyes he had ever encountered. He noted his challenger's fine clothes and magnificent stallion and knew he was in way over his head.

"D . . . don't shoot," he said, raising an arm in the air while trying, with difficulty, to keep his mare under control. "That bloke didn't pay me near enough money for the likes of this."

His pistol never wavering, the fancy gentleman released his reins and extended his velvety-gloved palm. "Then hand over the package and you'll have earned yourself more than you bargained for—your life."

"Fine . . . fine. Just don't kill me, sir. I've a family to feed,

1

and they are counting on me," the young man replied fearfully, reaching into his coat and pulling out the mysterious packet. He carefully inched his mare next to the stallion and placed the package in the gentleman's outstretched hand. "I can't see that there's anything really that valuable inside," he chatted nervously. "Just a paper and a funny piece of metal."

The thief narrowed his eyes. "Are you literate?"

"I don't think so, sir." He chewed his lip. "My wife makes me go to the King's church on Sundays."

"Can you read?" Stone-faced, the gentleman spoke patiently.

The young man's heart hammered in his chest. "N . . . no, sir. Never had the need to learn, sir."

The gentleman opened the packet and looked inside. Satisfied, he disengaged his pistol and stuffed the bundle and his firearm into his saddlebag.

"Maybe this is enough to be worthy of your silence." The lithe, finely clothed man reached under his elegant black riding coat, pulled out a large coin, and tossed it.

The young man's face broke into a wide gap-toothed grin. "Yes, sir! Thank you, sir!"

"Off with you, now, before I change my mind," warned the gentleman. The youth didn't have to be told twice. He took off, racing his mare as if the devil himself was at his back. Well, maybe he was. If so, thought the young man, he had an exceedingly fine tailor.

Chapter 1

Clouds drifted lazily overhead, intermittently blocking the sun and making shadows dance across the green meadow below. With her straw hat beside her on the grass, the cool breeze gently lifted Charlotte's long auburn locks and caressed her neck. She stifled a sigh. Coming to Southbridge had been a mistake. Charlotte resolved to weather this house party and keep a low profile, if that was possible with the matchmaking Balstrams. Still, it was lovely to be in the country again.

Having escaped the festivities, she sat atop a low-lying hill overlooking a small meadow and its surrounding clusters of trees. Charlotte felt as if she could be a million miles from London instead of a mere day's carriage ride. She drew idly in her notebook, lamenting Henrietta's influence in bringing her to this house party in the first instance.

"You must come to our gathering, Charlotte," her friend had avowed. "It will be *the* event—outside London, of course. Mama says there'll be many eligible bachelors at the house party and you must make haste, or Mr. Blanton will begin pressing his suit again. I would hate to see you married to a man you cannot tolerate."

"Do not pretend you're so concerned for my unmarried state, Henrietta," Charlotte chided playfully. "You just want the pretense of my attendance to mask your trysts with your darling Mr. Frickerby."

"What utter nonsense, Charlotte. I'm too polite by far to point out that you are nearly two years my senior and not getting any younger."

Charlotte crossed her arms and raised a dubious brow.

"And what if I do want to be with my beloved?" Henrietta answered candidly. "Would it hurt for you to be a little helpful while getting yourself out? It will be a whole week and Stuart and I can have many, ah, moments, together."

Charlotte suppressed a smile. "I'm quite sure your parents wouldn't appreciate your finer moments with Mr. Frickerby. Perhaps there is something to their dissatisfaction with his suit?"

"I know that with you there to ease Mama's and Papa's concerns, they'll learn to accept our union. You know how Mama and Papa adore you. They are forever going on about how 'Charlotte would never do this,' or 'Charlotte is such a proper young lady.' "

"I wish your parents would talk to my Aunt Sylvie about all my sterling attributes." She sighed. "Just this week she was telling me how improper it is for me to volunteer at the veterans' hospital."

"You know she's not opposed to your charitable work; she just prefers you do it less personally. I cannot argue with her there, Charlotte." Henrietta shuddered dramatically. "The one time you took me to that dreadful place nearly had me in the vapors. What a fright that horrible man gave me."

"That 'horrible man' was trying to direct you to the general's office. You were lost, if I recall."

"But he spoke to me!"

"How else did you expect him to tell you the way? Draw you a picture?" Charlotte shook her head, exasperated. "These men are facing terrible difficulties. Yet many do it with humor and great fortitude. I gain much from my friendships there."

"What could you possibly have in common with those men? What could you talk about?"

"You'd be surprised. I've learned some of the most fascinating things." She smiled mischievously.

"Such as?"

"Such as what happens between a husband and a wife."

Henrietta's eyes widened in shock. "They actually talk to you about such matters? Scandalous!"

"Oh, no. But if you spend enough time around the fellows, it is amazing what one picks up. These men have experienced much more than you or I."

"Of course they have, Charlotte. They are men." Henrietta said. "That's exactly why their experiences are not necessarily useful to us."

"I disagree. Why, just the other day, Lieutenant Freeman was teaching me how to defend myself."

Henrietta huffed, "Defend yourself? That's what gentlemen are *for*, Charlotte."

"You never know when you might need to fend off the overenthusiastic suitor, Henrietta. It's remarkable what one can accomplish with one's elbows and knees."

"I do not need to fend off anyone. I have my Stuart, and despite the unsavory habits you're developing, my parents are still under the impression that you are perfect. So will you help me or not?"

Charlotte hesitated; a week away with a house full of eligible bachelors and matchmaking mamas did not fit within her plans for remaining unnoticed. But Henrietta had whined, "Please, Charlotte? I am so much in love. Are you

going to deny me true happiness?" Charlotte somehow
doubted that what Henrietta felt for Stuart Frickerby was
more than a passing infatuation; she could barely stay at-
tached to anything from sunrise to sunset. Still, who was she
to stand in the way of her friend's great wish? Finally she relented, not only because of Henrietta's begging, but because
she wanted to avoid her Aunt Sylvie's displeasure.

As soon as Charlotte had completed six months of mourning for her father, Aunt Sylvie had campaigned for her to find
a suitable husband. "Charlotte, you must become more social, and this party is exactly the kind of engagement in
which to do so. I understand that the Duke of Girard himself
will be attending. He is the best *ton*. It is high time you took
the matter of securing a husband seriously. I will not have
you settling for one of your broken soldiers. You are a beautiful young lady, and you'd do so well if you'd only apply
yourself."

Charlotte's attempts at deflecting Aunt Sylvie did little
good. Even reminding her aunt of the difficulties of the last
few years, when her father lay ill and dying, did not help.
During that time, no one had questioned her lack of interest
in marriage. They'd just assumed she was too overwhelmed
with caring for her failing father and helping to manage their
numerous households to address her own needs. And she let
them believe this. For no one knew the unfortunate history
behind Charlotte's unique standards regarding marriage.

Between Aunt Sylvie's pressure and Henrietta's whining,
Charlotte had relented and agreed to attend the Balstram
party. Henrietta was thrilled. Charlotte had regretted the decision ever since. As soon as she arrived at the party, Lord
and Lady Balstram, lovely people Charlotte adored, began
trying to pair her off with one of their two sons. Either would
do. How could she explain that although their sons were
wealthy, titled, and well connected, they didn't suit Char-

lotte's specific requirements for a husband? At her first opportunity she took off on the long walk that had led her to this gentle hilltop.

The sun shifted toward the horizon. Charlotte sighed, knowing she needed to leave the peace of her surroundings and return to the festivities. Just then, she spied a movement in the meadow below. A young rider emerged from a cluster of trees, racing at full speed. He kept looking fearfully over his shoulder as if expecting pursuit. Charlotte was intrigued. The image of the frightened man racing through the wind was a welcome distraction and the perfect excuse to avoid returning to the house.

She flipped to a new page in her notepad and quickly sketched the escaping rider. As she drew, Charlotte kept her eye on the cluster of trees in the meadow below, waiting curiously.

Suddenly, James Morgan, the Duke of Girard, appeared from the trees, masterfully riding his stallion as if he and the black were one. Noting his olive complexion and raven dark hair, Charlotte recalled Lady Balstram's referring to his mother's Spanish heritage.

He was devastatingly handsome, had a body Adonis would envy, and was well polished, but for all his appealing attributes, Girard seemed inscrutable, aloof. That first day in the Balstram dining room, it was not his dark good looks or refined charm that had struck Charlotte, but his uniquely compelling eyes—a midnight blue so dark they resembled black diamonds. His glittering gaze did not seem to miss much, but offered little hint of the man inside.

As Charlotte watched him confidently gallop toward the house, she wondered at Girard's clandestine encounter with the frightened young rider. She had no doubt they'd met, and at this remote location. Charlotte well knew that it was a good hour's walk from the main house to this secluded spot.

Charlotte's heart jumped as Girard carefully scanned the horizon, spotting her on the hilltop and abruptly wheeling his mount toward her. His chiseled face was set in a cold, unreadable mask. *Not pleased to see me, but then again, he doesn't seem to be a particularly cheerful man*, thought Charlotte critically. Now that she was taking the time to consider it, she never once recalled seeing Girard laugh, or even smile. When he reached her, he halted his horse and dismounted.

He held his mount's reins loosely in his gloved hands. "Greetings, Miss Hastings."

She gathered her skirts and pulled herself up, not wanting to be at a complete disadvantage before him. She curtseyed. "Your grace."

"Lovely day."

"Quite." She didn't intend to fawn over him, as did the rest of the *ton*.

As his eyes traveled the length of her plain blue muslin dress, Charlotte withheld her grimace. Although her frock was embroidered around the collar and wrists, it was a simple yet serviceable walking dress, not the high fashion of most of the ladies in residence at the party. Self-consciously, Charlotte leaned over and lifted up her flowered straw hat, holding it in front of her, almost like a shield.

"I see no horse. Did you walk all the way from the house?" Girard raised his eyebrow, skeptical.

"Yes, your grace."

"By yourself?"

"That's the point of getting away to the country, is it not?"

He ignored her tone and commented thoughtfully, "It is quite a distance. It must have taken you some time." She gave no answer, as he seemed uninterested in hearing one.

"Have you been here long?" There. He had finally hit upon it.

"Yes, your grace." There was a pregnant pause and she

wondered how he would approach the topic of the fleeing young rider.

"May I?" He gestured to her notebook. Surprised, she nodded and handed it to him.

Girard dropped the stallion's reins and the horse stepped a few feet away, lowered his great head, and began nibbling the soft green grass. The duke opened the notebook, and perused her sketches of the veterans' hospital and the boys in varying degrees of laughter and distress. Her free sketching captured the precious moments she encountered in life, allowing her later to expand on the emotion back in her studio. Her art was her greatest escape in life, whether it was her watercolors, sculpting, or sketching. Girard did not look up as he spoke. "These are quite good."

"Thank you, your grace."

"Let us sit a moment, shall we?" Without waiting for her reply, he took her hand and led her to sit. Charlotte was shocked at the contact of his soft leather gloves with her skin; she had removed her gloves to sketch. Tingles raced up her arm to the rest of her body, causing the small hairs on her neck to stand on end. Unsettled by his sudden nearness and the intimate touch, Charlotte quickly removed her hand, swept her skirt up around her, and sat a little away from him. She set her hat down and pulled her gloves from her pocket, slipping them on.

If Girard noticed her discomfiture, he did not show it. He sat down, nimbly crossing his lean, muscled legs before him as if sitting on a grassy hilltop were commonplace for him. As he studied her sketches, she took the opportunity to study him. Although she had no interest in him, Charlotte could see what had women vying for the privilege of his bed and men contending for the benefit of his counsel.

He carried himself with an air of restrained power. It emanated not just from his title, but from the man himself. He was lean, well muscled, and agile, and he reminded Charlotte of a lion, ready to trounce any enemy threatening his pride. The only thing about his appearance that gave him any softness was his unfashionably long wavy jet-black hair. A stray curl hung on his forehead, making him look younger than his almost thirty years.

Everything else about him epitomized detached elegance. His well-made riding attire accentuated the tone of his slim waist and broad shoulders. His buckskin breeches were fashionably tight above his shiny black Hessians, making Charlotte's heart beat a little faster as she perused the strong, hard thighs of his muscled legs. My, the sun was suddenly getting hot.

Girard flipped the pages to view the various hospital patients, stopping at General Cumseby, the man who managed the financing and operation of the army hospital. With the war over, interest in veterans had waned. Still, the general championed their plight and ensured the hospital's operation.

"General Cumseby." Girard nodded in apparent approval.

"You are acquainted?" Charlotte asked, surprised.

"Yes. Excellent fellow. Do you know him well?"

"I consider him a dear friend."

He only nodded. Finally, he got to the end of the sketches and saw Charlotte's hasty but detailed sketch of the frightened rider. He looked up at her sharply, narrowing his midnight blue eyes, giving her a look that could freeze summer. Although her mouth suddenly went dry, Charlotte stared back at him, unblinking. He was the one having clandestine meetings; she had nothing to hide. As his gaze bore into hers, Charlotte licked her lips. He would not do anything untoward; he was, after all, a gentleman.

With absolute authority, Girard ripped the page out of her notebook. Charlotte's temper flared. He had not even bothered to ask her about the drawing.

"May I ask, your grace, what leave you have to tamper with my artwork?" she questioned through clenched teeth.

"I have leave to keep my business just that—my business," he replied dismissively.

Charlotte seethed with frustrated anger at his presumption. She had barely finished her thought when her mouth opened to suggest, "I will have to ask our lovely hostess about the man in my drawing. I'm sure he could be added to the party with little inconvenience."

His dark eyes glittered warningly and his chiseled features hardened further. He suddenly seemed . . . dangerous. Not necessarily a gentleman after all. They sat considering each other, the tense quiet disturbed only by the shriek of a scavenger bird in the distance.

"Maybe you should be mindful of your own interests," he cautioned.

Despite still being angry, Charlotte decided it would be prudent to regroup. "I would gladly provide you with any one of my sketches if you desired. Perhaps you should just ask for it politely instead of being so . . . forceful." She was proud she didn't use one of the other words in mind: arrogant, tyrannical, imposing. Girard looked affronted, ready to chastise her, but then he turned to look out over the horizon. Charlotte watched him warily.

He faced her, suddenly becoming all that was charming. "Miss Hastings. Maybe I was a bit . . . overeager about your artwork." Although she didn't move, Charlotte felt a palpable relief. He continued, "I'd appreciate having this sketch." He held it and said quietly, "And may I have your word you'll not discuss the events that occurred or anything you've seen today?"

"May I have your word of honor that you are not engaging in any nefarious, illegal, or immoral activity?"

Girard's nostrils flared and the muscle in his jaw jumped.

Looking him squarely in the eye, Charlotte sat awaiting his answer. She knew that she pressed him by daring to question his honor. He cursed under his breath and looked away.

"Excuse me?" she asked.

He shook his head, exasperated, and bit out, "I give you my word."

"Then you have mine, and the sketch," she replied, satisfied.

He folded the paper and placed it in his coat pocket.

Catching her gaze, he pursed his lips. "You are from Bury St. Edmunds, are you not?"

"Waveney, actually. Bury St. Edmunds is the nearest village."

"Did you know Mr. Richard Blanton?"

"Yes. But not very well. He was our nearest neighbor but spent much of his time in London. He passed away a few years ago."

"Five."

"I beg your pardon, your grace?"

"He passed away five years ago."

"Oh."

Silence. The wind picked up and the clouds began racing toward the horizon.

"You are acquainted with his son, Mortimer Blanton?"

She stiffened. "I am."

He frowned. Two birds twittered overhead, one chasing the other. Abruptly Girard stood and held out his hand. "May I escort you back to the house?"

Charlotte eyed his extended hand warily. She was not afraid of him; yet there were undercurrents between them that she did not understand. His actions today were uncommon, his touch disconcerting.

She shook her head. "That will not be necessary, your grace."

"I insist."

Charlotte placed her small hand in his larger one. He gent-ly lifted her from the ground as if she were lighter than a feather. She quickly looked down and brushed the grass from her skirt, hiding the heat that showed in her face. Even with gloves between them, touching the man left her feeling hot and giddy. It was irritating, to say the least.

He gracefully leaned over, lifted her straw hat from the ground, and handed it to her.

Charlotte set her hat on her head, tying the ribbons under her chin. Frowning, she touched her nose.

"What's wrong?" he asked.

"My Aunt Sylvie will have my head for each new freckle on my face." She sighed.

She tried not to blush as Girard's gaze settled on the little spray of freckles on her nose and cheeks. He shrugged. "I hadn't noticed." Looking down, pretending to adjust her skirts, Charlotte hid a small, knowing smile. The duke had not noticed anything about her until just a few moments ago.

"Your Aunt Sylvie is . . . ?"

"The Countess of Grandby. I know she means well, but she can be a little exasperating. She is forever after me to try all kinds of miracle cures to erase my freckles. Too bad freckles aren't the fashion." She shook her head. "So much fuss over twenty-seven little freckles."

He looked up from adjusting his sleeves. "You counted?" Charlotte blushed, certain her cheeks were crimson.

"I find that style has little to do with ever-changing trends," he commented. "It is the merit of a person that war-rants distinction."

"Do not judge a book by its cover." Her lips lifted at the corners as she accepted his proffered arm.

"A sound policy."

"I wonder how many members of the *ton* would agree with you."

He grimaced. "Point well taken."

A hare stood on its hind legs, warily examining their progress. The wind picked up and playfully lifted Girard's raven locks.

As they walked down the hill with the stallion, she looked up at Girard. "You do not seem to be a slave to fashion, your grace."

He raised an eyebrow inquiringly.

"Your hair."

He tilted his head in assent. "We all have our vanities."

"Some of us more than others."

Girard's lips curved into the ghost of a smile. He regarded her as if for the first time.

She looked up at him questioningly. "What?"

"Nothing. I am just . . ." He seemed at a loss for words. *Unused to smiling?* thought Charlotte. "Unaccustomed to hearing anyone joke so good-naturedly about her shortcomings."

She shrugged. "Life is amusing."

They continued on in companionable silence. She sighed contentedly, thankful for the company of a man who didn't insist on being entertained. He had an agreeable scent as well; sharp yet sweet—musky, that was it. He walked with catlike grace, managing to match her shorter stride with ease. All in all, he was a pleasant walking companion, and she couldn't help but feel a little flattered by his silent but insistent attention. She didn't fool herself that the man had any real interest in her, other than in keeping her quiet, but he was heart-beatingly attractive, in an objective sense, of course.

The clouds danced flirtatiously about the sun as the sky darkened and the air grew moist. A storm was brewing.

Chapter 2

That evening Charlotte avoided Girard entirely. Despite the pleasant walk back to the house, Charlotte felt that the duke was just too handsome for his own good. A man generally had to work harder to get her heart to skip a beat, and she was unwilling to allow this one to affect her further. Moreover, the time alone with him had been more than she'd spent with any of her "suitors," and she didn't want him to think she was one of his many followers.

At times Charlotte felt his eyes on her from across the room. He watched her curiously, as if she were a new type of specimen he did not fully understand. But she didn't dwell on Girard, as she was busy gently trying to discourage young Mr. Harold Balstram, while keeping his sister Henrietta from embarrassing herself over Mr. Frickerby. Finally, she had a respite from the Balstram *affairs de coeur* and sat beside Mr. Somersby, another guest with whom Charlotte felt comfortable. He was in his usual good spirits.

15

"I never did ask you, Charlotte—how is your brother Edward dealing with his duties?"

"I imagine as well as anyone could have hoped, for someone as young as one-and-twenty. At least Papa had time to prepare him."

"I knew your father." Mr. Somersby nodded. "A good man."

"Yes, he was."

"I am so sorry for your loss."

Her smile was bittersweet. "Thank you, sir. I miss him dearly. I still cannot believe he's gone. I still expect him to call me to his study or seat himself at the dinner table."

He replied sagely, "It will be that way for some time, my dear. But life goes on and so must we."

She looked across the room at Girard conversing with Lady Tinnsdale and asked tentatively, "I understand that the Duke of Girard came into his title at an early age as well."

"Yes, he did—very unexpectedly. The prior duke passed away suddenly, when young Girard was about nineteen, I believe."

"How horrible for him to lose his father and be responsible for so many duties, so many people depending upon him at that age."

"I'm sure it wasn't easy for him. As you well know, there's no good time to lose one's parent. I understand his uncle, Richard Blanton, helped give him guidance at the time."

She sat up straighter, interested in Girard's connection to her now deceased neighbor. "Richard Blanton was his uncle?"

"Yes. On his mother's side." Oblivious to Charlotte's sudden disquiet, he went on. "His uncle and I were old friends from Eton, you know. An honorable gentleman. We could use more like him. I paid a call shortly after his wife Lillian died. Beautiful lady." He shook his head, reflecting. "But troubled. He didn't marry again. He and the young duke did well together. They were very close. Then Richard died about the time my Gracie did. A riding accident, I was told. I never learned the details."

"Then Mortimer Blanton is the duke's cousin?" she asked carefully.

"Yes, why do you ask?"

She looked away, feigning nonchalance. "Just wanting to make the connection." Charlotte turned back to the older man and asked, "Does the duke know of your friendship with his uncle?"

"No. The man has enough people encroaching on his time to be bothered by me. Which reminds me—why do you spend so much of your time with this boring old man?"

She relaxed at the change in subject and smiled at him affectionately. "And miss all your wonderful stories?"

"Ah, you flatter an old man." He placed his hand over his heart. "If I were just ten years younger . . ."

"Ten?" She laughed. "Very well, ten," Charlotte teased.

Mr. Somersby's eyes twinkled. "But since I am not an option, do none of these young gentlemen interest you?"

"Do not be so quick to try to marry me off, Mr. Somersby. My sister, Margaret, will marry first."

"Is she not younger than you?"

"Yes; she is also the one coming out this season. Much delayed by family circumstances, I'm afraid. We only recently completed our mourning period," she explained, "yet she already has many interested suitors."

"Do not tempt the fates, Charlotte. Any man worth his salt would sweep you off your feet."

Charlotte smiled politely thinking of the last man whom she thought was worth his salt, Myles Wilmington. She had fallen head over heels in love with the vicar's charming young son, who had wooed her into believing that she was the most enchanting young lady in the world and that his heart was hers forever.

She was ready to run off with the ever attentive suitor until she found the letter Myles had written to a solicitor asking after Charlotte's diamond mines in South Africa. Upon confronting him, she saw his true colors, and the callousness behind his amiable facade mortified her. She would never forget the painful humiliation. She had sworn that she would not settle for any man who could not truly love her for herself. She had extensive criteria for the man she would marry, and trustworthiness, not charm or good looks, topped her list.

"So not even the handsome Duke of Girard can tempt you, Charlotte?" Mr. Somersby quipped.

"Do you see me with a man who is so aloof?"

Looking over at Girard nodding and listening solemnly to Lord Balstram, Mr. Somersby commented, "Granted, he does have quite a game face, so to speak."

"Game face? I wonder if his face would crack if he smiled."

"Is levity important to you?"

"Humor makes life bearable, Mr. Somersby. Without the ability to laugh at life's cruel jokes, one loses perspective."

"True. Still, is humor alone your basis for marriage?"

"Oh no, sir. I have a long list." Eyes twinkling, Charlotte smiled playfully. "A *very* long list."

Later that evening, James Morgan, the Duke of Girard, stood before his mirror as Collin, his valet and all-around man, assisted him out of his jacket. Collin had been in James's personal service since the duke had come into his title and had proved invaluable, particularly with what James called Collin's "special skills," winnowing out the most important information about people and judiciously sharing it with his employer. James considered him much more than a trusted servant; he respected the man and considered him a friend.

As James pulled at the knot in his cravat, he asked, "What

do you know of the Hastings girl?" Collin looked up from gathering his master's discarded clothing.

"Her maid, Anna, does not have any complaints." He pursed his lips thoughtfully. "One of the few belowstairs who does not. Although I am sure she is overstating it, she believes Miss Hastings kept the household going in the last years of Viscount Sheffield's life. Apparently, Miss Hastings and her brother, Edward, are anxious to see their sister marry well, which should not be difficult. They expect a match by the end of the Season."

James discarded the extensive neck cloth. "Miss Hastings is the elder of the two sisters?" Collin nodded. "What of her own plans for marriage?"

"Miss Anna spoke of their closest neighbor in Bury St. Edmunds being very interested."

He stopped unbuttoning his pants and looked up sharply. "How interested?"

"He has been attempting to court Miss Hastings for over a year now."

"And?"

"All she said was that he was exceedingly persistent, especially since she completed the period of mourning for her father. Apparently the fellow has set his mind upon marrying her."

He sat on the edge of his bed while Collin assisted him in removing his high black leather boots. This house party had been the perfect ruse to conceal his clandestine activities. Was the lovely Miss Hastings using the opportunity as well? But to what end? "Do you know if she has any connections in France?"

"I do not. Would you like me to make some inquiries?"

"Yes and keep an eye out tonight, will you?" he requested, standing up.

"On Miss Hastings? My distinct pleasure."

He ignored the joke, more pressing matters on his mind. "Don't worry, your grace. I'll be on my toes."

"As usual." He reached for the other set of clothes left out by Collin and began to dress. At his next encounter he would not be playing the elegant duke.

Chapter 3

Charlotte stood before the long mirror, as Anna carefully unfastened the silk-covered buttons of her high-waisted evening dress. She eyed her attire critically. What did it matter that her clothes were far from up-to-the-minute? Practicality and serviceability were her mainstays of fashion. There just had never been much time for frippery. There was Margaret to attend to, the servants to oversee, and her brother to assist. If she had any free time, she preferred perfecting her artwork; it had been ages since she'd had the opportunity to study with a decent instructor. And, when in Town, visiting the boys at the hospital took priority of her open afternoons.

But the memory of her first day at the Balstrams' burned her with humiliation. As the ladies had gathered in the salon, Lady Marchant had turned to Mrs. Littleton and whispered quite loudly so everyone could hear, "Why, I had no idea the young Viscount Sheffield was having financial difficulties. Can he not afford a proper wardrobe for his sister?" Mrs. Littleton had replied savagely, "That is what happens when one has no maternal guidance." The words still stung. That these ladies could bandy about the loss of her mother so callously appalled her. Charlotte had been wearing a plain but serviceable sturdy cotton print dress. Most of the guests' dresses were more elaborate, with sleeves puffed out, in muslin fabrics with colored stones, feathers, ribbons, and lace in abundance. Charlotte had felt unclothed by comparison.

She undid her garters, rolled off her silk stockings, and slipped her thin cotton nightdress over her head. Charlotte chuckled as she thought about her new friendship with Mr. Somersby. The elderly gentleman helped her maintain her sanity at these gatherings with his dry wit and descriptive humor. He called Mrs. Littleton "Little *ton* little" and Lady Marchant "the Merchant Lady" and affectionately referred to the lovely widows Tinnsdale and Summerlin as "Tweedle Don't and Tweedle Do." Charlotte pretended not to understand the innuendo. She could not wait to return to the hospital and share some of his stories with the boys. That was what she called the veterans, as if she could mend their souls and bring them back to the sunshine of their youth, the way they were before they faced the atrocities of war, before the insatiable hunger for power had overcome Napoleon. It irritated her to no end that her Aunt Sylvie referred to them as broken soldiers. They were heroes, and they deserved England's gratitude.

Charlotte thanked Anna and bade her goodnight. She stretched out in her bed, feeling fatigue wash over her. She gave thanks for the good in her life and prayed for the health of her family, her boys at the hospital, and her friends, as she did every night. Then she closed her eyes and tried to dream of the perfect man who would make her his bride. Yet tonight, the image of a man with olive skin, long wavy dark hair, and deep blue-black eyes kept disturbing her thoughts. He was unsettling enough in person; she did not need him invading her dreams. She pushed Girard resolutely out of her mind. Instead, she focused on a blond-haired, brown-eyed man she recalled from a book she had recently read. He loved her without reservation—her wit, her compassion, even her freckles. It was a wonderful dream as she drifted off to sleep.

James was breathing hard as he jumped from his mount and scrambled into the brush. He slapped Briar's rump and sent the horse racing off into the black night. Swiftly, he slipped behind a large oak tree, his dark cape blending into the shadows. He pursed his lips, willing his breathing to quiet. With his back pressed against the hard wood, he prayed that his ploy would do the trick. Four horses came rumbling into the nearby clearing, pulling up short just paces from his hiding place.

"Where'd he go?" growled the largest of the burly men.

"I think 'e went that way," pointed a lanky man having trouble controlling his mount. The horse nickered and bucked.

The man wearing a shabby gray overcoat directed in a French accent, "*Regardez*, you two go after him. Mason, stay here." Two men kicked their mounts and raced off after Briar. James squinted at the remaining pair through a parting in the trees, trying to assess their intentions. Carefully, he slipped his pistol from his pocket and his blade from the sheath at his ankle. Listening intently, he readied his stance and quietly inhaled and exhaled.

"I want you to go back to the house and watch," instructed the Frenchman. "Go to the east side. That's where the duke's room is."

"What about the girl with the big teets?"

"You're not to go anywhere near the lady. Do you understand?"

"But ya said we was to keep an eye on 'er," the brute complained. "I was hopin' for some fun."

The Frenchman impatiently pulled his horse's head up

from nibbling at the grass. "Your job is to find that packet. Search his room, follow his man. Whatever it takes."

"What if 'is man comes?"

"Kill him. Just make certain to cover your tracks. We do not want to alert the authorities." The Frenchman wheeled his steed. "And stay away from the lady. Do you comprehend?"

"I 'eard ya," the burly Mason grumbled. "Stay away from the skirt."

"Good. Now go." The Frenchman kicked his horse and raced off.

The brute sat unmoving for a moment. "Bloody hell. An' I love redheads."

James considered assailing the man but dismissed the idea as too risky. Even in the shadows, he could see that Mason was burly, and he was mounted.

Grumbling, Mason turned his horse and slammed his whip against the mount's side. "Move ya bloody bag a bones!" The steed neighed in protest and reared its head. "I'll punish ya, ya beast!" The whip cracked and, still protesting, the mount charged off.

James listened tensely to the sound of the horse's hooves pounding away. After many moments, he let out the breath he was holding and relaxed his muscles. A red-haired lady with large breasts . . . "Miss Hastings' hair is auburn, actually." He slipped his knife back into its sheath but kept his pistol handy. He stepped out from under the tree, his leather boots sinking into the soft mulch. "Whether you care for Mortimer or not, you are a fool to be involved with such villainy, Miss Hastings. But your mistake is my opportunity. I will have to take advantage of the special place you hold in the scoundrel's heart." He turned, resolute, striding toward the house. As he crafted his plans in his mind, he quelled the quiet cries of his conscience. "I will not put my man at risk, particularly not for the neck of a lady who has chosen so unwisely. Most especially not for a traitor, even if she is a beauty."

Charlotte woke abruptly. The moon filtered in through the balcony doors she had left open to enjoy the cool spring breeze. Something was wrong. She inched up, peered from under her covers, and spied a movement across her room.

Her breath froze in her throat. By the light of the moon she discerned the outlines of a man moving stealthily deeper into her room, before a cloud abruptly extinguished the moonlight. The man stopped and leaned against the far wall, keeping his eyes trained on the balcony doors as if expecting pursuit. Charlotte strained to hear of any rescue and heard nothing beyond the sweet whispers of the creatures of the night and the slight puffs of the scoundrel's breath. She lay frozen in the bed, wondering what she could do.

The man turned and looked at her. Charlotte slammed her eyes shut and pretended to sleep. Her heart hammered with terror. The sound of steady footsteps announced him crossing the room toward her bed. She willed herself to breathe normally. After an agonizing moment, she heard the footsteps recede. Her shoulders sank with relief. She opened her eyes and squinted into the darkness. She watched as the man slipped something behind the dresser and edging over, pressed his body against the wall and scanned the landscape through the balcony doors. Suddenly the clouds split, illuminating his profile.

It was James Morgan, the Duke of Girard! In her room in the middle of the night!

He turned to look back at her. Instinctively, her eyes shut. Interminable silence. When she had gathered the courage to peek through her lashes, the room was empty.

Charlotte lay frozen in her bed for some time. Had that really happened? Was it safe to move? But as the minutes ticked by, her curiosity overcame her fear. After what seemed like hours, she slowly rose from her bed feeling cramped but electrified. Inching her way toward the balcony doors, she leaned against the wall and peeked out. The scent of the misty country dew wafted in. No one was about. She quickly closed the doors, locked them, and leaned back against them in relief. She looked over at the dresser, trepidation thrumming through her veins.

Charlotte walked over to the dresser, stuck her hand behind it, and pulled out a mysterious bundle. She weighed it in her hands, turned it over, and felt it with her fingertips. It felt smooth along the edges and bumpy in the middle, as if there was something inside. It was risky, but she needed light. Her curiosity was too great. She lit a candle. The small flame trembled as she carried it to the floor by her bedside. She hoped her bed would block any light from leaking out the balcony doors as she unfolded the thick parchment. She held her breath as she opened the final crease and exposed an odd set of interlocking keys, the likes of which she had never seen before. They intertwined but did not separate. She placed the keys on the floor next to her and examined the parchment, squinting in the dim light. It was a map. *Napoleon ER I.— Depart Elba.* Napoleon and Elba? Whatever this was, it was not necessarily good for King and Country.

Why would Girard hide these things in her room? Charlotte blanched, considering the possibility of being branded a traitor for merely possessing such items. Thinking of the boys at the veterans' hospital and the horror they faced during the war, she felt her resolve strengthen. General Cumseby would know what to do. She just needed to get these articles to him. She bit her lip. She had no valid reason for leaving prematurely and departing now would raise more than a few eyebrows. Moreover, she did not have a carriage of her own as she had traveled with Henrietta to Southbridge. She would just have to try to lie low and wait for the earliest opportunity to escape. Mayhap Mr. Summersby could be convinced to return to Town early.

She would expose Girard's surreptitious activities and if necessary, set the authorities upon him. Charlotte was not about to let his nefarious dealings go unchecked, not when she had the power to do something about it. She quickly re-folded the keys into the parchment and considered where to stash the packet. These possessions were her proof, yet they could also be her downfall.

She looked at her jewelry case. Too obvious. Her armoire. No, her maid would go in there. Then her eyes rested on the thick volume "Arthur and Guinevere" on her bedside table. The book had been her birthday gift from Aunt Sylvie. The gap between the hard front and back covers of the tome and its binding was the perfect hiding place. Charlotte went to the table and found her thin little scissors and her glue pot. She had never understood the old style of wearing patches but found the glue handy at times. Sitting on her knees by her bedside, she used the scissors to undo the inside covering. It was tedious work, particularly in the poor light, and she concentrated all her energies into her agile fingertips. Years of working with clay proved valuable; slowly the paper separated from the cover and a sizable gap appeared. Charlotte gently urged the package inside. It fit flawlessly. She swept the glue brush along the inner lining, sealing the map and keys inside.

After cleaning up the excess glue and checking her work, Charlotte seated herself atop the book, using the pressure of her body to set the seal. She mentally applauded herself for her swift thinking and skill with the binding. Suddenly realizing how she must look, she felt a small bubble of nervous laughter burst from her throat. *Well, at least the house party was no longer boring.*

Chapter 4

The next day proved so beautiful that Lord and Lady Balstram decided a picnic was in order. They sent the servants scurrying to set up the area by the pond for an elegant party and ordered the kitchens to prepare a lavish feast. The enthusiastic Misters Harold and Richard Balstram decided that outdoor competitions would whet everyone's appetite for the meal. The brothers began organizing archery contests, horseshoe tosses, and even some equestrian activities. Excitement filled the air as the guests prepared to compete with one another for various prizes. The Balstram brothers, as they were affectionately called, maintained the level of enthusiasm by separating the men and the ladies. While the men competed, the women looked on, and while the ladies competed, the men made up the gallery.

Charlotte judiciously carried her "Arthur and Guinevere" book with her to the men's events. She was dressed demurely in a day gown of her favorite deep blue. Although it was not cut fashionably low, it was a classic Grecian design with lovely lilies embroidered along the bust line, sleeves, and hem. She wore a large, elegant straw hat adorned with a blue flower and a blue ribbon tied under her chin. Despite the lack of sleep, Charlotte's enthusiasm bubbled over at the thought of exposing Girard's mysterious actions and setting him to rights. Underlying her excitement was a small thrill of fear at the prospect of such a monumental mission.

As the Balstram brothers prepared the obstacle course for the first equestrian competition, Charlotte moved to stand next to Henrietta, who was practically jumping with titillation. With her lime green kid gloves, bright orange gown with yellow ribbons, and dark green straw hat trimmed with rose-colored ribands, Henrietta looked rather like a parrot. Charlotte hoped Mr. Frickerby liked exotic birds.

"Good morning, Henrietta."

"Oh, hello Charlotte. Can you see Mr. Frickerby anywhere?" She held her parasol high, straining to see her beloved in the bright sunshine.

The group of fashionably attired men primarily in black riding boots, riding britches, and coats congregated at the edge of the field earnestly discussing the rules. In a separate group, the stable master organized the rough and tumble stable hands and the horses. Like a magnet, Charlotte's eyes were immediately drawn to the lithe figure of the Duke of Girard. Her heart fluttered in her chest like a caged bird struggling to be free. She quelled the urge to flee to the safety of the house and took a deep breath. She need not fear him. He was in her sights, not the other way around. She forced herself to focus on the man as if he was a new specimen in need of analysis. She would learn everything she could about the scoundrel and pass her information on to General Cumseby and possibly the authorities. She narrowed her eyes in the glare and watched the proceedings with new vigilance.

A question arose regarding the placement of one of the

obstacles. Almost as one, the men turned to the duke to settle the dispute. Charlotte wondered if they would defer to him if they knew more about his nocturnal activities. Just at that moment, Girard raised his head, narrowed his eyes, and scanned the field. His sharp black gaze locked onto hers. For a breathless moment, everyone else faded into the background and it was as if they were alone on the field. A frightening thrill of awareness charged between them. But he couldn't know that she had taken his prize! Charlotte self-consciously broke the gaze and looked toward the stable master, the field, anywhere but at Girard. When she cautiously looked back at him, he was again conferring with Lord Balstram. She blew out a relieved breath.

The obstacle course competition began. As each rider passed, the ladies' group tittered with appreciative comments, assessments, and laughter. Charlotte stood next to Lady Summerlin and Lady Tinnsdale, two widows popular within Polite Society. She remembered Mr. Somersby's comment but could not recall which lady was Tweedle Do and which was Tweedle Don't. She did not really care one way or the other, she liked the ladies and they appeared to welcome her in their conversation.

"I understand that Mr. Grayson has taken a new mistress," Lady Tinnsdale stated dryly, watching the target of her comment canter past.

"Poor woman. I hope she does better by him than Joanne Sloan did. From the stories she is telling, it is more a burden than a benefit to play with Mr. Grayson," Lady Summerlin added jokingly. "If his performance below the covers is anything like his performance on the green, I can understand why." Both ladies giggled.

When Girard took the field, the ladies could not contain their explicit admiration. "Look at the muscles in his thighs," marveled Lady Tinnsdale.

"I like his broad shoulders and strong arms," commented

Lady Summerlin. "I understand that the good duke boxes at Manton's regularly when in Town."

Although she could not fault them, Charlotte was a bit irritated with their veneration. The man was a villain, and well-muscled thighs and gorgeous raven locks could not hide the fact from the world forever.

Lady Tinnsdale shuddered appreciatively, "Oohh, he is a masterful rider."

Her friend smiled naughtily. "So Maxine tells me."

Lady Tinnsdale, feigning shock, raised her hand to her mouth and cried, "Amanda, you are indecent!" Both women burst into a fit of giggles.

Maxine must be Lady Maxine Carlton, thought Charlotte, *the widow of the Baron of Dresford who died two years past.* She recalled Lady Carlton's beautiful classic features, blond hair, blue eyes, and fashionably pale and freckle-free skin. What she remembered most clearly, however, was her razor-sharp tongue. She wondered if Girard and Lady Carlton were still involved.

As she watched Girard jump an obstacle, Charlotte had to admit begrudgingly that he rode his mount with intrinsic grace and fine-tuned coordination. But that did not make him any less a rogue.

Lady Summerlin leaned in close to Lady Tinnsdale's ear. "Miss Druthers is not enough woman for him."

Lady Tinnsdale looked at Charlotte and then at her friend nervously. "Amanda, you forget yourself."

"Charlotte is not one to tell tales. Are you, Charlotte?"

"No, my lady, I am not," she replied, remembering the wheat-haired daughter of the late Lord Druthers. The girl was considered a beauty among the marriageable young ladies of the *ton*.

Lady Summerlin placed her hand on Charlotte's sleeve. "Please call me Amanda, dear. We need not stand on ceremony."

"Thank you." She smiled politely and asked, curious, "Are Miss Druthers and the duke betrothed?"

"Only in Lady Druthers' and the duke's mother's minds. The dowager is quite set on it, I hear. However, many do expect an announcement by the end of the Season."

Feeling freer to join in the gossip, Lady Tinnsdale added, "Miss Druthers will allow the dowager free rein."

"Surely the duchess need not be so cruel as to mistreat the dowager," Charlotte wondered.

Lady Summerlin waved her hand. "Not mistreat. However, many women would not appreciate the old dragon keeping her claws so deep in the management of the holdings and in the duke's life."

"I do not know Her Grace." Charlotte added, inquisitively, "She seems like a strong woman."

"Strong is not the word her enemies would use. You never want to get on her bad side," advised Lady Summerlin. "She is vicious when crossed."

Lady Tinnsdale nodded. "And totally unforgiving." She abruptly shrilled, "Is that a stallion or a mare the duke is riding?"

"When is Mr. Frickerby's turn?" Henrietta gushed, gliding up.

The three ladies abruptly straightened their poses from conspiring to casual.

"I have not yet seen him and am sure he will be brilliant."

Charlotte shared an amused smile with the widows and then turned her attention to the field. Henrietta was anything but subtle. Charlotte wondered what her friend saw in Mr. Frickerby. Granted, he was handsome in a moderate sort of way. His nose, mouth, and chin were all of adequate but not excessive proportion. His smooth features reminded her of some ancient Roman statues she saw at the National Gallery and lacked the kind of character she preferred. He had blond curly hair that he wore full and a little wild around his face, like an owl, and light blue eyes that Charlotte thought to be a bit dull. What she found most unappealing, however, was Mr. Frickerby's perspective on life. He was quite cordial and socially adept, but seemed to look at the world as if it owed him something. His mouth seemed always on the brink of a frown. She understood that Mr. Frickerby thrived on tearing down others, particularly those of wealth, title, or prestige.

Charlotte turned her thoughts to what the ladies had said about Girard and his mother. She had never met the duke's mother, but the dowager had attended various teas and gatherings where she, Lady Druthers, and Miss Druthers had been in attendance. She had the distinct impression that the dowager and Lady Druthers did not consider her family of sufficient social consequence to merit a closer association. Charlotte did not mind; in fact, she was a little amused by such arrogance. Although she was well versed in the fine art of social interaction, she really preferred not to have to pretend to be friendly with them. It gave her more time to confer with her intimate friends. She remembered something Aunt Sylvie had mentioned about traveling in different circles from the dowager but could not recall exactly what her aunt had said.

She turned to Lady Summerlin. "Have you seen Mr. Somersby?"

"He stayed back at the house, I believe," she replied distractedly.

"I shall join him," she noted, hoping to ask the good man about leaving at the earliest possible convenience.

"And miss all the excitement?"

Charlotte smiled to herself; defying the Duke of Girard and protecting her country were more than enough stimulation for her, as the bubbles doing a jig in her belly attested.

Chapter 5

Later that evening, after dismissing Anna, Charlotte had locked her balcony doors, placed a chair before them, and set a glass perfume bottle precariously on top. If anyone should try to get in, she would have ample warning. She walked over to her bedside table and again looked down at her "Arthur and Guinevere" book to reassure herself that all was safe. Thoughtfully she lifted the tall candlestick as a weapon. Yes, it would do nicely. It was hard, yet not weighty or too long.

She seated herself in her armchair and turned to watch the balcony doors. She stood up and shifted the chair to better face the balcony entry. She had dressed carefully in her plain cotton chemise and lacy dressing gown, the most modest sleepwear she had packed. The gown had a high neck and long sleeves, but still, it was a nightdress. Charlotte prayed that Girard would not return to her room tonight. Mr. Somersby had agreed to leave on the morrow, so she just needed to make it through the night.

She chewed her lip nervously. The man was so much larger than she. Was he a gentleman or not? And what if he were caught in her apartments? The scandal could ruin her. She had no illusions about whose word carried more weight in the world. She firmed her resolve. She would do what needed to be done. She just prayed that by doing so she did not wind up destroying her reputation, or worse, land in prison.

Charlotte shivered despite the warmth from the low glowing embers of the fire and the many candles she had lit. The smoky smell of burning wood and tallow filled the tiny space. For a moment she wished she'd asked Anna to sleep in her chamber tonight. But that would have raised Anna's concern. More important, she did not want Anna hurt—or anyone else, for that matter. Charlotte shifted in the armchair, making herself more comfortable as she held the candlestick. Looking around the room, she could think of nothing else to do. She was as prepared as she was ever going to be.

The tinkling of broken glass and the overwhelming scent of lilies roused Charlotte from her dozing state. In an instant she took in the low burning candles, the smoldering fire, and the candlestick on the floor by her feet, where it had rolled during her sleep. She watched in horror as a hulking brute of a man swiftly pushed aside the chair as if it were mere cotton. She jumped to her feet, groping for the candlestick, and opened her mouth to let out a blood-curdling scream. But no sound emerged as the man seized her and stuffed a filthy-tasting cloth deep down her throat. She grabbed at her mouth, trying to pry the foul rag out, only to be gripped from behind in steely hard arms and hoisted onto the bed. Her eyes widened in horror as the realization of her vulnerability assailed her. She had never expected another villain to enter her chambers, and this was far worse than anything she could have encountered with Girard. This beast could do anything

to her and no one would be the wiser. Her heart beat frantically, her blood pounded in her ears as terror gripped her and
held her hostage. She struggled desperately to breathe
through her nose, despite her rancid terror. She tried to calm
down, but her racing heart and burning chest protested. As if
she were someone else, she noted the brute's large muscula-
ture, his broad back, and the sharp, foul smell that emanated
from him. He held her down with his bulky arms, and lying
prone atop her body, he whispered harshly, "I was hopin' y'd
fight me a bit b'fore ya tell me where ya hid it."

Her eyes widened in horror. This man *wanted* to hurt her.
She saw the hunger and violence in him and terror gripped
her so strongly she feared she would die from it. She felt the
cold steel of a knife at her throat. Her body shuddered and a
small tear pushed its way out her closed lids.

He gently caressed her face with the blade. Then, leaning
his whole weight on her legs, he suddenly ripped her night-
gown, exposing her bare breasts. Goose bumps rose on her
milky white skin as the realization dawned that she had more
to fear for than just her life. Closing her eyes, she suddenly
wished for a quick death.

"Oh, yer a beauty. Oh, how I like me teets big." He
grabbed her left breast with his free hand and squeezed
painfully hard. Charlotte winced, but it was the slow burning
pain across her neck that shocked her need for survival. The
man had cut her. "Naw where is it?"

Her instincts took over. She had to get him to move off
her. Opening her eyes, Charlotte took in his dark, scruffy
face, then glanced over at the dressing table and quickly back
at her assailant.

He followed her glance and looked at the dressing table.
"No tricks now. I'll have too much fun havin' t'punish ya."
He eased off her, keeping the knife at her throat. He dragged
her by the arm to the dressing table and motioned toward the
jewelry box. "In dat?" Charlotte nodded. The brute leaned

over to get a better look in the box. She rammed her elbow into his throat. Her attacker grunted and pulled the knife back in surprise. She dropped to the floor, threw her dressing stool into his legs, and frantically scrambled toward the door. He tackled her from behind and mashed her face into the thick carpet, closing off her air. When he turned her over, she sucked in deeply through her nose, drawing air into her lungs. Straddling her chest with his large, powerful thighs, he placed his hands over her throat and slowly began to choke her. "I told ya I was wantin' some fun t'night. Fight me s'more, little lady."

The thought of giving this monster what he wanted nauseated her, but surrendering to his assault was worse. Charlotte kicked wildly at his back with her legs and tried pulling his hands off her throat, but to no avail. Pain thrashed through her neck and blood pounded in her ears. She heard screaming and a small part of her realized that it was only in her mind. She was shattering with the need for air, the need to live, the need to survive the next few moments. Brilliant stars played before her eyes and her world began to close in darkness.

Suddenly, her attacker was yanked off her and she was free. She struggled to wrench the awful suffocating thing from her mouth and after three attempts, finally succeeded. Shuddering with effort, she wheezed in gulps of air, trying to still the thunderous pounding in her head and the terrible burning in her chest. She heard muffled thuds and a struggle by the bed. Pushing herself up, she tried to scream, but resounding pain burned her throat and only a small squeak emerged. All she could do was watch the two figures ensnared in a struggle on the floor in front of her.

Girard.

Instantly she discerned the differences between the two men. Girard was shorter, leaner, and more agile. Her attacker was all bulk and brute force. Girard punched and jabbed, and yet her attacker still came. He threw Girard over the bed and the duke rolled onto the other side, landing crouched on his feet, fists raised. The beast, as Charlotte called him in her mind, clamored over to attack him. The man must have lost his knife in the fight since he was attacking Girard empty handed.

While she scanned the room looking for the weapon, Girard punched the intruder in the stomach and chest, but rather than yield, the man seized his neck and choked him. As he struggled, the duke was gurgling and groping for air. God bless Girard for trying to help her, but Charlotte saw that there was no way the duke would survive the encounter without aid. And if he fell, so surely would she.

Her every gasp was a harsh burn and her head felt as if horses had stampeded across her brow, but Charlotte heeded only one thought—*stop the beast at any cost*. She could not spot the knife, so she grabbed a heavy fireplace poker and circled behind the combatants. She squeezed the weighty metal in a death grip in her hands. Her heart pounding, her breath a shuddering wheeze, she quickly took aim, swung the poker back, and twisted her body, throwing her whole weight behind the blow. The poker smashed into the back of the beast's great head with a crack. The man blinked once in surprise, released Girard, and sank to his knees. Girard cocked his fist and let loose a massive punch to the man's jaw. The beast's head whipped back and he collapsed in a heap on the floor.

Charlotte and Girard looked down at the unconscious intruder and then up at each other in mutual relief. Panting, Girard leaned over and checked the man's pulse.

"Is . . . is he dead?" she whispered.

Girard shook his head. He stood, and placing his hands on her arms, looked down at her. "Are you," he cleared his scratchy throat, "are you all right?" She nodded in response, dazed but breathing.

A hard knock resounded through the room. "Miss Hastings?"

Charlotte looked up at him, frightened. To have him and the beast found in her room. She shuddered but lifted her chin. It could have been so very much worse. She swallowed and turned toward the door.

Girard pulled her around to face him. "Cover yourself!"

She looked down. The flickers of candlelight shined on her white breasts, exposed from her torn nightdress. Heat flooded her face. She spun and covered herself with her arms, mortified. She ran to her closet and pulled down a wrapper. Girard, meantime, was rolling and pushing the beast's great bulk behind the bed.

"Get him out of here!" she hissed.

"No," came his cold reply.

"Take him and leave." She pointed out the balcony doors. He ignored her and continued moving the body by the bed.

"We are coming in!" the voice shouted from behind the door.

Girard grabbed her hand and dragged her toward the entry. Racing past, she spied herself in the mirror; haunted blue eyes looked back at her, on a ghostly face veiled by a mane of red hair. Girard pushed her before him and swung open the door. Stuart Frickerby fell in, a small crowd of curious and concerned guests close behind. The duke propelled Charlotte forward, pressing everyone back out into the hallway. He firmly pulled the door closed behind them and placed his arm protectively around Charlotte's shoulders.

Mr. Glenridge was the first to speak. "Girard!" He looked over at Charlotte curiously. "Are you all right, Miss Hastings?"

Mr. Frickerby turned on Girard, pointing his finger accusingly. "What were you doing in Miss Hastings' room? And what was all that noise?"

Lady Tinnsdale and Lady Summerlin stepped away from

their doors and moved toward the commotion curiously.

"I merely fell over some furniture while I was entering Charlotte's room," Girard stated boldly.

The crowd hushed in appalled shock.

"It was a horrible mistake, of course, your grace." Lady Summerlin looked pointedly at the circle of faces in the hallway. "We all know you did not intend to enter Miss Hastings' room," she offered graciously, trying to give Girard and Charlotte a way out.

Girard hugged her closer to his side. "Yes, I did." The ladies gasped in surprise. Charlotte turned to him, her eyes wide with alarm.

"What is going on here?" Lord Balstram demanded, making his way through the crowd. He was in his dressing gown, his disheveled hair standing on end. Lady Balstram, looking flustered, followed in his wake. Henrietta trailed behind them, sleepily rubbing her eyes. Lord Balstram stopped in the center of the crowd. "Can someone please explain to me what everyone is doing in the hallway at this ungodly hour?" All eyes turned to Girard.

"Girard attacked Miss Hastings in her room!" Mr. Frickerby charged. Lady Pembrook fainted dead away. Her husband caught her, but no one else moved to help. Heads were filling with the anticipation of returning to Town with the juiciest gossip to spread.

Girard addressed his host and hostess, well aware of the crowd he played to, "We had not intended to tell anyone until we returned to London. Obviously, circumstances have altered." There was a pregnant pause. "Charlotte and I are engaged to be married."

Chapter 6

C harlotte's body stiffened at Girard's declaration. She would have pulled away, but he held her securely against him. He hinted forcefully to Lord Balstram, "I suggest we find some privacy to discuss the matter further."

Lord Balstram took in the scene and responded quickly, "As Miss Hastings is in our care, I expect a complete explanation. Come along, my dear," he motioned to his wife, "we shall retire to the library." The group, disappointed that they would be excluded from the full explanation, twittered among themselves. Charlotte was thankful for her high-necked dressing gown and her long loose hair, but otherwise felt exposed and vulnerable. She prayed that she could find her way out of this mess without her whole life falling apart. Her mind scrambled for options, but the arm around her shoulders was like a vise, keeping her pinned to Girard's side as he propelled her down the hall.

Collin appeared from the shadows. Girard pulled him

aside and said in a low voice, "Please straighten Miss Hastings' room and remove anything damaged."

"Yes, your grace." He nodded knowingly and swiftly drifted away. *Heavens, did the duke get into these types of situations regularly?*

Lord Balstram turned his head in question. Girard nodded. "I will, of course, reimburse you for anything damaged as I tried to find my bearings."

Hovering nearby, Mr. Frickerby yelled, "Bearings? You were at the wrong end of the bloody house." Girard sent him a look of sharp disdain, then turned away dismissively.

He looked down at Charlotte apologetically. "I was quite clumsy in my haste to visit, darling. Things will be much more convenient once we are married." She could not believe her ears. She tripped and would have fallen, but he held her up and thrust her along after the Balstrams. She mentally steadied herself by holding onto the belief that there had to be a simple way out of this mess that would not completely destroy her reputation. If Collin removed the beast from her room and Girard apologized . . . Girard had a lot to answer for. In her room. The mysterious packet. That beast. She shuddered. Granted, the duke had helped save her, but his declaration . . . the man must be insane. Unless his cousin Mortimer had told him about the diamond mines. Was Mortimer in on this with Girard? Charlotte looked up at the man hugging her close and drawing her down the hallway. Could he have planned that attack? No. He really *had* been fighting for his life. Instinctively, she doubted Mortimer would tell anyone about his humiliation and the diamond mines. What was Girard about, then? And what did this have to do with Napoleon and Elba?

As they entered the library, Lord Balstram seated Lady Balstram in a large chair before his desk and motioned to a sleepy footman hovering at the door to place two extra chairs next to hers. Lord Balstram lumbered over to the bar, stating baldly, "I believe we all could benefit from a drink." Girard seated Charlotte away from Lady Balstram with himself in between. Henrietta slipped into the room and secreted herself on the sofa near the windows. Without a word Charlotte accepted her brandy and held it clasped in her lap. Lord Balstram excused the footman and sipped his drink contemplatively as he sat down.

A funereal silence descended on the room.

Lady Balstram sniffed her glass and grimaced at the taste. Charlotte tried to bring the drink to her lips, but her hand shook so badly, she lowered it into her lap once more. Noting her difficulty, Girard removed the glass from her hand and set it on the desk. He folded her hand in his larger one and began speaking quietly to Lord and Lady Balstram. "Arthur, Claudia, I regret placing you in this situation. It is all my fault." *Here it comes*, thought Charlotte, *the explanation that will end this nightmare.* "You see," he continued in confidential tones, "I could not pass up this opportunity to see Charlotte. To be perfectly frank, it is actually a relief to be open with our commitment to each other." He squeezed Charlotte's hand hard. "As you know, in respect for her father, she only just completed mourning and my enthusiasm, well, it got the better of me. We had hoped to announce it at the end of the Season, but what is done is done." He leaned over and stroked Charlotte's loose hair, artfully covering her bruised neck. *Perfectly frank?* She blinked. She could not think past the comment. *Perfectly frank?*

"But you hardly know each other," Henrietta cried out from across the room.

Lady Balstram frowned. "You two do not seem to be well acquainted."

Girard turned to Lady Balstram and replied, "Actually, Charlotte and I know each other quite well. A mutual friend, General Cumseby, introduced us. He directs the army hospital off Clarendon Square."

Henrietta shuddered. "Ugh. That horrible place?"

Charlotte shook her head. "You don't understand—"

"That is the place exactly," Girard interrupted smoothly. "Charlotte does the most wonderful work there. I am really quite proud of her. She is so patriotic, don't you think? One would hardly believe her capable of any anarchist notions."

The comment was lost to everyone but Charlotte. She stiffened. He leaned toward her ear as if whispering lovingly and stated in a low, steely voice, "Do not even consider challenging me or I will ensure that you hang." An icy chill raced down her spine.

"No wonder you go there all the time," Henrietta crossed her arms and accused her friend. "You are there at least twice a week. I thought you were daft, spending so much time with those awful men. I had no idea you were meeting Girard. It all makes so much more sense now."

Charlotte fumed in frustrated silence. No one would believe her. Even her friends the Balstrams would be hard pressed to challenge the duke. From now on, her good works would be viewed in terms of ensnaring a wealthy, titled husband. More important, this conversation was entrapping her even more deeply into the lie of their engagement. She knew that engagements were broken on rare occasion, just as well as she knew that she would be ruined once she or Girard cried off. Well, she would be dished up if the strange objects were found in her possession. Deemed a traitor to her country. She had to get to General Cumseby. He would know what to do.

"Well, congratulations!" Lord Balstram raised his glass and saluted the couple. "You are a very lucky man, Girard. I had hoped Miss Hastings would tame one of my boys, but that is for another lady, another time. I can only pray that they will be as fortunate as you in your choice of bride."

Lady Balstram turned to Charlotte, "Yes, our sincerest congratulations, my dear." She glared pointedly at her daughter. "I always knew that you would do well for yourself. Your family must be thrilled."

The duke tilted his head charmingly. "We have not yet told our respective families. So you will understand when I tell you that we must leave as soon as possible and inform them before they learn of our engagement from another source."

"Yes, yes," Lord Balstram chimed in. "Can't have them hearing from the hired help, now, can you?"

"Why, we must celebrate the engagement. A dance tomorrow evening in your honor," Lady Balstram insisted.

"Unfortunately, we have to decline your gracious offer. We must get back to Town."

"So soon?" Lady Balstram asked, obviously disappointed not to be able to wallow in the glow of their good tidings for the remainder of the house party.

"Regrettably, yes. We will depart at first light. Let us retire so we can get an early start. Come, Charlotte, I will escort you to your room." He pulled her from her chair, none too delicately. She ignored the temptation to box his ears; her satisfaction would be short lived in front of the Balstrams.

Henrietta came over and hugged her friend, not realizing the discomfort she caused. "I am so happy for you." No one seemed to have noticed that Charlotte had not spoken or smiled throughout the interview. She suffered their congratulations as Girard bundled her out of the room and down the hallway.

Collin stood rigidly outside Charlotte's room. As they approached, the duke asked pointedly, "Is everything taken care of?"

"Yes, your grace. The offensive item was removed and locked away for safe keeping."

"Excellent." He nodded his approval, opened Charlotte's door, and pushed her inside. She stopped on the threshold, shocked. Her room was destroyed chaos. Her armoire was open, her dresser pushed away from the wall, and her drawers overturned.

Anna was rehanging her gowns and looked up as they walked in. She jumped up and curtseyed, "Your grace. My lady."

Girard's dark eyes narrowed as he quietly asked Anna, "Who did this?"

Anna looked at Charlotte and blushed beet red. "Well, err, I thought you did." Embarrassed, Anna added lamely, "I mean, your grace, that I'd heard . . ." Charlotte walked over, took her hand, and smiled. She turned back to Girard and glared. Someone had searched her room while they were in the library with the Balstrams. It could have been anyone, possibly one of the guests or one of the servants. There was no way to know. Girard noted Charlotte eyeing the dresser and her lack of alarm.

The duke turned to his manservant. "Collin, please help Miss . . ."

"Anna," Collin supplied.

". . . To order a bath and get some fresh linens. While you are doing so, why not tell her about Pennington House while I have a word with Miss H . . . Charlotte."

Collin led Anna into the dressing room and Girard strode to the overturned dresser and peered behind it. He walked back to Charlotte and grabbed her arm. "Is it still here?"

She pressed her lips closed defiantly.

He scowled. "Do not tempt me to summon the authorities and search the place. You would not like the amenities at Newgate," he whispered sharply. She had never been inside the renowned prison but had heard horrifying tales and seen the tall gray stone walls in passing.

"You are a vile scoundrel," she muttered harshly, conscious of Anna and Collin within earshot. "I should think the authorities would be very interested in your map and your underhanded schemes." She raised her hand to her lips, amazed at what she had exposed. She could no longer feign innocence of Girard's activities.

His glittering black eyes narrowed dangerously. "Where is it?"

Charlotte stepped back from him, alarm drying her mouth to dust.

He grabbed her arm and shook. "Where is it?"

She firmed her lips resolutely. There was too much at risk. He would not hear it from her.

"Just tell me that it is safe," he demanded.

Seeing the anger, frustration, and fear in his eyes, she nodded slowly. She pulled herself free of him and scanned the room. "It is safe," she stated hoarsely.

He nodded, relieved. "Can you see if anything has been taken?"

She searched the room. Distressed, she returned to Girard's side. "My jewelry is gone," she cried in a broken voice. "All of it. And the case." She thought of the cherished gifts from her parents. Even the case had been a present from her brother. She felt crushed and angry at the loss of her sentimental treasures.

"It is immaterial. So long as the other is safe," he replied dismissively.

Enraged, she shook her clenched fist at him. "It's not immaterial to me."

"Jewelry can be replaced."

That was it. "Go!" Charlotte forcefully pointed toward the door. "Get out!" she hissed, her throat burning with emotion and pain.

Stepping so close she could smell his leather boots and his tangy cologne, he towered over her. "I am not going anywhere until I have a full explanation from you."

"From me?" Her mouth hung open. "You must be mad!"

"Like a rabid dog, if I don't find out what I want to know."
He grabbed her arm. "How are you involved in this affair?"

She rammed her elbow into his chest. He grunted and
grabbed her other arm. "Tell me!"

"How can I tell you when it is *you* who dragged *me* into
this bloody mess?" she hissed. Ripping her arm out of his
grasp, she opened the top button of her dressing gown, exposing the angry purpling bruises. "This is all your fault! You
are how I am involved in this . . . *affair!* You are a foul, evil
blackguard . . ." The rest of her commentary was cut off by
Girard lashing her close and muffling her ranting with his
chest. Collin and Anna had appeared in the doorway. Girard
glared and Collin pulled Anna back into the dressing room.
"And another thing about Pennington House . . ."

Charlotte struggled against him, but he was too strong.
His arms held her in an iron grip, hugging her to his body.
She frantically racked her brain for something, anything, to
do to get away from the scoundrel.

"I am going to let you go now, Charlotte." He spoke as if
to someone with a diseased mind. "I want your firm promise
that you will tell me everything I want to know. Who sent you
and what is your purpose. How you found the map. *Everything.* Do you agree?"

She eyed him warily, but nodded. Slowly, he eased her
away from him and she opened her mouth to let out a horrific
scream. Too late, she saw the scarf in his hand. For the second time that night, her mouth was stuffed to silence. The
only saving grace was that this time the fabric was silk with a
faint taste of Girard's cologne, instead of the vile rag from
before. She kicked and struggled, but to no avail. He grabbed
her from behind and bound her hands with another scarf that
he'd pulled from the floor. He wrapped his strong arms about
her and pinned her to the floor. She was weak from the toil

and stress of the long, almost sleepless night, and she was no match for him. She ceased struggling and lay limp in his arms, her mind racing with potential means of escape.

Collin stealthily entered the room and squatted beside them. "I've sent Miss Anna off on some errands. She should be gone at least a quarter hour." Charlotte pleaded with her eyes, but Collin ignored her and nodded to his master. "What about her?"

"Give me the laudanum."

She watched terrified as Collin handed Girard the bottle with nary a word of caution or challenge. She increased her struggles mightily, kicking and heaving so much as to slam Girard's temple with her knee. "Hold the witch!" he commanded, and Collin obeyed. The manservant held her nose and she thought she would die. Girard ripped the cloth from her mouth and poured in the drink, choking her as she struggled to breathe. She was powerless to stop them. Tears of hatred, anger, and frustration eked out of her burning eyes and she glared hatefully at Girard. She despised him that moment. She had never hated a person so piercingly before. After a few moments, Girard eased the cloth from her mouth. She wheezed in air, her abused lungs burning with frustrated effort.

"Now, tell me who sent you, and for what purpose," he demanded, holding her shoulders. She wanted to spit in his face, but had no saliva in her mouth.

"Bugger off," she charged.

"Now, that is no way for a lady to speak," he admonished charmingly. "Where did you learn such language? From your neighbor in Bury St. Edmunds?"

Why was the madman talking about his cousin Mortimer Blanton? She narrowed her eyes and glared arrows at the scoundrel. She pressed her lips closed in a firm, hard line. She might be powerless to stop him, but that did not mean she had to cooperate with the bastard.

He shook her. "Tell me!"

"Go to hell." She tried to remember the more colorful expletives the boys used but was having trouble concentrating. Her eyelids dipped heavily and her head fell to one side. "Bloody hell," she mumbled angrily before crashing into unconsciousness.

Letting her fall back and running his hand through his hair, James cursed, "Bloody hell." He turned and looked around the room.

"What now?"

"Now, we search the room quickly and then get the maids to pack her things. We leave for London post haste. The luggage can follow." He stood. "I want her locked in my custody until I get some answers. I will not have her running back to her master, causing trouble for me."

"Are you so sure that she is one of the thieves?"

"She has to be involved somehow. There are too many coincidences. She stole the map and keys, and I mean to get them back and have my answers. All my answers. Then I mean to send my cousin to the hell of his own design."

James looked down at Charlotte and noticed the hideous bruising about her neck. He pushed aside any misgivings. "If Mortimer wants her, then I will be sure he does not have her."

"My sources seemed quite certain that your cousin is quite the ardent suitor. Still, your engagement to Miss Hastings was a bit unexpected."

He responded wryly, "To both of us."

Collin asked quietly, "Was it wise, your grace?"

"It was the perfect opportunity and will suit my plans amazingly well. Mortimer will have to go through me to get her." He fisted his hand. "I must admit that it is satisfying to take something of his, for a change." Charlotte was the perfect means to flush out his prey.

"Even if she is innocent, if I do say so, you did her a service, under the circumstances. Her reputation was at stake.

Whether it was you, that man, or both of you in her room, any way you look at it she would have been ruined."

James rubbed his chin. "It is odd about that brute, though. He seemed intent on hurting her. If Mortimer wants to marry her or if she is in on it with him, why would he attack her so?"

"Was it possibly a ruse?"

He shook his head. "No." Just the memory of that man sitting on Charlotte, choking the life out of her young body, made his blood run cold. "It was real. Too real." He touched his hand to his throat. "For me as well." He looked down at the unconscious girl. "She certainly has gumption. Few ladies would have had the sense of mind to hit that villain with a weapon as she did. She might just have saved my life. The man was powerful; I could not have held him off much longer."

"Mayhap there are more scoundrels to add to this witches' brew?"

"Perhaps," he replied. "Or maybe she is on the outs with Mortimer and I can use their falling out to my advantage. I will have my answers from her."

"Will she return with us to Pennington House?"

"She is my fiancée. No one will think it odd that she moves in with me. My mother is there to chaperone and her brother is out of Town. It is all quite proper, and convenient."

Collin's eyes widened in surprise. "So you will marry her?"

"Are you daft? I would sooner marry my own mother! I will not tie myself to a lying, deceitful wench for the rest of my days. Lord only knows what spawn she would produce."

His man frowned. "But my sources gave no indication that Miss Hastings was in any way involved, sir." He pressed, "I hate to point out the fact again, sir, but she may really be an innocent in this whole mess."

"She reacted when I mentioned Mortimer."

"So would most folk. The man's a mighty bugger. And I

can't quite see her," he pointed to Charlotte's sleeping form, "with the likes of him."

"Mortimer's men were watching her, and one, at least, was trying to protect her." He shook his head, refusing to accept that he might be doing the lady a terrible disservice. "There is too much at stake to take the chance. If I am wrong, I will . . ." He shook his head again. "On the slim chance that I am in the wrong, well, then, I will apologize and set her up in style. She can live anywhere she wants, with any funding she requires."

Collin frowned thoughtfully. "Granted, she does not appear overly thrilled with the prospect of marrying you. Ladies usually fall over their own toes trying to get to you, and most women would be flying high at the prospect of being a duchess. Maybe she is one of those blue stockings not interested in the married state."

"Regardless, Collin, we must move. You search the wardrobe and I will start over here."

For the next twenty minutes the men combed Charlotte's rooms without success. James tossed a blue bonnet onto the floor in disgust. "Where could she have hidden them?" He scanned the chamber once again and added brusquely, "I want *everything* packed, Collin. We cannot take the chance of leaving that map and keys behind."

"Yes, your grace."

He looked over at Charlotte lying on the bed where they had carried her. He grabbed a long green gown from the wardrobe. "Help me put this on her."

Collin looked dubious. "I am no lady's maid, but I doubt the dress is worn over a night garment."

"I do not care how it is supposed to be worn. I need her clothed and ready to go. It is bad enough to carry her around unconscious; I do not need her indecent."

He leaned over and gingerly rebuttoned her dressing

gown. With Collin's help, he sat her up and pulled the gown over her head. "How many buttons does this thing have?" he asked, annoyed.

"Ladies' attire does seem a bit complicated."

"I usually do not have as much trouble getting the damn clothes off," he muttered as he stretched and pulled Charlotte's garment past her tiny waist.

"But sir, the ladies you usually deal with wear a good bit less clothing," his man commented dryly.

"Yes, well, I prefer my women a bit more sportive as well."

"Your mistresses, you mean, sir. This is your betrothed."

James almost dropped her arm. He frowned. "Let us not pretend behind closed doors, Collin. The idea of being leg shackled to the brat for more than . . . well, it is not going to happen. As soon as I catch Mortimer, she will be gone."

After what seemed like a mighty struggle, they lay Charlotte back down on the bed.

Anna could be heard in the dressing room once again. James stood and looked down at the now somewhat properly dressed but disheveled Charlotte. He nodded, satisfied. "Deal with her maid. I am going to clean myself up and call the carriage around. I will have our things packed as well."

"Already done, sir."

He patted Collin on the back. "Good man." Shaking his head wearily, he confessed, "I do not know what I'd do without you."

"All of the great many things you already do, sir." Collin grinned. "Just a bit more slowly."

James frowned, lost in thought. Looking over at the lady on the bed, he realized that he was doing something that many would consider depraved. Kidnapping a young lady of consequence for his own ends. Although he knew that his intentions were sound, he understood with clarity that he had just increased the stakes mightily. There would be hell to pay, but he was willing to pay the piper if it meant stopping a murdering scoundrel from helping to finance another war. He would do whatever it took to stop Mortimer. Whatever it took.

Chapter 7

They departed just as the sun streaked over the dark horizon, spilling shadows across the grassy meadows. No one at the house stirred as the birds announced the new day with spirited chirps. Inhaling the crisp morning air, James barely saw the country landscape as he considered his strategies to ensnare, finally, his foul cousin.

It had taken him eighteen months to track the thefts from the War Office, and by then Edgerton was gone, and so were the stolen properties. His stomach lurched as he once again considered the magnitude of the thievery and the alarming possibility that the loot was being used to finance a new offensive by Napoleon. And it was all his fault. Although no one could truly blame him for the accounting system that had allowed the disastrous thefts to occur, if he had not been in charge of the Finance Division at the War Office, it might never have happened. His treacherous cousin had plagued him all his life, and Mortimer's deceptions had ballooned into a matter of national security. If the property was converted into funding to finance Napoleon's escape from Elba, many more would suffer the consequences. And it would be all his fault for not stopping his wretched cousin before now, for respecting and loving his uncle so much that he tried to ignore his cousin's misdeeds. But Mortimer had taken it all too far. There was no going back, and he meant to see Mortimer pay for his crimes, to atone quietly, and anonymously; there would be no trial, no hanging, in public that is. He felt too much responsibility for his family to have them endure that disgrace.

He looked over at the girl sleeping beside him. He could not quite fathom her role in this scheme. Was she supposed to have tracked the rider with the map and keys while in South-bridge? If so, he had inadvertently aided her in her quest when he'd hidden the articles in her room. Did she understand Mortimer's treachery? Did she appreciate the implications of her actions? Was she so in love with his cousin to be blind to his evil? He could not fault Collin's assessment. Intuitively he knew Charlotte was not interested in marrying any of the eligible men at the party. She did not flirt, make coy remarks, or prance about to show off her attributes, like other ladies of the *ton*.

While James had barely noticed Miss Hastings before yesterday, he had noted her since. He recalled the moments after the attack as she stood exposed, vulnerable, and half naked before him, holding the fire poker, heaving with effort. He could not quite get the memory of her flowing auburn hair and her succulent white breasts from his mind. In those few seconds, the shadows had played across her body, making her nipples look darker, her skin so white as to be almost translucent. Despite her small stature, she was tantalizingly curvaceous, albeit usually beneath the most unappealing attire he had ever seen on a young lady of consequence. And those freckles. None of the beauties of the day had freckles. It was unseemly. He did not mind the auburn hair, although he really preferred blonds. He recalled his fear and fury at entering Charlotte's room and finding that man throttling her to death. He was sore and hurting from his own confrontation. He could only surmise that she was feeling the effects as well.

He tapped the rooftop with his walking stick. "Stop at the inn in Darwick, John."

"Yes, your grace."

He turned back to study the girl. She would give him the map and keys. Once he had them in his possession, he would have irrefutable weapons to use against his nemesis: the keys to the treasure and Charlotte's hand in marriage. He suspected Charlotte would be the more effective tool against his cousin and he intended to use her to best advantage.

She cried out, and her eyes fluttered, then closed. She raised her hand, feebly scratching the air as if to deflect some unseen opponent.

He leaned forward. "Charlotte?"

Inclining heavily against the side of the coach, she inhaled sharp, hasty breaths. Her face contorted in terror, despite her sleeping state.

He slipped onto the seat beside her and gently shook her arm. "Wake up, it is just a dream."

Fresh wet tears slipped out through her closed lids, streaking her smudged cheeks. God, how he hated a woman's tears. But usually they were used to effect. Here, he begrudgingly had to admit that the chit had good reason for nightmares.

He awkwardly placed his arm about her. Lord, she was trembling like a leaf in a storm. "There, there," he said, in what he hoped was a soothing voice, feeling outrageously odd as he patted her shoulder.

She clutched his other arm and curled into his chest, pressing her face deep into the wool of his coat. She was warm and curvaceous and womanly in the extreme. Sighing, he tentatively wrapped his arms around her. Her quaking slowly subsided.

After a few long moments, he hesitantly pressed his nose into the silky tendrils of her auburn hair. The faint scents of lavender and laudanum floated about her. Not exactly exotic. But it was her heat and her luscious curves that held erotic appeal. Unconsciously, his hands crept downward, fondling the soft swell of her tiny waist. He liked the shape of her. Bountiful breasts, petite waist, and round, generous mounds for her derrière. She was built for carnal pleasure. He wrenched his hand away, realizing what he was doing. Good lord, he was mauling an unconscious woman. What depths would he sink to next?

He stiffened his spine but still held her gently in his arms. There was little harm in comforting the girl. She was fighting demons in her sleep, and she *had* saved his skin. Calming her was the least he could do after dosing the girl and kidnapping her.

She relaxed and snuggled deeper, sighing contentedly into his chest, warming him in the already steamy carriage. He would have liked to have opened the window, but he did not wish to disturb her.

Despite her possible nefarious involvement with his cousin, he could not help but feel a small kinship with the lady in his arms. If anything, she was as much a victim of Mortimer's schemes as he. He at least knew with what he was dealing.

She tilted her head back, muttering inaudibly, and dropped her upturned face onto his shoulder. He smoothed long tendrils away from her eyes, lightly caressing her velvety skin. She looked quite angelic in her sleep: thick, lush lips, small upturned nose splattered with freckles. Her long, dark lashes matched her rich reddish-brown tresses, which reminded him of a deep sunset in the heat of summer. Her brow was wide and smoothly relaxed.

His eyes were drawn back to that lush pink mouth. Tracing his fingertips across her sumptuous lips, he stilled when she parted them and unconsciously flicked her tongue to the corner of her mouth. He sucked in his breath as his loins heated. She snuggled closer. Good lord, he was in deep water, and the girl was out cold. Imagine if she actually tried to use her feminine wiles.

He noted his heavy erection and wondered if he and the girl might have a tumble before this misadventure was done. He grimaced, appalled with himself. Notwithstanding her involvement with Mortimer, she was quite possibly a lady of virtue, and he was not about to marry the chit. Heaven help him if he fell into that trap. The thought was enough to diminish his *enthusiasm*. Odd, he had never thought of his lady wife as a sexual partner. He had only considered the arrangements, the requisite bloodlines, and the necessary outcome: an heir. He had always pictured his betrothed as being blond, classically beautiful, inherently social, conventional, and proper. Nothing like the sensual and unpredictable girl in his arms.

Looking down at her, he realized that she was unlike anyone of his acquaintance. Ever since that meeting on the hilltop, she had surprised him, challenged him. Yet, he had to admit, he found himself drawn to her. Understandable, given her figure and her gumption. He had always been attracted to strong personalities—his uncle, his friends, his mistresses. He liked a lady with a spine.

What was he thinking? This woman was a bitch, likely designing to entrap him even more deeply into Mortimer's plot. He had to remain wary of her charms. He shook his head. A frumpy, unconscious woman, distracting him. It was laughable. But nothing about this situation was comic. Suddenly he realized how unsettled his life was becoming. Ever since he had discovered his cousin's treachery, his world had become volatile. While playing the charming duke in Society, inside, he schemed to destroy finally the one man who had vexed him to no end. And he needed to do it on his own, without anyone learning the deceitful beast his cousin had become. Looking down at the lady in his arms, he prayed that in fighting Mortimer, he was not becoming a monster himself.

Chapter 8

James shook her graceful shoulder gently. "Charlotte, wake up." She moaned, rubbing her eyes, then burrowed deeper into his chest. He delicately pushed her into a sitting position, but she fell back against the opposite cushion. Her long, flowing hair was in disarray, her dress wrinkled horribly, and her face flushed red with sleep. Strangely, it was an endearing picture.

The door opened, the footstool set, and Collin poked his head inside. "Is Miss Hastings still asleep? How much of that laudanum did we give her?"

James stepped down. "With luck, enough, but not too much." He reached in and pulled her toward him, and she fell limply into his arms. "I trust that you have procured a private salon?"

"The best available. I have ordered a cold luncheon."

Dismissing the innkeeper's inquiries after Charlotte's well-being, James carried her to the designated chamber and deposited her on a worn red low-lying sofa. She immediately curled up into a sleeping ball, mumbling lightly. He sent the flustered innkeeper to check on luncheon, locking the door behind him.

Collin stood worriedly over her. "I hope we have not poisoned her, sir."

"I am concerned as well, Collin. While she sleeps I will check her physical person. Hold off luncheon until I call for you."

"Yes, your grace. Please call me if there is anything I can do," urged Collin fretfully as he exited the room.

James walked behind him and locked the door. It was unlike Collin to be anxious. Perhaps the chit was affecting his man as well. James pushed aside the thought and purposefully strode toward Charlotte, pulling a short bench over to the sofa. He sat down, leaned over, and pulled her into a sitting position. She swatted at him ineffectively.

"Leave . . . alone," she mumbled, eyes closed.

"Charlotte, can you sit up for me?" Never opening her eyes, she licked her lips and nodded. "Good girl." He helped her sit up in front of him. Nimbly, he began unbuttoning the pearly buttons at the front of her high-necked gown. "I am better at getting the drat thing off," he commented, opening her dressing gown and exposing the pearly flesh underneath. Hideous bruises covered her throat and a long trail of blood caked part of her neck. "Good God," he muttered, horrified. He leaned forward and was relieved that at closer inspection, it was not nearly as bad as it first appeared. It was a very shallow cut, and unlikely even to scar. He carefully traced his hands over her body, searching for signs of broken bones. He was gentle but thorough.

Charlotte sighed sleepily. She opened her eyes a crack and her brow furrowed. He could only imagine her confusion.

"Charlotte, I am just assessing your injuries. Give me a moment more and I will be finished."

Her frown deepened. "Injuries?"

"Another moment." He ran his hands over the rest of her body, quickly checking for anything major to address.

"But we will be late for the party and I have nothing to wear," she slurred.

"Nothing to wear?" he asked, bemused. "Oh, do not worry. We have plenty of time."

"But my dress does not suit and Aunt Sylvie will be angry again."

Suddenly Charlotte leaned forward and whispered conspiringly through half-closed eyes, "You cannot tell a soul." He ignored her. Raising her finger for emphasis, she demanded, "You must give me your word."

"About what?"

"The great secret, of course," she insisted, smiling dreamily.

"What is the secret?" he asked expectantly.

"Shhh!" She held her finger to her lips. "Your word of honor."

He relented, "Of course."

"Good." She lay back down, fast asleep once more.

He gazed at her. Even her dream state was anything but tedious.

A tentative knock at the door. "Your grace?"

He stood, hastily covered Charlotte, then unlocked the door for his man.

"Bring in the brandy from the carriage, please." At Collin's questioning look, he added, "Not for me, for Charlotte."

"What is it?" his man asked, alarmed.

"A small cut. And she is badly bruised, but thankfully, there is nothing critical. I just want to be sure the cut heals properly. Now, go get the brandy."

Collin rushed to obey.

The moment the soaked cloth touched her laceration, the searing pain lanced her neck. Charlotte's eyes flew open and she cried out in pain, "Bloody hell!"

She pushed his hand away frantically.

Holding her head, Girard pressed the cloth firmly against her neck. "Lie still!"

"You foul bastard!" she hissed, and threw him off, scrambling into the corner of the couch, as far from him as she could possibly get. "Don't you touch me!" She struggled to clear the cobwebs from her head. Her mouth felt like cotton and tasted like dirt.

"So you are finally awake, my dear," he commented dryly. "I was hoping you would be more pleasant once you'd had your beauty rest."

"Go to hell!" She clutched at her open clothes, desperately trying to make sense of reality.

"Are you ready to cooperate now?"

"I'd sooner die!" She glared daggers at him.

"If you wish," he replied coolly. Her eyes widened and her already parched mouth went drier than the Sahara. Too late, she realized her situation.

Collin quickly covered her mouth and grabbed her in a grip of iron. She struggled, but it was like fighting a vise. He looked up at his employer.

Girard grabbed her legs. "Get something to cover her mouth and bind her hands."

She battled against the two pairs of strong arms that tried to wrestle her into obedience. She would not submit. She rammed her elbow into Girard's groin.

"Bloody hell," he growled through clenched teeth.

"She . . . is . . . a fighter, sir," the manservant choked out as she rammed her knee into his side. "Ooofff."

"Give me the rest of that laudanum!" Girard commanded as she thrashed about, trying to hit him between his legs again.

"Sir, ooofff! We shouldn't overdose her! She'll be sick."

Impervious to his man's alarm, he commanded, "Give it to me *now!*"

Reluctantly, Collin freed his hand long enough to pull the bottle from his pocket and pass it to Girard. Charlotte used the opening to ram her fist into Girard's neck. "Hold her down, man!"

The duke poured the remainder of the bottle down her throat as both he and Collin held her down. She tried to spit out the foul liquid, but Girard squeezed her nose closed and she choked for air. The awful fluid burned the whole way down. Charlotte shuddered with revulsion and bumps goosed every bit of skin on her body. Lord, how she despised being so puny. She struggled on but her labors weakened, her muscles spent. Her last thought was that if she lived through this ordeal, she would never cover her mouth or face again. Air, God, please, just let me breathe . . .

James continued to hold her down, even after her body stilled and her eyes closed.

Collin shook his head admiringly. "She fights like a little hellion." Frowning, he extricated his arms from hers. "That stuff certainly does the trick. But sir, too much of it can make one quite ill."

James stood, breathing heavily. "We had little choice in the matter. I cannot have her screaming her head off all the way to London. Regardless of our good intentions, we are kidnapping the girl."

Collin frowned. "I never fancied myself a lowly kidnapper. Patriot, more like it."

He straightened his sleeves and looked down at Charlotte's unbuttoned gown. Her breasts were mostly covered, but a glimpse of a rosy nipple could be seen through the thin chemise. "Straighten her up, will you, Collin, and let's quit this place."

For the first time ever, his manservant shook his head. "I'll not be touching the lady like that, sir. It's just not right. She is your betrothed, not mine."

He scowled. "Collin, I said before . . ." It was no use. "Fine. You check on the horses and bring the carriage around. We are leaving post haste."

After Collin closed the door, James stared dubiously down at Charlotte. He readjusted his pants, angrily probing the soreness between his legs. Tentatively at first, he redid her buttons and then, with more certain fingers, adjusted her clothing. She did not move a hair's-breadth. "There. You look just barely presentable." He leaned forward and awkwardly attempted to fix her hair; it was a mass of chaotic tendrils. She felt soft and delicate, a mere slip of a girl, really. "I will admit, you have pluck. And you fight dirty. I admire that in a girl." He rubbed his hands over his eyes. "Are you in love with Mortimer, is that it? I am told he is a handsome devil, but devil is what he is. You appear to be intelligent, can you not see the truth of the matter?" He lifted a loose curl that had fallen across her eyes. "Have you nothing to say for yourself?" Smoothing the soft curls behind her ears, he mused, "Oh, it is so gracious of you to apologize for smashing my cock. It was quite unladylike. Under the circumstances, well, I might just ask you to teach that move to my little sister." He blew out a sigh, stood, and lifted her easily into his arms. She really was well formed, with curves in all the right places. Too bad she had the misfortune to run in such bad company.

Chapter 9

~~~❦~~~

Horses' hooves clattered and her body rocked and swayed to the rhythm of a carriage ride. The rancid odors of refuse and human waste permeated the air, as did the muffled sounds of many persons. Charlotte pushed away the heavy cobwebs clouding her mind and tried to make sense of her surroundings. London . . . they must have reached London while she lay drugged and unconscious at the mercy of that lying bastard Girard. Just thinking his name made her want to scream, but she had learned her lesson. She lay unmoving with her eyes closed, trying to discern whatever details she could.

Her head lay across a strong muscled thigh, the soft wool of his britches gently rubbing against her cheek as the carriage clamored through the crowded thoroughfare. He smelled of man and cologne and . . . brandy. Tentatively, she tested the bindings on her wrists, but the knots only tightened. After a few breathless moments waiting for him to react, she relaxed slightly when he merely shifted in the seat, gently adjusting her head on his leg and resting his hand lightly on her shoulder. Ignoring his informality, Charlotte held her breath and then dared a peek out the slit of her eye. There was the door, with Girard's other leg stretched across her exit. His walking stick leaned against the opposite cushion, but that did not concern her. She cautiously wriggled her ankles. Thank heavens her legs were unbound.

Considering her options, Charlotte suddenly remembered something that Lieutenant Freeman had said, "Distract and then pounce. Feint, throw them off the scent. And when they least expect it, bam!" She needed to be subtle, crafty.

Charlotte's heart pounded as she considered a plan. Could she be so daring, so bold? Never in her life had she used her feminine wiles; perhaps this was the time to use what nature had provided her. Charlotte artfully rolled onto her back, shifting so that Girard's hand lay across her abundant breast. She felt him freeze, but he did not remove his hand. She did not know whether to chastise him or to thank her stars. His hand lay heavily on her breast, but then he seemed to think better of the position and started to remove it. She arched her back, moaned, then reveled when she heard his indrawn breath and felt his body tense. *Courage, girl. It is merely a game. A game of life and death.* She braced her feet against the carriage wall, and arching her back again, rubbed her head deep into his groin. He straightened.

"Charlotte?" Pause. "Have you come awake?"

She moaned again, rubbing her head against his growing member. *It is a pillow, a deep pillow.* She arched her back again, pressing her breast against his hand and her head into his lap. The walking stick clattered to the floor.

She parted her lips and licked her teeth. Her mouth tasted like old goat. "Mmmmm." *Steady, girl.* His feet were firmly planted on the carriage floor. Her heart was hammering a crescendo she was certain he could hear. She rolled her head from side to side, spilling her long hair across his thighs. He groaned. With her eyes closed and her feet braced against the wall, she arched her back slightly and moaned, gently lifting her head. Abruptly she slammed her head down, hard, into Girard's upthrust member. He roared. She rolled off him and plunged out the door before he could recover. She fell hard onto the dirty street, rolling, just barely escaping from under a passing carriage's wheels. She scampered up, diving into the crowd, and ran as if the devil himself were at her heels.

"Sir! Are you all right?" Collin stuck his head into the carriage. To his great alarm, his master sat scrunched in the corner, wincing in pain. "Shall I call a doctor?"

"No!" he hissed. "Get her!" He grimaced. "Get that bloody bitch!"

Collin stood atop the perch of the carriage and looked out into the busy thoroughfare, searching for a sign, a clue as to where she had gone. A myriad of colors, smells, and contrasts assaulted his senses. He stepped down from the box and ran through the crowd. There were too many faces, too many bodies. He tried one street, then another. He grabbed a lady in a long green dress. She swatted him with her parasol and he ran. He shook his head, frustrated. She was gone.

They went immediately to Charlotte's house in Hanover Square. Collin's discreet inquiries left no doubt that Miss Hastings had not yet returned from the country and was not expected back until the end of the week.

"What now?" Collin asked his master.

"You stay here and watch the house. I want her before she has a chance to speak to anyone. We cannot begin to know who is involved." James ran his hand through his hair. "You are certain that Mortimer is not in Town?"

"I have had no word from my eyes and ears. They have immediate orders to come to me at once and the rewards are too sizable for any of them to ignore."

"Where would she go?" He rubbed his chin, trying to remember anything of note about the chit. With her brother out of Town, would General Cumseby be of service? No. He was as straight laced as they came. A true patriot. The general would never involve himself with the likes of her unless he did not know he was being used. "I am going to the veterans' hospital. Send word if she shows." He called up to his driver, "John, Clarendon Square, as fast as you can get us there!"

Charlotte was exhausted, but she was too terrified to stop. Terrified and fuming mad. She would see that monster hang for his crimes. After traveling by back streets and roundabout ways, she finally neared the veterans' hospital. Once she was inside, she would be safe. Her spirits rose just thinking about the wonderful men who, despite their infirmities, would rush to her aid. They were her friends; they were heroes. Charlotte surreptitiously watched the entrance of the hospital for any signs of pursuit. Likely the bastard would wait for her at home. After a moment's hesitation, she scrambled across the street and ran through the welcoming doors.

She raced to General Cumseby's office only to find it quiet and empty. Her heart sank.

"Miss Hastings! Are you all right?" Young Mr. Gladson appeared from a hallway. Charlotte could only imagine how she must have looked—probably like a wild-eyed doxy.

"Gladson." She sighed with relief. "I am so glad to see you. Where is the general?"

"Are you unwell? Can I get you anything?" The enthusiastic young man, who had been infatuated with her since taking the job as the general's assistant three months before, rushed to her side.

"Yes. A knife. Cut these bindings."

His eyes widened. "Right away."

Trying to restrain the sense of urgency which threatened to overwhelm her, she followed him to his desk. She curled her fists in frustration as he fiddled with the scissors. "Where is the general?"

"He is in the gardens, my lady." Gladson coughed. "Ahh, having a smoke." He clipped the cords neatly. "There you go. Are you sure you do not need anything else?"

"I need the general!" she yelled over her shoulder as she ran down the hallway. Her salvation was only paces away, and she could not wait a moment longer to see him.

General Cumseby sat on a long stone bench in the inner courtyard that made up the area otherwise known as "the gardens." Few of the Quality would have considered the small green space a "garden" but to the inhabitants of the veterans' hospital, both patients and staff, it was a taste of nature in the pit of the city. The general puffed mightily from a long brown cigar while he observed a sparrow singing in the lone sapling nearby. He was a large man, tall and broad, with a shock of white hair that reminded many of an affectionate grandfather. Although he tended to have an absentminded air about him, the general ran a very tight ship. He somehow managed to get the best efforts from his hospital staff and squeeze the most money from his patrons.

"General!" Charlotte stopped short in front of him, her breathing labored.

"Lawks, Charlotte! You look as if you've seen a ghost!" The general tossed away his cigar and jumped from his seat. He was still agile, despite his years.

Now that she was here, she did not quite know where to begin. She fell into his arms, burrowed into his massive chest, and held on tight. Tears of relief, joy, and thankfulness washed down her face. Suddenly she could not breathe. She struggled to speak as a shudder ran through her fatigued body.

"Charlotte, dear. Please calm down. You are in shock. Let me call for help. Would you like some laudanum?"

She wanted to tear her hair out in frustration. She took a deep breath, willing herself to be composed. "I-I need your help . . . uhhh, uhhh, scoundrel, help me . . . please."

The general's bushy brow furrowed with worry. "Anything you need."

"Ah, there you are, darling." Girard strode smoothly into the courtyard. Charlotte dashed behind the general's back.

"Girard!" The general pushed up his spectacles. "What are you doing here?"

"Collecting my bride, of course." The duke nodded in greeting.

General Cumseby scratched his head. "Your bride? I do not know to whom you are referring."

"To Charlotte, of course," he replied evenly, a dangerous gleam lighting his dark eyes.

"Not on your life, you bastard!" she screamed from under the general's protective arm.

Girard stepped closer, moving like a lethal cat. "You are overwrought, my dear. Surely you do not want to bring the general into our little quarrel." He carelessly swung his walking stick to and fro. "We would not want to see anyone else implicated, would we?"

Charlotte glared with triumphant hatred, and in response, opened her mouth and let out a scream so blood-curdling her ears rang. It felt good to let that out.

The general covered his ears and Girard ran over and grabbed her arm. Men raced from all parts of the hospital. Workers, doctors, and patients stuck their heads out the windows and poured into the little courtyard.

"Let go of me, you bastard!" she hissed, her voice thick and scratchy.

"We are getting out of here, now!" he growled.

"Not with Miss Charlotte, you're not," called a loud baritone from the doorway. Girard looked up to see a gathering crowd of men. Wary, angry, fighting men. Many were lame, on crutches, some had missing limbs, but Charlotte could see from the look in his eyes Girard was not fooled by their injuries. These were her soldiers, her friends.

Lieutenant Freeman, a large brandy-faced man with a grizzled beard and salt and pepper hair, marched over. Despite his missing leg, he brandished his crutch boldly. "I'll have you step away from Miss Charlotte." She pulled back her arm from the knave's grasp and inched closer to the general. Inhaling deeply with relief, she glared at Girard victoriously.

"Charlotte happens to be my betrothed, Mr. . . ."

The man ignored him and turned to her. "Are you all right, Miss Charlotte?"

She bit her lip, overwhelmed with pride. "Now I am, Lieutenant Freeman."

"What is going on here?" the general demanded, looking down at her. "Now that you have called every man from his bed, pray tell us how we can be of service to you."

"Save me from the likes of him." She pointed at Girard, accusing loudly, "He drugged me and kidnapped me, and . . ."

"Charlotte is overwrought, General," Girard interrupted. "She does not know of what she speaks."

"You scoundrel . . ."

"Now, Charlotte." The general raised his hand. "I have known Girard since he was in leading strings. I find it hard to imagine him doing any such thing."

Appalled, she stared openmouthed. Even her dear general would take that fiend's word over her own.

"I have known Miss Charlotte since I landed in this place." Lieutenant Freeman moved closer. "And she does not lie."

A chorus of support rose from the crowd.

Girard eyed the men warily. Their anger and protectiveness were simmering into a cantankerous brew. He turned to the general. "General, if I may, I suggest that this can all be worked out if we just have the chance to discuss it rationally—say, in your office."

"Excellent. To my office, then."

She crossed her arms. "I am not going anywhere with him."

"Dear, if we are to get to the bottom of this, then we really ought to hear the man out. I am sure that there is a reasonable explanation for this misunderstanding, but we will not discover it standing here." The general waved at the assembly. "You come along too, Lieutenant. And Mr. Jones and Mr. Davenport as well."

Charlotte nodded, feeling reassured, and let the general lead her into the shadowy hallway.

Despite having her very own army by her side, Charlotte was feeling anything but cocky. Goose bumps were scaling her skin simply because the blasted duke was stalking behind her. She could feel his beady eyes on her back and had to suppress the urge to turn around and smack the satisfied smirk off his face. She finally peeked over her shoulder. Well, he was not exactly swaggering, but he was so wretchedly confident it made her want to scream. She drew herself up and sniffed. She would explain the whole awful mess and then have the man locked up for his crimes. The idea of the dashing duke behind bars gave her a small sense of satisfaction. She just feared that it was going to be very short lived.

Chapter 10

After steering Charlotte to his chair, the general urged gently, "Charlotte dear, please tell us what has you so distressed."

The cratered seat almost swallowed her; its size emphasizing her sense of insignificance compared to the olive-skinned scoundrel lounging across from her. The dratted man had the ability to make even a hard wooden stool seem like a throne.

She would not look at the rogue and instead ran her hands over the chair's arms, feeling the soft, bumpy, broken leather, smelling its rich scent, wanting this all to come out just right, so that everyone understood who the villain was in this piece. It did bolster her confidence that Mr. Jones and Mr. Davenport waited outside, and that her good friend Lieutenant Freeman stood sentry by the door. She drew herself up, resolving to state her case plainly and without emotional drama.

"That bastard is a traitor, and a liar and a scoundrel . . ."

"Charlotte, my dear, please just tell us what happened."

The general pushed his glasses up the bridge of his bulbous nose. "We cannot get to the bottom of this if we merely make accusations."

"Yes, the facts, please, Charlotte." The corners of the scoundrel's lips curled with wicked enjoyment.

Her face heated, but she managed to scowl at him. "The Duke of Girard entered my room in the dead of night while I was sleeping . . ."

"At your house?" the general asked, aghast.

"No, at the Balstrams' in Southbridge," the rogue answered dryly, as if he were commenting on the weather.

"So you admit it!"

"Please go on." He casually adjusted his shirtsleeves. "I cannot wait to see how your colorful story ends."

She glared daggers at him and turned to her friends once again. "He hid a map somehow relating to Napoleon in my room. I am sure that it was quite traitorous."

The duke sat up, alarmed. "You looked at the map?"

She turned her shoulder to him and continued, "The next night, I was attacked in my room by . . ." Her voice faltered as memory of the confrontation blared through her mind. "A . . . attacked by this . . . horrible man."

Lieutenant Freeman pushed himself away from the wall where he had been leaning. "Miss Charlotte!"

"I-I-I . . ." She was at a loss.

"You fought him well," Girard murmured quietly.

She smiled tremulously at Lieutenant Freeman. "I used some of those tricks you showed me."

"Good girl!" the lieutenant nodded, still scowling.

"And what happened?" the general demanded apprehensively. "I mean, I can see that you are fit, and, well, you are, aren't you?"

"Before any real damage could be done . . ." Girard prompted graciously. *Now* he was deciding to act like a gentleman and safeguard her reputation.

"Well." She frowned, not looking at him. "He came to my rescue."

The general leaned back in his wooden chair and whispered, "Thank heavens."

Heavy silence.

General Cumseby sat up straighter. "Now, that sounds more like the Girard I know."

She crossed her arms, irritated. This was not exactly coming out as she had hoped. "Well, then he attacked me and dosed me, nearly to the point of poison, and kidnapped me to London."

"You forgot the part about the engagement, Charlotte," Girard added mischievously.

"Yes, what about that?" the general asked.

Embarrassment flooded her cheeks and she bit her lip, knowing how it would sound. "Well, he told everyone that we were engaged to be married."

"But why would he do such a thing?" Lieutenant Freeman asked, scratching his graying beard.

"Because, my friend, if Charlotte had men in her chamber, her reputation would be in tatters," the general answered candidly. He turned to Girard. "Was the other man found in her room?"

"No."

"Thank heavens." The general nodded. "What happened to him?"

"He is in my custody," Girard answered slowly, "and will not be charged with anything specific, when," he added quietly, "I hand him over to the authorities."

The general thoughtfully rubbed his chin.

"You do not seem to understand, General," Charlotte insisted. "He manhandled me and took me against my will, bound and drugged, back to London."

"He hurt you?" Lieutenant Freeman leaned on his crutch toward Girard.

Girard raised his hand, hushing the group. "I have reason to believe that Charlotte might, possibly even without truly understanding what she is doing, be involved in a plot against our government."

"*You* are the traitor!" she charged, jumping to her feet. "You're the one who put the map about Napoleon in my room."

The general stood. "Girard, I do believe that it is time for an explanation."

The dratted man had the gall to ignore the general's request and simply sit there with his lips pursed and a contemplative look on his face. As if merely thinking about answering for his crimes was enough!

She was beginning to doubt that the man would ever admit to any wrongdoing. She glared down at her frumpy, wrinkled dress and raised her hand to her crazed hair, trying for some semblance of aplomb. It was not fair that he was so immaculately turned out, with not a wrinkle on his shirtsleeves, or a single crease in his coat, or even a scratch on his shiny black Hessians.

The general leaned forward and placed his hand on the duke's arm. "Girard, I have known you, and your father before you, well . . . almost forever. Charlotte is not a flighty girl given to fancies of imagination. If what she says is true . . ." He shook his head. "I must admit, it sounds more like your . . ."

The duke placed his hand on the general's, quickly interrupting. "I believe it is time for that explanation." He looked at the general and then at Lieutenant Freeman. "What I am about to tell you is confidential, and a matter of national security. I trust that the information will remain within these walls."

"Absolutely," the general replied.

Lieutenant Freeman smiled in agreement. "Yes, sir."

Charlotte almost rolled her eyes at the deference in their tone. "You must be joking."

"Now, Charlotte," the general chided.

Girard held up his hand. "Charlotte's animosity is understandable, given the circumstances. Based on your regard for Charlotte, I would consider that she was unaware of her role in the plot."

"Unaware?" she ground out. "How about uninvolved? Explain your stealing into my room in the middle of the night and your having the audacity to tell everyone that I am your betrothed."

"That," he smiled a small self-deprecating smile, "was a moment of inspiration."

"For whom?" she asked caustically, crossing her arms.

"At the time, it seemed the appropriate thing to do. I did not want that man found in your room, and neither did you. You must admit, it got us out of a problematical situation."

"Out from one and into another," she mumbled.

"What was that?"

She shifted in her seat, scowling with discomfort. Her neck still burned and her bottom hurt from her fall from the carriage. She was in no mood for his coy games. "What I want to know is what you were doing in my bedroom in the middle of the night in the first instance."

He shifted in his seat. "That, was, an . . . unavoidable occurrence."

"Unavoidable?" she cried hoarsely. "Sneaking into my room and hiding something behind my dresser in the middle of the night was unavoidable? Pray explain to me how that was anything but deliberate."

"Well, it was deliberate, but something done under trying circumstances."

Frustrated, she opened her arms wide as if beseeching the

heavens. "Enough of this circumvention. For all that is holy, please just tell me what you are about."

Girard faced the two men and then Charlotte and began speaking slowly but firmly. "I will tell you what I am at liberty to share."

She raised a questioning brow. "After all that you have put me through, I will accept nothing less than the complete truth."

"Charlotte, let us at least hear the man out," the general interjected.

The duke nodded. "To the point, I am trying to recover some trade properties that were stolen from our government and intended to help finance the war effort. I intercepted a rider who was delivering important keys to the location of the stolen property. Many men would have been extremely interested in securing these items for their own nefarious purposes, and I was not about to let anyone else get to the stash first."

"But why did you attempt to hide them in my room?"

"I was set to meet an informant and was ambushed. To be safe, I needed a good hiding place."

"My room, in the middle of the night, was a good hiding place?"

"At the time, it seemed so."

"Why?"

Girard shifted in his seat. "Well, no one would think to find them there."

"Let me consider this." She pressed her finger on her chin and looked upward, feigning contemplation. "Why would no one believe that your nefarious items were in my room?" She glowered at him. "Maybe because no decent person would dare put me and my reputation at such risk?"

His face closed. "I have other reasons that I am not at liberty to discuss."

"Well, find the liberty," she admonished. "It was my room, remember. My reputation, my life you risked."

"I have to agree with Miss Charlotte," Lieutenant Freeman interjected. "It seems you rightly drew her into the matter."

Girard frowned. The unflappable duke seemed perturbed at being questioned. Well, until he provided sufficient answers, he would just have to manage, Charlotte thought sourly.

"Let us just say I believed it would be a safe place," Girard explained.

"Why? Because I am not a thief?" she asked dubiously.

"It really is for a good cause, your Crown and Country."

"Why you?" Lieutenant Freeman asked.

"Because," he replied tightly, "the man who stole the items in question was under my command at the War Office. I should never have let it happen in the first place, and because of my, my . . . inattention, he was able to steal a small fortune from the Treasury."

The general added thoughtfully, "You did not see that he was stealing because you trusted him."

"Implicitly. To our government's misfortune."

"And your own," Charlotte added.

The duke reluctantly nodded. "Admittedly so."

Lieutenant Freeman leaned back against the wall, shifting his crutch to the side. "Why are you leading the investigation? You are a duke, for Pete's sake."

"There is a little more to it than stolen property," he replied. "The extent of the thefts was excessive, and the goods may easily be converted into currency which I believe is intended to finance another offensive by Napoleon."

Charlotte glowered. "Napoleon abdicated at Fontainebleau. He is exiled to Elba."

Girard replied gravely, "Sources indicate that Napoleon is seeking support financially and otherwise, to escape and resume ruling France. Recommencing the bloody warfare. That is why it is imperative that we quickly recover the stolen items so they cannot be turned into funding to support him."

She recalled the scratchy writing on the map. "*Napoleon ER I Depart Elba.*"

"You are a light sleeper," he commented dryly.

"I am unaccustomed to men sneaking into my bedroom in the middle of the night. If what you say is true, then you placed me in grave danger."

"I regret the necessity, but as I stated, the circumstances are unusual in the extreme."

She furrowed her brow, not quite ready to believe him. "Where was the map headed?"

"Mr. Edgerton, the scoundrel under my command, sent it to his wife. We were able to intercept it."

"Why not just arrest Mr. Edgerton and demand that he tell you all?" Lieutenant Freeman asked.

"Because Mr. Edgerton is dead."

Charlotte rounded her mouth. "Oh." The hairs on the back of her neck rose. She had to admit begrudgingly that there seemed to be more to this affair than she had considered.

"We must bear in mind Mr. Edgerton's co-conspirators. Additionally, we want to avoid drawing the notice of treasure seekers competing with us for the bounty. The more who learn of it, the more treacherous the matter becomes for everyone. So, Charlotte, I need you to give me the map and keys."

"Why did you dose and kidnap me?" she asked suspiciously, not ready to swallow his tale whole.

"Because I thought you were in on it with Edgerton's band."

"That's preposterous!" the general cried.

"Absolutely bloody unbelievable!" Lieutenant Freeman asserted, then looked sheepishly at her. "Sorry, Miss Charlotte."

"Think nothing of it, Lieutenant. These last few hours I've been saying the very same thing."

Girard shifted in his seat. "I may have jumped to some unwarranted conclusions."

She raised her eyebrow dubiously. "May?"

"Well," he defended reasonably, "you were there when I intercepted the rider carrying the map and keys. And for other circumstantial reasons, I was led to believe that you may have been involved."

She glared angrily at him. "*You* are the only reason I am involved."

"I must admit that I might have been a bit fervent in my attempt to stop the plot and return the property to the Treasury."

"Ha!" she cried.

"And now?" Lieutenant Freeman asked.

Girard straightened, his dark eyes glowing with purpose. "Now, I use the map and keys to try and uncover the hiding place. Additionally," he added in a steely-edged voice, "I am going to stop the scoundrels who are behind it all."

"What about Charlotte?" the general asked.

"Yes, pray tell, what is going to happen when word spreads that we are engaged?"

The general held out his opened hand. "You placed her in grave danger and put her reputation in jeopardy."

"And I saved it as well," Girard responded.

"Assuming you will marry Charlotte," came the general's quick reply.

"I would sooner marry my own brother!" she cried. "There's not enough scandal in the world to compel me to spend a moment longer in *his* presence!"

Awkward silence.

Girard leaned forward. "General, if I may have a word with you in private?"

The general pursed his lips, nodding.

Her hands fisted. "You are not excusing me!"

The general stood. "First I will speak with Girard alone, and then you, Charlotte. I believe that it is the best way to find a resolution to this dilemma."

"What dilemma?" She rose, her stance wide, her hands firmly on her hips. "The man used me abominably and put everything," she choked out the word, "*everything*, at risk."

"Exactly," he replied. "There is entirely too much at risk, and we must make it right. Is that not so, Girard?"

"Yes, sir."

Lieutenant Freeman glided over on his crutch and stood next to Charlotte, waiting.

Shaking her head in disbelief, Charlotte marched beside him from the room, feeling more than a little put out.

The door closed loudly behind the lieutenant. The general turned. "What aren't you telling me, Girard?"

He almost smiled. "One never could hide anything from you." He stood and walked over to the box of cigars on the desk. "May I?"

The general nodded. "I will join you."

After a few moments spent smoking in silence, James sat down and then stood again, agitated. The scent of tobacco filled the air, covering the other odors that emanated from the hospital—sulfur, illness, the sickly sweet smell of blood.

"My foul cousin Mortimer is behind the thing."

The general's eyes widened behind his spectacles. "Are you certain?"

"Yes, although I have no proof. Not only does it make perfect sense, given our past, but the scoundrel started sending me letters, taunting me with his exploits."

"He actually signed them?"

"No. He would not go that far. He ends them with 'CZN.' "

"Cousin," General Cumseby breathed. "I am almost glad that Richard is not here to see this."

James nodded. "Although I am loath to admit it, those are

my sentiments exactly. The idea of Uncle, of my mother, of my entire family seeing his betrayal . . ."

"Then you want to handle this quietly."

"Yes. And I need Charlotte's help."

The older man rolled his cigar between his fingers, frowning. "I cannot understand how you could come to the conclusion that that lovely girl was in any way involved in this scheme."

"Because Mortimer wants to marry her," James replied, blowing a long line of smoke into the air. "She was nervous when I mentioned him. She was there when I intercepted the rider. You add it up."

"I can assure you that Charlotte has nothing whatsoever to do with your cousin's scheme."

"Unknowingly, perhaps?"

General Cumseby shook his head, smiling. "Charlotte is too smart for that. She is quick and knowing. A bit too knowing for a young lady of her standing. No. Girard, you are dead wrong."

"Maybe so." He shrugged. "But I have made it known that we are engaged. She has little choice in the matter, really."

"You obviously do not know my Charlotte. She does not worry overmuch about what other people think of her. She does not tell me, but I know that she gets much grief for volunteering here. She is sunshine on a rainy day to these boys. She does what she would because she believes it is right, regardless of social consequences." He grimaced. "And that is what troubles me. Charlotte should have more of a care about her future." Leaning back in his chair, he eyed James thoughtfully. "A lady's reputation is not to be played with lightly, Girard."

James knew the general was right, but he needed Charlotte near him, in a best-case scenario with her playing the part of loving betrothed. Mortimer was never one to allow his face to be rubbed in the dirt. The engagement was a sure-fire method of getting Mortimer's nose out of joint, goading him into showing his hand. He rubbed his eyes. This was getting so bloody complicated. "I know. I just need her assistance until the end of the Season. I hope to have the matter concluded by then."

"And after the Season ends and everyone believes that you are engaged to be married? What about Charlotte then?"

He shrugged. "After the Season is over, I will provide for her."

"Provide for her?" the general asked, raising his snowy eyebrows skeptically. He harrumphed and stood, tapping his cigar in the tray on his desk.

Guilt washed over him as he considered how his actions must look to General Cumseby, a man whose opinion he respected. It seems he had been wide of the mark about Charlotte. Still, his intentions were well founded. Did that count for nothing?

"I must admit," James began tentatively, "if I had to select a person to assist me, she would make a superior choice. She is quite spirited." His brow furrowed as he considered how she had fought him and his man. "And intelligent. She was quick witted enough to come to you for assistance. And it could prove helpful that she does not care overmuch what people say about her."

"Did you not hear what I said, man?" Cumseby growled. "She needs to have more of a care about what Society thinks of her. As a lady her entire future depends upon her reputation. For you to bandy about the loss of her social standing as if it were something to be considered after the fact ignores the reality of her circumstances."

He looked down at his hands; suddenly it was hard to meet the general's gaze.

Grumbling under his breath, the older man began pacing the short room. He stopped in midstride and straightened, commenting carefully, "You could marry her."

"Did you not hear her? The girl thinks I am the devil incarnate."

"Charlotte is a reasonable child. If she understood that you truly were acting with the best intentions . . ."

He looked around the room as if searching for a way out of the noose that seemed to be tightening around his neck. "General, I confess that I wronged Charlotte. And I want to make it up to her. But wedding the girl? Her conduct is unseemly, she has no regard for propriety—"

"—I thought that was a desirable quality in your situation," the older man interrupted smoothly.

"I hope for this situation to be remedied shortly," he said through clenched teeth.

And there was the crux of the matter. He hoped, prayed, that this business with Mortimer would end with his foul cousin's untimely demise. He did not want the shadow of Mortimer's misdeeds to hang over the rest of his and his family's lives. That was the whole point to all this subterfuge.

The general pursed his lips and sniffed as if coming to a great decision. "Although I will do anything I can regarding the stolen property, I may not be able to help you where Charlotte is concerned."

He stood angrily. "I will not be blackmailed into matrimony."

"I am not the one who announced the engagement. That was *your* brainstorm."

James shook his head admiringly. "You were always one to take the bull by the horns, General. But you are forgetting something: I am in the best position to help her."

"Help her?"

"Charlotte may still be in danger."

James played his trump card. "You know Mortimer, if he wants something . . ."

"He stops at nothing until he has it," the general finished testily. He pursed his lips and asked, "So you mean to protect Charlotte?"

"Yes . . . protect her," he replied evenly. "That is why she must move into Pennington House. And that is why she must remain my betrothed."

"My point exactly. Anyone with muscles and a pistol can protect Charlotte's person, but you are the only one who can vouchsafe her reputation, forever." He placed a heavy hand on James's shoulder. "It is the only way to do right by Charlotte."

"I understand what you are saying, General, but I cannot marry the girl. She will not suit. She is too unconventional, too wild, too improper." He waved his hand. "The list goes on."

"Are you daft, man? She is so beautiful and kind, half the men here are in love with her. She is a rare individual of fine sensibilities and uncompromising morals. In that respect, she is an Original among her peers."

"I will have to take your word on that, General. In our limited acquaintance, I have found her to be outrageous, unseemly . . . why, she rammed me in the groin, not once, but three times!"

"And if your sister Elizabeth were in her place, would you not have wanted her to do the same?"

"It is different in a wife."

"Why?"

"You bloody well know why," he growled. "I cannot explain."

The older man sighed and removed his hand. "I never thought I would say it, but I am disappointed in you, Girard. I always thought you were one to cover your debts."

He looked up warily. "What debt?"

"To Charlotte."

James stamped out his cigar angrily. "I will do right by her. I just won't agree to marry her."

"It is your choice entirely," Cumseby murmured, then turned to the door and opened it. "Mr. Jones, please ask Charlotte to join us."

"Yes sir!"

After a few moments of uncomfortable silence, Charlotte walked guardedly into the room, her blue eyes darting warily from one man to the other. Her hair looked like a bat's nest and her clothes appeared as if they had been rolled in the mud. Still, she did have an endearing air about her, that was, until she wrinkled her nose at the smoky office. "Cigars, ugh."

"Ah, Charlotte, my dear. The good duke here would like you to continue on as his betrothed for the remainder of the Season."

"Absolutely not!" she cried. "The man is a beast, a monster, a depraved blackguard . . ."

The general turned to James, and peeking over the rim of spectacles, raised his eyebrows inquiringly.

"Fine," James growled. It seemed that the best means of trapping his vile cousin would also be his penance for his wrongs, and they were conveniently bundled in the chit standing frumpily before him. "I will do it."

"On your honor," the older man demanded. At the moment, he was anything but grandfatherly. He was "the general" in rank and manner.

"On my honor," he spat.

"And you will do everything in your power to make it so?"

"Yes, I will," he stated through clenched teeth.

Walking over to the general, James whispered for his ears only, "I can almost feel the shackles encircling my ankles."

"You will thank me for this one day. You would not be able to live with yourself otherwise."

He looked over his shoulder at the rumpled, randy-faced girl he had just agreed to woo into marriage. "Perhaps you are correct." He stepped back and bowed to the general, a worthy adversary and an even worthier ally. "But I doubt it."

The general turned to Charlotte, smiling winningly. "Charlotte, my dear, if I may have a word?"

Chapter 11

By the time they were off in the duke's carriage, Charlotte was sore, tired, hungry and more than a little irritable. James was looking as infuriatingly unflappable as ever. Nary a ruffle in his white linen shirt was out of place nor a wrinkle showed on his dark coat or his tight buckskin britches. The man had no right to be so drattedly handsome.

"I still do not understand why we must pretend to be so"—the words tasted sour on her tongue—"in love." If this farce was going to be anything near as tragic as her last venture with Venus, then she should just don her lace cap and blue stockings and call it a day.

"As the general and I pointed out, quite a number of times," he stated with obviously feigned patience, "it makes the story of our secret courtship while volunteering at the hospital more believable, and allows for a bit more leeway when you move into Pennington House."

She opened her mouth to challenge that issue as well, but he interrupted with an upheld hand, "It is for your safety,

Charlotte. This is not a game, we are dealing with cold-blooded scoundrels."

She crossed her arms and smirked, allowing the phrase to hang in the air.

"Yes, well, Charlotte, I already apologized for my poor treatment of you."

It had been quite an eloquent apology at that, she had to admit reluctantly. She sighed, looking out the window at the congested streets. She was finding it difficult to figure out who exactly the Duke of Girard was. Beyond his exasperatingly attractive demeanor, which tended to have an irritatingly unsettling effect on her nerves, the general had praised James Morgan to the heavens. If she had had to listen to one more rendition of his heroic efforts on behalf of King and Country, she had thought she would scream.

She peeked at him out of the corner of her eye. Maybe he was not a complete cad. Still, not every piece was fitting in this very curious puzzle. What gentleman would knowingly drag an innocent lady into this nasty affair? She did not accept his lame excuses about why he thought she was involved. There was more to this plot than he was telling, and she was determined to winnow out the truth.

She remarked, "I still do not understand why I cannot let my brother or Aunt Sylvie in on the charade. Allowing them to think we're truly engaged sets them up for a terrible disappointment."

"As we discussed at length with General Cumseby, it is unfair to ask them to pretend—and moreover, it probably would spoil the plan. People are notoriously bad at keeping secrets."

"You seem capable of handling more than your fair share."

He ignored the barb. "You agreed. I expect you to hold to your promise."

"Oh, I will keep my part of the bargain." Bargain with the devil that it was.

The carriage rolled to a stop and Charlotte looked out the window. "What are we doing on Piccadilly Street?"

"I will be just a moment," he stated, jumping down from the carriage. "Or would you care to join me?"

Charlotte looked down at her wrinkled green dress and raised her gloveless hands to her wild hair. She glared at him. "I am in no condition to be seen in public, especially without a chaperone, and you know it."

James merely called over his shoulder, "I will be back in a trice."

Her world was going mad and he was shopping! For almost a quarter hour, Charlotte fumed in the overwarm, stuffy carriage. Finally the door opened, and James gracefully seated himself before receiving a variety of packages from the footman outside.

"I hope your excursion was successful," she remarked caustically.

"Quite."

Before she could say another word, he pulled a lovely blue bonnet with green feathers from a hatbox on his lap and held it out to her.

"I cannot accept gifts from you."

"Oh, these are not gifts, Charlotte, really," he replied reasonably. "You cannot go home looking as you are."

She scowled. She could not disagree, given that she looked as if she had been rolled under a carriage. Well, she almost had. Being seen in her current state would raise too many questions, and showing up newly engaged on James's arm was more than enough of a shock. Plus, the bonnet was truly magnificent.

She looked away. "I do not believe that there is much that will help."

He shifted to sit beside her and tingles ignited her senses, suddenly making her feel skittish. She almost jumped across to the opposite bench, but tried for a modicum of composure.

"What are you doing?" she demanded with a mouth that had suddenly gone dry.

"Come, Charlotte, I will not bite."

Why did she suddenly feel so hot and giddy? Well, his nearness had always played havoc with her senses. Not for the first time, she thought that a man should have to work a lot harder to get such a reaction from a lady. She was a healthy female of almost three-and-twenty, but that did not mean she had to be completely susceptible to his charms. She straightened, resolving to be businesslike and to bear in mind how he had treated her just that morning.

James pulled out a pair of beautiful brown kid gloves and offered them to her. Tentatively, she took them; they were softer than butter. She held the gloves up to her nose relishing the rich, musky scent of new leather.

"It is probably a good idea for me at least to try to straighten my person," she admitted slowly. "But I will reimburse you, of course."

"Now, your hair," he stated matter-of-factly, as he set a box on his lap and pulled out a magnificent inlaid silver brush, comb, and mirror set. The silver was carved with an intricate array of roses and must have cost a small fortune.

"I cannot help but get the impression that you are trying to bribe me."

James looked up as if startled. His dark blue gaze gleamed with an emotion she did not quite recognize. He let out a long strained breath. "Actually, I am trying to make it up to you in some very, very small way. I am really quite sorry for all I've put you through and would like the opportunity to start afresh. To find a way to redeem myself in your eyes."

She bit her lip, not knowing what to say. It was not in her nature to lie, so she could not tell him that it was all water under the bridge. "Forgive and forget" was a lovely notion, but her anger, and yes, her hatred, were too fresh. His nearness unsettled her and she did not like that. Was she allowing his effect on her senses to cloud her reasoning? The general was quite effusive regarding the man's seemingly stellar qualities. Perhaps she was not seeing him as he truly was?

She studied him through lowered lashes. A thick black lock of his wavy mane fell over his forehead, making him appear almost boyish, vulnerable. He did seem to be trying to mend fences . . .

James rubbed his chin and added disarmingly, "Am I to understand from your silence that I have quite a road ahead to win your esteem?"

"Why do you care a fig about my approval?"

"We are engaged to be married, for one."

"It is a pretense. You said yourself that it should all be over by the close of the Season."

"Yes, well, to the world, we are betrothed, and I would assume that we would want to be on good terms, since we will be living together and socializing as a couple."

The idea of all of the balls and outings made her want to run into her studio and bar the door. She was safer with her clay and paints than being at the mercy of the dagger-tongued ladies of the *ton*. Just the thought of the challenge of appearing somewhat stylish while at the same time covered with bruises made her shudder with dread. It also reminded her that the duke was the one who had saved her from the beastly man in her room.

"It is just, well—we did not exactly get off to a good start," she offered.

"I was quite awful, wasn't I?"

"Yes, you were."

"An unfeeling blackguard?"

Unbidden, her lips quirked. "A monster, actually."

He grimaced. "I was doing a better job than I had intended."

"You are quite the effective villain, you know. You have a real talent for it." Her cheeks warmed. Heavens, was she flirting?

"I am not the only one. You certainly were capable of defending yourself; you made me think you had been professionally trained."

She suppressed a pleased smile. "Lieutenant Freeman deserves the credit. He is quite a worthy instructor. He really gets down to the meat and bones of it."

He shifted in his seat, adjusting his britches. "Yes, I know."

She looked down at his lap and then flit her eyes up to his face, aghast. Her cheeks flamed. "Ah, ah, ah . . ." Her tongue would not work and her eyes raced about the cabin, looking anywhere but at him.

He grasped her chin and turned her face toward him. "Do not worry, Charlotte, you did not cause any *permanent* harm."

He pressed his smooth lips to hers and her eyes widened as tingles lanced down her body. His mouth was soft and curved delicately at the edges, fitting her lips like it was designed specifically for her. His lips parted slightly and his tongue flicked playfully across her teeth and into her mouth, boldly caressing her tongue and causing the most shockingly titillating sensation quite a far distance from her lips.

Her heart skipped a beat and she pulled back, thunderstruck.

He watched her through hooded eyes. "Have you never been kissed before, Charlotte?"

She blinked. Good heavens! Myles Wilmington had never kissed her like that, and she had been in love with the rogue! She licked her lips, trying to collect herself, but it only revived the stirring sensation of his tongue touching hers.

"A true apology comes with a kiss, does it not?" he asked mischievously.

"Who is apologizing, you or me?" she sputtered breathlessly.

"It was a shared pleasure, let it be a mutual thing."

She raised her hand to her lips. "I, I do not think that we should do that again."

"Why not? This is an awful mess, we might as well make the best of a bad situation." He traced his hand down her cheek, causing her breath to catch in her throat. "Besides, we must learn to appear to be in love. It is only natural for us to exhibit affection."

She shook her head to clear it. "But it is an act, a performance for the public. So we should not do it when we do not need to." She wished her heart would stop beating so erratically. "It is too . . ."

"Improper?"

"Disconcerting" was the word she was thinking of. When James touched her, blast the man, or even came near her, her senses seemed to become overwhelmed. Kissing put her too much in his power. He was the experienced duke and probably had had harems of mistresses. Well, she was not about to allow him to add her to his list of conquests. "I just do not think that we should do it again," she stated firmly.

"I really am not a monster, Charlotte."

"I cannot imagine General Cumseby singing the praises he did earlier for a monster," she replied glibly, just wanting to shift to a safer topic.

"For the time being at least, we are betrothed. A love match. You must become accustomed to me touching you, Charlotte."

Straightening, she tugged on the gloves with a businesslike air. "Do not concern yourself, your grace, I will abide by my agreement."

"As will I," James mumbled under his breath. "No matter the challenge."

Chapter 12

A short while later, while sitting in the warm, soapy water of a lavender-scented bath, the fatal flaw to her plan to unearth the truth behind James's actions suddenly struck Charlotte; if she was shopping, attending balls, parties, teas, and the sundry activities of a Season in full swing, then she would probably be with James only in social situations, would not participate in his mission, would likely never uncover his underlying purpose. He would be off chasing after his treasure, and she would be left receiving Polite Society as the betrothed of the great Duke of Girard.

Charlotte slammed her hand in the sudsy bath in frustration, splashing water out of the tub. She was not about to go along with this colossal ruse merely to be "the Thing" one minute and scandal droppings the next. She scowled, annoyance and anger clouding her mind. How could she have been so thoughtless? Well, playing Society dame was not exactly her activity of choice, and shopping was fairly low on her list of priorities too.

She marshaled her thoughts. He still needed her to give him the map and keys. Although the odds were still against her, she was not about to fold her hand.

By the time the footman arrived with the supplies she'd requested to cover the hideous bruises around her neck, Charlotte was revitalized and refreshed from her bath. She sat down at her secretary and drafted preliminary sketches of the map and keys. She eyed her work critically. For a quick view in the middle of the night in poor candlelight, they were not half bad. They would have to do.

She quickly left her rooms and locked the sketches in her father's safe in the library. She was not about to take any more chances—particularly with the clever duke. He seemed to have every angle covered, and she was not about to let him shuffle her off to parties and the like while he traipsed around doing lord only knew what.

Once back in her chambers, she opened the packages, setting aside the fabric and lace. She tore open the accompanying note and read:

My Dear Miss Hastings:

It was good to hear from you after so long. Once again, I send you my deepest regrets over your father's death. I trust that the enclosed meets your very specific requirements. Per your request, I have forwarded the bill to the Duke of Girard. Please contact me if I can be of further assistance.

Faithfully, your servant,
Mr. William Frank

Charlotte looked down at the exquisite cameo in her hand. Mr. Frank had surpassed her expectations. It was an intricately carved portrait of a woman's profile, with fine detail, surrounded by a plentiful array of snowy white pearls. Just the thing to give her attire a touch of glamour and boost her confidence. Fashion was not her forte, and what she planned on wearing would be different, to say the least. She wondered how she was going to be received by the *ton*, and moreover by the imminently stylish dowager, Katherine Morgan. Charlotte looked at the clock. Well, she would know soon enough.

James tried to suppress his mounting frustration as his mother commented for the third time, "I do not understand why you did not consult me on this matter, James. I am your mother. Why did you rush things so unnecessarily?"

He replaced his teacup on the tray table between them and responded patiently, "Mother, as I have already explained, Charlotte is a wonderful girl, with excellent connections. Her father was the late Viscount Sheffield. Her family is good *ton* and her manner is all that is pleasing to behold." He almost grimaced, recalling her flair for kicking a man in the most damaging places.

Spine straight, arms crossed, the dowager, unrelenting, continued, "She is the niece of the Earl and Countess of Grandby. That does not speak well for her. If it were not for a quirk of fate, the Earl would still be a common horse breeder, you know. We do not associate with their kind." She pursed her lips crossly. "Granted, the family is acceptable *ton,* but really, James—you could do so much better. Take Constance Druthers, for instance. How do you think that Constance is going to feel about this?"

"I do not particularly care what Constance Druthers thinks about my engagement," he declared through gritted teeth. "Nor anyone else, for that matter. I have chosen Charlotte to be my wife. You should be happy that I have chosen so well. She is beautiful, well mannered, and gracious." He prayed that Charlotte would turn out to be as he described.

His mother flicked an imaginary speck of dirt off her billowing skirts. "I do not understand how you can see such attributes under such hideously unfashionable attire, James. The chit has no style."

He stood and walked over to the windows, remarking contemptuously over his shoulder, "Really, Mother, even you cannot be so shallow as to judge a person by their wardrobe."

Scowling, the dowager stood and walked to stand behind her son. "Does her family know that she frequents the army hospital in search of a husband? Or are they dying to marry her off and cover up her scandalous behavior? I thought Elizabeth would be the one to cause me grief, not you."

James's patience was almost at an end, but there was yet another hurdle to overcome. He turned and faced his mother. "I would have you be more discreet when you speak of my intended." He drew a breath. "Charlotte is to be my wife, and I want her treated with respect. I will not allow anyone to malign her. This is particularly true when there may be gossip about me being in Charlotte's room at the Balstrams' house."

"So *that* is it!" cried the dowager triumphantly, her finger pointed high to the sky. "She threw herself at you and forced you to propose. The dishonorable wanton! We will not stand for this entrapment. She undertook to disgrace herself, thus you lose no honor by refusing to succumb to her blackmail."

James held onto his temper, but barely. He spoke quietly, through clenched teeth. "Mother. You did not hear me correctly. I entered her room *uninvited*. *I* did it. *I* placed *Charlotte* in this situation. To be frank, she is not so enamored about having to marry me."

She blinked in disbelief. "She did not force herself upon you?"

"Definitely not," he answered firmly.

"She does not wish to marry you?"

"Let's just say that I do not need you or anyone else making the situation less palatable for her. I want Charlotte to be welcomed in our home. She is to be my wife and the mother of my children, your grandchildren. I would have her treated properly. Is that understood?"

His mother's steely eyes narrowed. She drew herself up, her manner anything but cowed. "If you will excuse me, James. I will speak with Cook about dinner."

James nodded and prayed that that would be the end of his troubles with his mother. Knowing her, he doubted it.

Chapter 13

Charlotte arrived at Pennington House at eight o'clock and waited tensely in a stately drawing room while her belongings were moved into a suite of rooms on the family's floor.

She took a deep breath, trying to stop herself from being so edgy. Yes, she was playing a decidedly different part, loving betrothed. But she was born to the role; why did it distress her so? Aside from the idea of living under the same roof with the handsome gentleman who had kissed her so daringly barely hours before? She looked down and realized that she was gripping her skirts and quickly unfurled her hands and flattened the muslin gown, hoping that she had not caused too much damage.

For something to occupy her mind, she turned and inspected the large portrait above the mantle. The artist had managed to capture the former duke's patriarchal air and the duchess's flair for style, in a subtle but tangible way. She stepped closer and examined Girard. He must have been fourteen or so then. His long black hair framed his face, delicately brushing his already broad shoulders. That same dark curl hung boyishly over his brow. You could see the promise of the man in the young lad, with his piercing blue eyes and aristocratic nose. Strong, detached, determined. There was little softness in him even then.

James paused on the threshold, suddenly nervous. Standing before the mantel was the lady who would be his wife, his partner, and the mother of his children. The enormity of what he had promised the general suddenly struck home, causing his heart to pound.

He wet his lips. Well, at least she was attractive, a bit too alluring, in some respects. He had not planned on kissing her in the carriage and did not even remember deciding to do so, but he was glad he had. It gave him a taste of the pleasures he hoped were to come. He recalled the feel of her generous curves and her hot responsiveness, and his body hardened. Her sensuality made him want to rush to bed her. Perhaps that was the way to force the marriage and keep his word to the general. He pushed the thought aside; from what General Cumseby had said, she would not let the threat of scandal dictate her future. He resolved to keep his distance. The chit was a bit too distracting for safety.

He must have made a sound, because she turned. Her astute blue gaze was wide and wary. She was dressed in a plain muslin gown of deep blue with a broad band of black lace lined in blue satin covering her neck. A beautiful cameo surrounded by pearls held the cloth in place. She wore long matching gloves of black lace with blue satin edging running down her arms. James had never seen such a style and he marveled at her resourcefulness.

"Good evening, Charlotte." He advanced deeper into the room. Hoping to present a confident air, he kissed her on the cheek. She smelled faintly of lavender and soap. "You look beautiful."

She stepped back, ostensibly startled by his intimate welcome. "Good evening, your grace."

"You must call me James," he chided gently.

She frowned and peered over his shoulder, whispering crossly, "I do wish you would stop this pretense when we are alone." She raised her hand to the jewelry at her throat, fretfully fiddling with it.

He stepped closer to examine the cameo and she inhaled a shaky breath. Lord, he must really have frightened her to make her so skittish. Well, he would do everything he could to make her exceedingly used to his presence. Like getting back into the saddle once you've fallen off a horse.

Touching the cameo delicately with his fingertips he commented, "Ingenious design."

She blushed and he watched the rosiness spread under her twenty-seven freckles and across her ivory cheeks.

So the plucky girl was susceptible to flattery.

"It suits her," came his mother's dry comment from the doorway. "She could certainly use a little sprucing up of her wardrobe, and it is a start." The dowager glided into the room. "Albeit a small one."

James took Charlotte's hand and turned. "Mother, may I present to you Miss Charlotte Hastings, my betrothed."

Charlotte curtseyed perfectly.

The dowager nodded graciously. "Miss Hastings, I welcome you into our home."

She rose. "Thank you, your grace."

"Regrettably, Elizabeth is not here to greet you as well. She will be returning next week from a visit to our cousins, Lord and Lady Falmouth. You are from Weveney. Is that not correct?"

"Yes, your grace."

"We have a cousin, Mr. Mortimer Blanton, whose home is not far from Bury St. Edmunds. Are you acquainted with him?"

"Yes, your grace. He is our nearest neighbor."

"I have not heard from him in some time. Have you any news?"

"Mr. Blanton spends much of his time away from Bury St. Edmunds, your grace." Charlotte artfully sidestepped the question.

Again, James wondered what she was hiding. Still, he did not want his mother dwelling on his foul cousin and quickly changed the subject. "I am sure you have much to discuss with Charlotte on the household needs, Mother."

The dowager kept her eyes trained on Charlotte. "When you have settled in, I will acquaint you with the staff and operations of the household."

"Thank you, your grace. I would greatly appreciate any assistance you might provide. Although," she looked at him pointedly, "James and I do have much work to do on a project for the veterans' hospital."

What was she talking about? James did not recall any additional promises to the general, and the investigation would occupy all of his free time.

"James informs me that you have been handling household matters in your mother's stead," his mother pressed.

"Yes, your grace."

"You were very young, were you not, when she died?"

"Thirteen, your grace," she replied politely.

The dowager looked penetratingly at James. "Then you will probably benefit from some guidance."

Charlotte added sweetly, "Although I had the benefit of my extended family's tutelage, I am sure there is even more I could learn from your incalculable experience."

The dowager started.

Did Charlotte just call his mother old? James coughed into his fist to stifle his chuckle. His mother opened her mouth to react, but the butler entered to announce that dinner awaited them in the dining room. James quickly extended his arm to his mother, effectively silencing her until the next parry.

Charlotte glanced across the elegant dining room table at the lady who was, for the moment, her mother-in-law-to-be. The dowager was a small, polished woman, with chocolate brown eyes lined with spidery wrinkles, gray-streaked jet black hair, olive skin, and tightly compressed lips. She held herself with a haughty, restrained air. Her small stature belied her large personality, which emanated from her like thunder before a storm. No wonder her son seemed without a soft side; she had probably hardened his temperament in the womb.

Charlotte examined James furtively through her eyelashes. He was dashedly handsome, with a crisp white collared shirt marking a stark contrast to his black formal jacket and skintight black breeches. He had been preoccupied through the last two courses, barely commenting as his mother prattled on like a harpy at a scandalbroth. It seems James had about as little interest as she in Viscount Marby's mistress's antics.

Charlotte looked down as the next course was placed before her on gilded china. Ah, veal in a white wine and cream sauce. Her last fine meal at the Balstrams seemed a lifetime ago, and at present the veal was more interesting than the dowager's gossip.

The dowager delicately parted her lips and declared, "I have it on good authority that the Countess of Grandby's daughter ran off with a common farmer."

Charlotte straightened her spine. That was her cousin the dowager was backbiting. Although as plausible as snow falling in summer, perhaps the dowager did not know of the connection. She licked her lips, trying for a reasonable tone. "Actually, your grace, your information is incorrect. *My cousin* Amelia has married Mr. Sherwin, the largest property owner in the Southern Uplands. Although he is not titled, he is highly regarded by all who know him and is considered a most respectable gentleman."

"A Scot." The lady shuddered. "Your family must be horrified."

She clenched her fists in her lap, willing herself to be calm. "Although my aunt and uncle were hesitant at first, now that they know Mr. Sherwin, they are quite pleased with the match."

She sniffed. "I suppose we can overlook your connections, knowing that you could not help your misfortune."

Charlotte bristled. "Misfortune? I feel privileged to be part of such a family. When my mother died I did not know what we would have done without the kindness of my relations."

"No need to get into a snit, child," she admonished. "Loyalty is an admirable trait when you know where to place it. Your circumstances have improved now, so you can put aside your prior allegiances and work on becoming part of a superior family."

Charlotte almost choked on her tongue. "If by superior you mean titled, Randolph is an Earl, for heaven's sake. But that is irrelevant. Accidents of birth and death may land a title, but the traits of integrity and honor do not necessarily come with it. Randolph and Sylvie Jaspers are all that is good and noble."

"The Earl," she said the term as if it were a disease, "was a mere horse breeder before the title accidentally fell his way." She dabbed a napkin to her tightly compressed lips. "The title should have gone to his cousin, Mr. Jefferies. He is by far the more deserving of the two."

Charlotte could not believe that this woman was sitting here, calmly insulting her family to her face. She stated through clenched teeth, "His cousin not only did not deserve the title, he is not worthy to be called a gentleman."

The dowager leaned forward, raising her voice. "How *dare* you challenge me? I have known Sylvie Jaspers since before you were born! If ever there was a pair undeserving of the title of nobility, it is them!"

Charlotte rose. "How dare *you* slander my family?"

The dowager stood and threw down her napkin. "James, how can you sit there and listen to this . . . *person* insult me? It is bad enough we have to suffer the veiled shame associated with your abrupt engagement. I will not suffer her insolence!"

James looked up from his veal, seemingly irritated that his dinner was being disturbed. Charlotte suppressed the urge to throw her fork at him. It would probably shatter against his stonelike countenance.

He coolly dabbed his mouth with his napkin. "I see no reason for such excitement."

"Of course you wouldn't." Charlotte glared at him. "Honor and decency are so commonplace to you."

The dowager nodded haughtily at her. "Your intended needs instruction on how to behave."

"Let me save you from the trouble of having to 'instruct' me, your grace." She turned and a footman rushed to pull back her chair. "If you will excuse me, I shall collect my belongings and be gone."

James stood, a scowl darkening his chiseled features. "Charlotte, your place is here, and you are not going anywhere."

She straightened her spine and raised her chin defiantly. "I am not one of your servants to be ordered about. I will not suffer the indignities of being in a house where my family and I are not welcome."

She spun on her heel and marched out the door.

* * *

James stood stiffly, his eyes on the passage through which Charlotte had exited. He knew that there was a long-standing feud between his mother and Lady Jaspers. He did not really care; he did mind, however, that his mother's arrogance and Charlotte's uncompromising loyalties were destroying his plans. Rubbing his chin thoughtfully, he recalled the general's warning about Charlotte's constancy. "Like a mama bear with cubs." Not a bad trait to have in your wife.

"You heard her," the dowager said severely. "I warned you, James. That girl cannot be a duchess; she does not have the quality or character. She is beneath us and unworthy of our name."

He glared, stone-faced, at his mother. "Last I recalled, loyalty was an attribute to be admired, not scorned. Charlotte appears to have the strength of character to stand up even to you, Mother, when it comes to her family's honor." He threw down his napkin, disgusted with his mother's theatrics. "And have no doubt that she will be my duchess. I have made a pledge and I honor my commitments. So the more mud you sling, the more you tarnish *my wife's* and thus our family's good name. Have a care, Mother," he warned, "for Charlotte is not the only one ready to defend her family's honor—no matter the adversary."

She reared as if struck, but rebounded, grinding out, "I will not have that woman in my household." At the look on his face, her eyes widened. "I speak of Lady Jaspers, not the Hastings girl."

Devil take it, he had enough troubles without having to play umpire to females. Still, if he did not do it, then who would? He tilted his head in assent. "In consideration of your . . . sensitivity, I will ask Charlotte to have Lady Jaspers visit when you are not in the house."

"That is unacceptable," she cried. "I am still running this household, and . . ."

"And Charlotte is to be my wife and your daughter-in-law. That is the end of the discussion, Mother." He strode out the door. Thanks to his mother, he now had more fences to mend with his betrothed. James wondered if he was ever going to be on the winning side of the scales with her.

Chapter 14

James paused before the closed door to Charlotte's chambers and took a long, deep breath to quell his irritation. He had more important things to do than woo a mulish girl into marriage. But aside from his promise to the general, he needed Charlotte to catch Mortimer; she was integral to his plans. And he would do whatever it took to achieve *that* goal.

He rapped twice, hard, on the wooden paneled door and listened to the shuffling of skirts inside.

The door opened a crack and the maid Anna peered outside. She blushed a deep pink and looked nervously over her shoulder at Charlotte, who was yanking dresses from the open wardrobe.

The maid curtseyed quickly and announced, "My lady, it is his grace."

Charlotte stopped her packing and walked to the doorway, effectively blocking his advance into the room. "What can I do for you, your grace?"

He looked pointedly at Anna and then at her. "A moment alone, if you would?"

"You cannot enter my bedroom. Despite the unusual circumstances surrounding our acquaintance, I must draw the line somewhere."

Now she was choosing to be virtuous and proper. She was going to drive him mad with her obstinacy. "We can speak in the sitting room next door," he ground out.

She seemed to think about it a moment, but then nodded. "Fine. Which way?"

He extended his arm. When she lightly touched his sleeve, he was gratified to see that she was no longer skittish around him. Heaven help him if he was going to need to keep her angry to be able to get near her without her recoiling. A love match, indeed.

James closed the door behind them, shutting out the curious eyes of the servants. A single candle glowed from above the mantel, just barely illuminating the rarely used room. James had little enough occasion to visit the cozy apartment during his life; it had been off limits to him and his sister until his father's passing. For the first time since moving into the ducal chambers, he studied the low brown leather couch, large plaid covered chairs, and small table with a critical eye. The furniture was a bit ratty and far from fashionable, not exactly the best scenery with which to convince Charlotte that it was in her best interests to stay. But it would have to do.

Charlotte turned around, her arms crossed, her stance wide, and her eyes skeptical. Her eyes flew to his closed bedroom door and then down at her interlaced arms as she tried to conceal her rosy blush. Gold highlights glinted in her auburn hair from the reflected glow of the candle.

"Sit down and let us speak for a moment." He indicated to the brown leather sofa.

She did not move. "I do not know that we have much to discuss."

James tried to keep his irritation in check. He had always considered himself a rational, composed man, not given to fits of anger. But between Mortimer, his mother, and now his strong-willed betrothed, he was finding it harder and harder to keep his emotions from boiling over. He stated through clenched teeth, "We have an agreement, Charlotte, and I expect you to keep to it."

"I will not sit by and allow my family to be maligned." She glared. "I, at least, have some sense of honor about how I treat people—within earshot and otherwise."

Had she just dared to question his honor? If she were a man she'd be meeting him on the field at dawn. Well, she was not as free-spirited as she might think. "Do you have any idea about the speculation that will arise if you move in and out of my home on the very same day? Especially after what happened in Southbridge?"

"There are worse things than Society's disapproval," she retorted.

His jaw clenched. "It will be more than mere disapproval, and you know it. You will be given the cut direct from everyone of consequence and your family will face censure if they stand by you."

"After what I have been through, perhaps it is worth taking my chances. At least I need not worry about scorpions in my own home."

His anger seethed. "You will remain in this household and play your part, just as you agreed." Two could throw stones. "Or perhaps is it *you* who lacks the principle to keep your word?"

Her lush bottom lip dropped open with disbelief, her face flushed red, and her blue eyes sparkled with fury. At any other time he might have found the picture alluring.

"You are the one who lacks principles, you lying, conniving . . ." She grabbed a book resting on the small table and hurled it at him.

He shifted quickly, but not fast enough in the small space. The sharp corner of the leather volume cut him across the temple with a harsh burn. He saw red, and not just from the blood dripping into his eye.

He lunged for her and grabbed her arm, growling, "You little hellcat!" All thoughts had fled beyond the need to shake some sense into her. "You are the most maddening, vexing, fractious . . ."

"Don't you touch me!" she hissed.

He was going to shut her up once and for all! He ground his mouth down onto hers, savagely assaulting her sumptuous lips, plunging his tongue deep into her hot open mouth, wanting her to taste his fury.

Searing heat raced from his mouth straight to his groin. He heard a groan and realized that it came from deep in his belly. God, she was on fire. The hands latching onto his arms were not fighting him, but pulling him closer still. She was hot and soft and curvaceous and was kissing him with a passion that left him wanting desperately to be inside her.

In a distant part of his mind, James heard the call to heed, but she was too sultry, too sweet. He savored her honeyed mouth, the erotic twining of their tongues as her sumptuous breasts pressed against his chest. The taste of her was intoxicating. When she shuddered with passionate response, his desire flared and he deepened the kiss, while sliding his hand to her ample breast. He squeezed lightly, gently rubbing her nipple with his thumb. A small moan escaped from her lips. Wrapping his other arm around her, he caressed her luscious bottom, grinding her into his hard member. He leaned in to kiss her neck, but encountering the expansive cloth instead.

Charlotte pushed against his chest, crying out in dismay, "Stop. You must stop!"

James froze. He let go of her so abruptly, she almost fell,

but he caught her lightly. She pushed him away, her eyes wide with horror. His stomach turned over. He truly was a monster. He walked away from her, trying to recover his composure, trying to stop the rushing beat of his racing heart. What had come over him? Was he losing his humanity? Or merely his mind? His body still thrummed with restrained passion. Was she so unaffected? He looked at her over his shoulder; her breasts heaved with emotion, her face was flushed and rosy with . . . desire. He saw the heat in her eyes and remembered her fiery response to his touch.

The yearning in Charlotte's eyes was quickly replaced by blaring anger. Standing ramrod straight, she cried angrily, "Do not dare attempt to intimidate me by such brutish force!"

She thought it was a ploy, a maneuver to get her to stay. She had no idea how badly he had lost control.

Patting his temple with his handkerchief, he was gratified to note only a couple of drops of blood. No, the real damage was to his self-control. He turned to her, commenting coolly, "Intimidation? More like I was giving you a taste of the benefits you might enjoy in my home."

"You conceited beast!" Her hands clenched and unclenched, and he was glad that nothing else was within her reach as a weapon.

He moved closer. She seemed to be arguing with herself as to whether to step back. Decisively, her shoulders straightened and she crossed her arms protectively in front of the bosom he was so boldly caressing just a moment before.

"Come, Charlotte. We are both healthy adults and this is a nice boon to a decidedly odd situation." He reached out and she inhaled a sharp breath but did not move. With his finger, he coiled a tendril of hair behind her ear, delicately tickling the lobe. "Why not allow the sparks between us to flame?"

He watched the redness in her cheeks deepen. So she recognized the passion simmering between them. But he would let her believe that he was in control of his desire, when he was feeling anything but, where she was concerned.

She licked her lips and asked breathlessly, "What are you talking about?"

"I am simply saying that we are betrothed for a purpose. We have a mission . . ." He traced his finger across the line of her jaw. "Or have you forgotten already?"

She blinked and her eyes flickered with anger and . . . embarrassment. So, in the heat of the moment, she had forgotten as well.

"Ah, so you remember now why you are here, why we must remain engaged. Unless, of course, you are going to break your promise."

She ground out through clenched teeth, "I have never broken my word in my life."

"Then you are not packing to leave?"

"That is not fair! Circumstances have altered. When I agreed to this ruse, I was under the impression that I was going to unmask a . . . a . . . group of vile scoundrels and help stop a war. Not sit at your fractious mother's knee and learn about household accounts and listen to her scandal mongering about my family."

"Do you still want to help me stop the scoundrels and avert a possible war?"

"Well, yes."

"What if I limit your dealings with my mother and ensure that your family is welcome?"

"Not enough. I want to be included in the investigation, as a full participant."

"That is ridiculous, Charlotte. It is too dangerous and you well know it."

"What? The mighty Duke of Girard is afraid of competition from a lowly woman?"

"Competition has nothing to do with it!" he snapped.

"Then you found the map and the keys?"

He tempered his simmering anger. "You will give me those possessions. It was part of our agreement."

"I agreed to the charade of our engagement, I promised to help, but I did not specify about the map and the keys."

"Why, that is the most persnickety, barristerlike, foolish argument I have ever heard. You will give me those items!"

She raised her eyebrow, taunting, "And if I do not? What will you do, maul them out of me?"

The air almost crackled between them.

He bit his inner cheek just to keep from shaking her. But it was too perilous, as his self-control seemed near to breaking, where she was concerned. He needed her. He needed that map and key. He was nowhere without all three. And he could not keep his word to the general if Charlotte left in an angry huff, or worse yet, thought him a lecherous rake. Devil take it, he was trapped and had little choice.

"So what will it take?" he ground out.

Her eyes widened in surprise. So she had not thought that he would agree.

"I want to be your partner. To share in all of the information, the efforts to recover the stolen goods, in, well, everything."

"I will not have you prancing about, chasing after common criminals."

"From what you said, these criminals are anything but common."

On that front, at least they could agree. "I will allow you to participate in the investigation, but I cannot have you in dangerous situations." She opened her mouth to argue, but he held up his hand. "Moreover, you are supposed to be acting like a duchess. You must comport yourself properly. We cannot afford to have a scandal distract us from the mission."

Charlotte glared at him. "I will not stop visiting the boys at the hospital."

"Fine. But in all other respects, you must conduct yourself like the lady you are. I do not need any additional complications. It will only cause acrimony between us and we are on the same side, remember?"

She huffed. "I will do as you say, if I am a full and complete partner in your efforts."

"And give me the map and keys."

They eyed each other a moment longer. Charlotte was the one to look away first. "Agreed."

"Agreed."

He let out a long breath.

Opening the door to the hallway he pronounced grimly, "I will go handle my mother." Charlotte nodded and sank wearily into the sofa. She was so strong, yet, this had to be wearing on her. Suddenly inspired, he added, "And I will have some of the almond cheesecakes and custards sent up on a tray. Cook's sweets are divine."

As James strode down the hall, he begrudgingly admitted to himself that she had grown in his estimation. She was formidable, intelligent, loyal almost to a fault, and a hard-nosed negotiator. If she just did not drive him to distraction, he might have been contented to have her as a wife. Almost.

As Charlotte spooned the buttery custard into her mouth, savoring the rich vanilla flavor, she let out a blissful sigh. If James had any idea how much she loved sweets. Thinking of the exasperating man made her frown. She should be pleased. She had negotiated an agreement granting her everything that she needed, without really having to give up anything new. Her father would have been proud. If only it were not for that kiss. Kiss? It was more like an assault on her senses. One moment she hated the man mightily and the next she was wantonly lusting in his arms.

Her cheeks colored just thinking of the bold thrusts of his

tongue in her mouth. Suddenly the sugary vanilla did not compare to the delight of his scandalous touch.

Why did she respond to him with such intense ardor? Myles Wilmington was a raindrop compared to James's typhoon and she had supposedly loved Myles. Myles's kisses had been titillating, nervous little touches compared to the avalanche of sensations that overtook her when James held her close. She would do well to stay as far away from him as possible. But to achieve her goals, she had to do just the opposite.

Could she be with him day in and out and not recall the fiery passion between them? He had called it "sparks to flame." How could he have been so nonchalant about the whole thing? As if firestorms of passion erupted for her every day. Her cheeks heated. She felt depraved, as if her body betrayed her in some way, making her weaker, more vulnerable. She shook her head, resolute. Tomorrow was a new day. She would do what she needed with a no nonsense manner. She had practically run her family's household since she was thirteen, dealt with a host of turbulent issues, difficult people, great loss . . . she could do this. She had to. It was just the challenge of facing her own traitorous body that daunted her.

Chapter 15

The next morning James had Collin bring Charlotte's belongings to his study. With the men watching judiciously, Charlotte selected her book from the open trunk and turned to James. "Do you have a knife?"

He leaned over and pulled a blade from a sheath at his ankle. Raising an inquiring eyebrow, she took it silently. The dagger was well balanced, with a leather grip and a razor-sharp shiny edge. "Careful," he cautioned.

She smiled sweetly. "I know how to handle a knife."

Watching her, he could see that she did. She opened the book and, using the knife, peeled the paper off the inside cover. Collin watched with fascination as she widened the gap, exposing the packet inside.

"Ingenious," breathed his manservant.

"Quite resourceful," James agreed, rubbing his chin. "Apparently a lady of many talents."

She pulled the packet out, unfolding it and examining its contents.

"On the desk," James directed, gesturing. Charlotte laid the map flat. Placing paperweights at the four corners, James scrutinized the drawing.

"Napoleon ER I.—Depart Elba," Collin read aloud.

James indicated a wavy patch on the map. "This is likely the Channel."

"It would make sense to hide the spoils near water for ease of transportation," Collin concurred.

"And to remove to Elba."

Collin pointed to the corner of the drawing. "But what is this section here in the middle of the water? It could be a legend, but one that makes no sense."

Stepping over to the other side of the desk, Charlotte studied the map. Then she moved back behind James's shoulder, continuing to peer at the marks.

"This map is clearly not drawn to scale," he remarked, frowning.

"Maybe this," Collin stated, gesturing to the grouping, "is a small island?"

"No." Charlotte stood over the map and declared with conviction, "It is not a legend or an island. It is another map."

James looked up at her. "What is that, you say?"

"It is a map within a map." She stared at the drawing, nodding. "Imagine making a map of a tenant farm at your family seat. First, you might make a general sketch of the entire property to orient yourself. Then, maybe even on the same paper, you draw the specifications of the farm."

"By God, she's right," Collin asserted.

James studied the parchment, narrowing his eyes. "Then this was made for someone who already knew the general location of the hideaway but just needed some additional markers?"

"Exactly." She asked, curious, "You said that this map was intercepted on its way to Edgerton's wife?"

"Widow," James corrected. "I see what you are saying."

He nodded. "Maybe it would make sense to her." Pausing, he shook his head. "She came forward to inform us of Edgerton's actions. She is an honest woman." He rubbed his chin thoughtfully. "Still, she might be able to give us information on Edgerton's background, the places he was familiar with near the water."

"Excellent notion," Charlotte declared. So she was caught up in the chase as well.

"I have a few other leads that may pan out." James stamped his fist on the desktop earnestly. "Finally, some progress."

"Let us see if we can identify more of these symbols." Charlotte looked up at him and beamed brilliantly. Her luscious pink lips bowed wide exposing straight white teeth, her blue eyes sparkled and her whole countenance shimmered with rosy radiance. Men would lay down their lives just to glimpse such a smile.

"What?" She raised her hand to her face.

He shook himself. He had been staring at her instead of the drawing. "I was just thinking that it was a lucky thing that you were here to view the map with us. You have an artist's eye."

Her cheeks reddened. Turning back to the diagram, she was only partially successful in hiding her pleased smile. "I think that this is some sort of rock formation."

He pulled up a chair and offered it to her. "Yes, well then, let's get to it."

The sun was shining brightly through the tall windows by the time the clock chimed the hour, startling Charlotte from her concentration on a particularly confusing part of the map.

"Good heavens, is it past two already?" She blinked, surprised. She pressed her hand to her exceedingly empty belly.

"I asked Collin not to have us disturbed," James commented distractedly as he jotted down notes.

A lock of his raven black hair kept falling over his fore-head and he negligently pushed it away. His dark blue eyes glimmered with a boyish exuberance that Charlotte found contagious. She had been so caught up in the excitement of solving the puzzle that she had not realized how closely she and James hunkered together behind the great desk. Aware-ness of him suddenly settled in, and his proximity raised tiny tingles along her skin, titillating her senses. Curious, she sniffed delicately. Underneath his spicy cologne and the scent of leather from his shiny black Hessians was that dis-tinct aroma that Charlotte now knew was *James*. She licked her lips and leaned a smidgen closer. Heat radiated off his strapping body like clouds before a storm, ample warning to get away before it was too late. She abruptly stood, banging her knee into his heavy chair. "Ouch!"

"Are you all right?" He looked up.

"Fine." She rubbed her stinging knee. "I am just hungry."

He shook his head as if surprised. "No wonder, we have certainly been productive this morning."

Two knocks thumped on the door.

"It is Collin, sir," came the call from without.

"Come."

"I apologize for disturbing you, sir. But her grace was most insistent." Collin stepped inside. "Her grace requests yours and Miss Hastings' presence in the south drawing room. Lady and Miss Druthers have called."

James frowned and Charlotte suppressed a groan.

Turning to her, James sighed. "We should probably get this over with."

She nodded. She had signed on for this and was resigned to the inevitable. "I would prefer to make a short appearance and then have luncheon. If that is acceptable."

James proffered his arm. "Then appear we shall."

* * *

As they walked down the heavily carpeted hall toward the drawing room, Charlotte whispered to James tentatively, "Rumor had it that there were some expectations that you might wed Miss Druthers."

He leaned close to her ear, his breath tickling her skin. "You are the only lady I have ever been betrothed to, Charlotte." He added teasingly, "I trust you have not been engaged to another before me?"

She stiffened and the toe of her slipper caught on the carpet edge. He tightened his grip on her arm, helping her keep upright.

His eyes narrowed and she quickly looked away. Despite the recent exuberance of sharing an exciting chase, Charlotte forced herself to remember her objective: to uncover the truth behind James's curious activities. She had to be wary not to fall into the trap of believing that the scoundrel actually cared one whit for her. He was single-minded enough in his purpose to endanger her life, and now seemed quite intent on having her near. But to what end?

She leaned away from him and set her back up, replying matter-of-factly, "Let us recall that we are not truly engaged, your grace."

"With you reminding me all of the time, Charlotte, I can hardly forget." He eyed her thoughtfully and then pulled her closer to his side, coiling his arm about her waist.

She pushed him away, hissing, "Unhand me!"

"Since we will have an audience, I suggest you recall that this is a love match, *darling*."

She glared at him. "I can play the role acceptably, but that does not mean I must be subject to your lecherous mauling."

"Most women seem to find my *mauling* quite stimulating."

Her stomach lurched just thinking of him and his harems of women. "Extolling your exploits will not endear you to my heart, your grace," she ground out, wishing she was not so deeply affected by him. His nearness and the muscled hand hugging her waist was causing the most unholy heat to unfurl in her belly. This was just another reminder to keep away from the rogue.

"You did not seem to mind my kisses," he teased.

"That will *never* happen again."

" 'Never' is a very long time."

"Not so far as you are concerned. I suggest that you keep your hands to yourself, or I will show you more of Lieutenant Freeman's tricks."

"Come, Charlotte." He squeezed her waist. "I am jesting. I just love watching how your face gets all rosy and your mouth puckers in a scowl and even your freckles seem to glow when you are angry."

She struggled with the notion that the stone-faced Duke of Girard was playfully trying to provoke her, and succeeding quite admirably at that. Well, he certainly had found the gap in her armor; she was quite put out by how irritatingly responsive she was to him. "I am not your chum and do not appreciate your teasing," she chided defensively.

He stopped and placed his hands on her shoulders. She stared into that blue-black gaze that suddenly was anything but comical. "Regardless of your distasteful feelings toward me, Charlotte, you agreed to being my thrilled and loving betrothed."

Suddenly she felt a bit guilty for her iciness. The man had only been joking for heaven's sake. Why should she care if he bedded other women? "I will uphold my end of the bargain," she stated abashed.

She looked around the empty hallway and lowered her voice to a bare whisper. "Speaking of our mission, have you learned anything from . . . from that . . ."

"It seems that Mason, the man who attacked you, is a

hired gun, so to speak." He scowled. "The bastard knows nothing, cannot identify anyone and is a sorry excuse for a human being."

She swallowed. "And where is he now?"

"Newgate."

She bit her lip and looked down at the colorful oriental carpet.

James gently lifted her chin with his finger. His dark eyes shimmered with intensity. "He will never, ever have the chance to get near you ever again, Charlotte."

She nodded slowly. And if he did, she would do whatever it took not to be in his power. James was studying her worriedly. She forced herself to be businesslike once more. "And the other leads?"

His eyes shifted away and he dropped his hand. Charlotte felt a slight draft on her chin where his warm finger had been. He shrugged noncommittally and adjusted his sleeves. "We should not keep them waiting overlong in the drawing room," he commented dryly.

"The way I understand our agreement, we cooperate on all fronts. Need I remind you that we are in this matter together?"

"How could I forget?" he asked sardonically, turning her toward the drawing room.

She drew herself up. Out from one firestorm and into another.

James and Charlotte entered the south drawing room side by side and the dowager's discourse cut off abruptly upon their arrival. Charlotte pasted a smooth smile on her visage, hoping to get out of this encounter unscathed. This was her first meeting with James's mother since their argument last night.

Lady Druthers, a heavy-set woman of middle years with meaty jowls and dark brown hair sprinkled with gray, looked up expectantly. She wore a large turban in the same peacock green as her gown, with a billowy orange feather perched above. The wheat-haired waiflike Miss Druthers sat stiffly across the room as if not quite party to the conversation. Her reserved and quiet demeanor contrasted sharply with the daringly low-cut purple day gown she wore. Like her mother, Miss Druthers favored the fashions of the east, and she wore a wide violet turban with indigo feathers.

James bowed. "Hello, Mother. Lady Druthers, Miss Druthers. I believe you know Miss Hastings, my fiancé."

Although the dowager looked away, as if seeing Charlotte was distasteful, she nodded regally and commented, "I was just telling the ladies of our good fortune."

So it would be a truce of sorts between them, with no overt hostility. Well, Charlotte could live with that.

Lady Druthers stood, commenting with false cheer, "Congratulations, your grace. Miss Hastings. Constance and I are so pleased for you both." She sent a sharp look of warning to her daughter. "Is that not right, Constance?" It seemed Lady Druthers was determined not to have anyone believe that her Constance had been overlooked.

Miss Druthers stood, curtseyed, and mumbled her congratulations without meeting anyone's eyes. Feeling a pang of distress for her, Charlotte hoped the girl was not in love with James. Maybe after this entire affair was over, Miss Druthers could have her duke. The dowager would likely dance a jig.

Lady Druthers continued to flush effusively. "Such a surprise, your grace. I understand from your mother that you are quite decisive when you make up your mind about something."

"Actually," James held up Charlotte's hand and kissed it, "I have been intent on marrying Charlotte for almost as long as I have known her."

"And how long is that, your grace?" Miss Druthers asked, raising her gloomy gray gaze and watching them from across the room. If eyes could have thrown daggers, Charlotte would have been bloodied and dead. Charlotte decided to retain her good hopes for someone else.

He replied smoothly, "General Cumseby is responsible for our match."

"From that hospital?" the dowager asked, frowning disapprovingly.

"Yes, Mother. Charlotte has been an invaluable resource for the general, and although it is not widely known, I am a great supporter of the facility."

"You must tell us more about how you came to be engaged," insisted Lady Druthers. She bobbed her head, jiggling her jowls, as she reseated herself on the chintz sofa.

"Yes, please," added Miss Druthers, glaring spitefully.

"Another time perhaps," Charlotte replied. "I wish to refresh myself before the midday meal." She smiled tightly at James. "With your permission, my darling?"

"Yes, of course, my dear. I will walk you out. I need to check in with my man-of-affairs." He inclined his head in salute. "Mother, Lady Druthers, Miss Druthers. It was a pleasure seeing you again."

As she and James walked out, Charlotte could feel the hard stares of the three ladies on their backs. She realized that she had better get used to it, as Polite Society was going to be quite diverted with the news of their abrupt engagement. She suppressed an inward groan. Well, she had signed on for this misadventure and would pay any price to uncover the scoundrels in this case. She just prayed she might make it out of this mess without her reputation completely in tatters. But between her sham engagement and her infuriating weakness toward James, somehow she doubted that was possible, no matter what the general had promised.

Chapter 16

The next day the notices were posted in all the appropri-ate papers, mandating the requisite five o'clock ride in the park.

After traveling barely half a lane, James and Charlotte were besieged by the curious, the solicitous, and the envious well-wishers of the *ton*. Charlotte was thankful that she had just received a new driving suit, ordered for her by Aunt Sylvie. The striking red ensemble with matching hat, gloves and short red veil gave Charlotte the added confidence to withstand the scrutiny of the crowd. Apparently her up-bringing had trained her well for the role, and playing loving wife-to-be was not as difficult as she had feared. Charlotte watched James charm both the men and ladies of the *ton*, en-suring that there was no hint of the potential scandal that had precipitated the engagement announcement. She wondered if James was going to be so enchanting when they broke it off.

* * *

Manton greeted them as they entered the foyer. "Miss Hastings, her grace requests your presence in the east drawing room."

Charlotte looked at James, and he suggested reasonably, "I will gladly join you, if you would prefer."

"Ahem."

"Yes, Manton?"

"Her grace is with another. A modiste, I believe."

James grimaced. "Perhaps not."

Charlotte sighed. Wonderful. Now she had to face the dowager and a hawker.

At the look on her face, he commented, "Be nice, Charlotte. She *is* trying."

She smiled wickedly. "Yes, she is." She handed her driving coat to the waiting footman and followed Manton down the long corridor.

James watched her go, thoughtfully considering his plan. He had accomplished phase one of his strategy; being seen by all and letting it be widely known that he and Charlotte were in love. Polite Society was the perfect showground for his stratagem. Now he just needed to await his prey, for his unsavory cousin would doubtless be too tempted to let Charlotte go. He frowned. Suddenly the idea of using Charlotte as bait seemed a little ruthless, a little risky. Well, he would do what had to be done to stop his murderous cousin from hurting anyone else. Surely that was more important. He had promised the general to marry the girl. What more could one ask of him? He turned toward his study, wishing he were feeling more cheerful about his plans.

Charlotte entered the east drawing room and found piles of cotton, lace, muslin, velvet, silk, and dresses of all shapes and sizes. The dowager stood in the midst of it all, talking to a red-haired, big-bosomed woman with pins in her mouth and scissors in her hands. The woman stopped speaking when she noticed Charlotte standing in the doorway.

The dowager turned, asking firmly, "How was your drive in the park?"

"Quite pleasant, your grace."

"Good. You need to make the right impression." She waved at the woman behind her. "This is Madame Clavelle. She is the most extraordinary modiste. French, of course. And she has graciously agreed to assist us on extremely short notice."

"Assist us with what?" Charlotte eyed the fabrics guardedly.

"With getting you some decent clothes, my dear. You are going to be a duchess. You need not necessarily set the style, but you must have some."

She pressed her hands together to hide her agitation and stated resolutely, "Your grace, I thank you for your kind offer of assistance. But I prefer my own modiste and my own clothing, if you please."

Madame Clavelle sashayed her lush bulk over to Charlotte, circling her and examining her from head to toe as one would an interesting exhibit. "But *ma chèrie*, you are beautiful," Madame Clavelle stated in a French accent with a slight Cockney inflection. "You have zee sensual figure any opera sing-aire would covet. But zees." She pointed dismissively to the new riding outfit Charlotte adored. "Does not do you justize. You are meant to be sultry, stylish, yes, yes, mysterious. In this, you look like a . . . how you say it? A red fish."

The woman had just called her a fish. Fighting the sensation in her middle that felt uncomfortably like embarrassment, Charlotte stuck her chin in the air defiantly. "I love this outfit. Aunt Sylvie selected it especially for me."

The dowager snorted.

The modiste smiled indulgently and spoke as if to a child. "But it ees the wrong color. Your hair is the color of hot sunset before zee night. And I love your freckles, just enough to add freshness, youth, *vitalité*."

Charlotte could not believe her ears. No one had ever spoken favorably about her freckles or her figure before. Throughout her entire life, she had felt imperfect, unequal to the classic beauties of her world. This woman did seem to be a professional. Maybe she could help Charlotte work with her attributes instead of trying to alter what could not be changed. "What do you have in mind?"

Madame Clavelle and the dowager exchanged a knowing glance.

"I see you in somezing more like zees." She pulled a shimmering bronze silk jacquard dress from the pile on the sofa and draped it majestically over her arm. Its only ornamentation was an outline of tiny bronze beading set in gauze around the low V-shaped plunging neckline.

She stared in amazement at the lovely dress, wondering if she could dare to wear something so bold, so modish, and so chic. She raised her hand to her neck and suddenly remembered her bruises. She turned away self-consciously. "I think that you are a gifted modiste, Madame Clavelle. But I do not believe that your fashions suit my style."

"You have no style!" the dowager insisted.

Madame Clavelle ignored her and stepped closer to Charlotte, saying gently, appealingly, "Then tell me about your style, how you wish to appear."

She looked away, unwilling to engage in the exercise.

The modiste was no fool. She had obviously noted Charlotte's expression upon seeing the dress. She asked patiently, "Just tell me what you like about deez dress and what you do not prefer."

She turned back reluctantly. "I love the color and the simplicity. I just cannot wear such an immodest dress. So much exposed skin."

"But your breasts are *magnifique!* Do you not like your body?"

She shrugged. "It suits me well enough."

"Then it ees the neckline? But that ees simple to fix! You will tell me what you like and what you do not and together we will create a new style, just for you!" Madame Clavelle declared enthusiastically, smiling broadly.

She looked at Madame Clavelle and back at the dress on her arm. "Well, I suppose there is no harm in trying . . ."

"Excellent! Go behind the screen and I will work my magic on you. Wiz your beauty and my artistry, we cannot fail."

Once behind the screen, Charlotte called out, "Please hand me the dress, Madame. And maybe a scarf?"

The modiste popped her head behind the screen and froze. Her eyes were wide with mortification. "*Merde!*"

She gasped, struggling to cover her bruised neck.

"What is it?" the dowager demanded from her seat on the couch. "Does it not fit?"

Charlotte bit her lip, transfixed. There was no doubt the modiste had seen the ghastly bruises and marks encircling her neck. Dear lord, her reputation would be destroyed forever.

"It is nussing, *Madame*," Madame Clavelle commented quickly. "I just jabbed myself wiz zee pin." She leaned behind the screen and whispered urgently, "Do you need help?" Her accent had miraculously disappeared. "Just say the word."

Charlotte's mouth widened into a great white tremulous smile as relief flooded her belly. "I thank you. I truly thank you. But it is not what you think."

She glowered. "It never is."

"I thank you for your concern, Madame Clavelle. But I assure you, the man who did this to me has been taken care of."

"By your fiancé?" she asked suspiciously.

Charlotte nodded. "And me. He will never touch me again."

"You are certain?"

"Absolutely." She dropped her hand. It seemed that catering to the cream of the *ton* was not the modiste's only talent.

"From what you say, you make me believe that you run across such . . . matters often?"

"More than I would like to say." Madame Clavelle shook her head. "These poor women suffer so horribly and are frightened almost to the point of madness."

"I-I would like to help," she offered sincerely. She derived great benefit from working with the soldiers at the veterans' hospital, and had never considered assisting the women who fought private battles of their own.

"What in heaven's name is taking so long?" the dowager cried impatiently. "Are you having trouble with the gown?"

The modiste peeked around from behind the screen. "Just a moment, *Madame*."

Charlotte whispered urgently, "I understand your hesitation, Madame Clavelle. Rest assured that I am sincere in my desire and my ability to help. Financially and personally. Most of my efforts are at the veterans' hospital off Clarendon Square."

"I know the place."

"Yes, well, the general there is wonderful. You may send word to him and we will do whatever we can." She laid her hand back on the older woman's and looked her square in the eye. "I mean it."

"I have heard of this general. A good 'un, I'm told."

Charlotte squeezed her hand. "Please let me help."

"You could have dressed ten ladies by now!" the dowager complained, standing.

Madame Clavelle swept out from behind the screen with a flourish. "No, Madame. We must keep Miss Hastings hidden until zee final show. It eez for zee effect, *oui?*" She walked over to the fabrics and pulled out a rich chocolate cashmere bundle. "And I have just zee thing."

Later that night, at the Earl of Rawlston's ball, Charlotte felt like a princess at her coming out. For the only time in her memory, she felt beautiful, fashionable, and elegant. Her shimmering bronze silk jacquard gown accentuated her every curve. She loved the feeling of the slightly puffed short sleeves above her tight white kid gloves. Madame Clavelle had taken the original silk gown and wrapped a soft chocolate brown cashmere scarf around Charlotte's shoulders and neck, leaving the deep V-shaped plunging neckline with gauze and beads to draw attention to her ample bosom. Madame Clavelle had been wonderful, designing everything for Charlotte's particular needs and without letting the dowager suspect a thing.

Charlotte was amazed by the designs and surprised by the appreciative stares she was receiving from the gentlemen present, including the enthusiastic Mr. Axelrod, who was trying to keep from looking down her cleavage as he explained the dynamics of various feeds in breeding stock. The topic was interesting, for the first two minutes of Mr. Axelrod's fifteen-minute oratory. Suddenly Charlotte felt a large, strong arm snake around her waist. She gasped in surprise and spun around.

"Oh. It is you." She blushed so furiously she thought her face might flame. She had to keep remembering that she was supposed to be in love with this man. She looked around, embarrassed to see that many eyes had turned toward them, curiously noting James's demonstrative embrace. Thus far, he had used every opportunity to touch her, whisper in her ear and otherwise display his apparent affection. It was embarrassing. It was disconcerting. It was also a bit flattering, even though she knew it was a charade.

"Hullo, darling." He wrapped his other arm about her waist.

She arched back and looked toward Mr. Axelrod who was staring, fascinated. "Ah, you are acquainted with Mr. Axelrod?"

James never took his eyes off Charlotte. "Axelrod. If you will excuse us? This is my dance."

"Yes, of course," Mr. Axelrod replied, bowing and smiling broadly behind his hand. "Congratulations, by the way. You are a very lucky fellow."

He swept Charlotte away toward the dance floor. "Yes, I know."

Charlotte had always loved to dance, but between her father's illness and her own reticence to be courted, it seemed like forever since she had last set slipper to hardwood floor. Yet even if she had danced just the day before, it would not have prepared her for the wave of sensation she felt as James twirled her about the crowded ballroom to the stirring rhythms of a waltz. The orchestra's resonance faded into the background, as did everything else beyond the strong muscled arms of the lithe body holding her so scandalously close.

She did not even have the decency to blush, she was so deeply caught in the magic of the moment. They moved together almost as if they were shaped for this motion, for the press of hard powerful chest against sensitive soft breast, the brush of thigh against hot muscled thigh. Firm muscles bunched beneath her gloved hands. Even the soft wool of his garments could not hide his masculine strength. The spicy musky scent of him was almost intoxicating.

Her heart beat wildly and heat suffused her whole being. Her breath became heavy with wanting; her body was filled with desire. She peeked at him through lowered lashes, her gaze fixing on the soft curve of his pink lips—those delicious lips that had pressed against hers and opened her mouth and her senses to scorching passion. Heaven help her, she wanted to feel the caress of his tongue in her mouth again, to know the taste of him once more.

Watching her through hooded eyes, his dark gaze glowed

with blue-black fire. Could he know what she was thinking? He had to feel her heat, recognize the passion simmering between them. He slowed, shifting her slightly away. Disappointment welled inside her. It was over so soon! Awareness of the crowds, the stares and the sounds of clattering voices, entered her consciousness. Her cheeks heated. She prayed that she had not betrayed herself too shamefully.

James escorted her off the dance floor and brought her to his mother and her crony Lady Wells. He leaned close.

"I will return to you shortly," he whispered, brushing her cheek with his velvety lips. Was it a promise or a threat? He stepped away, bowed and touched a hand to his hat in farewell. He slipped off into the crowd, the dashing duke, her betrothed. He looked grand in his elegant full-dress outfit. His dark black tuxedo sharply contrasted with his white vest, accentuating his broad shoulders and muscled arms. Tonight, instead of boots, he wore black shoes with decorative buckles. He was the epitome of masculine elegance. Too bad he was an underhanded scoundrel. The thought brought her back to reality. She needed to play the part of loving bride-to-be, not become it.

Trying for a modicum of cool, Charlotte turned to the ladies with a serene smile. Lady Wells's eyes glowed appreciatively while the dowager's gaze narrowed with shrewd calculation. The dowager tapped her fan in front of Charlotte's face. "I must admit, I have never seen James so attentive with anyone before."

Lady Wells beamed. "I think it is quite romantic, the way Girard is so adoring. And in public, no less."

"Yes, romantic," she replied ironically. "Well, we are thrilled and in love."

Lady Wells missed her tone entirely.

"Thrilled and in love? Why, how marvelous!"

Lord Fairbanks sauntered up to them, frantically waving his lacy fan. "Why, if I had not seen it myself, I never would have believed it. We used to call him Mr. Wooden, he was always so unaffected."

"Mr. Wooden?" Charlotte asked, curious. She peeked over at the dowager and Lady Wells engaged deep in conversation with Lord and Lady Willowby. She turned to Lord Fairbanks, guiding him a step away from the group for a modicum of privacy. "Do you know him well?"

He closed his lacy fan and placed it over his lips dramatically. "Do not repeat that I told you that nickname, Miss Hastings. He did not like the reference, of course, but there were many worse, of that I can assure you. I knew of a man who was referred to as . . . well, never mind. We used to say that Girard's blood was made of ice. He was so cool about everything—cards, sports, and the women!" He waved his hand. "The man is a real lady-killer. You must have fairy blood if you are able to get Girard besotted."

"Thank you, I think, Lord Fairbanks."

"Oh, you must call me Maxwell, dear." He placed his monocle over his eye. "We are going to be great friends, you and I. I need to know everything about you. You see, everyone wants to know about your great love affair with the duke."

"I would prefer, Lord Fairbanks, if you told me more about Mr. Wooden. I am curious, you see, about the man I am engaged to marry. You understand, of course, that I wish to know him better than anyone else does."

"Well, that would be easy for you to do, my dear, since there are so few who truly *know* the man. Why, of all of the people in our class at Eton, about Town, there are maybe a handful who have a true sense of him. Girard always holds his cards so close to his chest, never letting anyone know what he is about." He leaned in close, tapping his fan in the air. "Quite unsociable, if you ask me." He reopened his fan and waved it around the room airily. "Not that I am one to judge, mind you. I would not dare." Lord Fairbanks adjusted his lacy cuffs. "He was always close to Plankerton, though."

"Plankerton?"

"Lord Avery Plankerton. He got married, too. Fell hard, that one. They just had a baby. Or is it their second?"

"Getting back to Girard. Is there anything else you can share with me, confidentially, of course?"

"He does not cheat at cards. Unlike Lady Haverty, well, she . . ."

She quickly asked, "Does he have any bad habits?"

He scrunched his face up, thinking aloud. "Does not drink too much. Boxes at Manton's regularly. I hear that he is quite good. I myself have no taste for the sport." He leaned in and whispered conspiringly, "Always seemed so uncivilized, if you ask me." A wave of his lacy fan. Then, catching Charlotte's eyes, he whipped it closed and let it hang idly by his wrist.

"Let's see. A decent shot. I heard something recently about him being under the hatches, but he does not appear to be hurting financially, and I need to hear a tidbit from at least two reliable sources before spreading the intelligence." He blinked and leaned forward, all that was sly. "Perhaps you can elucidate on that bit of buzz?"

"From all indications he is quite sound financially . . ." Her voice trailed off as she realized she might have hit upon the reason for the forced engagement. Was the Duke of Girard a legacy hunter? If so, with his looks and standing, he could certainly do better than her, unless, of course, he knew about the diamonds.

"I will keep my ears open on that one, and you will be the first to know of any exposé." He looked around nervously. "Now I must be running off. I cannot let anyone think that I am scandal mongering. I am quite closemouthed, and everyone knows it. Best of luck to you, my dear."

As Charlotte watched Lord Fairbanks scoot off into the crowd, she marveled again at how Society viewed her inscrutable betrothed: noble, decent, and without vice. But she just knew that there was more to him than met the eye. If only the view were not so confoundedly appealing.

Still, the matter of his financial situation was interesting. From all indications—the house, the staff, the tallow, the dishes served—the duke did not seem to be pinching pennies. He had paid for all of her new clothes, an issue she found a bit irritating, but he had refused to take money from her. Was it all for show?

She scanned the crowded ballroom. Where was her unfathomable fiancé, anyway?

"Ah, Miss Hastings, my hearty congratulations. Have you yet purchased your trousseau?"

Suppressing her grimace, she pasted a serene smile on her face and turned. "Hello, Mr. Arnold." She dragged her mind away from James and tried to focus on the uninspiring duties of a bride to be.

A few paces away, James lounged behind a tall pillar, watching his betrothed. Although she was probably unaware of his prowling, he hovered close to Charlotte, unwilling to stray too far. She was valiantly attempting to appear engrossed in Mr. Arnold's diatribe, which undoubtedly pertained to the latest fashions; the man had room in his head for little else. Poor Charlotte. Arnold could not have found a less interested audience.

She was holding up admirably for a woman unused to triviality. He was finally beginning to get a glimmer of the woman beneath her ladylike veneer, and he was delighted by the contrast with most of the females of his acquaintance that she presented; she was anything but frivolous and self-involved. Still, understanding her had thus far proved elusive, but he was growing fond of the mystery.

Charlotte was looking exceedingly delectable in the daringly low-cut number his mother had orchestrated. It emphasized her womanly figure while leaving much to his very active imagination. His eyes roved the crowd. It seemed that other gentlemen were admiring her attributes as well tonight. He shifted his shoulders uncomfortably. Well, that was the point of tonight: parading his love match with Charlotte so that his foul cousin would take the bait. Then why was he feeling anything but pleased?

Pushing himself away from the pillar, James resisted the urge to rip Arnold's lecherous eyes out. He coiled his arms about Charlotte's waist and hugged her close. "How are you, darling?"

She blushed a rosy red and shivered delicately. How he loved to rattle her with his intimacies.

"Ah, fine," she sputtered.

He glared at Arnold and the wise soul quickly took off.

She turned in his arms, deftly unwinding from his embrace. "You certainly chased him away."

"Do you mind?"

She yawned delicately behind a gloved hand. "The man seemed unable to discuss anything beyond his tailor."

On the pretense of giving her a break, he pulled her toward his trusty pillar and set her back against it, lounging his arm protectively above her.

She let out a little sigh. "Much better, thank you."

"Do not fail me now, Charlotte. We still have the Worchester ball to attend."

"I am fine. Frankly, I am just unused to all the attention."

"Soon the *ton* will tire of our story and move on to the next titillation." Someone brushed against his back and he pretended as if he were pushed too close, pressing his chest against her soft bosom. The scent of lavender floated delicately around her. She bit her luscious lip, flustered once more. This was too enjoyable by far.

Her brow furrowed and she seemed quite preoccupied with his tie. "Ah, are you pleased with our reception?"

God, how he'd love to trace his finger in the plunging neckline of her gown. "It is proceeding perfectly as planned."

She looked up, her astute blue eyes narrowing. "So there is a plan?"

He tore himself back to reality. "Well, I, ah, meant that I had planned on there being no scandal resulting from what happened in Southbridge."

She seemed suddenly on edge, her brow furrowed with worry. Did Mason's attack still plague her mind? He was trying to think of something to say that was reassuring without raising her hackles when she straightened her back and stated in a no-nonsense tone, "With your mother leading the battle cry, there probably will not be any talk resulting from the house party. She really is quite good at this."

Following her lead, he stated casually, "Years of training, I assure you. She used to feel that she had to live down her Spanish heritage. Now, she reigns over Polite Society. She did well by you tonight. You look beautiful, Charlotte."

"You seem surprised."

"I just have never seen you in such attire."

"Yes, well, during the last few years being fashionable was not precisely a priority. I had neither the time nor the inclination to follow the continually changeable styles."

"As I told you that first morning, being fashionable is about more than following styles, Charlotte. It is about creating an effect." James leaned closer, shielding her from anyone else's view. He traced his index finger slowly down the V of Charlotte's tantalizing bosom, relishing the plush, velvety softness. "I very much like you this affecting."

Her eyes widened and her delectable mouth dropped open and her rosy cheeks reddened. Her blue eyes sparkled with anger as she scanned the crowd while at the same time chastised in a harsh whisper, "Enough is enough, James! I find your *performance* entirely too warm."

"I am besotted, Charlotte."

"Having escaped the scandal of Southbridge, now you create gossip of another kind."

Charlotte was too perceptive by far.

She continued, her voice barely above a whisper, "I still have no idea how on earth I am going to get out of this mess unscathed."

He squared his shoulders. "Come. Let us find Mother and head out. This grows tiresome."

"You seem to forget that I am more than something for you to use for your own ends and then discard."

James barely stopped himself from cringing. Her comment hit a little too close to home. That was exactly what he had intended to do. But that was before.

Something hard jabbed at his back. He looked over his shoulder. His mother stood behind him, scowling condescendingly. She waved her fan like a dagger. "I am tired of this, James."

He got the message. He was playing the besotted fiancé all too well. Heavens, what was happening to his self-control?

Charlotte slipped out from under his arm to stand by his mother's side. "As am I," she stated pointedly. He suppressed a groan. He was not ready to withstand them teaming up.

"Are you finished then?" His mother raised a haughty brow.

"Not even close," he mumbled, resignedly extending his arm.

Chapter 17

Charlotte slept poorly that night, tossing and turning, agitated by James's touch and the fact that she was so susceptible to his charms. She awoke tired and crabby. What she needed, she decided, was a vigorous ride in the park.

She dressed quickly in her new green riding habit and donned her small black beaver hat and kid gloves. Relishing the added benefit of an early rise, she looked forward to avoiding members of the Polite World, who surely still lay abed, sleeping off the effects of the revelry the night before. The house was quiet and James and the dowager were still tucked in their apartments when Charlotte called for a carriage and took her leave. She was headed to her family's stables to ride her mare, Henny, as she felt uncomfortable going to James's stables by herself.

As she stepped into the carriage, she paused, realizing that this was her first excursion out without James by her side. She knew it was ridiculous, but not having him near made her feel a bit vulnerable. She shook her head, disgusted with herself. He was the one she was trying to trip in lies.

Still, she turned around, went back inside, and wrote a brief note advising James of her plans. She also resolved to ask for two grooms to join her for her ride, instead of one. There was little harm in taking precautions and little benefit in taking chances.

As Charlotte galloped down the lane, she felt her spirits revive. The morning sun added a touch of warmth to the brisk spring air, making her want to laugh with the joy of it. Trees were budding and flowers were blooming, giving off the wonderful scents of springtime. Harry and Jake, the largest, meanest looking grooms in her family's service who were actually quite kindhearted, followed close behind, but not near enough to infringe on Charlotte's sense of space.

Suddenly, a sharp *crack* resounded overhead. Henny reared and bucked in fright. Snorting loudly, she tore off madly down the lane. Trees, branches, and sky whizzed by as Charlotte fought to hold her seat as Henny raced frantically through the woods. With her heart in her throat, Charlotte lay low, holding on to Henny's neck with all her might. Her every muscle strained, and blood pounded in her ears. Henny reared and kicked, and Charlotte just could not hold on. She felt as if she were suspended in midair for the longest time until she landed with a hard *thump*! into a cluster of bushes. She lay very still, waiting for the world to stop spinning, her heart to stop hammering, and her breath to return. Staring up at the clouds that had finally ceased churning, she heard carriage wheels and horses headed her way. Tentatively, painfully, she sat up. A black carriage was bearing down the lane toward her.

The driver and his companion, two swarthy-looking fellows, searched the area intently. Instinctively, Charlotte lay below the brush line to see what they were about. She did not trust her legs to function and prayed that these unsavory men moved along soon.

"Where'd she go?"

"She canna 'ave gone far. See, there's 'er horse and 'er hat."

"Miss Hastings! Miss Hastings!" Harry and Jake. Relief washed over her.

"I danna see 'er anywhere. The Master'll be angry, and I am not goin' to tell 'im that you shot at 'er. I am not getting kilt over some chit, I tell ya."

"We danna get paid enough for the likes of this," grumbled the other. "Where can she be?"

Harry came barreling through the trees. "Miss Hastings!"

"The Master'll slit our throats fer sure if we get nabbed. We have to go!"

"Fine. But yer gonna be da one tellin' 'im, not me."

"Jus go!" The whip cracked in the air. "Haya!"

The carriage wheels rumbled as they flew past.

Charlotte peeked above the bushes. She noted that the crest on the carriage was covered over, but she did get a good look at the two men. She closed her eyes and tried to memorize their faces. What she would have given for her trusty sketchbook and coal.

When they were gone, she called out, "Over here, Harry!"

"Miss Hastings! Are you all right?" Jake jumped off his horse and ran to help her.

"Shaken but fine, Jake. Please check on Henny."

"Harry's got her, my lady."

Jake carefully helped Charlotte rise and extricate herself from the branches that had broken her fall. She sent a silent prayer of gratitude for the limited damage caused. Her bottom and her right hip and arm were sore, but nothing was broken. It could have been so much worse.

"Can you ride, my lady?" Jake asked, his broad face scrunched with concern.

She nodded. "How is Henny?"

"A bit jittery, but seems no worse for wear," Harry replied as he led Henny back to her mistress. "How about I ride her back and you take Patches?"

"That is very considerate of you, but I will ride Henny. I will not allow anyone to scare me off of my own horse."

"You think someone did that on purpose?" Jake asked, picking up Charlotte's beaver hat, brushing it off and handing it to her. "They do allow hunting in the park, my lady."

Charlotte gently placed her hat on her pounding head and lay her hands on Henny's neck, stroked her horse soothingly. "There's a girl," she crooned. Charlotte stood nose to nose with Henny and leaned against her horse, allowing herself a moment to recover. She stood still, murmuring to Henny and absorbing the mare's calming affection. "We had best get back. I have yet to break my fast and I want to give Henny an extra bag of oats."

The three riders mounted their horses, Charlotte gingerly and achingly. By the time they returned to High Street, she could not wait to take a long hot bath and wash the incident from her mind. Before that, though, she decided to send a note off to the general post haste. He would know what to do.

James stood over Edgerton's map ready to pound his desk in frustration. The bloody diagram was really quite detailed, except for the small fact that it could depict any shoreline from Blyth to Bristol and beyond. He scowled, wanting to pull Edgerton from his grave and shake some answers from the rascal.

A knock thumped on the door. "It is Collin, your grace."

"Come," James ordered. He rolled the tension from his shoulders, hoping his man would have some good news to report. He looked up expectantly.

"You wanted to know if Miss Hastings sent off any letters." He held up a small white folded paper in his gloved hand.

"Its direction?"

"General Cumseby."

"Send it off, then." He waved his hand and returned to the map.

"Ahem."

"What is it, Collin?"

"Miss Hastings was looking a bit unwell when she returned from her ride in the park. In fact, sir," he grimaced, "she had footmen bring her writing instruments to the drawing room across the hall. She seemed unequal to the stairs."

James stiffened. "Where is she now?"

"Right here, your nosiness," Charlotte replied sardonically from the threshold. She was leaning heavily against the doorjamb, as if to keep her weight off her leg. She looked peaked and pale. Her eyes did not sparkle as they normally did and her brow furrowed as if she were in pain. James felt a twist in his gut.

She stepped gingerly into the study, chiding wanly, "I asked that that missive be sent to the general directly. I should have known that you scoundrels would stoop so low as to read another's post."

Well, she had her sarcasm; she could not be completely bad off.

James watched her carefully. "Thank you, Collin."

Collin slid the letter on the desk and closed the door soundlessly behind him.

She slipped into one of the leather armchairs, favoring her left hip. She winced as her bottom adjusted in the seat.

James placed his arms on the desk and leaned forward, asking intently, "Are you all right, Charlotte?"

"Fine," she answered dismissively, "just a little shaken up. Although I am sure that I will be feeling this misadventure tomorrow."

He scowled, trying to keep the fear from his tone. "What misadventure?"

"Do not raise your voice." She rubbed her temple. "I do not know the social niceties of describing an attempted kidnapping."

He stared at her dumbfounded and then closed his eyes. God help him for placing her in danger. But she was sitting before him, chastising him; she had to be all right. He took a deep breath, opened his eyes, and very carefully placed his palms on the desktop. "Please tell me what happened, Charlotte. Every detail."

She sighed heavily, as if greatly put out by his concern. "While riding in the park, I was shot at, Henny took off in fright, and I was thrown. Two men were trying to kidnap me."

"You are unhurt?"

"Fine." She waved her hand dismissively. "I had even taken the added precaution of having two grooms with me . . ." Her voice trailed off.

"Charlotte?" James demanded gently. "Did you injure your head, darling?"

"Um, where was I? Fortunately, I fell into a large row of bushes." She smiled tremulously. "Sometimes I do believe that someone has been watching over me. There have been other pretty close calls, and yet everything turned out all right."

"You are certain that you are unhurt?"

"Thankfully, most of my weight fell on my hip and side. But anyway, the strange thing is that these two swarthy men, unless there was another in the carriage . . ."

Razor sharp alarm seared his gut. "What did the two men do?"

"Oh, yes. I seem to be having trouble staying on track. Sorry. Anyway, the two men could not find me as I was in the bushes and not that interested in moving at the time. Jake and

Harry came along shouting my name and frightened them off."

"Did you get a look at them? Did you recognize them?" he asked with bated breath.

"Yes. No. I mean, I did not recognize them, but I did get a good look at them. Later, when I am feeling better, I will draw a sketch."

The slow fear building in his chest amplified. "Are you not feeling well, Charlotte?"

"Oh, I am just feeling a bit muddled. Nothing, really."

"Are you sure that you did not bump your head?"

Grimacing, she raised her hand to her forehead. "Quite certain. But the important fact . . . um, a master!" She raised her hand in triumph. "That was it! They said something about a master, and not getting paid enough. Sounded like an awful fellow, slitting throats and the like."

The hairs on James's neck stood on end as he recalled that Mason, Charlotte's attacker at the Balstrams', was found dead at Newgate prison just the day before, his throat slit open. He shook off the chilling feeling and focused on Charlotte. "Do not worry yourself about it, Charlotte. Maybe this is all a great misunderstanding. As you said, you are confused."

She straightened her spine, affronted. "Do not treat me like an imbecile. I was almost kidnapped, I tell you, and I need to tell the general." She stood. "Odd." She raised her hand to her head. "The room seems to be spinning . . ." She dropped back into the chair with a *thump*.

James dashed to her side. "Charlotte!" A thin layer of sweat lined her brow and her face had turned a grayish green hue. "Charlotte? Speak to me!"

"I suddenly . . . am feeling a little . . . ill."

He quickly scooped her up out of the chair and rushed her to the sofa.

"Is there a specific place you feel pain?"

"Everything hurts, but mostly, I am queasy."

"When was the last time you ate or drank?" He laid her down gently and swept her hair from her face.

"Last night at the ball. I was not very hungry this morning. Just the thought of food . . . oh, I do not feel very well at all."

"No wonder. I will be right back. Do not try to get up or move." He jumped to his feet and ran out the door, crashing directly into Manton. James pushed past him.

"Manton! Get me a cloth and a basin of water immediately."

"But your grace, there are callers."

"Let my mother deal with them! I am busy and do not want to be disturbed!" James charged down the hall toward the kitchen.

Manton ordered the basin with water for the duke. Next, he went to inform the dowager that Charlotte's brother, Edward Hastings, Lady Sylvie Jaspers, the Countess of Grandby, and Robert Clark, Viscount Devane, had come to call on Miss Hastings and the duke, and that the guests were waiting, unattended, in the south drawing room.

James raced into the kitchen, shouting, "I need some bread or scones or something!" The cook stopped midmotion with a spoon held in midair as he hovered over a big pot, speechless. The staff stood frozen with shock. The duke had never entered the kitchens before in anyone's memory.

"Quick! Bread, something easy to eat!" James commanded, frustrated and tense with worry. He did not want to leave Charlotte alone for long.

Like puppies abruptly set free, the staff jumped to respond. "Your grace, may I bring you . . ." "I would be happy to bring you . . ." "Did you ring, your grace?" "Let me, your grace . . ."

"Just give me something, now!"

Amidst the confusion, Gunter, the young kitchen hand, went to the larder and returned, shoving some rolls into James's hand.

"Good job, man!" James patted the boy on the back. "Bring me some tea in the library!" He ran back out the door. The kitchen erupted in chaos, everyone trying to make sense of the unusual display and rushing to respond to the urgent command.

The dowager stormed to the south drawing room in a rage. "I will not have that woman in my house! I will not stand for it!" She entered the room ready for battle. She stood, legs apart, finger pointing angrily at Sylvie Jaspers. "You are not welcome here! Take your leave, or I will have you thrown out!"

Lady Jaspers stood stiffly, hands clasping the back of the chair, yet she replied coolly, "You always were one for bullying, Katie. But we are not leaving without seeing Charlotte."

No one had called her Katie in over thirty years. The dowager saw red. "My son will hear of this! There will be hell to pay!"

The dowager stormed out, shouting, "James!"

Edward turned to his aunt. "Aunt Sylvie, you said that you and the dowager had an unfortunate history, not that she hated the mere sight of you!"

Sylvie quickly strode to the door. "Come along. I will not have us ejected before we get a chance to see Charlotte and find out what is going on."

Kneeling before Charlotte on the couch, James hand-fed her tiny pieces of bread. With her eyes closed, she opened her mouth like a baby bird, delicately nibbling on the morsels.

"Tea is on its way," he assured her, worriedly pushing her auburn hair from her face with shaky fingers. "Any better?"

Her lids still shuttered, she nodded. "I never faint; I am

quite sturdy, most of the time. I do not know what came over me."

He continued caressing her curls with his fingertips, almost more for his own comfort than hers. The general would kill him if Charlotte were harmed. Was that why he was so disturbed? "You have been through a lot these last few days. I do not know any ladies who could have done so well."

"I do not seem to be dealing that well now." She frowned, opening her eyes. Her clear blue gaze locked with his. "Your eyes are so beautiful," she stated breathlessly, a hint of wonder in her voice.

He blinked. Then he almost smiled. "Now I know that you bumped your head, Charlotte."

She flushed red and tried to sit up. "I believe I could use some air."

"Here, let me open your jacket to allow you to breathe better." James slowly unbuttoned the top of her jacket, gently easing the stiff cloth away from her throat. He winced. The bruises on her neck looked gruesome.

At that exact moment, the dowager charged into the room with Sylvie, Edward, and Robert close behind.

The dowager shouted, "James! I will not stand . . ." She froze in mid-sentence, appalled by the scene of James kneeling before the bruised and exposed Charlotte. The newcomers stood in shocked silence, and then chaos erupted.

Robert Clark pushed past the dowager and charged James, yanking him away from Charlotte and throwing him across the room. "You animal!" he roared.

James slammed into the far wall, rolled away, and stood warily.

"You bloody dog!" Robert growled and rushed at him again.

Edward jumped between the men, arms on Robert, holding him off. He declared, "She's my sister. I'll hear an explanation before I kill him."

Lady Jaspers ran to Charlotte's side. "My darling! What has he done to you?"

"There's no acceptable explanation for what he's done to her!" Robert yelled over Edward's shoulder, eyeing James angrily.

And the dowager stood transfixed in the doorway, for once in her lifetime shaken into silence.

Chapter 18

"**I** am really just fine," Charlotte stated quietly in the tension-filled room. Sitting up slowly, she closed her jacket self-consciously.

Edward chided angrily, "You cannot protect him, Charlotte. We all saw the damage he has done."

His eyes never leaving the men, James asked softly, "Are you feeling any better, Charlotte?"

She raised her eyes to him. "Yes, thank you."

A spoon clattered on a tray and all five heads turned to see Mrs. Bloom, the housekeeper, standing in the doorway, tentatively holding a tea tray, and Manton standing behind her with a bowl and towel. The housekeeper did not move as she eyed her master, the two gentlemen pushed against one another, and the ladies watching nervously.

"Please put the tea on the desktop, Mrs. Bloom," Charlotte directed. "And the rag and bowl as well, Manton. Then, please close the door as you leave."

"Shall I bring more tea for your guests, your grace?" Mrs.

Bloom asked James, as she backed toward the door.

James did not relax his stance or take his eyes from Robert and Edward. "No. That will be all."

The servants walked out of the room, nervously eyeing James and the dowager. The loud click of the closing door filled the silence.

Charlotte could barely contain her smile as she watched the door shut firmly. Now those closest to her could know the truth. She turned to James. "They have a right to know. Or would you prefer that they believe you beat innocent young ladies?"

He lowered his fists. The muscle in his jaw jumped, but otherwise she could read nothing in his stony features. "So you agree that it is my tale to tell, on my terms?"

Charlotte frowned, comprehension dawning. "I will abide by . . ."

James held up his hand, cutting her off. "Just so we understand each other." He spun on his heel, walked over to the windows overlooking the garden, and leaned his hands on the windowsill. Edward looked at Robert, who looked at Sylvie, who looked at Charlotte. No one paid any attention to the dowager. The clock chimed the half hour loudly on the mantel. James turned and gracefully propped himself on the sill. Almost lounging, he stretched his legs before him and studied the assembled group. Casually, as if entertaining, he invited, "If everyone would be seated?"

The tension in the room lowered a few notches. Aunt Sylvie gracefully dropped into the sofa, and Charlotte sat down beside her. Aunt Sylvie hugged her close, cloaking her in a warm, rose-scented embrace. Her father's sister was a tall, broad woman who carried her physique with effortless grace. Even though she was almost five and forty, she was handsome and well shaped. She had long brown hair twisted into a chignon, with patches of gray at her temples. Her deep brown eyes and long, slightly rounded face always seemed on the brink of a smile. She whispered in Charlotte's ear, "Just so long as you are well, Charlotte."

Eyes watering, Charlotte realized how much she had missed her aunt. So much had happened, and she really needed that complete love and acceptance.

Slowly, Edward released Robert and the two men stepped back and stood along the wall closest to James's desk. Robert crossed his muscled arms, his remarkable golden brown eyes never wavering from James. God bless him, he was a bear when his loved ones were in danger. The flamboyant viscount had been a best friend to Edward since boyhood, and despite his belonging to a mighty lineage through his father, the Earl of Swathmore, Robert had adopted the entire Hastings family as his own.

In contrast to Robert's contained fierceness, Edward stood tensely, his fingers nervously fiddling with the shiny gold buttons on his coat. Two dearest friends could not be more different. Where Robert was tall and broad, Edward was compact and well proportioned. Perhaps it was losing his parents and appreciating the dangers in the world that caused Edward to be more contemplative and wary than his friend. Robert was always the first to jump to action, fearing nothing but the shackles of marriage.

Robert pushed a stray lock of his pale chestnut hair out of his eyes. After all these years of palling around, Charlotte was almost immune to Robert's striking good looks. But she was female, for heaven's sake, and his tall stature, well-muscled chest, and square-jawed face did make for an enticing view.

The dowager barely gave the men a spare glance as she seated herself haughtily in a high-backed chair. Her lips were pursed and her brow raised in query.

James looked at each person. "I need your word of honor that you will not repeat what I am about to tell to you."

"How can you ask that when we do not even know what you are about?" Robert challenged, shifting his stance.

Edward intoned, "I agree. I cannot give you my word on an issue before knowing what is at stake."

James shook his head emphatically. "I will not discuss anything with you unless I have your word. There is so much at risk that I can assure you it is more than a matter of honor."

Sylvie declared, "You have my word, so long as no one will be hurt. I want to understand what is going on."

Edward and Robert looked at one another and silently communicated their assent.

"On my honor. So long as it is not illegal or dishonorable," Edward said. Charlotte was surprised; Edward usually followed Robert's lead. She sniffed back a tear; her brother must really be concerned about her.

"And the same conditions on mine," Robert added.

James turned to his mother. She stiffened her spine and adjusted her skirts. "Do not be absurd, James."

"I will have your word, Mother," he spoke intensely, "or I will have you leave."

The dowager stood, affronted. "How dare you speak to me this way, especially in such company?"

Stone-faced and determined, he stated, "It is your choice entirely, Mother. I will force you to quit the room if you do not agree."

Although it obviously galled her, the dowager sat back down stiffly. "Fine. I hope you are happy."

"Far from it," he replied sourly, "but I will not have the matter leaving this room. Therefore, on your honor, I will tell you about a clandestine investigation I am conducting on behalf of His Majesty's government." He let out a long breath. "During the war, I worked in the War Office, generating the financing needed to support our troops. A man under my command, Sylvester Edgerton, embezzled a large quantity of property. I am charged with recovering that property, or the funds it has been converted into, before it can be used for disreputable purposes."

Charlotte saw the disbelief in Robert's golden eyes. She reassured, "General Cumseby has vouched for James and his mission." She blinked. Why was she suddenly defending him? She realized that as far as recovering the stolen property, she believed that James's intentions were honorable. That he meant what he said. It was what he did not say that had her suspicious.

Edward nodded. "Well, the general would certainly know about such things, and if he says that this is aboveboard . . ."

"Where do you believe this Mr. Edgerton is hiding out?" Robert asked.

"Sylvester Edgerton is dead."

Shocked silence.

Robert had the audacity to ask, "Did you kill him?"

James shook his head firmly. "No. Although I would have liked to have gotten my hands on the scoundrel. Mr. Edgerton may have tried to betray his own band."

"Then there are more men involved?" Sylvie asked nervously.

Rubbing his hand over his mouth, James stared out the window at a robin perched on the outside. Seeming to come to a decision, he faced the room again stating quietly, "I do not believe that Mr. Edgerton was the mastermind behind the operation. I am after the man who planned and directed the thefts and his men seeking out the treasure."

"Who is this mastermind?" Charlotte asked bluntly.

"For now, you need to understand that I am under considerable time pressure to recover these items."

"What is the rush?" Robert asked dubiously.

James looked him square in the eye. "We are concerned that the property has already been or will soon be converted into funds to support another offensive."

"By whom?" Edward asked.

"Napoleon."

"Surely not!" cried Sylvie.

"Sources indicate that Napoleon will be attempting to flee Elba. He believes that his men will flock to his banner once he succeeds. Still, he needs resources." James added cynically, "War is not cheap."

Edward opined, "Exile to Elba always concerned me. The man should have been made to pay for his crimes."

"But what does this have to do with the Hastings girl?" asked the dowager, frowning.

"Charlotte." James looked over at her. "Well, Charlotte has been assisting me with the investigation, and regrettably was injured in the process."

"Why on earth do you have a mere girl assisting you with your investigation?" Robert challenged. "Sorry, Charlotte, I know you like to believe that you are made of sturdy stuff, but a man has been murdered, for God's sake!"

James set his lips in a firm, hard line. "It was an unfortunate string of events that led us to this juncture." He stood, looked over at Charlotte and tilted his head in salute. "And Charlotte *is* made of sturdy stuff. Her help has proved invaluable."

She stared at him, baffled. The man constantly seemed to shift the ground beneath her. One day he was a vile monster, and the next he was honorable and handfeeding her bread.

"But why was it necessary for you to become engaged?" the dowager demanded.

"It was necessary for Charlotte and I to become engaged, because . . . well . . ." He shifted his shoulders. "Because Charlotte's reputation was at stake."

Robert recrossed his arms forcefully and asked, "Really? And how did that 'unfortunate' event take place?"

"In escaping an ambush, I wound up in her room at the Balstrams', at night. That is all I have to say on the subject."

So he was not going to disclose anything about the black-guard who attacked her.

"I always knew there was more to it than you let on," the dowager noted smugly. "You had to agree to marry her to save her reputation."

"You could have figured something else out—like the truth, for instance," Edward supplied.

"Of course he had to propose." The dowager spoke as if Edward were an idiot. "No man would have had her after the scandal."

"I would marry Charlotte no matter what the circumstances. Any man with a brain in his head would do so," Robert declared firmly.

Charlotte looked at him appreciatively and smiled. "Thank you, Robert. I know I can always count on you."

James's eyes narrowed warningly. "The matter has been settled."

"That is very honorable of you, my dear," his mother observed, "but that may not be necessary, now that the viscount is here."

"I will decide what is necessary," he growled. "The issue is not available for discussion."

"But I still do not understand how Charlotte was hurt." Sylvie frowned with concern. "How did she get those terrible bruises?"

James looked at Charlotte. "It was an accident . . ."

Her eyes never leaving his midnight gaze, Charlotte murmured, "I was attacked in my room by a vicious brute."

Sylvie gasped and clutched Charlotte's hand.

James rushed on, "I stopped him before he could do anything but bruise her."

Edward began pacing the room. "This is a lot to digest." He looked at James and insisted, "Then you caught the scoundrel?"

"Yes."

"You handed him over to the authorities?" Robert ground out.

"For crimes against the Crown."

Edward sighed with relief. "And no one knows about Charlotte?"

"No one who will let on."

Sylvie squeezed Charlotte's hand. "I do not like you being involved in this, Charlotte. The man attacked you because of this investigation."

"That room was a regular thoroughfare," the dowager commented dryly.

James glared at his mother.

Edward resumed his pacing. "But you said that Charlotte was merely bruised a bit. Why was she ill today?"

James looked at Charlotte and then around the room, uncomfortably. "Charlotte fell from her horse."

"I did not fall from my horse, James. I was thrown," she corrected him. "And it would not have happened if those men had not shot at me."

"What!" Sylvie exclaimed.

"Who was shooting at you?" Robert demanded.

James answered smoothly, "You yourself said you were confused, Charlotte. We do not know exactly what happened."

She bristled. "I have sense enough to know when someone is trying to kidnap me, thank you."

"Kidnap you? But why would someone want to do that?" Sylvie asked.

Charlotte and Edward exchanged a glance. Not even Sylvie knew about the diamond mines that comprised Charlotte's sizable dowry. It had been Charlotte's idea to keep it a secret. Myles Wilmington had been a hard but well-learned lesson on love and matrimony. Not about to partake in a cream-pot marriage, she would make her own choices, not have someone snare her for her fortune.

James asserted, "Whatever happened this morning will not occur again, you have my word on it. Charlotte will be protected at all times."

"Indeed. She will not be unguarded again," declared Robert. "Not while Edward and I are available. We see how well she did while under your protection."

"I can protect Charlotte well enough," he replied stonily.

"Attacked twice in the short time of your association. Very effective protection," Robert derided him.

Edward added, "Precautions should have been taken."

"I took Harry *and* Jake with me, Edward," Charlotte replied defensively.

"You need to be more vigilant," her brother answered sternly.

James stood. "And we will be. Charlotte is in my care and I give you my word that her protection will be foremost in all of my considerations."

Robert and Edward exchanged a glance that spoke volumes. "That is most beneficent of you, and quite appropriate under the circumstances," Edward replied reasonably. "I must insist, however, that you share the duty with Robert and myself. That will free you to conduct your investigation without additional distraction."

"I do not mind Charlotte distracting me." James stopped as if suddenly realizing what he had said. "What I meant is that Charlotte and I are engaged to be married. Given that fact, it might raise a few eyebrows if the viscount here spends every waking moment with her."

Charlotte tilted her head, exceedingly interested in hearing James's opinion on this issue. "So you do not mind Edward's escorting me about?"

"He is your brother."

"And Robert is one of our dearest friends," she countered. He shifted his shoulders.

"Do you not trust Robert?" she probed.

"When I cannot attend you, I will gladly welcome assistance from either of them."

Robert spoke purposefully, "We will expect you to call upon us at any time, day or night."

James walked over to the men, his hand extended. "Agreed." Edward shook his hand. Robert reluctantly followed suit.

Edward added, "We still have the matter of yours and Charlotte's engagement to discuss."

He nodded. "I suggest we discuss it, ahem, more privately."

"I still do not understand why you feel that the engagement must stand, James," the dowager interrupted. "There are other alternatives, you know. It is not as though something like this has never happened before."

"Enough, Mother."

"Fine," she harrumphed and turned away.

"Now that everything is settled," he offered, "would you care to join us for luncheon?"

The dowager rose. "There is another matter yet to be settled." Sylvie visibly straightened. The dowager looked only at her son. "I will not have that woman in this house when I am in residence. That was our agreement, James, and I would have you enforce it."

"Is that really necessary, Mother?" he questioned gently. "Obviously Charlotte and her aunt are close."

The dowager stood stiff and unyielding. Her mouth was set in a firm line. "I will have it so in my own home."

James looked at Charlotte and Sylvie apologetically.

Charlotte was not about to let the matter stand. Sylvie was her family, for heaven's sake. "That is unaccept—"

Sylvie rose from the sofa gracefully interrupting her, "Do not waste your time, Charlotte dear. This is not your battle to wage. Frankly, I am surprised that we were not evicted before this. Katie has always had difficulty not getting everything exactly her way."

The dowager glared at her hatefully. Aunt Sylvie ignored her.

"So long as we have seen that Charlotte is safe and well cared for, we will take our leave." She leaned down and kissed Charlotte, the scent of roses floating around her. "Go get something to eat and some rest, my dear."

Disappointed, Charlotte got to her feet. "I should be home at some point in the next few days. I will send word and we can have a visit then, shall we?"

Sylvie beamed at her affectionately. "That would be lovely." She curtseyed to James and swept out the door, giving the dowager the cut direct. Hurrah, Aunt Sylvie.

Robert leaned forward and brushed his lips across Charlotte's forehead, taking her aback. He had never before shown such affection. He whispered for her ears only, "I count on you to call upon me if there is anything you need, Charlotte."

Impulsively she kissed his cheek. "Thank you, Robert. You are the dearest friend to us."

Edward turned to James and the dowager. "I would like to stay and have a word with you and Charlotte, if I may."

James nodded quickly. "Of course. Please join us for luncheon. I would like to get some solid food into Charlotte."

Charlotte scoffed, chagrined by his concern. "I am not a child."

"No, just a greenhead," her brother teased. "You know how you get when you do not eat."

"Do not tempt me, Edward." She narrowed her eyes playfully. "I have very sharp teeth."

"I know," James answered, leading them out the door.

Behind James's back Edward raised his eyebrows incredulously at his sister.

She ignored him, suddenly wanting to focus on something other than the tall, handsome gentleman striding beside her. It must be the need for food unnerving her. For what else could be making her heart beat so erratically?

Later in the dining room, James gently patted his lips with his napkin, satisfied that he had not had to divulge any more to Charlotte's family and friend. Nothing had changed, really, except now he had others available to guard Charlotte. It irked him, however, that one of those extra sets of hands seemed intent on doing more than simply protecting her. James resolved to remain by Charlotte's side at every opportunity, thereby ensuring that the viscount's services were not required. No use allowing the man to think that he stood a chance with Charlotte.

James watched Edward and Charlotte from across the dining room table. The siblings shared the same sparkling blue eyes and facial structure, Charlotte's finer and more delicate, of course. But there the similarity ended. Edward's coffee brown hair did not compare to Charlotte's fiery auburn locks. Her skin was finer than porcelain, despite the freckles, while her brother must spend a great deal of time out of doors, giving him a ruddy complexion.

James sensed the personality differences as well. Edward tended to fiddle with things; his coat buttons, utensils. There was an air of wariness about him. In contrast, Charlotte was a lioness, bravery facing harrowing conflict. No one would have guessed that just a few hours before someone had shot at and tried to kidnap her. He should be pleased that his plan was working, that Mortimer was taking the bait. But the cold meat in his mouth suddenly tasted like wood and he pushed his plate away in disgust.

Edward popped a slice of fruit into his mouth and commented, "The abrupt news of your engagement had the household in an uproar, your grace. Why, I had to order my staff not to follow me to London, they were so provoked." He toyed with his fork. "I had not heard that you were in need . . . well, in the market for a wife."

James raised his brow but chose not to reply.

"From your comments, am I to understand that you intend to marry Charlotte?"

James looked pointedly at Charlotte. "Yes. I do."

She made a face, but thankfully, Edward was looking at him.

"We can all agree that the scandal of a broken engagement would not suit any of us at this time." Edward dabbed his mouth with his napkin. "Still, we do not want to rush to judgment. It is marriage, after all." He looked at his sister meaningfully. "A very serious undertaking."

Surprised, James lowered his goblet from his lips, carefully watching the man.

Edward waved his hand. "I am not opposed to the union, you understand. I just want everything to be done with the right intentions. First and foremost is Charlotte's happiness."

"Has Charlotte done or said anything to make you believe that she would not be content married to me?" he asked slowly. He doubted she would break her word; she was too upstanding for that. But she was astoundingly good at finding loopholes. Charlotte met his gaze with wide, innocent eyes.

"Oh, no," Edward declared. "She has not said a thing."

"Then what is your concern? I would think that you would be glad for the match."

"We are, we are," he rushed to assure as he sipped nervously from his goblet. "We just want to be certain that Charlotte has time to assess her options."

Dear lord, was Edward angling for a marriage between Charlotte and his friend the Viscount Devane? If so, it was time to nip it in the bud—diplomatically, of course. Nothing could interfere with his plans; he had to stop Mortimer at all costs. Then there was his word to the general to consider.

James commented carefully, "I do not want any gossip or innuendo associated with our engagement."

"Certainly not." Edward looked at his sister worriedly. "Charlotte's reputation and her happiness must take precedence over other considerations." He licked his lips, nervously suggesting, "It would probably be a good idea if at some point we discussed terms."

"I do not expect a dowry. Any other issues are minor details that we can work out as the need arises."

Edward's eyes widened. "No dowry?"

"Although I am sure Charlotte is well taken care of, under the circumstances, however, I feel that she need not bring anything further to the marriage, other than herself, of course."

The siblings exchanged a glance.

Sensing their distrust but not understanding, James spoke up again, elucidating a new idea. "We can still put the funds to good use, for instance, by creating a charitable trust for the veterans' hospital."

Edward scratched his head. "An interesting idea. What do you think, Charlotte?"

"We have plenty of time," she replied coolly. "Let us address the issue at the end of the Season, when we know better where we stand."

James smiled wickedly. "As agreed, we will be standing side by side, darling."

She glowered.

Edward watched them uncertainly. After a moment he commented, "So, Charlotte, you are coming home tomorrow; we can catch up."

She rolled her eyes teasingly. "Yes, Edward, I will help with the household accounts."

"And while you're at it, can you tally the ledgers, too?"

"Not on your life!"

Grinning, Edward turned to James. "You must not underestimate our Charlotte. She is quite brilliant, and when she leaves us to marry, I do not know how we will get along without her."

"Oh, you are not getting rid of me anytime soon, Edward," Charlotte said. Then James caught her eye, glaring. She licked her luscious lips. "I mean, Margaret will marry first."

"Thank heavens." He smiled and added half-jokingly, "I do not even want to be in the district when you tell her that you are engaged."

"Oh, no, Edward. You are the head of the family, and I will not let you abdicate your duty."

James raised a questioning brow.

"Margaret is . . ." She shrugged. ". . . excited about the prospect of finding a husband."

Charlotte, obviously, was not.

"A little too excited, if you ask me," Edward commented, tossing down his napkin. "I do wish that she would be a bit more circumspect. Just because a gentleman dances well does not make him a good candidate for a husband."

"Nor does having a title or connections," Charlotte asserted. "We must be diligent and guide her, Edward."

"As I have told you a thousand times before, Charlotte, we will not let her marry a scoundrel."

"Sorry." She smiled ruefully. "You know how I get, on that topic."

James scowled. She bit her lip and commented airily, "Do give me the news at home, Edward. It feels like a lifetime since I was there."

As Edward shared local tidings, James listened with half an ear, more focused on the auburn-haired beauty sitting across the table. For the first time, the novel notion entered his head that after all was said and done, Charlotte might reject his suit. He pushed the unsettling thought away. She was nearing three-and-twenty, for heaven's sake; if he wanted her, he would have her. Suddenly he realized that the thought of having her was growing on him like moss to stone. Unlike everything else in his life, it seemed a natural and artless occurrence. Novel, indeed.

Later, staring out the window in his study, James was pondering the tangled web his life had become, when Charlotte moved to stand beside him. "What do you see deep in the rose bushes, James?"

"Why, the future, Charlotte! Didn't you know that rosebuds foretell the future, if you look hard enough?"

"But how can you read anything if they will not flower until summer?"

He shrugged. "There is much I can see, and much more that I cannot."

"It looks like we will be having some rain before the day is out," she predicted lightly as clouds raced swiftly overhead.

James watched her from the corner of his eye. She was still favoring her side, but otherwise did not appear to be suffering additional ill effects from her fall. Her eyes somehow looked bluer in the sunshine. The light emphasizing the reddish highlights of her auburn curls. Her freckles were almost the same color as her hair. All twenty-seven of them. He almost smiled. "I want you to keep to our bargain, Charlotte, with everyone, including your family."

"My family and friends will not divulge your secrets."

"You agreed."

Silence.

"I got the distinct impression that your brother is exceedingly particular where you are concerned." James looked down at his fingernails. "Much more so than most gentlemen of my acquaintance would be."

"We are not typical Quality."

"That is patently clear," he murmured, still not satisfied. "Still, I would have thought he would be more eager to see you well settled."

Looking down, she swept some lint from her skirt. "Well, Edward has always wanted me to marry Robert. With him we always know where we stand."

"Unlike with me."

She ignored the lure.

He rubbed his chin thoughtfully, changing tactics. "The Viscount Devane is very protective of you."

Looking out the window, Charlotte smiled affectionately. "I was amazed when he charged you like that, but he can be a bull when crossed. He really is quite sweet most of the time. A very kindhearted man."

"So you care for him?"

"Of course."

"Your aunt would undoubtedly be pleased if you and Robert wed?"

"Aunt Sylvie has always favored Robert. He has been a stalwart support through some difficult times. Aunt Sylvie says that a real friend shows her true colors on a rainy day. She is such a wise soul. I cannot understand the animosity that she and your mother have for one another."

"How do you feel about it?"

"I wish I knew what happened between her and your mother."

He put his finger under her chin, capturing her surprised gaze. "Not about my mother, about you and the viscount."

She frowned, blinking. "You think that it had something

to do with Robert? Does your mother even know Robert?"

"I am asking about you! How do *you* feel about marrying the Viscount Devane?"

"Marry Robert?" She pursed her lips. "Well, by any account he is dashedly handsome, and he comes from an excellent family. Lord and Lady Swathmore are quite lovely. But I get the sense that Robert prefers his clubs and his chums to the rustle of silken skirts. He is forever at our estate, crying off the marriage mart as a hunting ground where the prey devour the supposed predators."

So she had no idea of her allure. James would bet the bank that the viscount was not so oblivious to her charms.

Her eyes narrowed. "Are you going to try to marry me off to Robert at the end of the Season?"

James's face was a controlled mask. "That is highly doubtful."

"Good. Because I will not be forced into a marriage simply because it is convenient, even if it is to Robert."

"If not for convenience, why else would you marry?" he asked curiously. "Do not tell me that you take to the foolish notions of love and romance, Charlotte? You seem too levelheaded for any such nonsense."

She folded her arms and replied, "I will marry when I find the right man. One who has all of the qualities of an honorable, decent gentleman."

"Unlike myself, of course."

"You know better than I do."

"Yes." He looked down at her intently, dark eyes flashing. "I do."

Their gazes locked. The world dissolved and he was caught in the twin whirlpools of brilliant blue, sucking him in with their enchantment.

She tore her eyes away. "If you will excuse me?"

He pulled himself back to reality. There was no magic,

only cold hard fact. And the fact that Charlotte was unwilling to consider him as a potential partner was a bit galling. She turned to leave, but he was not finished with her yet. He grabbed her arm and drew her close. Her mouth opened with a sharp intake of breath, giving him just the opportunity he needed. He wrapped his arm about her tiny waist and kissed her lush lips, savoring the honeyed sweetness of her mouth. He realized that he'd wanted to do that all day.

She shuddered, and leaning into him, pushed her soft breasts against his torso. Her tongue boldly caressed his; there was the fire beneath his lioness's veneer. Heat infused his being, with the nexus swelling between his thighs. He wanted her lying under him, wrapping her curvaceous legs around him. He wanted her to want him. The way he desperately wanted her.

Collin's voice traveled down the corridor through the open door of the study, "I am sure his grace is ready to see you now, Mr. McArthur."

Bloody hell, not his solicitor, now, of all times.

He reluctantly ended the kiss and pulled back. Her luscious lips were swollen and parted, her blue eyes glazed with desire. Good. He knew at least on this front, he was making headway.

"Your grace?" Collin stood in the threshold, blocking Mr. McArthur's view. He wore an expression of pained contrition. If James did not know better, he would have thought his man was amused.

"A moment, Collin," James ordered. He looked down at the beauty in his arms. Her cheeks were stained bright red and her mouth puckered into a scowl. He spoke quietly, "There is no need to be embarrassed, darling. We are engaged."

"Shall I return at another time?" Mr. McArthur peeked from behind Collin's massive back.

Charlotte pushed out of his arms, gliding toward the door.

With her back ramrod straight, she did not even give him the benefit of a by-your-leave.

Suppressing a sigh, James turned away from the doorway to collect himself a moment. He looked out at the garden. If only those roses could tell the future . . . for he would surely like to know if Charlotte was to be in his.

Chapter 19

The next morning James dropped Charlotte off at the house on Hanover Square, saw her securely inside, and left to attend to some business at his club.

She knocked on her brother's study. He looked up from his review of the ledgers and smiled broadly. "Charlotte. Come in. How do you fare this morning?"

She walked in and dropped into the comfortable seat beside his desk, shifting slightly to keep her weight off her left side. She was still sore from her fall. She sighed, contented. Ever since Papa's death last year, this was their usual arrangement—he at the desk, she positioned nearby. "Better, thank you."

"You gave us quite a scare. I kept thinking about it all night. I find it all so hard to believe. The thefts, the attacks—I must confess, I am worried, Charlotte."

"You are not the only one."

"Getting engaged to the duke did resolve some of the more pressing issues, though. So a man actually exists who can fulfill your 'list'?" he teased.

"If I had used that list before falling for Myles Wilmington, well, I never would have fallen for Myles Wilmington."

"Or anyone else in the world, Char." He leaned forward. "Maybe your marrying Girard is not such a terrible thing to come out of this horrid business."

"Papa and I agreed that I would choose my husband, my marriage. You promised me that as well. Do not fail me now."

"He seems set on marrying you."

Her pact with James uppermost in her mind, Charlotte wondered, "I just want to know whether or not the entire situation is a stratagem of some sort."

He scratched his chin. "You've lost me, Char."

"The engagement. I do not believe James is a corrupt or unscrupulous man, mind you. I just cannot discern his true motives on insisting we marry."

Edward asked gently, "Did you ever consider, Char, that he may be in love with you?"

A loud guffaw erupted from her throat. "Ahem." She put her hand in front of her mouth. "I do not think so."

"Stranger things have been known to happen."

He suddenly sat upright, the chair screeching in protest. "He cannot know about Southern Africa?"

"My concern exactly."

"But how could he? Except for you and me, the solicitor and the agent . . ."

". . . And Mortimer Blanton."

"And Mortimer Blanton," he finished faintly. He shook his head. "No. Mortimer would be too embarrassed or too greedy to tell anyone."

"Mortimer is James's cousin."

Edward fiddled with his quill. "I must admit I was concerned that Mortimer might have been behind the attempted kidnapping yesterday."

"The notion crossed my mind as well. But I thought Mortimer was staying in the country. The last I spoke to him, he was considering a trip to France, now that the war is over."

"That was when you rejected his suit."

"Yes. I was quite emphatic that I would never marry the man. I cannot imagine sharing a meal with him; forget my life or my . . ." Charlotte shuddered disgustedly. ". . . Anything else."

"Until we hear definitive word that he has left the country, we cannot rule him out. I do not trust him."

"I agree. I would not put the kidnapping attempt or anything past him. But whatever he might try," she smiled resolutely, "I would rather face ten scandals and life in a convent than consider marrying him."

"I cannot imagine you in a convent, Char. You would drive the nuns mad, organizing everything, ordering everyone about."

"Am I that horrible?"

"No, you are that *wonderful*." He looked down at the ledgers before him. "I do not know what I am going to do without you."

She stood and placed her arm across her brother's shoulders. "You are the master, Edward. I just help a bit here and there. You will be just fine. And besides," she smiled broadly, "I am not yet ready to be shuffled aside for the new viscountess."

Edward's smile faded to a frown. "Oh, no, Charlotte. I am not about to throw myself on the mercy of the marriage mart just because you might leave."

She replied playfully, "Miss Annavelle certainly seemed smitten."

He bobbed his head assuredly. "I am certain that I can handle things well enough on my own."

"I am confident you will manage everything just fine. And regardless of what happens, I will never go so far away."

"Where are you going?" asked a sweet, high-pitched voice.

Margaret stood in the doorway, looking as doll-like and beautiful as ever. Her chocolate-brown hair was coiled bouncily around her head, accenting her wide, kittenish brown eyes.

"Margaret! You are back," Charlotte exclaimed, opening her arms to welcome her little sister.

"Yes. It was a lovely party—dancing, picnics, just lovely."

The congenial siblings shared hugs and greetings.

"Any news, Margaret?" Edward prompted.

She floated over to the window in a cloud of peach-colored muslin and lace. "I am now preferring Lord Manfield to Mr. Willowby. He was very gallant and much better at cards."

Charlotte and Edward exchanged an unfavorable glance. Since Margaret undertook the task of landing a husband as a kind of game with the husband as the prize, her siblings bore the burden of winnowing out the profligates from the acceptable suitors. Although Charlotte was tempted to tell Margaret about her dreadful experience with Myles Wilmington, she did not wish to dampen her sister's lighthearted spirit.

"Lord Manfield has a bit of an unsavory reputation," Edward assessed gently. "I would have trouble envisioning him as a good husband."

"Oh," Margaret accepted, smiling. "His breath did leave something to be desired."

Charlotte barely stopped herself from rolling her eyes. "Bad breath, proficiency at cards, these are your standards for a husband?"

"Do not be silly, one must consider good looks, and a fine tailor, too." At Charlotte's scowl, she giggled. "I am only jesting, Char!" Charlotte did not know whether to be relieved or irritated.

Edward cleared his throat. "Well, Charlotte has some good news, Margaret, and I will let her tell you."

She swiftly snaked her arm around her brother's waist and squeezed him hard. "As the head of the family, I will let you do the honors."

Margaret looked at him expectantly and he announced with cheer, "Charlotte is engaged to James Morgan, the Duke of Girard."

Margaret's smile widened. "Now it is *you* who are jesting with *me!*"

"It is true, Margaret," she insisted softly.

Margaret's smile faded. "But I had no idea that you were even thinking of marriage."

"Well, I am nearly three-and-twenty," she replied affably. "You seem to be the only one not rushing to see me wed."

Margaret seemed to struggle with how to respond. "Do you love him? Is that it?"

She released Edward and walked over to her sister. Taking Margaret's hand, she spoke gently, skirting the question. "I know that you wanted to have the attention this Season with becoming engaged to be married. And you deserve it. Heaven knows it was difficult enough with Papa so ill, and then the mourning these last months. I am sorry that you are disappointed but this is the way it must be, for now, Margaret. You will probably be happily with child before I have even walked down the aisle."

Emotions played across her pretty face. "It's not just that, Char."

She heard the "just" and knew she had hit upon an issue plaguing her sister. "What is it then, dear?"

"It's just, well, I just never thought you would marry and leave us."

Charlotte was astounded and slightly insulted. "You thought that I would never marry? You believed that I would be an ape leader?"

"Oh, not that, nothing like that." She rushed to assure her.

"It's just that I never saw you leaving us and Greenwood Manor."

"And what did you think would happen to me when Edward married and the new viscountess moved in?"

"Oh, that." Margaret waved her hand dismissively. "That will not happen for many years, and by then she will probably be so green compared to you that you will still take care of everything."

"I *will* still take care of everything," Charlotte repeated softly, comprehension dawning. She could not believe her ears. She looked at her brother.

He held his hands up in mock surrender. "I am not getting in the middle of this."

Never marrying, always being there for the family, never having children of her own or a man who loved her, for herself: the thought gave Charlotte pause and caused her more than a little discomfort. She pushed the issue aside for examination later. For now, she wanted to understand her sister and make a point of her own.

Margaret curled a tendril of hair around her finger. "Kind of like old Cousin Maude."

Being compared to the loving but dowdy matron who had cared for them in their youth made Charlotte wince. She dropped her sister's hand and paced the length of the office.

Margaret's brow puckered. "I just never saw you as the type to fall in love."

She stopped in her tracks. "Why on earth not?"

Edward put his head in his hands.

"You are too practical, for one thing," Margaret replied reasonably. "And your standards are so high. You are loyal and caring, but certainly not romantic." There must have been steam coming out of Charlotte's ears, because Margaret suddenly found tact. "I mean, you are extremely loving and everyone loves you. It's just not the husband–wife kind of loving."

She set her hands on her hips. "What kind of loving is that?"

Margaret blushed a deep pink. "You know, the kind Lord Byron writes of."

"You mean romantic love and . . . physical love?"

Edward covered his eyes with his hands. "I cannot believe the way this conversation is heading." He looked up hopefully. "Maybe I should leave you two to discuss . . ."

Charlotte pointed at him sharply. "Do not move a hair, Edward Hastings!"

"Well, I am going to sit down, at any rate." He sat down, his chair squeaking loudly.

"I am going to say this once, and I want you both to understand. I will marry, the man of my choosing, when I am good and ready. And although I will miss you dearly, I will be living elsewhere with my husband and, I hope, my enormous horde of children." She stared hard at her sister and enunciated clearly, "And I will love my husband on all levels *in all ways*. I am not made of stone."

Margaret smiled sweetly and walked over. "No need to get a knot in your skirts, Char. I just never thought about it much, and, well, I just always wanted you near me. That is all."

"Well, now that that is settled," Edward said pleasantly, "how about having first crack at the tenant ledgers?"

She crossed her arms, still annoyed. "Now that I am shortly to be gone for good, why not have the first run yourself, Edward? I have some projects to work on in my studio."

Chagrined, he asked, "Then I am destined to go it alone?"

Her stance softened. "I will help after luncheon. In fact," she raised her hand to her chin, "if we put our minds to it, we can start working on finding you that viscountess . . ."

"Go!" Edward yelled, and Charlotte glided, smiling, out the door.

Chapter 20

Charlotte entered her sanctuary with no small sense of relief. Just the smells of damp clay and paints relaxed her. She loved her studio at Greenwood, but she favored the architecture of the London workroom, its high ceilings and tall windows admitting ample light from the southern exposure.

She took some clay from the bin in the corner and slammed the mound down on the wooden table, to get out any air trapped inside. A spinster! No physical love? She hammered the clay with her fists. *I am not made of stone.* She pounded at her little sister's presumption. She hammered at the dowager for making her feel ill equipped. At the beastly men who had attacked her.

Charlotte grew warm with her efforts. She smacked at James. Unreadable, enigmatic, provoking wolf. *Slam!* A thin line of perspiration built on her brow. What was she supposed to do about this inscrutable man who plagued her dreams and her nightmares? She hated feeling like she was in a spider's web that was shrinking closer and closer around her.

Abruptly she stopped. Papa would have known what to do. A wave of loss overwhelmed her. She missed her mother; the comfort, the love. And her father. Well, if he were alive today, he would protect her, provide her with invaluable advice and assistance in this difficult situation. She rubbed at the ticklish sensation on her nose, leaving a smear of gray. She grabbed a cloth and wiped her face.

Papa always had an answer, a new way of looking at a problem, a solution to provide. He had been her mentor in all things, household and otherwise, her standard to aim for. Although his legacy lived on, she missed him dreadfully.

Breathing heavily, and with her arms and shoulders aching from her efforts, Charlotte worked with the clay. Finally, the shape emerged. It was a naked woman, sitting tall and proud, her left arm curled protectively about her stomach, as if safekeeping her womb, and her right hand lay flat over her heart. Tears watered in Charlotte's eyes. Edward teased her about her list of requirements for the perfect husband. Margaret assumed that she would always stay. Was she setting herself up never to leave home for a life with a husband and children? Was she a coward, forsaking her future for fear of her past mistakes?

The bright morning light poured golden rays into the room as Charlotte sat wearily on a bench by the windows. She let the welcome heat soak through her clothes into her bones. The birds chirped playfully outside. Inhaling a deep breath, she watched a small brown bird jumping precariously from one high, slender limb to the next. The little creature made it look so easy.

Resolve flushed through her. She was not going to allow that knave Myles Wilmington and what he'd done ruin the rest of her life. Energized, she stood, returned the remaining clay to the bin and wiped her hands on a cloth. She feared loving the wrong man, choosing unwisely. But if she failed to choose, she stopped herself from having the life, the pleasures, the joys she really wanted. She would finish her Season as James's betrothed. But then she would find her husband. One who would love her for herself alone. No compromises.

A gentle knocking sounded at her studio door. She adjusted her hair. "Come."

Margaret poked her head inside. "We have a visitor, Char. Mr. Frickerby."

Charlotte frowned. What could he possibly want?

"He is quite handsome," Margaret gushed. "I sat next to him at Lady Klondyke's musicale and had difficulty paying attention."

Mr. Frickerby probably wanted to discuss the Balstram house party or Henrietta. Either way, Margaret should not be privy to the discussion.

"Margaret, please give me a moment alone with Mr. Frickerby. Then, come join us." She walked toward the door and when passing her sister added, "By the by, he will not be staying for tea."

Margaret looked at her oddly, "Is it proper? I mean, he is an eligible young man. And why not invite him to join us for tea?"

She patted her sister's shoulder and headed out the door. "I believe that Mr. Frickerby would like to discuss something . . . sensitive about . . . Henrietta, and it should take only a moment." Charlotte was in no mood for more. "Also, James is joining us for tea and I want it to be just a family affair. We all should get to know one another better. He is my betrothed and you are my favorite sister."

"I am your only sister."

"Yes, a pity, isn't it?" she noted, as she headed down to deal with Mr. Frickerby.

Mr. Stuart Frickerby was waiting on the blue chintz sofa in the blue salon. Sporting a bright green waistcoat and colorfully striped vest, he appeared to Charlotte like a skittish bird ready to fly when he jumped at the sight of her. No doubt she and Henrietta had quite different taste in men.

"Miss Hastings!" He sauntered over, grabbed her hand, and squeezed.

Charlotte gently but firmly pulled her hand from his moist grasp and stepped back. "Mr. Frickerby." She nodded politely to him and indicated the sofa from which he had flown. "Please sit down."

His lips curled. "What is wrong with your face?"

She raised her hand to her nose self-consciously. "They are called freckles."

"Not that, the gray stuff."

"Oh." Charlotte pulled a handkerchief from her pocket and scrubbed her cheeks. "I was working with clay." She hoped he might believe that her reddened face was from friction, not her mortification. She stuffed the kerchief back in her pocket. "To what do I owe the pleasure of your visit today, Mr. Frickerby?"

"With that terrible happening in Southbridge," he placed his hand over his heart, "I am concerned about you."

"I appreciate your concern, but it is misplaced. I am fine, as you can see for yourself."

Mr. Frickerby surprised her by swiftly moving his large frame around the table between them and crouching beside her chair on bended knee. He clutched her hand and held it tightly against his chest. "Miss Hastings . . . if I may be so bold . . . Charlotte. You must know that I care for your well being. If Girard has hurt you in some way, if you are in difficulty, I am at your disposal. Just tell me what I can do."

"I *insist* you conduct yourself *appropriately*, Mr. Frickerby!"

To her horror, instead of removing himself, the man leaned into her, pulling on her hand, trying to draw her closer. His musty breath slithered across her cheek. "I have learned to care for you in the short time we have been acquainted. Please let me be of service to you. I am a man of many talents and limitless potential."

"Unhand me this instant!" she cried as she shoved him away. He toppled unceremoniously onto his bottom with a dull thud.

She jumped to her feet and stepped behind her chair. She was shaking with anger and indignation. She could only pity Henrietta for caring for this Jack-a-dandy. "Never presume to be familiar with me, Mr. Frickerby!" She straightened her dress and glared at him. "I suggest you leave, as your services are neither required or desired."

"And what services might those be?" James asked in a steely soft voice as he stood in the threshold, looking powerful and controlled, like a leopard poised to pounce. His dark eyes glistened dangerously and his mouth was set in a hard line. Charlotte's heart skipped a beat; she was so glad to see him.

Mr. Frickerby picked his large body up off the floor and straightened his puffy jacket sleeves. He looked up and nodded warily. "Girard."

James stepped further into the room with Margaret trailing curiously behind.

He purred dangerously, "I ask again, what services did you offer my betrothed, Frickerby?"

"Mr. Frickerby was just making sure that I did not suffer any ill effects from the quick trip back to London." Charlotte looked pointedly at James and then at her sister. "Margaret, please be a dear and call for tea. Mr. Frickerby was just leaving."

Frickerby and James eyed each other like lions from rival prides, neither moving a muscle. James called quietly, "Lieutenant Freeman?"

With remarkable grace, the lieutenant entered the room. His salt and pepper hair was trimmed neatly around his ears, he was clean-shaven, and he wore livery of the Duke of Girard. "Yes, sir? I mean, your grace."

"Please show this man out."

"He's not a footman," Frickerby charged. "He is lame!"

James asserted dangerously, "He's perfectly capable of *handling* anything required, including you."

Charlotte was so flush with pride she thought she might burst. She slipped her hand neatly into the crook of James's arm, admiring him so much she wanted to kiss him. "Lieutenant, if you would do the honors?"

"Certainly Miss . . . I mean . . . Lady . . . I mean your . . . odsbodkins! Yes!"

The good lieutenant nimbly grabbed Mr. Frickerby. The man wildly shook his blond curly hair as a dog might shake off water. "Now, see here!" Mr. Frickerby blubbered and flailed, but the stronger man won over and Mr. Frickerby was settled out on the street, roughly rubbing his derrière.

Chapter 21

"**S**he is beautiful, Charlotte. So proud, powerful. I love it." Aunt Sylvie stood in front of the statue Charlotte had created the day before and shook her head in wonder.

"Thank you."

After a moment, Charlotte asked plaintively, "Aunt Sylvie, why do you and the dowager hate each other so?"

"Hate Katie? I am horribly, horrifically, furiously angry with her. But I do not hate her."

"What happened between you to cause such animosity?"

Her aunt took a deep breath and began walking around the room, stopping at a figure here and a statue there, examining them, then moving on. Charlotte could tell that although she looked at the artwork, her aunt's mind was elsewhere. Finally, coming full circle, the older woman began speaking slowly. "Katie and I were once the very best of friends."

She raised an eyebrow in disbelief. "Now, that is hard to imagine."

Aunt Sylvie smiled. "I know it is from the way we be-
haved yesterday, but we were so close—closer than sisters,
even. Our land lay adjacent to her family's, you see. Growing up, we played together, and celebrated many holidays
together. We even shared many of the same tutors." She
smiled again, distantly, remembering. "When it was time to
prepare for our first Season, we shared our dancing instructor, the same modiste, and even chose similar designs. We
traveled to Town together and shared the excitement and joy
of our first Season. We were both a success, the lord be
praised, and our parents were thrilled. Their goal was to
have us happily settled with titled nobility after our second
Season." She chuckled. "Katie and I used to fantasize about
marrying dukes or even princes, and in those dreams, our
husbands were the best of friends and we were always close.
We even imagined what it would be like if our children married. Then we would really be family." Sylvie paused and a
wistful smile crossed her face. "Then I met Randolph, and
everything changed."

She smiled at Charlotte. "You know most of the story.
Randolph came to sell my father two mares. I remember
them so clearly, Merriweather and Star. At that time, Randolph was already four-and-twenty and he rightly took my
breath away. I think that I loved him from the moment I saw
him that cold winter's day. My parents would have none of
it. They were set on me marrying well, and despite Randolph's good breeding, he had no title and not much money
to speak of when we fell in love and married. No one could
have foreseen the earl and his sons dying at sea. Randolph
really was only a distant cousin to an earl. Nevertheless, I
loved him fiercely. And no one understood that, least of all
Katie."

Staring out the window, she commented quietly, "Looking back, I can see now that Katie felt threatened by my
relationship with Randolph. She had always been my

closest friend and Randolph became my best friend, confidant, and lover. I went to Katie before we ran off and I asked for her blessing. She was angry and said some terrible things. So did I. But the worst was the betrayal." She shook her head ruefully. "She set my parents upon us. She probably thought that she was 'saving' me. Randolph and I barely escaped my father and his men. After traveling all night, we married at Gretna Green. The best decision of my life."

"It took a lot of courage to follow your heart."

"Not really. It was our destiny to be together."

"Did you ever see the dowager again?"

"Before the title came to Randolph, I tried to reconcile with her. She had married the duke by this time and they would have nothing to do with either of us. Although, to give the duke his due, I do not know what Katie told him about us." She scratched her chin. "As a matter of fact, now that I think back on it, when that scoundrel Jeffries was trying to prove that Randolph was unfit for the title, we heard that the old duke told him to accept his lot and live with it. Since then, well, although I try to ignore Katie, she has plagued me quietly for years. My balls are not quite the height of fashion, my parties do not draw the best *ton*."

She paused and then beamed happily, "But frankly, Charlotte, I do not really care. Katie got her duke, and I got my horse breeder. And I am happy. Although I appreciate the benefits involved with being a countess and the money is immensely helpful, I would have been content with Randolph without the Earldom. To this day, we hate to be apart. If it were not for your sudden engagement I would be back home right now."

Charlotte grimaced guiltily. "I am sorry. There really was no need for you to have come."

"Nonsense. I could not let an event like this go without ensuring that all was proper. I must admit, it was odd hearing that your intended was Katie's son. I wondered if she would accept you, knowing our connection. And then I had heard that she had chosen Miss Druthers as her 'successor.' "

"I had heard that intelligence too, but before last week, I had no inclination to be involved with the Morgans and they seemed disinclined to know me as well." Charlotte shook her head. "Now we are all thrown together like seamen at a port in a storm."

"Your betrothed reminds me of the old Katie—restrained and all that is proper on the outside, with just a hint of the devil on the inside." She sighed. "Although it's ridiculous, I still miss my old friend."

"Do you ever see reconciling with her?"

"I will certainly never try again. But if she came to me . . . well, we will never know, because Katie would rather eat her own shoe than admit she might have been wrong." She wrapped her arm about Charlotte's shoulders. "For now, I just want her to treat you well. But based upon her comments yesterday, I get the sense that she has taken you in dislike because of me."

"I believe that James has her on a tight rein. It is helpful that now I can understand her disapproval a little better."

"So you can deal with her as your mother-in-law?"

Charlotte smiled ruefully. "First let me settle upon marriage and a husband, then I can worry about the relations."

"Are you thinking of not going through with it?"

Aunt Sylvie was quick. Charlotte bit her lip. "It is all so new. The attack, scandal, the investigation. I am just beginning to sort it all out."

"I had no hesitation with Randolph. Maybe this marriage is not for you."

She hated lying, so she sidestepped the question. "Few people are as fortunate as you and have the benefit of instantaneous love and mutual affection."

Speaking earnestly, Aunt Sylvie took her hand. "You are

like me, you need to be loved and cherished. You need that sense of belonging to a man, as a partner, as an equal, not as a possession." She paused. "Do you believe you and Robert could be happy together?"

"Why does everyone suddenly want to marry me off to any man who might just suit?" James's idea yesterday of pawning her off on Robert still bit in her craw. It was not even near the end of the Season yet, and he was already trying to wash his hands of her.

Her aunt gently rubbed her back. "You will see, Charlotte— destiny will play its part."

Charlotte withheld her harrumph. Thus far, destiny was being a bit too playful, as far as her love life was concerned.

Heading back from the stables with James by his side, Edward inquired, "Where does your investigation lead you now?"

"I want to interview Edgerton's widow and find out some additional background on the man. Obviously I did not know him as well as I thought."

"You are not responsible for someone else's lack of morals."

"I can blame myself for not catching onto the scoundrel sooner." *In addition to not noticing that he was such easy prey for Mortimer's temptations.*

Edward swung his walking stick along absentmindedly. "Where does she reside?"

"In Spalding, just south of Boston."

"When do you leave?"

"As soon as possible. Arrangements need to be made before my departure, however. You know how it is," he added companionably, "always so many loose ends to tie when you need to get out of Town." James did not admit, even to himself, that he was putting off leaving because he did not want to leave Charlotte.

"Well, you need not trouble yourself about Charlotte. Robert and I will not let her out of our sight."

That was what worried James: the viscount's enthusiastic protection.

Edward added thoughtfully, "Say, it might be a good idea for her to move back home." At the scowl on James's face, Edward hurriedly added, "For the interim, of course. Just while you are out of Town. That way, I am available and Robert practically lives in our house."

There was no way James was about to let that happen. "Charlotte will be accompanying me to Spalding." He could not believe that he had actually uttered aloud the idea that had just popped into his head. Well, it was a good plan.

"I know that you are officially engaged, I read the notice in the papers myself. But as her brother, I have grave concerns about Charlotte's reputation. I believe that her good name would suffer from such an overnight excursion."

"Charlotte will accompany me and her reputation will not suffer in the least." Edward opened his mouth to argue, but he held up his hand. "Charlotte and I will visit Spalding and then continue on to Leicester and spend a night or two with my dear friends Lord and Lady Plankerton, who are home with a newborn. She will be perfectly safe, and so will her good name."

"That is true . . ." replied Edward, distractedly fiddling with his coat buttons.

"We will not let on where we are going and I will have my men follow to ensure that all is safe." James was liking the idea more and more. He would have Charlotte to himself for a few days without the annoyance of his mother or the viscount and he'd see Avery and Georgina and the new babe.

"Shall we?" He gestured to the house, effectively indicating that the conversation was at an end.

Edward nodded and flipped up his stick. "Yes, of course."

The two men stepped inside as the butler promptly opened the door.

Sylvie was telling Charlotte about her daughter Amelia's new home with Mr. Sherwin in the Southern Uplands when Edward and James crossed the studio's threshold.

Charlotte's breath caught in her throat just watching James stride into the room with catlike grace. A man should really have to work harder to get her heart to stampede and her breath to quicken. She clenched her fists, remembering the unholy feeling of raking her hands through his long wavy raven black hair. Her face heated with the realization of the effect his simple presence had on her. He was like a compelling force that was building in its impact, and she was growing heady with the stimulating effect.

James approached and her mouth went dry. She fiddled with her skirts, heat suddenly erupting all over her being. Part of her was euphoric to have him near. The more intellectual part was screaming to run and hide. She pushed away her ruminations and looked up; she could at least enjoy gazing at the man she was supposed to marry. He really was quite easy on the eyes.

"Are you unwell, Char?" her brother asked. "Your face is all red and splotchy."

She licked her lips, trying for a modicum of normalcy. "What did you think of Edward's new stallion? He is so proud of his purchase, one would think he had birthed the horse himself."

"Samson is a fine specimen," replied James good-naturedly.

"He should be, for what I paid," her brother commented. "But I cannot take all the credit. Robert helped me pick him, and if anyone knows horseflesh almost as well as Randolph, it is Robert."

"Or Aunt Sylvie," Charlotte chimed in.

Her aunt replied modestly, "You cannot spend almost thirty years with Randolph and not learn at least something about horses. I thank my lucky stars I had at least some interest, or I fear Randolph would have left me years ago and run off with his head groom."

Edward guffawed. "I'll have to tell Robert that one."

Charlotte chuckled. Turning to James, she asked, "Do you wish to depart?"

"Yes, if you are ready."

She kissed her aunt and brother good-bye. "I will see you soon, I am sure."

"In a few days, anyway," replied Edward.

She raised a questioning eyebrow.

"You and your betrothed will be going out of Town for a few days, I believe."

"Actually, Charlotte and I had not yet had the chance to discuss it. We will let you know as soon as our plans are settled." To Charlotte's chagrin, James nodded his good-byes and quickly shepherded her out the door, forestalling further conversation.

Once they were safely ensconced in the carriage, Charlotte, clearly a little piqued, asked, "What was Edward speaking of?"

James adjusted his coat and straightened his sleeves as he procrastinated telling her his idea for the trip. He did not want her to say no. He looked her in the eye and said charmingly, "I would have preferred to discuss it with you first, but Edward had asked me about the investigation and I told him my plans—our plans."

She leaned forward eagerly. "Have you found the location detailed in the map?"

"Not yet. That is the reason for a trip north. As you so cleverly pointed out, it may be worthwhile to visit Edgerton's widow and find out more about the man. That way, we may learn of the places he frequented, the areas he knew. It may well lead us to the location on the map." James added as persuasively as he could, "Having you present for the interview with the widow may encourage her to speak more freely. Will you join me?"

She looked out the window. "Is she far from London?"

"I estimate getting to Spalding and questioning Mrs. Edgerton should take us most of a day."

"I cannot go with you."

"We can stay with my old friends Avery and Georgina Plankerton. They live in Leicester, not too far from where Mrs. Edgerton resides."

"But will it not be impolite to drop in on the Plankertons with such short notice, even if they are old friends?"

"Avery and Georgina will be disappointed if I do not stop by. They are my dearest friends, and I would like for you to meet them. Georgina will be thrilled for news of the *ton* and Avery—well, Avery just does not care about having notice."

Eyes twinkling, Charlotte leaned forward, teasing, "Why should he care? It is the women and the servants who will be dashing about arranging quarters, adjusting meals, and the like."

He was chagrined by her description. He replied light-heartedly, "I believe that if it were left to the men, so long as there were brandy and cigars, we would gladly live in caves!"

She sat up, playfully feigning shock. "Your grace, you made a jest!" The corners of his mouth quirked into a smile. "You are smiling! Stop it!" Charlotte continued on like a carnival caller, "Contact the newspapers! The great Duke of Girard broke into a smile! Will wonders ever cease?"

He brushed his hand across his mouth self-consciously. "Is it really so rare?"

She continued teasingly. "You are quite stoic, James. But underneath it all . . ."

He straightened abruptly. She had called him "James." The sound of his name on her lips was a honeyed triumph; she could not hate him terribly if she could call him by his Christian name.

James moved across the carriage to sit beside her on the small seat.

She shifted over, adjusting her skirts. "What are you doing?"

"The view here is much more pleasant," he commented, looking at her.

"I do wish you would not be so informal with me." Rosiness spread across her porcelain cheeks.

"We are engaged."

"For public consumption."

"We are engaged," he stated firmly, placing his gloved finger under her chin. Her sparkling blue eyes widened. "This is an awkward situation for both of us, Charlotte—"

"—I do not see how it is awkward for you," she interrupted.

"Well, for one, I never would have imagined you as my betrothed. You are sauce mouthed, improper, and unconventional, to say the least—"

"—You certainly know how to flatter a girl."

"If you would allow me the courtesy of finishing a sentence . . ."

She pressed her lips closed.

"But you are also loyal to a fault, sharp-witted, brave beyond bearing, and breathlessly beautiful. An exceedingly odd and yet compelling combination. I cannot help but like you, Charlotte."

"You can save your hatchet flinging for your *other* female companions," she grumbled.

"I do not flatter, I speak truth. And the truth is, Charlotte, I find being around you . . . provoking." He shifted closer, his mouth pausing just a finger's width from her luscious lips.

"And for the record, I have no *other* female companions."

He lowered his mouth to those soft, full lips, praying she would not spurn him. The simple contact swamped his body with heat. Dear God, she was open and waiting for him. He plunged his tongue into her honeyed mouth, and when her tongue tentatively touched his, he almost jolted from the fiery shock. He could taste her desire like a heady elixir, scorching through his veins all the way down to his toes. Excitement flushed his body and he pulled her closer still, wanting more warmth from her fires.

The scent of lavender and woman wafted around her, a powerful aphrodisiac. She raised her hand to his face, the buttery leather pressing gently against his cheek. He shuddered and groaned. She wove her other hand into his long hair and pulled his head down closer, pressing her soft body deeper into his hardening form.

The carriage lurched to an abrupt halt. He reluctantly pulled away, trying to settle the fantastic racing of his heart. He swallowed hard. "We will continue this later, Charlotte."

She blinked, her normally bright blue eyes clouded with desire. She licked those delicious lips, murmuring breathlessly, "Is that a promise or a threat?"

He straightened her lopsided hat. "Both. I promise that we will finish this later, and if we do not, then I will be ready for Bedlam; and where I go, you go."

The footman opened the door and set down the stool.

Charlotte gathered her skirts and stepped out of the coach, asking breathlessly over her shoulder, "James, was that another jest? Two in one afternoon? One would hardly recognize you."

James descended through the door. "These days I can hardly recognize myself."

Chapter 22

They left two mornings later. At Charlotte's insistence, James sent a messenger ahead to inform the Plankertons of their impending arrival. As the carriage carried the couple and their entourage north, Charlotte and James once again went over their strategy for interrogating Edgerton's widow. They were firmly agreed that they would not show the widow the map, but were undecided on whether or not to show her the keys. They finally agreed that Charlotte would carry the keys in her reticule and would only bring them out if the need arose during the conversations. Both of them had spent a considerable amount of time trying to understand the odd, interlocking shapes that made up the keys, to no avail. They hoped that they would learn their relevance soon.

The carriage pulled up in front of a dilapidated old house that looked as if its best days had come and gone. The garden was overgrown, the door looked as if it had not seen a paintbrush in years, and the one shutter still hanging appeared ready to drop with the faintest wind. The hodgepodge of flat stones assembling the walkway were loose, and some were missing. James escorted Charlotte toward the front door with his arm wrapped protectively about her waist. Even though it was a simple gesture to ensure that she did not stumble, her blood quickened excitedly at his touch.

As they walked toward the house, the curtain in the front window was thrust aside and an anxious face peered out. James knocked and from behind the door came a rough woman's voice, challenging, "State yer business."

James looked at Charlotte, his eyebrow raised at the rude reception. "Open the door, if you please."

The entry opened a crack and the top of a dirty blond head peeked out.

"What's a gentleman an lady be wantin' with me?" asked the voice, suspicious but not hostile.

"If you let us in, you will find out," replied Charlotte assuredly.

The door edged open wider to reveal a large woman with dirty blond matted hair, light gray eyes, and sallow skin. She touched her hand to her disheveled hair as if to straighten it, but it did not look as if anything would help except a soapy scrub. Her rumpled gown, once dark blue, had faded to a pale imitation. The woman's calculating eye narrowed slightly, in a heartbeat noting everything superficial about James and Charlotte—their clothes, the carriage, the attendants. Charlotte felt as if she were being sized up for auction.

"Mrs. Edgerton?" James asked.

"Who's wantin' to know?" asked the woman guardedly.

"James Morgan, the Duke of Girard, and Miss Hastings, my fianceé. Are you Mrs. Sylvester Edgerton?"

"No, she is not," announced a soft voice, "I am." A small woman stepped from the shadows of the dark hallway, gliding lightly on her toes. She reminded Charlotte of a child ballerina, except this little figure wore a high-necked long-sleeved dress in darkest black. The only thing not black in her ensemble was the white lace kerchief clutched tightly in her small hand. She moved toward them slowly, her small frame forcing her to look up at James. "You are from the War Office. I remember Sylvester talking about you."

He grimaced slightly. "Yes. Your husband worked under my supervision."

An uncomfortable silence ensued.

Mrs. Edgerton shook her head disapprovingly. "I knew that this matter was not nearly at an end. You are here about the gold, aren't you?"

James exchanged a glance with Charlotte. "May we come in, Mrs. Edgerton?"

"Yes, of course." She turned and led them into a small, shabby parlor. The room smelled of cat and lemon cookies. She faced them and nodded toward the larger woman. "This is my sister-in-law, Mrs. Laura Vane." Both James and Charlotte sent the woman polite nods, then turned their attention back to Mrs. Edgerton, who waved her white handkerchief toward the shabby but clean furnishings. "Please sit down."

They sat side by side on an old flowered couch faded with age. One of the legs showed signs of a busy cat; it was shredded to the wood. The widow sat across from them on a tall-backed gray armchair. Mrs. Vane stood behind her sister-in-law, her arms resting on the back of the chair. She carried herself with an aggressive air, as if waiting for an opening to pounce.

"Can I offer you some refreshment?" Mrs. Edgerton asked.

"That would be wonderful," replied Charlotte, smiling politely. "It was a long ride from Town."

"All the way from London. Bet it weren't a bad ride in a fancy gig like that," sneered Mrs. Vane.

Mrs. Edgerton sent her sister-in-law a harassed look. "Laura, please."

"What? If it weren't for you fessin' up to the government, we might be ridin' in nice gigs and dressin' in pretty clothes just like these Fancy here. They're no better than us, just richer."

Mrs. Edgerton gave an exasperated sigh. "Laura, please bring in some lemonade for us. And some cookies."

She waved her hand indignantly. "I am not their servant."

"Of course not, dear. If you would please bring us *all* some refreshments." Mrs. Edgerton narrowed her eyes warningly. Despite her small stature, she seemed a tough little lady. Her sister-in-law paused for a moment and then left with a harrumph.

The small woman turned to James and Charlotte apologetically. "You must excuse Laura. She usually is a dear. Her husband passed away last year, leaving her in great debt. Then, her brother just recently . . ." She trailed off, her thought unspoken but heard. Then she added, "She has been particularly down these last few weeks. I cannot account for it, but who could blame her?"

James cleared his throat. "We want to extend our most sincere condolences on the death of your husband."

She smiled sadly. "It is strange. To mourn a man who cheated, stole, lied, and left me. I do not know what disappoints me most about Sylvester. Whether he was such a greedy soul or whether he was not willing to share his treasure with anyone, not even me."

Charlotte asked gently, "Mrs. Edgerton, do you believe you could have lived off the treasure in good conscience, knowing it was stolen?"

She looked into the distance, deep in thought, and sighed. "At one point in my life I think I could have done anything, so long as Sylvester was with me. But he was a different person then and would not have injured a fly. It seems like forever ago that he changed; nothing satisfied him, nothing was good enough. Sadly, not even me. I think you may be right, Miss Hastings. I do not believe I could have been at peace with myself or with Sylvester, for that matter, knowing what he'd done. He had turned into someone I did not care for overmuch. Is that a terrible thing to say, now that he's dead?"

"Of course not," James said. "Death does not change who a man was. His value, his merit is the sum total of his good deeds, his successful undertakings, and his family left behind."

Charlotte heard echoes of prior Dukes of Girard in that statement. She speculated that James must have had those sentiments drummed into his head since he was in short-coats.

Mrs. Edgerton looked him squarely in the eye and suggested cynically, "Under your estimations then, your grace, Sylvester would be worth very little."

"I am not here to judge, Mrs. Edgerton. I am here to correct a wrong and keep the stolen property from falling into unsavory hands. Being a woman of strong moral character, you stepped forward and exposed the thefts. We still need your help. What did you mean about the gold?"

"Well," she began slowly, "things were taken, or 'redirected to better use,' as Sylvester used to say. But you know that."

"Yes. Thanks to you, we were able to trace many of the stolen items." He paused dramatically. "But most of the property has yet to be recovered."

"Well, you aren't the only ones looking for it, I can tell you that."

"Who else is looking for it?" Charlotte asked, leaning forward expectantly.

James stiffened beside her.

"Mr. John Brown," she replied. "But I suspect that is not his true name."

"Tell me, Mrs. Edgerton, what did the man look like?" asked Charlotte.

"I don't recall. He was blond, tallish, I cannot really remember. I am sorry."

Oddly, James seemed to relax upon learning almost nothing about the man's identity. Charlotte shifted in her seat. There was an undercurrent to this interrogation she did not understand. Her stomach fluttered, almost not wanting to recognize that James was keeping secrets from her still.

Mrs. Edgerton continued, "Came here a few weeks ago, claiming to have been a friend of Sylvester's. He said he was willing to share the bounty with me if I could give him the map."

Charlotte and James exchanged a meaningful look. "Did he say what the map depicted?" asked James.

"No, just that it was a map of his and Sylvester's and he needed it. I didn't speak with him for longer than a few short minutes. I knew right off that he was one of the thieves. I sent him on his way."

James straightened his back, concern lighting his handsome features. "He did not give you any trouble?"

"Actually, when I didn't help him, that's when he started talking about the gold. He offered to share some of it with me if I helped him recover it."

"Not the stolen trade goods?"

"Gold. That's what the man said. I told him I couldn't help him and sent him on his way."

"Have you seen him since?" asked Charlotte.

"No. He left so readily. I was surprised. He left me alone and has not been back since." She frowned worriedly, the white kerchief clutched tightly. "Should I be concerned, your grace?"

He considered the issue seriously for a moment and then slowly shook his head. "I believe that the man would have been back by now if he believed you knew something more. Frankly, I'm relieved he gave you so little difficulty. He must have known somehow that you were telling the truth."

Mrs. Edgerton smiled ruefully and spanned the room with her hand. "I asked him if he thought I would be living here if I had a map leading to a treasure of gold. He left shortly after that."

"They've no more right to the gold than we do," Mrs. Vane charged, carrying a tray full of lemonade and lemon cookies.

James stood as Mrs. Vane set the tray down on the unvarnished wooden table. "As I was Mr. Edgerton's supervisor in the War Office when the thefts took place, I have assumed responsibility for correcting the transgressions."

Mrs. Vane unbent her back, wiped her hands on her skirts, and scoffed, "Wantin' the loot fer yerself, more like it. Yer all the same, the Fancy you are. Needin' this and needin' that."

James sent the offensive woman a look that could stop a storm in winter. "Any property recovered will be returned to its *rightful owner,* the English government. That money belongs in the Treasury, and I will see it returned there and not put to nefarious use."

Charlotte put a gentle hand on his sleeve; she heard a discordant note in Mrs. Vane's complaints. "Mrs. Vane," she asked, "I seem to have torn my hem. Would you be so kind as to provide me with some needle and thread to fix it?"

The woman frowned, taken aback by the abrupt change in topic. She nodded and spoke slowly, "I have what yer needin' in the salon."

Charlotte rose. "If you will excuse us, your grace, Mrs. Edgerton. I would repair this hem before it tears further."

"Yes, of course, my dear," he replied stiffly.

She followed Mrs. Vane. As she reached the threshold, she leaned over and covertly tugged at her hem, tearing it quietly.

She looked up and caught James's blue-black gaze. He was staring at her as if she had suddenly sprouted horns.

Playfully she winked at him. He blinked and straightened and she had to suppress a giggle as she followed Mrs. Vane to the parlor. It was fun to rattle *him* for a change.

Bewildered and then amused, James sat back down with Mrs. Edgerton. His fiancée was proving to be as enigmatic a puzzle as he had ever encountered.

Looking up from pouring a cup of tea, the widow commented quietly, "Miss Hastings seems lovely, your grace. If I may be forward, why is she here with you?"

"She is my fiancée."

"Have a care, your grace. Sylvester traveled in some disreputable circles."

"Where my betrothed is concerned, I will take every care, Mrs. Edgerton."

She sipped her tea. "She is helping you with the recovery effort?"

"Yes."

"I must say, it seems odd for a lady of her standing to be involved in such corruption."

"Charlotte is anything but typical, Mrs. Edgerton." A fact he was learning to admire more and more.

"If I may again be so bold, are you in love?"

He shifted his shoulders. "We suit."

"Perhaps it is better if you are not in love. It causes one to lose sight of the other person sometimes. Like me with Sylvester."

James withheld his scowl. He and Charlotte were nothing like the Edgertons. They had mutual respect, admiration, compatible values, and . . . secrets. Could he and Charlotte ever have a solid relationship if it was founded on his darkhearted craving to pilfer what his cousin wanted? Unwilling to dig too deep into his feelings about Charlotte, he pushed aside the thought.

"Tell me, Mrs. Edgerton," he asked tentatively, "did your husband ever mention anyone else in the plot?"

She studied her cup and, spotting a chip in the china, frowned. "He made reference to a master, but I know nothing of him. Sylvester was so terrified of the scoundrel, he feared to even breathe the man's name."

James was pleased that no one else knew of his cousin's involvement, especially not Charlotte. Mortimer was a dastardly villain, deserving punishment much worse than anything James would mete out. Still, it would have been nice to have *even more* confirmation before he considered killing his own flesh and blood.

Mrs. Edgerton held out a plate full of cookies. "Please have a lemon cookie. Laura baked them and they are quite good, if a little sour."

In the salon, Charlotte seated herself on the long sofa across from Mrs. Vane. The widow reached over, dragged a sewing basket from the corner, and pulled out a needle and thread. "I hope that black is all right. It's already in, an' all."

"Black would be wonderful, thank you." She peeled off her gloves, modestly picked up the hem of her gown, and held the torn strip in place. She smiled warmly. "If you would be so kind as to keep me company, Mrs. Vane? I do so hate to sew alone."

"Well, I certainly have my share of stockings to darn." Mrs. Vane hauled some old stockings from the sewing basket, licked her fingers, and began threading another needle. Charlotte slowly mended the tear in her gown, silently thanking her lucky stars for her years of keeping Mrs. May company while she tended to her mending. Her stitching was passable, but she did not think Mrs. Vane was watching her too closely. Charlotte asked nonchalantly, "It must have been quite a scare for you to have that man come around asking after stolen gold."

The widow's gaze reflected anger and . . . pain, but she shook her head and frowned. "Scared? No. He was not the frightnin' sort."

"I know that I would have been frightened if a strange man came around after all that has happened. I would venture to guess that he was horrible inside and out."

Mrs. Vane stopped her darning, a small smile playing on her lips. "Oh no. He was not bad to look at, at all." Her eyes turned suddenly dreamy. "He was so tall, and well, manly, if you know what I mean. So strong, smooth, and dapper." Mrs. Vane shook her head regretfully, as if to shake the memory. "Dressed dandy and talked all kinds of pretty talk."

Charlotte smiled at her, genuinely sorry for the woman's pain. "Did he mistreat you, Mrs. Vane?"

The woman shook her head ruefully, knowing Charlotte understood exactly what had transpired. "Just my pride, Miss Hastings."

"He told you he would marry you?"

"Lied through his teeth, the rotter. I should've known all he wanted was the gold. Kept askin' after the map, the gold. I was a fool." She frowned down at her stocking, noticing that she had missed a stitch, and tugged at it.

"You are not the first woman fooled by an unconscionable man."

"I knew what he was about. I was foolin' myself. I have no one to blame but myself."

"Still, I am sorry. It must have been very upsetting, having him lie to you."

"Just so, just so." She nodded emphatically.

"Is there anything more you can tell me about him? Do you think you could describe him to me?"

"Well," started Mrs. Vane, "he was tall. A real looker. Handsome as anything. Blond 'air, blue eyes. A real charmer. Fine clothes. Definitely Fancy."

"Had you ever seen him before?"

She shook her head.

"Did he have any distinguishing features or markings?"

Mrs. Vane blushed.

"I assure you, Mrs. Vane, I am not here to judge you."

"Well, he had this scar, see." She held up her right arm and pointed to her triceps. "Right along under his arm. Said it was from a duel. With swords. Romantic like." Her cheeks reddened further. "And there was his mole. A red one. Right here." She lifted her hair and pointed to the back of her neck just below the hairline. Charlotte could not imagine for her life what chance Mrs. Vane had to see such a mole or a scar, but she was glad for any information on the man.

"Was there anything else that was distinctive? Did he say anything, anything at all, about Mr. Edgerton or the stolen property?"

She seemed to struggle to remember. "He said he was goin' to be rich as a king. Talked about goin' to the Continent. France, in particular. Said I would love Paris. I don't agree, I don't like frogs an' all, but it sounded nice. Talked a lot about the gold."

Charlotte looked down at her stitching to hide her disappointment. She had hoped for some insight as to the location depicted in the map. Still, she was not about to lose this opportunity.

"Where were you and your brother raised, Mrs. Vane?"

"Falmouth."

"To the south."

"Yes. A world away from here."

"Is it on the water?"

"Yes, blistery cold and bitter, that sea. We were always cold, even in summer."

"And your brother lived with you growing up?"

"He was with us until he went north to Truro for work. That's where he met Alice." She grimaced. "Pity for her. If he wasn't my own brother, I would've killed him for what he did to her. She's an angel." She pulled out a stained handkerchief and noisily blew her nose. "I don't know what I would've done if she hadn't taken me in."

Charlotte felt for the two women. At least they had each other. "I hope that I get along as well with my in-laws." Barely focusing on her stitching, she scrambled to think of additional questions. "Is Truro on the water as well?"

"No. It's inland."

She was curious. "How did you wind up in Spalding, so far from your home?"

"Was Sylvester's idea. He didn't want us in Town with him, just wanted us near enough to visit, but not near enough to be any trouble to him." She sighed. "He'd already gotten a little big for his britches by then."

"Did he visit often?"

"Off and on. Was always needin' to be off on government business." She glowered. "Dirty business, if you ask me."

Charlotte looked down at the hem in her hands. Her stitching was abominable. Anna was going to have to rework the entire hem. Mrs. Vane began to put away her stockings and supplies.

"One last thing, Mrs. Vane. Did Mr. Edgerton ever leave here briefly while visiting, or head somewhere other than London after his visit?"

Her brow furrowed. "I remember a time or two, Sylvester headin' north instead of south, back to London. Said it was business. He'd be gone a bit and then back a time or two as well." She shrugged. "Even if I knew where to look for the gold it wouldn't do me any good without the map. I turned this place upside down tryin' to find it." Realizing what she had admitted, she blushed again.

Charlotte ignored the admission and smiled pleasantly. "Thank you, Mrs. Vane, for the needle and thread and for your company."

Mrs. Edgerton walked them to the door.

James nodded graciously. "I appreciate your time, Mrs. Edgerton. Mrs. Vane, your cookies were delicious. I thank you for them."

The widow smiled shyly. "Thank you, your grace."

"I wish I could have been more helpful," Mrs. Edgerton replied sadly.

Charlotte really wished there were some way she could help the lady. Standing on the threshold, she turned to Mrs. Edgerton. "Have you ever considered, Mrs. Edgerton, that your husband was murdered because he opposed his co-conspirators and tried to do right?"

She smiled. "It is kind of you to consider my feelings on the matter. Actually," she raised the kerchief to her mouth and smiled tearfully. "It does make me feel better to think that my husband saw the error of his ways and repented. One can always have faith that he found the right path."

Charlotte smiled sympathetically. "It may well have happened."

"Thank you, again, Mrs. Edgerton. Mrs. Vane." James nodded and escorted Charlotte from the house and into the waiting carriage.

As the coach rolled toward Leicester, James remarked, "I am amazed and impressed with your investigative abilities, my dear. I never would have guessed that Mrs. Vane was the 'woman scorned' by our mysterious Mr. Brown." He shook his head in wonder. "What was your clue?"

"She obviously had a bone to pick with someone and I just knew there had to be more to it. Also," Charlotte added, "I was surprised that our Mr. Brown left Mrs. Edgerton alone so readily. I knew he would have to have been sure that she did not have the map before leaving. What better way to have the premises searched? Mrs. Vane seemed the perfect candidate."

"Has anyone ever told you you have a devious mind?" he teased, looking down at her.

She smiled modestly. "So now we know about Mr. Brown's identifying marks, and," she paused dramatically, "we might know where to focus our efforts regarding the map."

"Charlotte!" He leaned forward excitedly.

"Well, do not get too provoked, James," she tempered. "I know that we have to search north of Spalding, a short ride away, near water. It's not terribly specific, but it limits our hunt more than before."

"If memory serves, the closest shoreline is *the Wash*, just northeast of Spalding. It is somewhat expansive, but it is progress, my dear. Progress indeed." James smiled, an act that was almost habit where Charlotte was concerned. "When we return home we can begin plotting the territory and will find that monstrous cave. Excellent work, Charlotte. Excellent."

As the conveyance rocked and swayed, the muted sounds of the countryside barely entered the carriage under the din of the horses' hooves. James was so glad that he'd thought to bring Charlotte along, for more reasons than finding out the new information. She was surprisingly engaging company and was proving more than a bit resourceful.

Charlotte's lush lips turned down to frown. "I do feel sorry for Mrs. Edgerton and Mrs. Vane. They do not appear very well off. Is there anything that can be done?"

"Today I informed Mrs. Edgerton about the fund for widows and orphans for personnel in the War Office."

"What fund?"

"The fund that I created this afternoon."

Spontaneously, she leaned over and kissed him on the cheek. "James, how lovely of you!"

Amazed, he gently raised his fingers to his face, touching where she had kissed him. Her action was so lovingly heartfelt. Heat warmed his cheeks, and if he did not know better, he would have thought that he flushed from her esteem. But that was impossible; a chaste peck on the cheek could not unnerve him. He hid his discomposure by coughing into his hand. "Ah, well, Mrs. Edgerton is a woman of grace and fortitude. She and her sister-in-law have suffered enough by Mr. Edgerton's actions. A little financial assistance is the least I could do."

"Do not make light of it, James. I do not know many members of Society who would help two unconnected women." She blessed him with a brilliant, earth-shattering smile. "Well done, James."

It was the first time she had granted that remarkable, dazzling smile just for him. It made him want to shout to the rooftops with triumph.

Adjusting his sleeves, he schooled himself to stop being so emotional. He had never been so demonstrative. Perhaps the investigation was getting to him. He peeked at his betrothed out of the corner of his eye. Or perchance it was someone else's influence.

Again he was struck by how refreshing Charlotte was when compared to other ladies of his acquaintance. Most would have considered Mrs. Edgerton and Mrs. Vane insignificant. He knew with certainty that Constance would never have deigned to sit with either of the women, let alone share refreshment with them. He marveled at the fact that not only did Charlotte accompany him on his investigation, but she did so with an energetic, excited spirit of adventure and ingenuity. No wonder Mrs. Vane had opened up to her. She had the quality of making you want to be with her, to share her joy of life for a moment in time.

And James found himself wanting to be with her more and more; a worrisome thought, when you considered the underlying cause of their betrothal. Under the same circumstances, another woman would be gratified enough by having landed the Duke of Girard to turn the other cheek to any manipulation by him. But Charlotte cared little for wealth and title, he was learning. Again he worried over his plan. What was done needed to be done. Still, did the ends justify the means?

He was looking forward to confiding his concerns to Avery; he just prayed that his friend did not despise him for his misdeeds.

As if reading his thoughts, Charlotte asked, "What will you tell the Plankertons about us?"

"They are my dearest friends, but I have not yet decided how much to share," he admitted candidly.

She seemed to ponder that for a moment. "I have no strong opinion on the matter since I do not know them, nor do I know about your relationship. Or much about you, really . . ." Her voice trailed off.

"In reality, Charlotte, although we are engaged to be married, we hardly know one another."

It was a hard truth.

"You and Lord Plankerton were at Eton together, were you not?"

"Yes. We managed to get into some trouble in our school days. That was, until Father passed away."

"That probably just saved you from being sent down," she teased gently.

He marveled at how she seemed able to put a new face on a difficult issue. "You are probably correct. In my younger day, I was known to get into a tangle or two," he replied unrepentantly.

"Ah, the ramblings of an old man."

"I am almost one-and-thirty," he noted with feigned solemnity. Unbidden, his lips lifted wide at the corners.

She laughed even harder. "One would think you were one step in the grave, the way you speak."

"Sometimes, particularly lately, I am feeling almost in my dotage."

She chuckled quietly and wiped her eyes. "I wonder if after all is said and done we will be friends in our advancing years."

The smile vanished from his face. That she could speak so easily about leaving him left him cold. James turned away, looking out the window but barely seeing anything. He closed his eyes, a wave of tiredness suddenly swamping his limbs. "We will be there shortly, Charlotte. Maybe you would like to rest your eyes a bit before we arrive."

"Certainly," she replied quietly.

He could feel her gaze on him, but tried to shut out her presence and wrap the familiar stoicism around him, like armor against her humor, her heart, her appeal. But he feared that she had whittled away at the cracks in his long solid shell, cleaving them into a chasm that could not be restored.

Chapter 23

"**O**h, I do hope that she likes me," Georgina whispered, nervously tucking one of her wild red curls behind her ear as she and her husband stood on the front steps awaiting their guests.

Avery looked down at his beautiful freckled wife and challenged teasingly, "Name one person who does not like you."

"Fredrick Nickers!" they shouted in unison, laughing.

Georgina looked up at her husband, smiling, her dark green eyes shimmering with mirth.

"Oh, you always know how to make me realize when I am being foolish," she sighed. "I have not thought of that scoundrel in ages."

"It took 'that scoundrel' for me to finally realize how much I loved you," he commented dryly, hugging his wife close. Years before, Fredrick Nickers had stolen Lady Cladridge's diamond necklace and framed poor Alfred Sickamore. Avery still remembered the day Georgina, the passionate vicar's daughter, had stormed into his study, demanding to know what he was going to do about the injustice. Her pluck, loyalty, and fiery beauty had left him breathless, and from that morning forward he had set his sights on marrying her.

"It was only a matter of time, my dear," Georgina quipped. He tickled her and she shrieked, her fair skin flushing a deep pink. "I am so pleased that spring is finally here. I cannot wait to show Miss Hastings the garden and maybe the pond, oh, and I hope Cook has finished the apple tarts."

"Stop worrying, love. She will like you, and our family, and we will have a lovely visit."

"I know. I just want us to remain close to James. If his wife does not care for us, we will probably see less of him."

"I cannot imagine James letting anyone alter his affections for us."

"You know what I mean, dearest. It will just make everything more difficult."

"James would not choose a wife who would cause him grief. It is not in his nature. He is too controlling by far."

"One cannot control love," she stated definitively.

"Not that he would, but he did not mention anything akin to love in his missive. Just the potential scandal at the Balstrams'. Miss Hastings' being involved in his investigation somehow. We will learn all soon enough."

"Oh, I do hope James finds love. He so deserves it."

"I do not know if I would wish that on my dearest friend," he joked.

"Not amusing, Avery."

The carriage pulled up before them and the pair prepared to greet their guests.

Alighting from the coach, James took Charlotte's hand. She appreciated the comfort of it as he introduced her to his dear friends. "Lord Avery Plankerton and Lady Georgina Plankerton, may I present Miss Charlotte Hastings?"

"Welcome to our home, Miss Hastings," Georgina greeted warmly, her green eyes shimmering with excitement. Her dark red curls bounced in the spring breeze, giving her an air of youthful befuddlement, yet keen intellect shone from her eyes. "I trust that your ride was not too dreadful."

"We bid you welcome, Miss Hastings." Avery bowed. With his long brown hair tied neatly back, deep chocolate-brown eyes, and a broad, friendly face, he was disarmingly appealing. "It is a pleasure to make your acquaintance."

"The pleasure is mine. Thank you for having me at your home, My lord, my lady."

"Oh, you must call me Georgie," Georgina exclaimed. "Why, we are to be almost family. James is like our . . ."

"Family dog?" Avery interjected. He wrapped his large arm about James's shoulders. "We love him like a cherished pet." Avery's playfulness represented a surprisingly different side of James. Obviously, the men shared a great bond.

"Well, this pet could use a treat, Avery," James joked back as they entered the foyer. "We have had a long drive."

"Luncheon awaits your pleasure," Georgie assured them. "Let us proceed to the dining room at once."

As they entered, a loud screeching noise assaulted them, coming from somewhere down the hall.

Avery cringed. "Georgie, please ask Miss Mirtle to cease the violin lessons until after the meal. My delicate stomach cannot handle it."

"We must encourage Albert," Georgina chided him. She turned to Charlotte and James. "You must excuse Avery. He does not appreciate the finer arts. We brought Miss Mirtle from London to teach our Albert the violin."

Strings could be heard screeching. Avery shuddered. "Can we send them back there for the lessons?"

Georgina winced as the wailing strings escalated. "Perhaps I will ask them to rest a bit during the midday meal."

After having availed themselves of the cold game, pickles, cakes, and tarts from the dining room sideboards, the couples enjoyed a pleasant and satisfying repast. Suddenly, the sounds of a squalling baby filtered into the dining room.

Georgina shifted uncomfortably in her seat and then rose quickly. "That is my call. I will be back in a trice." She returned just a few moments later carrying the sleepily satisfied baby Eve.

The little luminary enchanted everyone, and James even put off his favorite dessert to gush over the child. "She is so tiny and pink, and delectable," James declared. "I may choose to eat her instead of my apple tart."

"I always knew you were an ogre," Avery ribbed.

"Why, she is beautiful," Charlotte admired. "She looks just like you, Georgie."

Georgie asserted, "I think she looks like Avery."

"Heaven help the girl," James commented dryly.

"Say what you will, James. I know that she is beautiful," Avery replied.

"Yes, Avery. Just think of all of the rakes and rakehells you will have to fight off when she makes her debut."

He groaned. "Do not think I have not considered that. You and I will have to practice our marksmanship, James. As her godfather I expect you to do your share of protecting."

"Oh, I will do my part. Mostly by holding you back from condemning every man who attempts to speak with her. I know you, Avery—you will be like a bull in a china shop, ready to charge at every potential suitor."

"You are probably correct. You will just have to keep me well into my cups most of the time to help me through it. Speaking of which . . ."

"Oh, you two go on," Georgina admonished. "I will help

get Charlotte settled. Just do not do so much damage that you sleep through dinner."

"Do you see how she humors me?" Avery sighed dramatically, as if greatly put out. "She might lead one to believe I need her permission for a little relaxation with my old friend."

"I am glad you finally realize the reality of the situation, Avery, dear."

Georgina turned to a bemused Charlotte. "You must forgive them. They are like brothers, and cherish their time together. James gives Avery a sense of companionship that he needs from other men. That, and the excuse to imbue fine spirits in the middle of the day."

"Here, here," Avery intoned gregariously as the men escaped arm in arm.

Walking down the hall, James asked half-seriously, "Have things changed so much that now you require permission?"

"No, James. But now I can do as I please with a clear conscience and feel good about it."

"Would it not feel good if Georgie did not approve?"

"It would feel about a tenth as good during, and absolutely awful later."

"And this is what I have to look forward to?" he asked as they entered the library. "Small pleasures, once in a while, by my lady's leave?"

Avery patted him on the back. "Oh, this and so much more, my friend. If your Miss Hastings is anything like my Georgie, you are in for the most joyous, wonderful, and infuriating ride of your life. And you are going to love it, even if only half as much as I do." James raised his brow dubiously. Avery only smiled. "You will see, my friend. I cannot believe you are finally falling into the parson's mousetrap."

"I can hardly believe it myself," he noted sardonically as they moved deeper into Avery's sanctum.

As it was a chilly spring day, a fire burned low in the

hearth in the library, the smoky-smelling wood warming the room considerably. Avery poured James a snifter of brandy and joined him by the fire. James helped himself to a cigar and then handed one to his friend in exchange for the drink. Sitting down in the deep leather chair and savoring the rich smoky flavor in his mouth, James felt a little of the tension in his shoulders ease.

Through a stream of fragrant smoke, Avery studied him from the opposite chair and mused aloud, "You look like a man in need of fortification. I have not seen you this tense since your father's death."

Leave it to Avery to see through James's impenetrable veneer. "I have had much on my mind these past few weeks."

"Is it about Miss Hastings?"

He stared at the fire for a long moment. Avery, who understood how hard it was for James to open up, waited patiently for him to air his concerns. James studied the burning tip of his cigar. "It is about Charlotte, and yet about so much more. Please do not share this with anyone, even Georgie. Can I ask that of you?"

"I do not share everything with Georgie." At his friend's dubious expression, Avery added, "Well, not *everything*. She is so insightful, it is a great help to hear her thoughts on matters. But yes, you can trust me not to share what we say together with anyone." He sat up a little in his seat. "This sounds grave, James."

He placed his snifter on the table and rubbed his hand over his eyes. "I am so tired, Avery. Tired of worrying about my family, about the possibility of another war, about the consequences of all of my actions, about whom to trust and what to do. About how to annihilate my cousin without hurting everyone in the process."

"You still believe that he is behind the thefts at the War Office?"

"Yes. I just have no way to prove it, aside from his irritatingly innocuous notes." James rubbed the back of his neck with his hand. "The connection between him and Edgerton is there, but that is not enough to condemn the man. I know in my heart that he was behind the whole thing. What I cannot fully grasp is the Napoleon connection. I never knew him to be a great admirer of the man."

"Is it not true that you have spent little time with your cousin in many years?"

"Yes, we've not truly seen each other since we were children, and then even less after Uncle died. I swear, I cannot fathom how a man as honorable and decent as my Uncle could spawn such a . . . a viper."

"Often times the adage about the apple and the tree is only that, an adage. Assuming you are correct, why risk his reputation, the gallows? Maybe he has fallen under Napoleon's spell? Certainly many others have."

"Who knows? He does many things simply because he enjoys hurting others. He was evil even as a child. He did the most heinous things to the servants; to anyone he could get under his power. He is deranged. He hides behind the facade of a gentleman, but he is sick in heart and in spirit." Perhaps that was why his cousin wanted Charlotte so badly, to ease his diseased mind. Just the notion of Charlotte in Mortimer's clutches made James shudder with anxiety.

"So what now?" Avery asked gravely.

"Well, I was able to intercept a map and keys that were being sent to Edgerton's wife. I believe Edgerton may have intended to double-cross Mortimer."

"And he wound up dead for his trouble."

"Yes. Although frankly, I find it hard to mourn a man who betrayed me so. Still, he left behind a decent woman."

"Did you learn anything on your visit?"

"Not really." His lips quirked into a bemused smile. "But Charlotte did."

Avery leaned forward, interested. "Do tell."

"She actually gained the confidences of the widow's sister, who had a dalliance with someone after the map."

"Mortimer?"

"No, thankfully. Probably one of his accomplices. He usually gets others to do his dirty work."

"Why thankfully? Do you believe Mortimer would have hurt her?"

James frowned. "You never can know what Mortimer will do. But no, I was thankful because I did not want Charlotte to find out that Mortimer was behind this whole madness."

Misunderstanding, Avery commented, "Keeping it quiet even with your fiancée. You always were one to keep your cards close to your chest. Still, if there is another accomplice, maybe he can lead you to your cousin?"

"Or at least implicate him. I would gladly wring a confession out of any of Mortimer's colleagues."

"So in addition to her great beauty, Miss Hastings is proving to be a lady of resources."

"Yes," James stated dejectedly, drinking deeply from his glass. "She is really quite quick-witted. Intelligent. Charming, even." He set the snifter down with a hard thud.

"The way you say it, it sounds like a list of her shortcomings."

James rubbed his hand through his hair and then, covering his mouth with his hand, he looked at his friend, assessing what to tell, afraid of sharing his secret. Fearful of what his friend might think of him.

As if reading his thoughts, Avery asked, "Is it so terrible? Do you not love her?"

"Love has very little to do with why I asked Charlotte to be my wife."

With that pronouncement, and nothing further forthcoming from James, the men sat in somber silence. "I can see that you are distressed and I really want to help." Avery sat back and sighed. "How many years have I been recommending that you marry, James? Two? Three?"

"Actually, four and then some," he replied, lost in thought. "It began shortly after you met Georgina."

Avery smiled ruefully. "Georgie *does* have a way of getting me animated about things. But still, there are so many advantages to a good marriage that I just wanted you to enjoy the same benefits as me."

"It takes finding the right woman for the match to be as beneficial as yours."

"And the alliance with Miss Hastings is not?"

He sat silently looking into the fire, as if examining his soul. Beseechingly, he asked, "Tell me, Avery. Can a marriage be good when its foundation is based on a lie?"

Avery puffed thoughtfully on his cigar. "I guess that would depend upon the nature of the lie."

James's reticence took hold once more. He feared exposing his transgression, even to his closest friend.

Into the quiet, Avery ventured, "You did write that Miss Hastings had been attacked and that you were found in her room. Under the circumstances, I cannot see what you have done that plagues you so."

"I should not have even put that on paper. I would not want anyone thinking that Charlotte was compromised in any way."

"By anyone other than you, you mean?" his friend asked shrewdly.

"Yes, of course. Well, I did ask her to marry me," he replied defensively. "But about the other man. I feel dreadful about that."

"Many would argue that you acted honorably."

James stood and walked to the fire. He picked up the poker and jabbed at the burning wood, sending a cloud of smoke billowing at his ankles. "Yes, well, it was not very honorable of me. I caused the man to be in her room. It was my fault that she was attacked, and I was the one who placed her in physical danger and compromised her reputation."

"James, you assume much responsibility for what occurred. Please explain yourself."

He stabbed angrily at the embers, as if skewering a smoky ghost. "I was just so confoundedly determined to get Mortimer. At any cost."

"You have lost me, James. What does Miss Hastings have to do with your cousin? And what could you have possibly done that would have so endangered her?"

He replied harshly, as if the words were torn from his throat, "I planted the stolen map and keys in Charlotte's room. Her attacker came for them."

"Why would you do such a thing?" Avery exclaimed.

"I did not believe anyone would look in her room. I thought, well, I thought Mortimer would not allow anyone into her room."

"Does Miss Hastings have a relationship with your cousin? Does he care for her?"

Through clenched teeth, he ground out, "Mortimer wants to marry her."

Avery was clearly stunned. "You said when you hid the items there you did not expect her to be placed in jeopardy. With hindsight, surely you would have acted differently, but you did nothing dishonorable. You saved her from her attacker, did you not?"

"Who never would have gone near her if it were not for me."

"Still . . ."

"Stop defending me, Avery!" he snarled. "You still do not understand." He shook his head and stood facing his friend. "I asked Charlotte to marry me because Mortimer wants her. I was willing to go to any length to draw him out, to take what he wanted. I do not know . . . to hurt him." He shook his head as if to dispel the ugly truth and looked at his friend, his anguish seeping out of him. "There is more."

Avery tensed. "What?"

"I had no intention of marrying her. I-I planned on discarding her once I finished with Mortimer."

Avery frowned and forced the point. "That is not like you."

James scowled. "Like me? I can barely recognize myself these days. I thought, well, at first I believed that Charlotte was in on it with Mortimer."

"Why would you think such a thing?"

He shrugged. "It was a foolish notion. Perhaps to make myself feel better about involving her in the dirty business. But even when I knew the truth of the matter, I still hoped to use her to my advantage, and then, even after her reputation was ruined from the broken engagement and the scandal, I merely intended to set her up in the country or some such— never truly considering the risk I put her in, the harm I would do to her reputation, to her life." He looked up at Avery, grimacing in shame. "I was so bloody blinded by hatred for my cousin. I set out to stop him, but I am no better than he."

Funereal silence.

"But now you do intend to marry her?"

"I gave my word to General Cumseby that I would do everything in my power to convince her to marry me. But I fear that Charlotte might see me as the monster I truly am. She wants an honorable man who will treat her with the dignity she deserves." He added glumly, "In sum, not me."

"So Miss Hastings knows your reasons for asking for her hand?"

"No, she does not know about Mortimer, and I do not want her ever to know. My actions are despicable. And the fact that Charlotte is actually a fine, decent, lovely woman makes it all the more difficult."

"How so?"

"Do you not see? The scoundrel tried to kidnap her while back in London. He still wants her. Now, more than ever, because I have claimed her. It is like when we were young, both vying for Uncle's affections. I have made her into a prize he covets, and now he will stop at nothing to have her."

"Does she prefer him?"

"I do not know. I dare not even raise his name in her presence. Yet I continue to place her in jeopardy. I want to draw Mortimer out, to catch him in the act, to get closer to exposing him and his misdeeds and dealing with him soundly. He still wants her, and if I know my cousin, he will stop at nothing to get her. Good God, when they tried to grab her they shot at her and she was thrown from her horse."

Avery's mouth dropped open. "James, this is a very serious situation. I know you understand that. You must tell her. You must protect her."

"I will do everything in my power to protect her, Avery. I have already taken extensive precautions." He shook his head emphatically. "But I will not tell her."

"You must."

"I cannot."

"Why in heaven's name not? Her life may be in danger."

"No," James replied slowly. "From what Charlotte said, the shots were in the air and her horse bolted. I do not believe Mortimer wants to hurt her. Or else I could not bear to live with myself. No. Mortimer desires her, safe and sound, for himself. And to take her from me, of course."

"Just as you took her from him."

"Yes. Do not look at me that way. I deserve it, I know. Yes, I am out to stop the funds from reaching Napoleon, but it is much more than merely a competition with my cousin. He is a menace to all we hold sacred. He must be stopped." He looked up at his friend, seeking understanding. "Avery, I believe Mortimer may have killed Uncle."

Avery crossed his arms. "That is a very serious accusation, James. And it happened years ago. How can you prove anything?"

"Exactly. There is little I can do except nail him to the ground with his misdoings now. I just wish I did not have to abuse Charlotte so abominably to do it."

"You have much to offer a lady in marriage. Title, wealth, connections. You can still make a good match."

"Did you not hear me? Charlotte wants an honorable, trustworthy gentleman. I have done her a grave disservice."

Avery grabbed James's arm, imploring, "Then tell her. You said she was a fine, decent lady. Maybe she'll understand."

"And show her what an honorable gentleman I am? No. She will leave me as fast as she can and not even wait until the end of the Season. If she leaves I cannot protect her and . . . and . . . she just cannot leave."

"So she means more to you than a mere pawn to get at your cousin."

James threw himself back into the deep leather upholstery, frustrated, angry, confused. "She is a good woman, Avery. An intelligent, honorable woman. She even has a sense of humor that I find interesting. She continues to surprise me with her character, her wit, her heart. She has a good heart."

"Those are not compliments that you toss around lightly, James." Avery sat down and studied the fire, then looked up intently. "You will not tell her because you cannot stand the thought of her being disappointed in you or leaving you?"

"Well, yes," he replied forlornly.

A slow, wolfish grin spread across Avery's face.

"Do not pretend to tell me that you would not feel the same way if the situation were reversed."

"And Miss Hastings was my Georgina? I would feel absolutely wretched. And I would tell her. I would not be able to have the lie between us. Obviously you must care for the girl if you are comparing her to me and Georgie, James."

When James made no reply, Avery walked over to stand in front of him. "Well, do you care for her or not?"

"I am not made of stone, Avery."

"No, just wood," Avery joked gently. He rubbed his chin, dearly considering all he had learned as he stared into the fire. James anxiously waited for some word from his friend. Censure, certainly. Anger, contempt? Well, he deserved it. Suggestions? James hoped.

Avery smiled. Then slowly, in fits and spurts at first, he began to chuckle, then finally to laugh out loud. Soon he was guffawing like the village idiot and holding his stomach from the effort. Tears of laughter ran down his flushed face.

"I find little amusing about this matter," James charged. "This is a serious affair. Charlotte's person and reputation are at risk, and we may be at war again soon. My cousin is a danger to us all. And I still need Charlotte's help to expose him. What, pray tell, is so amusing to you?"

Avery sniffed gleefully. "What do I find so amusing?" He straightened his coat, trying to assume a serious demeanor, with a broad stupid grin pasted to his face. "This is a serious business, James. It is just." A chuckle escaped his compressed lips. "Here I spent years trying to get you to marry and you treat marriage as an unwelcome obligation you were dispassionate about assuming. Then you go and take upon yourself responsibility for saving the Crown's property, stopping a war, capturing a potential murderer, and at the same time, falling in love with the one woman in all of England who does not want to marry you. Could you have made it any more difficult for yourself? It is priceless."

"I did not fall in love," he insisted. He added guardedly, "I like spending time with her. She is a good companion."

"You can deny it until you die, James, but I know you. You care little for what others think of you. If you did not love Miss Hastings, you would not care overmuch if she knew the truth of the matter. You must love her."

Looking down, James straightened his cuffs. "On this point you and I must disagree. I do not want her to know because I do not want her to be unprotected. That is all."

Avery tutted and shook his head knowingly. "You still have much to realize, James, and little time to learn it. But maybe Georgie and I can give you a little help while you are here."

"What kind of help?"

"The kind that will assist you in landing yourself a wife."

"I am engaged. The notices were sent to the papers. Remember?"

"James, if a woman does not love you, or prefers another, then she will break off the engagement and suffer the scandal without remorse. Do you want that to happen?"

"No," he vowed resolutely. "What can I do?"

"My first suggestion would be to tell her the truth. If she is worthy of your love, then she will ride the tempest with you."

"Absolutely not an option."

"Then, only because I love you, I will try to help you enthrall Miss Charlotte Hastings to the point where she loves you in return. That is the best I can try to do for you. The rest, well, you are on your own." He leaned over and squeezed James's hand. "You must do right by her, James. And that means more than a pension and a cottage in the country. I know you, you will not be able to live with yourself otherwise."

"Tell me what I can do."

He looked at James thoughtfully. "You are a man who likes things to be under control, systematic, rational. Courtship when one is in love is stormy, unpredictable, and even sometimes unreasonable. A woman in love is the most irrational being one can encounter."

"But Charlotte does not love me," James stated emphatically. "Of that I am sure. In reality, we have not had much of a chance to get to know one another."

"Yet you have grown to care for her," he pointed out judiciously.

James shrugged.

"Do not worry, my friend, with me and Georgie helping you, your Miss Hastings will soon be pining for you."

"I thought we agreed you wouldn't tell Georgie anything."

"I assume you'd be willing for me to tell her you require some assistance in wooing your bride-to-be?"

James frowned. "I am not a charity case, Avery."

"Of course not. Still, do you want our assistance or not?"

"Well, yes."

"This might actually turn out to be fun."

"Maybe for you," James grumbled.

"No, James—for you. And Miss Hastings."

Chapter 24

Charlotte joined Georgina in the salon and sat down to share a bit of bohea and biscuits. She adored the black china tea and gratefully accepted her cup. "Thank you . . . Georgie." Charlotte was still unused to the familiar term.

Georgina nibbled on a biscuit. "Oh, I almost wish Juanita was not such a wonderful baker." She patted her middle. "I should be more regimented, but Avery does not seem to mind the extra 'me' since the children." She held up the plate of treats.

Charlotte smiled graciously but shook her head. "I am still quite full from that wonderful luncheon."

Georgina sighed. "I do not recall the last time I was not hungry. Particularly when nursing I find that there is always too much time between meals."

She nodded politely, sipping her tea.

"So tell me, Charlotte, how did you finally land James? Avery and I have been trying to get him to settle down for years. He seemed completely uninterested in the undertaking."

She smiled noncommittally, not knowing how to respond.

After a small uncomfortable pause, Georgie smiled reassuringly. "No need to feel uncomfortable around me, dear. I know about what happened at the Balstrams'."

She looked over the rim of her teacup to hide her surprise. "You do?"

"Yes, James wrote to us. We know about James and that scoundrel in your room. Nothing to be ashamed of. We know that you and James stopped the brute."

"Well, then, you know why we are engaged."

"All we know is that after James was found in your room, he asked you to marry him."

"What more is there?" she asked innocently.

"Why, the truth."

"The truth?"

"I know James. If he were found with a vestal virgin he would not ask her to marry him if he did not want to. He would extricate himself somehow. He would take care for the lady's reputation, of course; he is a gentleman through and through. But he would marry only if he wanted to. And before you, he did not want to go anywhere near the parson's mousetrap. What did you do to change his mind, Charlotte?"

"I really did not *do anything*, Georgie."

"Nothing?" Georgie asked doubtfully.

"In fact, I would like to know why he asked for my hand as well," she replied candidly.

Georgie seemed taken aback by this intelligence. Apparently she had anticipated meeting a woman who had campaigned vigorously to land James as a husband. "I had such hope that someone finally helped James to experience some of the higher emotions," she added faintly, sipping her tea.

"Well, then," Georgie commented. "How about a turn in the gardens?"

"That would be lovely," she replied, relieved.

"Excellent. Let us not tarry then. We cannot leave the men alone for too long. No telling what trouble they will cook up."

Charlotte and Georgina strolled down a long lane of low-lying bushes with lovely white flowers budding toward the sun. A faint sweet scent wafted up. Bees buzzed lazily and birds chirped overhead.

"The gardens at Greenwood Manor have been sadly neglected ever since Papa's death, but I remember when they were glorious. I miss walking them," Charlotte commented wistfully. Seeing Georgina's concern, she added, "He was ill for a long time and died just last year."

"I am so sorry for your loss."

After they stopped to examine some recently installed new hedges, Georgina asked gently, "I do not mean to pry, Charlotte, but is your mother gone as well?"

"Yes. She died when I was young."

Georgie sighed. "I honestly cannot imagine it. It must have been very difficult for you. To this day my mother drives me daft, but I do not know what I would do without her."

"We all do what we must."

"Is that why you agreed to marry James?" Georgie asked quietly. "Because you felt you must?"

They stopped before a row of tall shrubby rose bushes. "What a wonder these must be when they are in bloom," Charlotte admired appreciatively.

She nodded, apparently accepting Charlotte's reticence to confide. "It is a feast for the senses."

"I heard once that if roses flower too early, it is bad luck."

"Nonsense." Georgina shook her head. "Nothing could be bad about roses. They come when nature wills it." She gently brushed her fingers along the leaves of the bush. "Love is like that, too. It took me many months to figure out that Avery and I belonged together. Please be patient with James." She added slowly, "Although it is a bit difficult for him to . . . un-bend, he is a good and decent man."

Charlotte agreed. It was just that he was so confoundedly pokerfaced. One moment he was straightforward, candid al-most to the point of being rude; the next he could have been in the adjacent county, he was so distant. She sighed; nothing was turning out as she had expected. James was not a scoundrel, yet he was hiding something unsavory, she just knew it. His interest in her dowry appeared minimal, but what else could it be? Maybe Georgina could provide some intelligence on her betrothed, because Charlotte was cer-tainly at a loss to understand him.

"He is quite guarded most of the time," she noted cau-tiously.

"Well, who can blame him? He did not live in a home where love and the grander emotions were particularly val-ued. Honor, respect, responsibility—those were the qualities eschewed by James's parents."

"Do you believe his intentions are honorable?" she probed.

"Undoubtedly."

They strolled down the lane in silence for a moment.

"As far as his reserved countenance, that is his way with almost everyone. Except Avery, and sometimes me."

Charlotte felt a small sense of satisfaction knowing that James was indeed capable of opening up, as rare a feat as it might be.

"I probably should not tell you, but you could hear it from any of the gossipmongers if you asked," Georgie said. "James's father was not what one would call loving. I under-stand he was quite dictatorial—old-fashioned in many ways. He was deeply involved in politics, to the point that he spent many months in London while James and the dowager stayed at Montrose. Then James was sent off to school at what I consider a very early age. I cannot fathom sending away my Albert when he is eight, but then he is only four and I cannot imagine him being eight years old."

Charlotte shook her head. "James told me his father died when he was only nineteen. They had little time those last years together. What a loss for them both."

"Yes, well, that was why it was so wonderful that James's Uncle Richard took such a strong interest in him."

"Uncle Richard? Do you mean Mr. Richard Blanton?"

"Why, yes. Did you know him?"

"Not well. Although a close neighbor, he spent most of his time in London."

"So you know James's cousin Mortimer?"

"We are acquainted," she replied noncommittally.

They walked along together in silence. Charlotte was trying to figure out a polite way to ask if James was in dire financial straits when they arrived at the end of the lane and were at the edge of the garden terrace.

"Shall we?" Georgina motioned toward the house.

"Of course." She nodded, relieved. For some reason, she did not want to hear that James desired her for her diamonds. She stepped into the shade of the house wondering if she would ever understand James and his enigmatic intentions. Or if she even wanted to.

When she entered the drawing room for dinner, the discussion ended hastily, leaving her feeling more than a little out of place. James looked quickly away, Avery walked over to the bar, and Georgina flushed crimson enough to match her dark red mane.

Charlotte stood uncertainly in the doorway, her hands clasped tightly before her. "You did say half-past seven, did you not?"

"Yes, my dear," Georgina rushed to reassure her. "The three of us were just a bit early and were catching up on a few things." Her dark green silk dress brought out her eyes, which at this moment were shining with unease. She glided forward and gestured for Charlotte to enter the room, the intricate ivory lace bordering her ribcage and sleeves flapping gently with her every stride.

James gracefully approached and bowed; his raven hair tied neatly in a leather cord shone black in the candlelight. "Good evening, Charlotte."

Her heart began the familiar gyration it performed especially for him. Charlotte felt the attraction between them like a cord tightening around her chest, tugging her to him. Instinctively, her feet trod closer. She licked her lips, roving her eyes across his wide shoulders encased in black silk formal attire, down the expanse of his broad chest swathed in a deep burgundy waistcoat, but as her eyes trailed down to his fashionably skin-tight black pants, her mouth went dry. Dear God, it should be illegal to show that much masculinity without first giving her a fortifying sip of wine.

She dragged her eyes up to meet his blue-black gaze, and if she did not know better she would have thought that they twinkled with amusement. He could not know what she was thinking, could he? Her traitorous cheeks colored.

"Good evening, Charlotte. You look lovely." Avery ambled over, a snifter of golden brown liquid in his hand. He made a grand show of kissing her gloved hand. It was only half past seven; was he deep into his cups already?

James grimaced and grabbed her hand from his friend with a flourish. He pressed his lips to her wrist, sending delicious tingles racing up her arm. What on earth was going on with these two?

Signals seemed to be passing from one man to the other and Charlotte was growing dizzy with the effort to make sense of them.

She was relieved when Avery announced, patting his flat belly, "I, for one, am famished and am dying to break into that case of French champagne."

James raised his eyebrow. "You dare?"

His friend waved him off. "From before the embargo. That is why we must finish the whole lot of it. Can't have anyone pointing any fingers, now, can we?" He led his wife out the door and commented wickedly, "Come along, my dear, you know how you get when good bubbly is served."

Suddenly being alone with James made Charlotte feel less than up to the mark. She had prepared herself with special care this evening to impress James's friends, and she had to admit, James. What woman would not want to tempt a magnificent man like him?

She brushed her gloved hand along her hip, hoping that her silk gown appeared as lovely to James as it had to her in her rooms. The Princess Elizabeth Lilac did enhance her blue eyes and made a nice contrast to her auburn hair. Although the gown was form fitting and evocative, it had long sleeves and a high neck. Thus, no need for ever-bothersome accessories.

The silence stretched long as James studied her with hooded eyes. She raised her hand to her curls self-consciously. "What is it?"

"I am savoring the view, Charlotte. You look positively delectable." He tucked her hand into the crook of his arm and whispered in her ear, "If we were not in Avery and Georgina's company, I might consider skipping dinner and dining on you."

Her pleased blush warmed her all the way to her toes. "You are quite presentable yourself, your grace. But I would not like to eat you. Too much chance of a bellyache."

"Do I not even warrant a handsome out of you?"

"You do not need compliments to enhance your bountiful self-esteem, James."

He crossed his hand over his heart dramatically. "You are brutal."

"Brutally honest. You have every lord and lady of the *ton* fawning over you."

"I would prefer some fawning by you."

"Come, now, James," Charlotte chided. "Why do you need my compliments?"

He was suddenly serious. "Because I want the favor of your approval, no one else's. The important question is, do I please *you*?"

She eyed him warily. The man barely had to walk into a room to make her want to lay herself down and . . . dear heavens! Where did that thought come from? She bit her lip, abruptly fiddling with an invisible hair on her skirts, fearful that her face might expose her wanton thoughts. She took a calming breath and straightened. "You know that you are beautiful. Why make me say it?"

"Beautiful," he mouthed the word as if tasting it. "No one has ever called me beautiful. Handsome, elegant, attractive, desirable. But not beautiful. You find me so?"

"Do not make fun of me, James. It is not nice."

"When I am with you I have no wish to be nice. I wish to be charming, attractive, and undeniable."

"Undeniable? You flatter yourself. No one is undeniable."

"Avery is to Georgina."

"Pray tell why was he making such a show of kissing my hand?"

He grimaced. "He was making a point."

She raised her brow questioningly.

He did not meet her eyes. "I am trying to be . . . a better betrothed."

She blinked. "Why bother?"

"Because, well, I want you to like me."

Heavens, James was like any other man; he wanted to be liked for himself. Charlotte certainly knew how *that* felt.

"I do like you, James," she admitted quietly. It was true. She enjoyed his company, relished the flip-flop that her stomach did when he came near, and liked conversing with the handsome devil. She certainly liked him enough to allow him access to her increasingly passionate person.

He awarded her with a slight smile. It opened up his face, making him more boyish, more approachable. It also made him devastatingly handsome.

"We must work on getting you to smile more often, James. When you smile you truly are beautiful."

"And you, my dear, are undeniable to me. Let us join our friends."

Charlotte felt a warm glow in her cheeks and a tickle in her middle that had little to do with Avery's jest. She blinked as realization dawned. She was foxed. Her hand lifted to scratch her nose and she missed it and traced her cheek. She suppressed a small giggle and peeked across the dining table at James. His dark cheeks were a bit flushed, but he seemed none the worse after, how many was it? Five or six bottles of some of France's best bubbly. He brushed his dangling curl off of his forehead. God, how she loved his hair. And those lips. She'd just die to kiss him again. He raised his goblet to his mouth. Even the man's bloody hands were gorgeous. She watched his fingertips delicately trace the line of the crystal wishing that those fingertips were caressing her.

Her face heated. Could the man know that every night she dreamed of him touching her and lying with her? The blasted rogue had no right to be so bloody attractive. She looked down at her hands. Would it be such a terrible thing to marry James, even if his intentions were not wholly honorable?

"Did you not hear me, Charlotte?"

She blinked. He was suddenly standing by her side. "We're off for a tour of the portrait gallery."

"Oh, yes," she murmured. She stood and the room spun crazily.

He grabbed her arm and steadied her. "Are you all right?"

"F . . . fine."

She let him guide her behind their hosts and was quite proud of her performance as they traversed the gallery. She nodded sagely whenever he spoke, but for her life she could not tell a thing he had said. She rarely overimbibed and was enjoying the experience too much to wonder where Avery and Georgina had disappeared to or how they'd gotten to the ballroom.

Candles were lighted strategically around the great room, giving hints of light while keeping the room cloaked in shadows. Charlotte thought the Plankertons not very frugal with their beeswax to leave the room lit, but did not say so. She looked around the elegant room decorated in gold and beige with beautiful carvings painted with gold leaf on the ceiling and graceful pale statues adorning the corners. Leave it to Georgina to have everything set to rights even if no one was expected.

The sound of a violin drifted in from another part of the house, a gentle breeze of song.

Charlotte smiled. "That's definitely not Albert."

"Miss Mirtle, I presume."

"It's a waltz . . . lovely."

James extended his hand and bowed before her. "May I have the honor of this dance, my dear?"

She raised her gloved hand to her lips self-consciously and giggled. "Here? Now?"

"Absolutely. I am not one to miss the opportunity to dance with the most beautiful lady in the room."

A little thrill tickled her middle. "I don't know, James. My dance card's quite full."

"Ahh. You force me to have to call out your partner. The coward runs. He does not know the value of a waltz with my Charlotte."

He swept her into his arms and skillfully swung her into a

turn about the room. She laughed, gleefully enchanted by the gesture. Candles whirled by and she struggled to catch her breath as they circled the room. They danced, plunging in and out of the pools of flickering candlelight.

The violin sang as they moved, and Charlotte was no longer laughing. She was quiet, her senses thrilling with the vibrations reverberating through her body. She relished the feel of being in James's arms, of the lovely music guiding her steps, and of their heady contact. For the first time, she fully understood the danger in the waltz. Why, some still believed it should be disallowed in Society. Thigh lightly brushed thigh, her full breasts pressed gently but tantalizingly close against his hard chest. A deep and heady exhilaration raced in her veins, making her feel as if her feet could fly.

She closed her eyes and savored the deep pulsing in her veins that made her feel thrillingly alive. How she loved the spicy, musky scent of him! He held her tightly, possessively, in the circle of his strong arms. He swung her wide and drew her even closer, pressing his powerful hard thighs against hers, causing heat to unfurl in her belly with shameless pleasure.

For a stolen moment, she pictured James as her husband, *her real husband*, and imagined the intimacy of his touch, the press of his warm, hard body against hers as a man takes his wife. He would kiss her with his open mouth as he did so deliciously well, stroke her tongue, caress her breasts, and make her body tingle with that incredible heat that felt as if a smoldering fire was creeping up her bare skin. Her mouth went dry. Her heart was hammering so loudly, he could probably feel her pulse under his hands.

She peeked up at his darkly handsome features. He must be enchanted, for no other man caused her flesh to quiver with need and her mind to race so yearningly toward sin. When he was near, it was patently clear that she was not like one of her clay horses. She was definitely not made of stone.

They slowed, swaying gently to the whispering violin, leaning into each other, the heat of their bodies mingling and intensifying. Her skin was alive, aware of his every breath. He was breathing harder than usual, as if slowing down after a long race. For the first time she wondered if the unflappable Duke of Girard felt anything like the storm of sensations pulsing through her being. Curious, she slipped her hand under his black silk coat and velvety soft vest. She reached up, her fingers skimming up the smooth linen shirt toward his chest.

Under her fingertips his heart was thundering like a stampede of raging bulls. She swallowed, and tilted her head to look up at him.

"I am not made of wood, Charlotte," he whispered harshly. "You have no idea . . . how you make me feel."

Her favorite dark curl hung down over his forehead, matching the gleaming blackness in his eyes. The raw desire in them stole the breath from her throat. Time froze. Nothing existed outside his searing gaze of blackness burning with a heat that made her want to jump into the flames.

She felt as if she were hanging on a precipice. Her body ached for more of him, to taste him, to feel him. She was somewhat mortified by her compelling desire, but even more horrified by the possibility of not knowing more, not experiencing further this heady elixir that only James seemed able to supply. She licked her lips. "Is this common, the temptation, this yearning . . ."

"Good God, Charlotte. I have never in my life wanted anyone so badly." A muscle worked in his jaw. "You lure me to do things, to break taboos . . ." He brushed his lips across her forehead. "You are so captivating in your innocence."

"I am not a child," she exclaimed. "I am nearly three-and-twenty."

"But in the ways of man and woman?"

She bit her lip. She was miffed that he did not consider her enough of a woman and yet apprehensive at the possibility of becoming one. Still, she was so confoundedly fascinated. "I know some things . . . but I must confess, they sounded quite unaffecting until . . . well, nothing like what happens when you kiss me."

Everything about James seemed to set him apart from the ordinary. Perhaps it was the champagne, but searing insight suddenly pierced her awareness; her whole life had been more poignant, more affecting, more . . . colorful since her association with him. Instinctively she knew that his touches and kisses belied a more powerful encounter that awaited them. Her body clamored for it and she desperately wanted to know.

"Is it possible, James, to . . . explore the attraction between us?"

He sucked in his breath, his arms tightening around her. "You do not understand what you are proposing."

"I think I do." She was coming to the awful conclusion that her life would never be the same after James, that once the season ended, she could never fall into the insipid arms of a less magnificent man.

"This is not a decision to be made lightly, or," he grimaced, "after imbibing champagne. Let me escort you to your room."

Dear lord, *now* he was rejecting her? After she had just told him how much she wanted him? She did not know where her bravado came from, but she tilted her head back and mocked, "Don't you want to know how I might feel lying beneath you?"

He stiffened, his whole body hardening, particularly a central spot pressing heavily against her belly.

"This is not a game, Charlotte . . ." he ground out.

"Or are you afraid that you might just succumb to the higher emotions when you thrust yourself inside me? Myself, I wonder what it will be like to taste you underneath your clothes—"

"Bloody hell, Charlotte!"

His mouth claimed hers with a ravishing fervor that exploded through her body. His power, his strength and his
overwhelming need left her quivering. Seeking balance, she
reached up and clutched at his hair, loosening the leather
strap and setting his wavy mane free. Almost unconsciously,
she glided her fingers through his dark locks, feeling the silk
fall through her fingers. *Like a river of night.* She allowed
herself to fall deeper and deeper into the intoxicating kiss.

She did not recall making it to the wall. Suddenly the
couch was underneath her as he pressed against her, ravishing her mouth, running his hands up and down her body with
shameless abandon. Her senses cried with glory, relishing his
every touch. She heard moaning and realized that it was
coming from deep within her. Nothing existed in time or
space beyond his touch and the exploding sensations drum-
ming through her body.

He withdrew from her and she cried out in protest. He
ripped off his coat and yanked at his cravat, sending his shirt
falling to the floor in a cloud of white. The glow of candles
silhouetted his form, cloaking his olive skin in a golden halo.
Her breath caught in her throat; she had never seen a man unclothed, and nothing had prepared her for the magnificence
of his broad shoulders, brawny chest, muscled arms, and flat
stomach.

He lay back down on her and she could not help but smile
as she ran her fingers down the smooth flesh of his back, en-
thralled by the texture of him. She pressed her mouth to his
bare shoulder, feeling the solid muscle underneath her parted
lips and tasting the salty, musky flavor that was James.

His lips found hers and the tide of passion swelled all the
way down to her toes as she rubbed herself against him, crying for more. Her body was on fire and the intense pressure
building between her legs was *divine.* Dear lord in heaven!

He fumbled with the gown's buttons at her back, cursing

his clumsy fingers. He whipped the thin chemise over her head, and finally free, the air skimmed across her nakedness, raising bumps all along her skin.

He gently leaned her back on the couch and kissed her neck, her shoulder, trailing his long locks across her sensitive skin. Good God, what was he doing to her breasts? His licking and sucking and caressing would drive her to madness! She threw her head back and clutched his hair, wallowing in the ecstasy of his touch. A small voice in her head clamored that this was folly, but she pushed it away, knowing that this was a recklessness worth savoring.

When his smooth member touched the sensitive flesh of her inner thigh, she shivered not with fear, but with longing. She arched her back and moaned. He sucked her bottom lip as he clutched her derrière and guided the head of his manhood to the vortex of her heat. The warning voice in her head suddenly began shouting. She shifted beneath him. "J-James . . ."

Electricity rocketed through her veins from the hard sensitive nub between her thighs straight to the tips of her curling toes and back to the ends of her hair. All thoughts fled. She cried out from the searing force of pleasure as her body erupted in a frenzy of heat and tremors. He rubbed himself against her again and again, sliding up and down in her wetness. She was panting, crying, begging, her mouth wide open, her eyes locked closed. She sucked in her breath, holding on tight to the sleek flesh of his hard muscled shoulders. She arched her back, wanting, yearning, waiting . . . for something . . . holding on for dear life . . . heaven . . . something surged inside of her. She threw her head back and screamed. Her insides pulsed and spasmed, shooting waves of ecstasy crashing over her body again and again. Her breath came in short, harsh gasps.

He plunged deep into her and something ripped inside. She felt stretched and opened beyond her capacity. Fear crashed into her consciousness like a wave of ice water. She struggled and pushed against him, her heart charging wildly. But he was in thrall, rocking and thrusting inside her. Suddenly he cried out and pumped himself into her, again sending pulses of delight spasming inside her innermost core. She was astounded. In his release, she relived her own, losing any sense of discomfort and rekindling her taste of ecstasy.

She lay fixed, her heart hammering with apprehension, her mind racing with the realization of what she had just done. She had given away her maidenhood, and quite cheaply, at that. But just like everything else with James, it was beyond her imagining, incredible past dreams. He was the eye of her stormy passion and she could not fault her desire; it was a spectacular passage to womanhood.

He was breathing harshly, his heart still hammering against her chest, but he was relaxed and unmoving. Slowly he raised his head and looked down at her, his blue black eyes gleaming with contentment. He kissed her swollen lips tenderly, their hot breath intermingling. He smiled and dropped his head onto her neck.

At least she did not repulse him with her wantonness. She sighed. Aside from the misgivings over her future, she felt incredible, warm, and sated. Her muscles relaxed into the couch with delicious weariness.

She stroked his glorious silken hair and watched the shadows dance across the gilded ceiling in the flickering candlelight. The scent of beeswax and the heady musk of their lovemaking filled the room.

He slowly peeled himself off her and sat beside her on the divan.

"No more music," he commented, lazily brushing his hair from his eyes.

The violin was gone. She sat up and a gush of dampness rushed between her legs. She looked down. A small trail of pink wetness lay on her inner thigh. Heat warmed her face and she wanted to die.

He handed her his handkerchief. His initials were embroidered in black on the lacy white linen.

"I do not wish to stain it . . ."

"Don't be ridiculous. I am sorry for . . ." He leaned forward and curled a lock of her hair around her ear. ". . . The pain I caused."

She used his offering, gently cleaning up, and straightened her rumpled clothes. How on earth was she ever going to look him in the eye again after *that*?

He grabbed her hand. "I do not wish you ever, ever to have to suffer again."

She bit her swollen lip. "Well, it was not all suffering . . ."

He smiled and wrapped his arms around her shoulders, kissing her lightly on the forehead. "From what I am told, it only hurts the first time. After that, well, if I do my duty, then it will hopefully only be pure pleasure. For both of us."

She had so many questions. There was so much she wanted to know. She pushed aside her discomfiture and asked, her cheeks flaming, "Did you feel that . . . that . . . crashing, pounding . . . thing that happened . . ."

He smiled from ear to ear, his white teeth gleaming in the candlelight. "Most definitely."

"Is it like that every time you . . ."—she blushed, but continued bravely—". . . do that?"

"If all goes as planned." He sighed and dropped his chin against her tousled hair.

She nodded slowly. "Fascinating."

"I am glad you find it so." He rose and donned his wrinkled shirt and buttoned his pants. "We will have many opportunities for things to go as planned, once we are married. I have no intention of maintaining separate chambers. We will share *everything*."

A small trickle of trepidation iced down her spine. The old dread of being wanted for her dowry and not herself reared its ugly head. She peeked up at him through thick lashes. "Well, actually, if we wed, then everything that is mine will be yours."

"That is the whole point, is it not?"

The knowledge that he wanted her for her dowry slammed into her chest like an anvil. She adjusted her gown, hiding every bit of pink flesh from his view. Why should it hurt so much, if she already suspected the ugly truth? Still, she wanted to hear him say it. "Why did you ask for my hand in Southbridge?"

"Now, don't start with me, Charlotte." The little muscle jumped in his cheek. "It is irrelevant."

Her anger flared. It was humiliating enough to be in this situation; he did not have to treat her like a greenhorn. "I have just as much say in what is relevant. Or perhaps if this is an indication of how you will treat your wife, I might reconsider taking the position."

"We just made love, for heaven's sake." He clenched his hands and looked ready to spit nails. "There is nothing to reconsider. You are mine. I had you and I will continue to have you."

Her eyes narrowed. "I am not a bloody possession, James. I make my own choices and I will not be bullied into marriage."

"You have little choice in the matter, Charlotte." He grabbed the pink stained handkerchief from the couch and held it up triumphantly. "You just gave up your . . . *last option*."

It appalled her how right he was about her situation; still, she would not accept all the blame. "It is not fair. Well, I am . . . *was* an innocent. You are experienced . . . probably had more women—" The idea of him bedding other women made her stomach clench. She swallowed. "I was not thinking about matrimony . . . or much else . . ." Her voice trailed off.

He ran his hand through his hair. "I must admit, my judgment was a bit hampered by . . ." His lips cocked into a small grin. "By your tantalizing gameness. So, we were a bit tipsy—"

"—Drunk as an Emperor—" The excuse sounded lame even to her own ears.

"So where is the harm? We are engaged to be married. We can just go ahead with it—"

"I still insist on knowing why you asked for my hand."

"What does it matter?" he asked sharply.

"It is the foundation of . . . well, everything." She shoved an errant curl behind her ear. "I mean it underlies our expectations, our prospects—well . . . everything."

Charged silence crackled between them.

"I need to know the truth, James."

It was as if someone had dropped a carriage on his head, hammering him into the ground. He stood frozen. His heart was stampeding once more, but this time with fear, and his mouth was so dry a camel could cross it. He hated to do it, but he tore his eyes away from her brilliant blue ones and stared at the black shadows splayed across the far wall. "You were there in Southbridge," he replied harshly. "You know very well what happened. There is nothing more to say."

She was silent so long, he wondered if she had heard him at all. She sat stock-still, her luscious lips pressed together tightly and a frown marring her lovely brow. The pain in her eyes tore at his gut.

He stepped away and then turned back, his hands fisted by his sides, his mind racing to make sense of her unachievable demand. He had to try to make her accept the situation without insisting on knowing the truth.

"I just asked you to be my wife, Charlotte. My duchess. To avoid all the scandal that will inevitably erupt if we break the engagement. To be with me, lie with me. I am offering you a life, Charlotte, as my wife and the mother of my children."

She straightened her shoulders and rose. "What you offer me, James, is not good enough."

She turned on her heel and walked out of the room, the pat of her slippered feet echoing softly on the hard floor.

James watched her go, powerless to stop her. He just could not bear for her to know the monster he had become. He felt her loss like a hole in his chest that might eat him from within. He turned and looked around the empty room. Everything had been going so well. So fantastically, amazingly well. And then she had asked him to share the one truth he was unwilling to expose . . .

He noticed the small leather strip from his hair lying on the hardwood. Crouching, he picked it up, rolling the soft leather between his fingers. Looking up, he spied the lacy pink-stained cloth on the couch where he had dropped it. He had bedded her. She had given herself to him. Willingly, lovingly. She had loved him, physically, anyway. He pressed the leather strip to his lips, smelling the comforting scent of buckskin. War was not won overnight. He would let the idea settle upon her. Then he would campaign. He would campaign with everything he had, for suddenly he realized that he fought for more than her bed, or even her hand. He battled for her trust. Despite this crazed mess, he would prove that he was trustworthy. And if Charlotte could trust him, could care for him, could . . . love him, then he would not be a monster after all.

Chapter 25

James and Avery walked their horses slowly, side by side, along the trail flanking Nancy's Creek as they returned from visiting the mill. Avery was showing James some of the improvements he had recently made around the estate.

"So how is your campaign of passion faring with the lovely Charlotte?"

A small bird flew overhead. Another followed. James watched their progression, trying to sort through his encounter with Charlotte the night before. "I believe I pressed my advantage a bit too soon."

Avery looked over at his friend disbelievingly. "You would sooner force your attentions on a woman as cut off your arm."

"Not that. I asked her to marry me." More like insisted. His gut clenched with shame, recalling how he had brandished her maidenhood like a golden chalice.

"You didn't."

"I did."

"What happened to our plan? Woo and entice, court and pursue, and let her come to know you and care for you."

James ran his hand through his loose hair. "I cannot seem to stay in control where Charlotte is involved. She makes me impulsive, more volatile."

"Well, what did she say?" Avery sidestepped his horse around a deep rut.

"She wanted me to tell her why I asked for her hand in Southbridge."

"And what did you tell her?"

"Nothing."

Avery's eyes widened. "Nothing? The girl gave you the opening to end this entire charade and you told her nothing?"

He gritted his teeth. "I told you. If she knew the truth of the matter, she would leave."

Avery sighed. The men walked their mounts along in silence.

"The love of a good woman and the children you have together make life worth more than just living," Avery avowed. "And you are giving it all up out of an overblown sense of fear."

"I am not ready to give up. I just need to regroup."

Avery shook his head and adjusted his seat. "I do not mean to chastise you, but—"

"Do not let me stop you," he interjected glumly.

"You must be honest and true to your lady *in all things*."

"Wait one moment, Avery." He pulled his mount up short. "Are you telling me that you will never take a mistress?"

Avery reined in alongside his friend. "It can only hurt my family life, and I am not willing to take that chance. Besides," he half-joked, "Georgie told me that she would rather kill me than see me with another woman. And you know her . . ."

"She would do it," supplied James with a wry grimace. "I have no mistress at present. For now, Charlotte has my full attention. But for the future . . ."

"So Maxine is history?"

James allowed Briar to lower his head and nibble the grasses along the lane. "Very much so. She was too demanding by half." He patted Briar's neck affectionately. "It was becoming a bother."

"All the more reason to settle down."

He smiled ruefully, pulled Briar's head up, and began walking him toward the house. "As you so graciously pointed out, I have yet to procure a bride."

They turned the corner, their path joining the wider lane.

Avery nodded. "Despite destroying our plan, I still have hopes that you can convince Charlotte to marry you."

"Why?"

"Because you always get what you set your sights on. You always have, ever since I have known you."

James admitted slowly, "Nothing has ever seemed as important or as difficult before."

The men walked along in silence, the song of the mockingbird filtering through the trees.

"I wonder what the ladies are doing?"

"Missing Charlotte already? We have been gone for only a few hours," Avery teased.

"Enough of this laziness. Let's ride. Or have you gotten too soft?"

Avery laughed and kicked his mount into a trot and then a swift canter. James raced Briar after him, the two friends relishing the speed and the excitement of running free.

Charlotte's legs were leaden as she approached the drawing room where James and Avery waited. She was desperate to see James, but simultaneously loathed to face the man who had tempted her to risk everything for a stolen night of passion. She was still slightly sore between her thighs, but that did not diminish the memory of those fantastic sensations coursing through her body. Nor did it reflect the nightmares about her future that had plagued her until dawn. She had roused to the inescapable conclusion that if she were unwilling to marry James Morgan, the man who made her heart race with desire, then it was unlikely she would marry at all.

She paused before the entryway, drew herself up, and prepared for the worst. Coldness? Disdain? Or would he simply cry off now and not wait until the Season's end? The thought of never seeing him, of never again knowing his touch, left her more than a little dispirited.

She inhaled a deep breath and stepped into the parlor.

James stood tall and magnificent with his back to the room, the sun from the lofty windows outlining his body in bright silhouette. His black riding clothes enhanced his manly form, emphasizing his broad shoulders and slim waist. Her heart began the prancing gait reserved uniquely for him and her cheeks heated, mortified by his effect on her.

He turned. His face was a mask of refined beauty, exposing nothing of the man within.

"Greetings, Charlotte." His voice was silky smooth.

Did nothing affect him? Her mouth was too parched to reply. She licked her lips. "Your grace."

He scowled, demanding crossly, "James."

Avery rose from the chaise, sending a look of rebuke to his friend.

James straightened his coat and asked more pleasantly, "Did you enjoy the morning?"

"Yes, how were the children? Did my little rascals behave abominably?" Avery inquired.

Charlotte resolved to follow James's lead. If he could be nonchalant about one of the most momentous experiences of her life, then so could she.

She turned to Avery smiling. "The children were just wonderful. Little Eve is a treasure, and Albert read me his favorite portions of the most brilliant story about William Wallace."

"Jane Porter's *The Scottish Chiefs?*" James raised an innocent brow.

"Oh, you know it?" She faced him, surprised.

"I have only read it to him a hundred times. And that was
on one visit." He shook his head good-naturedly. "I found
myself dreaming of the man and his exploits."

"I expect you liked the story as much as I did," she challenged. She felt a sudden itch to punch the man.

"Oh, pray do not tell the members of my club that I enjoy
reading children's stories," he teased, raising his hand to his
heart, dramatically horrified.

"Oh yes, it is not fashionable to be loving with children,"
she replied sarcastically.

Georgina glided into the room. "Fashionable? I heard
something about fashion and I have been meaning to mention to you, Charlotte, how much I admire your fashion
statement."

Charlotte blinked, her attention wrenched away from
James. "Excuse me?"

"Oh, I love how you abandon accessories. You really keep
it simple. I so admire that! It took me until my second child
to have the courage to discard some of my more cumbersome
accoutrements. Well, not all of them, of course."

Embarrassed, she did not know what to say. She did not
believe that Georgina was making sport with her, but how
could any person on earth deem her stylish?

"Oh, Georgie, you love being the fashion maven," her
husband chided. "Why, I have spent more money on pelisses,
fans, reticules, scarves, and gloves. How can anyone spend
so much money on ribbons?"

Georgina slipped her arm into his. "What about my stockings and high heels, Avery? I do not hear you complaining
about those."

Avery's mouth split into a wicked grin. "Maybe I need to

investigate those stockings and shoes, Madame? To get a better understanding of the accessories, of course."

Charlotte looked at James questioningly, suddenly feeling like an extra on the stage, not quite part of the story.

Her heart skipped a beat as he leaned close and whispered in her ear, "Marriage talk." His spicy, musky scent combined with the aroma of horse and leather, teased her senses. "Charlotte. I wish to make amends for last night." His breath tickled the hairs on her neck as he spoke softly for her ears only, "I realize that I changed the rules in mid-game. Would you allow me the pleasure of your company for a ride this afternoon?"

She eyed him warily. She had to admit, he was behaving quite amiably, under the circumstances. And where was the harm? She nodded slowly. "That would be . . . fine." Butterflies suddenly fluttered in her middle; to be alone with James was both alarming and tantalizing. Well, if she was not going to marry, she might as well enjoy her engagement while it lasted.

The energetic young steed loped along underneath Charlotte, a shower of gravel flying from beneath his clattering hooves. As she inhaled the perfumed scent of wildflowers, she felt like singing aloud for the joy of the ride. The soft breeze lifted the curls poking out from her bonnet, contrasting with the warm sunshine soaking through her burgundy riding habit. The combination was in one instant exhilarating and relaxing.

She peeked at James, galloping gracefully on his mount beside her. The man really did have a marvelous seat. But she had recognized that the first occasion she had seen him ride. She could not believe that it was only a short time ago that she had watched him meeting the frightened young rider in Southbridge. Would she have run as if the devil were at her heels if she had known all that would transpire from that auspicious encounter? She could not say yes with complete honesty.

He reined in his mount, slowing the stallion to a walk. "You enjoy riding."

"I cannot imagine anything better on a glorious day like today."

He looked out across the meadow speckled with multicolored wildflowers. "Somehow, it seems more exquisite than on my last visit."

"Everything looks more lovely in the springtime."

James watched her. "Perhaps that is the reason."

Their eyes locked and Charlotte felt ensnared in the depths of his midnight blue gaze. The birds stopped chirping, the breeze fell silent, and her breath seized with yearning. She would venture that if she were able to press her hand to James's chest, his heart would be charging to the same deafening beat as hers.

Her mount stepped languidly aside and swooshed his tail, breaking the spell.

"Come. Let us walk a bit," he commented, looking away.

She nodded and allowed her horse to fall in step alongside him.

"Over there," he directed with his gloved hand, "is the pond where Avery and I used to fish in summer." She tried to visualize him as a young boy, but the image of his broad bare chest gleaming in candlelight kept interfering with her thoughts.

"Are the fish abundant here?" she asked in a breathless voice, scrambling for an innocuous topic.

"We would catch our share," he commented wryly. "But we used it more as an opportunity to be lazy than to be sportsmanlike."

"Did you swim as well?"

"Bare as the day I was born."

Her stomach flipped over and she thought her cheeks might sizzle from the heat of her blush. She peeked at him through thick lashes. The bastard was trying quite unsuccessfully to contain his grin. Well, she could set her mind to bland subjects just as easily as he.

"Do you return much to . . . Montrose, is it?" she asked, quite proud of herself.

His eyes twinkled with mirth, but he had the good grace to pretend that this was a normal conversation. "Because of my duties at the War Office I remain primarily in London. Perhaps soon I will be able to concentrate more on the estate and some of the renovations I have been hoping to make."

"I find it interesting that so many gentlemen of property like to build, and add on to their existing buildings, creating some remarkable architectural assembly." That was an excellent comment, coming from a woman who kept picturing James buck-naked, gliding through water.

"Yes, we gentlemen of property do like to stake our claims and also like to have something as testament to our time on this earth."

"Children are not sufficient?"

"Children are integral. Without a family line, the buildings are meaningless."

James's children. Her stomach tightened. No. This would not do. She pushed away all thoughts of James, his bare bottom, and his offspring. She focused instead on the small group of cows munching lazily on the green grass in the meadow below.

"Do your mother and sister usually reside in Montrose while you are in Town?"

"Although Mother can be . . . difficult, she really is a lovely lady." He mistook her meaning. Charlotte was actually feeling somewhat charitable toward the old dragon. Despite the underlying irritation behind the gesture, the dowager had done her a good turn with Mrs. Clavelle's designs.

James patted Briar's neck. "And my sister Elizabeth is . . ." He was searching for the right description.

". . . Very accomplished."

He chuckled. "That is the most politic thing anyone has ever said about Elizabeth. Mother assures me that she takes after the Gordon side of the family. Their family motto is 'Conquer now, reflect later.' "

She squinted through the bright sun at him. "I was referring to her piano playing. I heard her at a musicale. She is really quite good."

"Well, yes, there is that. Although I prefer my music a little more . . . tame."

Her lips lifted into a wide smile as she recalled the rowdy ditties that Miss Elizabeth clearly loved to play, shocking people in the process.

"She certainly did have a way with lyrics. I recall something about France and aunts and Lanc-elot. It was quite witty."

"Witty she is. She just manages not to insult anyone in particular, most of the time, that is. Although I do keep my pistols ready just in case. I do hope she did not offend you, Charlotte."

"Actually, I found her quite . . . refreshing."

"Members of Polite Society usually try to hint, judiciously, of course, that I 'oversee' her better."

"And do you?"

"No. She will grow up eventually. No need to hasten the process."

She stole a glance at the man sitting atop his horse beside her. Perhaps James was giving his sister an indulgence he never had?

He turned his mount down a narrow lane alongside an array of spiky green bushes. The air cooled as the trees thickened around them, providing welcome shade from the afternoon sun. A small cottage appeared around the next bend.

She asked warily, "What is this place?"

"Georgie and Avery set it up for us. They suggested that during our ride we give the horses a rest and refresh ourselves as well." He stopped his mount at the edge of the clearing and looked at her questioningly. "If that suits you, of course."

Charlotte's stomach jumped. To be alone with James in a house in the woods. She licked her lips, her heart thrumming to the licentious possibilities. Well, she was already ruined. Where was the harm, indeed?

James waited patiently, his horse swooshing its tail to swat at a bothersome fly. She pressed her lips but nodded assent.

He dismounted and then approached her. He gently removed her booted feet from the stirrups, his touch sending tingles rushing from her ankles all the way to the crown of her head. He clutched her waist and pulled her off, delicately sliding her down his hard, lean form. Her heart settled somewhere in her throat, making speech impossible.

Looking down, he coiled a wayward curl behind her ear. Her mouth went dry and the rapid pounding of her heart suddenly escalated, excitement merging with apprehension. He leaned forward, his lips open and expectant. Impulsively she jumped back, thumping into her mount. The feathered plume of her riding hat slipped down over her eyes.

He straightened and stepped away, a frown marring his handsome features. "Let us go inside and talk, Charlotte."

She could only nod, a combustion of emotions roiling in her uneasy stomach.

She blinked in the sudden dimness. Diffused light peppered the cabin through the open windows. The room was sparse, yet housed clean furnishings. Set on the table was a wonderful array of fruits, sweets, and cheeses. She turned to James questioningly.

"Avery and Georgina escape here sometimes to get away from everyone. They graciously arranged for us to enjoy the quiet today."

"Yes, well," she said nervously. "We certainly are away from everyone."

He went over to the table and lifted off a cloth to uncover a bucket containing a bottle of champagne. She gingerly seated herself on the small sofa. While James uncorked the bottle, Charlotte used the opportunity to peruse his broad shoulders, his muscular frame, and his hardened thighs encased in snug buckskin breeches. She clenched her hands in her lap, the itch so strong to reach out and touch him. Dear lord, she was more skittish than a newborn colt.

He handed her a glass, the bubbles tickling her nose. Tensely, she raised the flute to her lips and sipped down a gulpful, coughing and sneezing.

He patted her back, sitting beside her. "Are you all right?"

She nodded, coloring with embarrassment.

"Charlotte, I am sorry to have made you uncomfortable in my presence. That was not my intention after, well—after last night." He blew out a gust of air. "I wish to speak frankly with you, if I may?"

Here it comes. She swallowed. "Please do."

"This is an odd situation indeed. To the world we are engaged. Yet things are . . . unsettled between us. I propose that for the time being we not consider the future and simply get to know one another better."

Relief flooded through her. So he was not going to cry off the engagement. Nor apparently was he going to confess the secrets she just knew he was hiding. On that point, she could not decide if she was irritated or relieved. "H-how do you see that happening?"

"As friends, for the moment, at least. Then see how matters . . . progress from there."

She bit her lip. Camaraderie with the man who had . . . her mouth went dry just thinking about lying beneath him, spreading her legs with fiery desire . . . if she were a proper young lady she would be telling him what to do with his friendship and instead be demanding a wedding. But since she had already faced the unavoidable conclusion that she would probably not marry, why not enjoy her remaining time with James? But as his chum?

"That, that would be nice," she said instead.

He leaned forward, speaking intently, "You've proven to be an invaluable partner in my investigation, Charlotte. I admire your courage, your steadfastness. Last night, I just got a little carried away."

"You were not the only one," she admitted ruefully.

A whisper of a smile graced his lips. "*That* I did not mind at all."

She looked away, trying to dismiss the delicious heat unfurling in her belly. He lifted his flute to his mouth. Her eyes flew to his delectable lips, remembering their silky touch. The man had no right to be so bloody gorgeous.

"Nothing about our relationship thus far has been conventional," he offered.

She sipped her champagne. "Far from it."

He spoke casually, "So too, our friendship need not be bound by the usual societal restraints. We are working closely together in the investigation, and . . ." He peeked at her from half-closed lids. ". . . Enjoying close contact. Let us speak freely, Charlotte. We cannot undo what has already been done. Last night was extraordinary. As for our immediate future . . . where is the harm in a bit more of such pleasures? Now that we have already crossed that bridge, so to speak."

Her heart jumped and the breath caught in her throat. So James's idea of "friendship" paralleled her own desire. Did she dare confess that she wanted to taste the erotic fruits of last night's pleasure again?

He slipped off his glove and traced his fingertip along her lips. A shiver ran down her spine. He leaned closer, his breath caressing her cheek. He smelled musky, masculine. Smoldering heat infused her face and raced down her body from her hairline to her toes.

"It will not hurt this time?" she whispered, not daring to look into his eyes.

He leaned forward and gently traced his velvety lips over hers. "Only pleasure from now on for you, Charlotte."

He captured her "oh" in his mouth as he pressed his lips to hers, his tongue plunging in with demanding precision. His arms wrapped tightly around her in a grip of silken steel, pressing his hard body lengthwise against hers and igniting titillating memories of the night before.

She twined her tongue with his, sucking, licking, moaning with the pleasure of a wanton kiss. Heat pumped through her veins, rousing her senses to awareness of everything about him. The soft wool of his coat, his musky scent, the prickly roughness of his cheeks chaffing against hers, his muscled arms gently squeezing her close.

He tenderly laid her back onto the couch, but she protested and pushed against his muscled torso.

"What is it, Charlotte?" he asked, pulling away, his midnight blue eyes burning black with need.

"You lie down," she ordered, shocked by her boldness but intuitively certain of what she wanted. Her frustrations, her fears about her future, her loss of control made her chomp at the bit to *take* her pleasure, not just accept it as a gift he bequeathed. She would have her way with him and have her pride, if not her chastity.

A small smile played at his lips, but he reclined, watching her through hooded eyes.

"Take off your jacket."

He slowly yanked the coat off revealing his white ruffled shirt topped by a knotted neck cloth.

She licked her lips; lord, he was a sight to behold even with clothes on.

"Now the cravat and shirt."

With emphasized slowness, he undid the intricate cloth and peeled off the cambric encasing his golden form. Blood thrummed through her veins and she was hotter than burning cinder. God, how she wanted to touch him.

She tugged off her gloves and dropped them to the floor. Leaning forward, she traced her fingertips along the velvety hills and valleys of his trunk, paying particular attention to the firm muscles of his chest. His mouth dropped open and he began to pant as she slowly circled his nipples, the erotic exploration causing her own to raise and harden. He sucked in a deep breath as her hands grazed his flat belly and tickled the black hairs trailing down toward the bulging hardness of his manhood.

She smiled, a sense of shameless fervor fanning the flames of her escalating passion.

"I want to taste you," she murmured, leaning forward and pressing her open mouth to his chest. She would give him a sampling of what he did to her the night before. She lavished his nipples with her tongue, sucking, licking, teasing as he squirmed beneath her. The wetness in her mouth did not compare to the mounting excitement between her thighs. As she laved his body with her tongue, he gently pressed his knee between her legs, rubbing her at the focal point of her agitation. She rocked and stroked against him, stimulating herself to shattering heights of yearning.

She moaned, her breath coming in short, harsh gasps. She reached lower and dared to press her hand against his stiff member, his rigid shaft growing rock-hard under her agile fingers.

"This is nothing like clay," she whispered breathlessly.

He choked out, "I should hope not!"

She stroked and squeezed. He groaned a deep growl of

pleasure and placed his hand over hers, showing her how to please him.

He tilted his head back, licking his lips. "Dear God, Charlotte, let me give you pleasure before I embarrass myself."

She was on fire for him.

"Show me," she demanded fervently.

His lips split into a wide, wicked grin. "By your leave, my lady."

And he did, quite fruitfully, to be sure.

Chapter 26

❦

Their leave taking from the Plankertons' was a quick but heartfelt good-bye, with many promises for a return visit, although Charlotte had no idea how that might occur. Avery and Georgina treated her with obvious regard, and Charlotte realized that when the Season was over, when her adventure had ended, she would miss more than just James.

As the coach rolled toward London, she marveled at how no one seemed to perceive the changes within her, now that she had tasted the pleasures of womanhood. Servant, host, hostess, and James alike all treated her as if she was the honorable Miss Hastings, when underneath it all she was a newly minted fiery vixen. She smiled and closed her eyes, taking a moment to relax to the rocking sway of the carriage.

Exhaustion overtook her stimulated senses, and amazingly, Charlotte slept during most of the ride back to Town.

Miss Elizabeth Morgan came charging at her brother the moment James crossed the threshold of Pennington House.

"How could you?" she exclaimed, pounding on her brother's broad chest. "I go out of Town for one little week and you go and get yourself engaged! How could you do it, James?"

Manton tried to get James's coat while the footmen scurried to keep out of Elizabeth's way.

"James!" The dowager came barreling down the staircase, waving a crumpled letter in her fisted hand. "I will not have that, that *person* dictating how my son commemorates his engagement. The nerve of that woman!" She slammed her fisted hand into her other palm. "James, you must attend to me at once!"

Elizabeth broke in, "Mother said it is a forced engagement and that there was a potential scandal. Are you truly going to marry her?"

Charlotte slipped behind James and let him take the brunt of the assault. After the quiet comfort of the carriage, she was jarred by the loud and provoking onslaught. She would gladly leave James to his relatives.

"Is that her?" Elizabeth spied her trying to be innocuous and pushed past James. "Come out here at once, Miss Hastings."

"Enough!" roared James. "Neither my fiancée nor I will be spoken to this way! Into my study, both of you!"

Elizabeth straightened her spine, but a small pout emphasized her youthfulness. Although she was olive skinned and dark haired like her brother, there any similarity ended. She was willowy like a swan, with a long neck and delicate arms. Pout in place, she turned and walked demurely toward the study. Drawing herself up, the dowager followed suit. Charlotte used the opportunity to try to scurry up the stairs unnoticed.

"You too, Charlotte," James directed softly. "I would speak with you as well."

Looking up the stairs at her lost escape, she sighed and turned to join them in the study.

James closed the door behind Charlotte and walked to stand behind his massive walnut desk. He placed his fists on the tabletop and glared hard at his mother and sister. Charlotte was thankful not to be on the receiving end of his wrath.

"I will not have anyone, and I mean *anyone*," he looked at his mother pointedly, "saying that I was forced into this engagement. Do I make myself clear?"

Elizabeth opened her mouth. "But Mother said . . ."

He held up his hand and growled in a tightly controlled voice, "Stop, Elizabeth, before I get really angry." She immediately closed her mouth and glowered at her mother.

"What on earth could possibly warrant such hysterics, particularly in front of the servants? You, Mother, were always the first to insist that all family discussions be behind closed doors and between family members only. Half of London will be hearing about our welcome by hour's end. Is this how you greet Charlotte?"

Duly chastised, the ladies turned to Charlotte. Elizabeth curtseyed gracefully. "Please pardon my behavior, Miss Hastings."

The dowager tilted her head regally. "I too, made an error in judgment. It will not happen again. However," she added, holding in her fisted hand a crumpled letter, "there is a matter of grave concern that we must address."

Charlotte immediately recognized Aunt Sylvie's stationery and prepared herself for the worst.

"Your aunt plans on hosting a ball in yours and James's honor to celebrate your engagement."

Charlotte's eyes widened in dismay, and then she smiled. "Why, that is so sweet of her." Aunt Sylvie was attempting to stand in for what her own parents would have done.

"It is not sweet." The matron said the word as if it were poison. "It is an insult."

"I do not understand." Charlotte looked at James uncertainly.

"It is an insult to me. It is for *me* to throw a ball in your honor. Not someone else. It is uncalled for."

"But Sylvie is family," she insisted.

James stated decisively, "Mother, under the circumstances, since Charlotte's parents are no longer with us, it is not so extraordinary for Lady Jaspers to host such an event. In fact, it is a lovely gesture. Do not turn this into something about you."

"But it is about me," she asserted, brandishing the wrinkled paper. "Can you not see that? She is trying to humiliate me because I have not organized a ball in celebration of the engagement."

"And whose fault is that, Mother?" he asked quietly.

Silence descended upon the room.

The dowager crossed her arms defensively. "Under this state of affairs . . ."

"What state of affairs?" Elizabeth cried, waving her hands in the air in frustration. "All you would say is that there might have been a scandal, but James hushed it up with the engagement." She turned to her brother. "Are you getting married or not?"

"Yes, I am getting married. To Charlotte. End of story. And we will be delighted to accept Lady Jaspers' generous offer."

"But I will be the laughing stock of the *ton!*" raged the dowager. "You cannot allow it!"

He slammed his hand on the desktop, his olive skin darkening even more. "I have heard *enough* about your little quarrel with Lady Jaspers."

The dowager closed her mouth into a hard, firm line, her eyes narrowing dangerously. She and James glared at each other across the desk, neither willing to back down.

"Ahem." Charlotte cleared her throat. "I may have a solution that would be acceptable to all parties." When no one replied, she went on, "Edward and Margaret can host the ball at our house. It will be perfectly lovely and we all can attend."

"No," said James firmly. "Lady Jaspers has offered, and we will accept. If Mother wants to redress the issue, she can host a ball of her own. I will not repay kindness and generosity with pettiness. It is undignified and below us."

Charlotte felt a rush of appreciation for him. He was willing to infuriate his mother to do the right thing by Charlotte's family. Given that the engagement was going to be short-lived, it was a particularly magnanimous gesture.

"This is not the last of this matter." The dowager glowered at her son and left the room in a huff.

James stared at his mother's receding back. "Elizabeth. Give me a moment with Charlotte."

"Certainly, James. But first there is something I must do." She glided around the big desk and threw her slender arms about her brother's neck. She kissed him noisily on his chiseled cheek. He blinked and then smiled, wrapping his arms around her willowy form. "It's about bloody time, James. No matter the circumstances." She released him slowly and pointed her finger at Charlotte "I want a rambunctious brood of nieces and nephews. Five of each, at least."

Charlotte's lips split into a grin. Elizabeth was anything if not audacious.

"We will do our best, Elizabeth," he rejoined, smiling.

"You do that." She curtseyed, spun on her heel and left the room.

"I am sorry that you had to be subjected to all that, Charlotte."

"Family can be vexing sometimes."

"Yes, well, particularly when it is my mother. I seem to have trouble convincing her that I am the duke and not her." He blew out a long breath. "Be that as it may, I want to talk with you a moment about your security, now that we are back in Town." He indicated the chair in front of his desk. "If you would?"

She sat down and he followed suit.

"Now that Lieutenant Freeman has had an opportunity to familiarize himself with Pennington House and his duties, I would ask that you take him with you everywhere you go where I cannot escort you."

"I would actually prefer that he escort us even if you are with me." She shifted in her seat. "If the villains know about the map and know that it is in your possession, you are in as much danger as I. I would feel much better about the whole thing if you took special precautions as well." She rubbed her chin thoughtfully. "Like being armed and taking your man Collin with you. He seems a sturdy bodyguard, and that big footman, what was his name?" She looked up and noticed that he was smiling broadly. She crossed her arms. "Do you find something amusing?"

His lips bowed and lifted as he tried to suppress his grin.

She frowned and admonished like a school marm, "This is not a laughing matter. Do you believe that you are indestructible, unsusceptible to pistols or knives or runaway carriages?"

"No, Charlotte," he replied, gently tracing his lips with his fingertip. "I am finding myself quite susceptible."

"Well, then. About that rather large footman . . ."

"Thomas."

"Yes, well, Thomas would be a good guard, do you not think?"

He stood abruptly and moved swiftly around the desk. He pulled her out of her seat and into his arms.

She looked up into those deep dark pools of midnight, a pleasurable swell of anticipation unfurling in her middle.

"I do not need anyone to guard my body." He nuzzled her ear. "Other than you."

She leaned back and licked her lips. "I am being serious, James."

"So am I." He traced his tongue along the inside of her ear. She shivered and clutched his arm, delicious anticipation warming her to her toes. He pushed his hand into her hair, freeing a bounty of pins from her curls. She barely heard them drop onto the thick carpeting. "You fight dirty, like any bodyguard should. I never want to be on the receiving end of your wrath."

"Again," she murmured.

"Ummm?" He kissed her jaw. Small butterfly kisses moved toward her lips.

"You never want to be on the receiving end of my wrath again," she replied huskily as she turned, her mouth eagerly leaning toward his.

"Umm, yes." He spoke the words into her open lips. "I almost forgot about that."

Knock.

"Go away," he commanded without turning.

"Your grace." Collin stepped in self-consciously. "Ahem."

"Not now, Collin."

Red faced, Charlotte pulled away.

The manservant shifted his feet, but stepped closer into the room. "Yes, well, sir, sorry to interrupt, but you wanted to know as soon as we heard anything about, well, you know."

James looked up angrily. "Stop speaking nonsense and spit it out, man."

"That person you wanted to know about?" He raised his eyebrows, as if willing James to understand.

James frowned and then his eyes widened. "Oh." He stepped back. "Yes, well, Charlotte, um, if you would excuse us?"

Her eyes narrowed. "Is this about the gold?"

"No. No, of course not," he replied hastily, looking over at Collin. "Just some Ducal business that requires my attention."

She crossed her arms. "We had an agreement."

He put his hand on her back and propelled her toward the entry. "And I will let you know as soon as I learn anything. Duty calls and I must answer." He swiftly shuffled her out into the hallway and shut the door.

Charlotte stood glaring at the closed door until she heard a loud *click* as the lock fell into place. Her eyes narrowed and she wanted to press her ear to the keyhole so badly. Instead, she turned and stomped up the stairs. If he thought that this was how their new "friendship" was going to progress, he had another thing coming. What, she could share his bed but not his business? She resolved to keep to her agreement with James the same way he kept it with her, maybe in word, but certainly not in spirit. Friendship, indeed!

Chapter 27

~~~

Aloof. That was the only way James could describe Charlotte's demeanor over the next two days; ever since he had locked her out of his study. She played the role of bride-to-be satisfactorily, but her smiles were polite, restrained affairs. None of her brilliance shone through. She did not laugh with him. Did not tease him or draw him out. And she rarely touched him, only when absolutely necessary. Every time he had tried to get her alone, she had gracefully demurred.

He did not like it. Not one bit. Aside from missing the taste of her honeyed lips and the softness of her skin, he felt as if he had lost something elusive but very real. This was a major setback in his campaign to win her trust. If only he were not so abominably terrified, now more than ever, that she would discover the truth of the matter; that he was so cold-hearted and calculating as to insist on the engagement to wound his cousin, take what Mortimer wanted, and then after, dispose of her like a useless cast-off.

It sickened him to think that he had considered warm-hearted fiery-yet-tender Charlotte expendable, not worthy of his concern. His gut wrenched with shame every time he recalled telling the general how he was going to "protect" her and set her up once the quest was finished, never once considering the irreparable damage he was doing to her reputation, to her life. Even more chilling was the knowledge that it was not his own sense of honor that made him change his plans, but the general's demand, under oath, that he do right by Charlotte.

These revelations overshadowed his progress in the investigation. Plotting out his strategy to find the loot was moving ahead nicely. One of the men who matched Charlotte's drawing of the unsuccessful kidnappers had shown up dead in the Thames, his face slashed and his body hideously disfigured. James was not hopeful that they would find the other man.

Without additional leads to Mortimer, James found himself vying with the clock to reach the stash before anyone else. Although it was worthwhile work, he was feeling adrift, as if he had lost his moorings. And he could trace that sensation back to the moment he'd shut the door in Charlotte's face, denying her the opportunity to learn that Mortimer was behind the whole dastardly business.

He was finding it increasingly difficult to lie to her. He needed to make amends, breach the gap, and regain some of the footing he'd lost when he'd locked her out of his study. So he arranged for some guards for the house, left his maps and drawings and plans in his study, and was now escorting his mother, sister, and supposed bride-to-be to the Cavendishes' ball.

Charlotte looked enchanting in her tight-fitting gown of crushed burgundy velvet with black lace. The velvet scooped daringly low over her breasts; through the lace, one could see a hint of the bounty beneath. The deep burgundy color brought out the reddish highlights in her hair, which was arranged in a pile of loose curls on top of her head that bounced jauntily with every move she made. The coiffeur gave her additional height and a touch of glamour. He could not tear his eyes from her. The memory of their lovemaking not only haunted his dreams, but was beginning to press on his mind every time he looked at her, and that was as often as possible. The whole mess was driving him to distraction and making him inordinately irritable. He knew that he was hovering, but could not find the good sense or inclination to leave her side.

James was wondering if he should swat the dandified peacock yapping at Charlotte's ear when Lord Fredrick Styles casually sidled up to him and spoke above the din of the ballroom, "I cannot believe my eyes. The great Duke of Girard paying homage to the goddess of matrimony is one thing, but playing jealous husband is quite another."

"I am not jealous." He frowned and turned to his friend, whispering, "And I am not yet her husband. Thus the need to watch over her."

"Are you so concerned that she might get away?"

He straightened imperceptibly. "Let us just say that I will not take any chances where Charlotte is concerned."

Styles raised his monocle the better to view Charlotte and asked solemnly, "So she is different from the others?"

"Exceedingly so." Many a time, the two men had mused over a brandy about the interchangeability of many of the ladies of their acquaintance, and the notion of finding an Incomparable for a wife.

Styles looked at Charlotte with renewed interest. "I am so glad for you, Girard. I can think of no one more deserving. You must introduce me."

James leaned over and touched Charlotte's arm. She turned toward him expectantly, and noting the gentleman by his side, smiled brightly. "Lord Styles, how good to see you again." At his look of confusion, she explained, "We met briefly at Countess Grandby's musicale in Bedford, Christmas past. 'Quite abominable to treat the partridge so poorly,' I believe you said."

He raised his handkerchief to his mouth, his cheeks reddening. "Certainly sounds like me, but I must confess that I do not recall it."

"Oh, do not take it to heart, my lord," she reassured him, gracefully. "You seemed more focused on the lovely widow, Mrs. Parsons. I, for one, would have preferred her company to mine on that particular night, as well. I was in no mood for festivities, but Aunt Sylvie insisted that I get out. Quite an unremarkable evening, even for me."

"I remember now. Your father had recently died." He bowed. "My apologies. I only beg for the chance to make it up to you." He took her proffered hand, brought it to his lips, and kissed it with an overblown sense of drama.

Red-hot jealousy tore at James's gut and he clenched his fists to stop from snatching Charlotte's hand away.

Styles continued on, oozing charm enough to sicken the room, "I assure you that it will not happen again. Especially since I will always be able to recognize you by the great oaf that I venture to guess will forever be hovering by your side. May I take this opportunity to wish you my most sincere felicitations on your impending marriage?"

"I see that you have the look of matrimony about you as well. Where, pray tell, is the lucky lady?"

He blanched. "You can tell? Just by looking at me?" He glanced around in fear and hunched over. "Not a soul knows!"

James leaned forward, thrilled for his friend and himself over not having a rival. "It is true, Styles?"

"Well, almost, not quite . . . well soon." He confided in a whisper, "There was a scandal, you see, with her sister, and I helped out a bit, and well, we want to wait for everything to quiet down and the matter to be settled before we make it public." He looked at Charlotte nervously. "How on earth did you know?"

"Rest assured that if I can see it, so can every matron of the *ton*."

"Thank you for the warning. I must get out of here before I am found out. You will not tell anyone?" he begged. They shook their heads, Charlotte smiling, James frowning. He bowed quickly and ran off in the direction of the stairs.

"How could you tell?" Bemused, James watched Styles scoot past several imposing matrons with barely a hello.

"There is a look about a man who has found that kind of contentment. A sense of ease with the world. It is wonderful to see, particularly in a reformed rake."

James stared into her astute blue eyes, wondering if that was how she saw him, a rake worth reforming? She tore her gaze from his and peered into the crowd. He lifted her chin with his finger, forcing her to meet his eyes. He spoke in low tones for her ears only, "Be my friend again, Charlotte."

"I am not your friend, your grace. I am your betrothed."

"You know what I mean."

"If you will excuse me a moment?" She stepped away, without looking at him.

"Of course." He nodded, frowning.

Charlotte made her way toward the retiring room, returning greetings and making small talk on her way, all the while her thoughts ruminating on her stunning but exasperating fiancé. James had been frustrated and brooding ever since he realized that she could close doors in his face too, figuratively speaking. As if it were her fault that he was a lying knave. After several attempts to make it up to her, he had finally gotten the message that she was not a toy to be played with and discarded at will.

Weaving through the crowds, she examined the array of mostly eligible males around her. For the life of her, she kept comparing them to her maddening betrothed. They seemed so lifeless and uninspiring. James, in contrast, was the height of masculine elegance this evening, from the tips of his black buckled shoes to the top of his pomade-drenched shiny black hair. The man had no right to be so dashedly handsome. When near him she could even discern his smell from amongst all of the perfumes and colognes of the crowd; spicy, musky, masculine *James*. Charlotte felt his attraction like a compelling force of nature, drawing her near, like a moth to the flame. Well, she was determined not to get further singed.

Charlotte raised her hand to her hair and irritably pushed back a bouncy curl. She needed to get away from James and the unsettling effect he was having on her. The man was too appealing by far, and she found herself forgetting why she needed to keep her distance.

She entered the ornately decorated salon with relief and nodded to the other ladies attending to their needs. She sat down on a small sofa in the corner and ordered some water and a towel.

"Charlotte!" cried Lady Tinnsdale, who was just then entering the room with Lady Summerlin following behind.

Lady Tinnsdale walked over to her, smiling brightly. "So good to see you, Charlotte. I so want to extend my congratulations to you and the duke." She grabbed Charlotte's arm. "Let us go find him, shall we?"

"Actually, I was enjoying a moment to myself, thank you," she replied, chagrined. "Why not join me?"

Fretfully waving her fan, Lady Summerlin squeaked, "Oh, but it is so much more exciting outside. Let us remove ourselves *at once*."

"I am not going anywhere," she steadfastly replied. "Why in heaven's name would you want us to leave when you only just . . ."

Lady Maxine Carlton swept into the room like a tiger on

the prowl, glowering arrogantly. Her fair eyes roamed the room, fixing on Charlotte and narrowing menacingly. Charlotte withheld a groan.

Maxine sashayed over to the long mirror, her thin-lipped mouth tightening into a sly grin. The ladies in the room quieted, tension gathering like clouds before a storm. Maxine was on the hunt and Charlotte the likely prey. Outwardly calm, Charlotte prepared herself for a confrontation, bubbles of anticipation mixed with fear tightening in her belly.

Maxine examined her reflection, proudly running her hands down her soft muslin dress of pale blue, accentuating her willowy frame, slim hips and small breasts. She raised her hand to her fine golden hair piled high on top of her head and adjusted the large gold and diamond-encrusted comb. She was like a diva on the stage, playing up to her audience of ladies of Society, apparently wanting to lash out, even if Charlotte had never done a thing to injure *her*.

"So many little virgins here tonight," Maxine commented contemptuously, her blue eyes flashing around the room. "I do find the marriage mart so tiresome. Little girls pretending to be refined, when in fact," her malicious eyes lit upon Charlotte, "they are quite low minded enough to sink to any depths to catch themselves a titled husband." A gasp exploded from one of the ladies.

Charlotte was actually unimpressed with the jab. She knew the truth of the matter and in her mind, anyhow, it just made Maxine look like a sore loser. She steeled herself to be dignified and not lower herself to Lady Carlton's level. The ladies of the *ton* would just have to find their fodder elsewhere. Unperturbed, Charlotte coolly turned to the mirror and dabbed her forehead with a towel and adjusted a curl.

Maxine frowned, obviously disappointed. She pointedly began toying with the gold and diamond bracelet on her wrist. "Have I shown you my new bracelet, Olivia? It was given to me by an *ardent* admirer." She looked up and glared viciously at Charlotte.

Charlotte's cheeks heated as a searing jealousy nipped at her composure. That this caterwauling brassy had the benefit of James's touch, his kisses . . . She desperately wanted to hit something, preferably Maxine's face, but she refused to debase herself. She noted the looks of titillation and yes, pity around the room. Although she knew that soon every one of these ladies would be exchanging the tantalizing scandal of her and James's broken engagement, she just could not sit back and let this shrew get away with her insults.

She took a deep breath, stood casually, and adjusted her velvety burgundy skirts. The room hushed in anticipation of the confrontation between the intended and the ex-mistress of the Duke of Girard.

Smiling luminously, Charlotte turned to Lady Tinnsdale. "Ex-traordinary evening, is it not?" she declared. "Ex-quisite music. Ex-emplary entertainment. Ex-citing conversation. Ex-travagant food. Ex-cruciating crush. So many exes. I always knew them to be so common, so un-ex-ceptional." She turned her back on Maxine and eyed the older woman in the mirror. "Ex-asperating and vexing, in fact, *or so James tells me.*" Two of the ladies giggled at the implication. Maxine gritted her teeth, glaring at her back.

Charlotte picked an invisible piece of lint from her sleeve. "Anyone with any taste would just discard them as one would yesterday's rubbish." She turned to Lady Tinnsdale. "Now, Olivia, you wanted to congratulate my betrothed, did you not? He is attending me in the next room and awaits my return." She smiled. "And I do not like to keep my love waiting. *He so despises self-indulgent, vulgar behavior of any kind. He says that it is quite unsuitable for marriage.*"

Another round of gasps and giggles erupted from the spectators as Charlotte glided elegantly toward the exit. Lady

Tinnsdale and Lady Summerlin scampered to follow. They knew which way the wind was blowing.

A bright red flush of anger washed Maxine's pinched features. She screeched to Charlotte's receding back, completely losing her composure. "You think you are so privileged, you mousy little bran-faced sappy? Marriage or no marriage, he will come back to me and warm *my* bed." Lady Tinnsdale gasped and Lady Summerlin gaped.

Immediate shock and disapproval resounded through the room. Maxine was just as Charlotte had stated: vulgar and self-indulgent. One did not insult distinguished ladies, or demand marital infidelity or flaunt one's affairs like common trifles. It was unseemly, it was boorish, it was badly done. The ladies made their disgust and their censure plain. Almost as one, each and every lady filed out of the room, rigid backs toward Maxine, noses and chins in the air.

Lady Tinnsdale turned to Charlotte, stating coolly, "By tomorrow her name will be slashed from every invitation list. She will not dare show her face in Town again."

Lady Summerlin shook her head. "I doubt many will miss her."

Just so long as James did not miss her, Charlotte reflected grimly. There was only room for one woman in his bed, and even if she was unwilling to warm it, Charlotte was not yet ready to relinquish her place.

There was talk of little else that night. By the end of the evening, Charlotte was being credited with every honorable attribute known to woman and Maxine was being portrayed as a short-heeled scapegrace. Charlotte found the whole business tiresome and was relieved when James called for the carriage to go home.

As the coach pulled away from the curb, James closed the curtain, muting the light from the streetlamps and muffling the rowdy sounds of merriment and caterwauling. Charlotte relished the darkness, thankful for the momentary quiet.

Still excited, Elizabeth practically bounced in her seat. "I wish I could have been there when you put Lady Carlton in her place, Charlotte." With that remark, Charlotte's hopes of James not learning of the confrontation vanished.

"How dare she insult you and hope to get away with it?" Elizabeth raved.

"Elizabeth, that is enough," admonished the dowager, patting her daughter's hand beside her.

"What?" Elizabeth shrugged. "It is not like it is a secret. Everyone at the ball was talking about it." She faced Charlotte across the carriage, asking eagerly, "Did she really try to rip your gown?"

"Leave Charlotte alone, Elizabeth," James ordered harshly, his lips pressed in a firm, hard line.

She took no notice. "Whatever did you see in that woman, James? She is quite lowbrow, you know."

"I said enough!" he snapped.

Charlotte kept her counsel, but she also wondered what he had seen in the woman. Granted, she was beautiful in the classic sense, but she had a meanness that Charlotte noticed from the first. Even before tonight's escapade, she had held Maxine Carlton in fairly low regard.

Elizabeth clapped her hands. "Huzzah! We are going to get to hear all the details tomorrow when the world comes to call."

Charlotte just barely contained her groan. Mayhap she could pretend that she was ill. Better yet, she might just take off and go back home. Remove herself from the fray. Could she in good conscience leave the dowager to deal with all her false admirers?

In the dim cabin Charlotte could make out James's scowl. "You do not like callers?" she asked, curious.

"I dislike being party to a drama where my private life is exposed for the amusement of the *ton*."

"It is not my fault," she declared resentfully. If he had not bedded the vulgar hussy, there never would have been a scene.

He waved his hand dismissively. "Of course not. In fact, you kept your wits about you and handled the incident . . ."

"—With panache," the dowager finished for him.

Charlotte blinked. So the tough old bird did not consider this yet another disgrace brought on by "that Hastings girl"? She did not miss that the dowager had yet to call her by her Christian name.

The older woman nodded. "Granted, her style is not the ordinary sort. Be that as it may, it worked well tonight. She knew exactly what buttons to push with Lady Carlton, an invaluable skill in Polite Society."

Charlotte would have felt more gratified with the compliment if the dowager had not spoken as if she were not there.

"But what exactly did you say when Lady Carlton talked about debauching James?" Elizabeth asked audaciously.

The dowager hissed and Charlotte's face heated.

"Close your mouth now, Elizabeth, or there will be hell to pay," James warned through clenched teeth.

She pouted. "No one tells me anything."

The coach rocked and swayed in blessed silence, quiet in the eye of the storm.

Chapter 28

Early the next morning Charlotte knocked lightly on the open door to James's study.

"May I come in?"

"Yes, of course, my dear." James and his man of affairs were working together as she glided into the room. "Mr. Clayton and I were just finishing up."

As Charlotte seated herself facing James, she noted that Mr. Clayton, a lean, bookish man of middle years, apparently favored the severe, old-fashioned attire of knee britches and stockings. He stood rigidly beside his employer, jotting notations in a book.

She could not help but smile at the transformation in James since last night, aside from his coiffure and attire; there was a boyish exuberance to him that was unabashedly appealing. He obviously enjoyed tackling the challenges of his role as duke, and she would wager that he was very good at it, just as he seemed to be with everything else.

James had an air of competence about him that made one

feel as if things were in good hands. Unconsciously, her eyes fell to his broad olive-skinned hands skimming nimbly across a ledger. They were so large, and yet smooth, with long, graceful fingers that had the most sensual caress . . . Her heart skipped a beat. She tore her eyes away, her flaming cheeks facing the unremarkable bookshelves lining the far wall. But the volumes could hold her attention for only a moment and she peeked back at her betrothed, hungry for more of him.

She preferred his hair as it was this morning, his wavy raven locks loosely held back in a short black ribbon. Not the more severe, slick coiffure of last night. Her favorite curl hung playfully on his forehead. She closed her fists and locked them in her lap, just itching to wind the supple coil around her finger. Charlotte recognized that her body was not the only part of her drawn to James. She was finding it more and more difficult to retain her distance; the man was so blastedly charming. If only . . . she sighed. There was no point in hopeless musings.

James shifted in his seat, uneasily wondering why Charlotte was studying him so fixedly. He pointed out a notation on the ledger. "We need to redirect the laborers to the east end of the house and have them concentrate their attentions on the roof repairs."

"Yes, hum," Mr. Clayton crooned as he scribbled.

James wondered what caused Charlotte to get out of bed so early. "And please give Mr. Simon the list of supplies he requested. I see no abnormalities and would like him to make his repairs before the weather turns."

"Yes, hum." Notation.

He hoped she was not upset about last night. That she understood his affair with Maxine was long over. That if he could go back in time he would never have gotten involved with the insufferable woman.

"Oh, and Mr. Clayton, please direct payment to Mr.

William Frank in the amount noted." He handed over the invoice.

Mr. Clayton frowned at the missive and looked pointedly at Charlotte, who stared innocently back. "Certainly, your grace."

"You may go now, Mr. Clayton, and thank you."

"Thank you, your grace." The man gathered his notes and exited silently.

"I am well worth it, you know," Charlotte commented teasingly.

"Of that I have no doubt," he parried. "In fact, I must remember to send Mr. Frank a bonus." He nodded to her, asking cautiously, "You are up early, Charlotte. Did you not sleep well?"

"Fine, thank you. I am up early because I am going home today."

His heart froze in his chest. She could not leave him. Not yet, not ever.

She waved her hand. "I know that it is not really very nice of me to leave when we will be beset by all of the gossip-mongers salivating over the most recent uproar, but"—she shook her head emphatically—"I must insist that I return home today, James. Your mother will be in her element and will deal with the visitors admirably. I will be back by dinnertime and no one will have missed me at all."

He released the breath he did not know he was holding. He was so relieved, he was lightheaded. He did not care one whit about the callers today. She was not leaving him; that was enough.

"James?" She cast a worried frown at him. "Are you unwell?" He did not know how long he had sat there, contemplating his fear.

He placed his palms down on the solid walnut desk replying gruffly, "I am sure Mother can handle anything that comes up. So long as you are properly escorted there and back." He blew out a long breath. "It looks like I may be leaving London for a few days. I can stop by your brother's to say good-bye."

"Have you had any luck?"

A thrill of excitement swelled in his chest. "I believe that I may have found Edgerton's hideout. It is a good lead, I just have to confirm it."

"Really?" She clapped her hands, delighted. "How wonderful!"

"Yes, see here." He walked around the desk and placed the diagram before her. He pointed to a spot on the map with multiple diagrams and numbers. "Based upon my calculations, this is likely the best place for us to find a cave of the size and depth to house the property stolen. It is within the Wash, just a short drive from Mrs. Edgerton's home. Even if it has been converted to gold, we can hope that Edgerton still used the area as his hiding place."

"This is just wonderful, James!" She beamed up at him.

"Hopefully soon this whole bloody affair will be finished."

She froze. Their gazes locked and the world stopped.

"Charlotte, I . . . I did not mean you."

She tore her sparkling eyes away. "Be sure to send the general word. He will be most eager to hear the news." She stood stiffly.

James stepped back, imploring, "We, you and I, need to discuss the future, Charlotte."

"We will get to that point soon enough," she commented quickly, then spun on her heel and escaped.

He watched her go, feeling . . . adrift.

Collin stepped through the open door. "Is Miss Hastings unwell?"

"Why do you ask?"

"She nearly ran me down in the hallway and she appeared flush."

James frowned, frustration and fear festering inside him.

"I came to report, your grace, that your cousin was seen entering a house down by Skidmore Street."

James was totally averted. "By the Thames?"

"By Skidmore Pier."

James locked the map away in his desk and pocketed the key. He went over to the cupboard and pulled out two pistols. He checked the sights, carefully examining each weapon to ensure it was loaded. "Let us pay my dear cousin a visit then, Collin."

"By all means," he replied enthusiastically.

A dirty street urchin sitting unobtrusively in the stairwell across the lane watched as James's handsome carriage sped away. He observed another carriage pull up in front of Pennington House, and a beautiful young lady alight with the help of a one-legged footman. The boy blinked. *The Fancy usually spat upon the likes o' them*. He waited for the coach to pull away and then raced off to deliver a message. He ran as fast as his shoeless feet could take him, fresh blunt foremost in his mind.

Margaret was sitting at her secretary, drafting a note, when Charlotte walked in.

"Hello, love. How are you?" Charlotte walked over and kissed her sister on the temple.

Margaret's porcelain cheeks reddened and she quickly shuffled aside her papers. "I did not expect you home, Charlotte," she said derisively. "Is James out of Town?"

"What a nasty thing to say, Margaret!"

"I did not expect you to visit after last night. Edward told me all about it," she added. "Why, you will miss all of your fans."

"What is wrong with you, Margaret?"

"Me? What on earth could be wrong with me? I have the most wonderful sister in the world who catches herself a duke and routs a viper in the retiring room. Simply perfect."

Realization dawned. Her sister was jealous! She wanted to be the only one receiving the attention of the Polite World. Charlotte was exasperated by her sister's shallowness. She had not contrived to land James. She did not plan the encounter with Lady Carlton. She was hurt that Margaret was casting her as someone who purposefully manipulated the situation to her advantage. Did her sister not know her at all?

"I am frankly tired of the attention I have been subjected to, Margaret. Her grace can deal with the *ton* today. I just want a nice visit at home with you and Edward, and then I want to do some work in my studio. Tell me, Margaret, how do you fare?"

Margaret sulked, but seemed mollified. "Well, if you are asking about my suitors, I do have some interesting news. Mr. Frickerby has asked Edward for permission to court me. He is so handsome, don't you think?" She did not wait for her sister's response and went on animatedly, "He has the most lovely eyes. And he told me that I am by far the most beautiful lady in the *ton*. I do believe he is in love with me. Is that not just wonderful?"

"Wonderful" was not quite the word that Charlotte had in mind. She remembered her last unpleasant encounter with Mr. Frickerby and did not relish the idea of him as Margaret's husband. "But we threw him out, Margaret, do you not remember?"

"Oh, that." Margaret beamed. "He explained it to me. You misunderstood his concern."

"I thought Mr. Frickerby was taken with Henrietta Balstram." Charlotte dug for help from any quarter.

"Stuart, I mean Mr. Frickerby, says that Henrietta is a bore." She giggled. "He says I am prettier by far, and much more interesting."

Charlotte was concerned for her friend Henrietta and likewise worried about her sister's infatuation with the capricious Mr. Frickerby. Knowing that she was treading on shaky ground, she began slowly. "Margaret, dear, just a few short weeks ago Mr. Frickerby was declaring his love for Henrietta. Do you not think that vacillating between eligible ladies as he has done displays a certain weakness of character?"

Margaret stood, charging angrily, "Just because he is not titled does not mean that he is not an honorable gentleman. Not all of us are willing to sink to your depths to land a duke."

The words stung, but no more than her venom. Charlotte took a deep breath and stated grimly, "Despite what you believe, Margaret, I have only your best interests at heart."

"Stuart told me that you would not approve of him."

Lord only knew what else Mr. Frickerby had told Margaret.

"Margaret, I want you to consider how well you know Mr. Frickerby and how well you know me. Talk to the people you know and love, like Edward and Aunt Sylvie. Then think long and hard about your future, because what you do now and how you conduct yourself will affect the rest of your life. I am leaving to find Edward."

She quit the room angry and irritated with her little sister. She was trying to be magnanimous, but deep down she could not help but feel that Margaret was a spoiled brat. Her judgment was unsound and her criticisms were unfair. Whatever had happened to her sweet little sister?

Charlotte found Edward at his desk in the library, busy working on the books and ledgers. She sank into the old leather couch and stretched. She needed a little brotherly support this morning.

"Hello, Char," Edward greeted her distractedly. "What are you doing here?"

"Am I no longer welcome in my own home?" she asked, annoyed.

He raised a quizzical brow.

"Sorry. I am a bit peaked this morning."

"Of course you are, after what happened last night. But why are you not receiving the multitude that will inevitably come to fawn over you?"

"I am hiding out here in the hopes of avoiding some of the histrionics. I had enough of them last night."

"You can blame no one but yourself."

Charlotte sat up straight. "Excuse me?"

"You should not have let her provoke you."

"How can you blame me?" She shook her head and replied angrily, "As if you would have kept your mouth closed under the same circumstances!"

"It was undignified."

She stood and walked to the windows, staring at the leaden sky. "Would you prefer that I slapped her cheek and demanded pistols at dawn?"

"Now *you* are the one being ridiculous." His seat squeaked loudly as he leaned back.

"You really should get that chair fixed."

"It does not bother me. I like it, actually. Makes me feel like I am not alone when I am here doing the accounts. I am leaving shortly for the Beckersvilles' for luncheon," he commented. "I am certain they would not mind if you joined us."

"I will return to Pennington House," she declined, feeling a little out of place. She moved to leave. "By the by, I would not encourage Mr. Frickerby's suit for Margaret."

"Really? Margaret seems quite taken with the man."

"He is not up to snuff. Last week he was enamored of Henrietta; this week it is Margaret. He is too fickle by half."

"Margaret is not exactly constant in her affections."

"Trust me on this, Edward. I just do not like the man." And with that she left, feeling as if she was no longer at home in her own house.

* * *

She pushed away her negative musings as the carriage rolled languidly through the streets of London. The vehicle slowed to a standstill as Charlotte heard angry shouting, horses braying, and a sundry of loud noises.

Lieutenant Freeman's features filled the tiny window. "There appears to be some kind of accident ahead, Miss Charlotte. Shall I go see if I can help?"

"Certainly. I am undoubtedly not going anywhere."

She waited in the warm carriage, hoping all was well and wishing she had brought along a maid when suddenly the door burst open and Mortimer Blanton stepped inside. She was so shocked she barely had time to scoot over on the bench as he seated himself beside her.

"Hello, my dear." Mortimer smiled his oily, sharp-toothed smile that seemed more like a sneer, and slammed the door behind him.

"How dare you?" Charlotte cried, affronted. "John Driver!"

"Oh, do not bother calling your man, Charlotte, my dear. He is indisposed at the moment."

"John Driver would never leave his post."

"Maybe not voluntarily," he retorted.

Dear God, what monster had her childhood companion become? "I insist that you leave this carriage at once!"

Mortimer leaned back against the cushion. "Oh, but do you see the lengths I must go to to visit you, my dear? My mongrel cousin has been keeping you all to himself." He crossed one lanky leg over the other, effectively blocking the door.

She froze. If she screamed, she would not be heard over the din outside. She would just have to hold the man off until Lieutenant Freeman returned. Charlotte shuddered. Her skin still prickled in Mortimer's presence, like a cat whose fur had been swept the wrong way. She stood and quickly shifted to the opposite seat, trying to keep as much distance from him as possible. "Again, I must ask you to leave."

"We were once friends, you and I."

"That was a *very* long time ago." Before Mortimer had begun his strange antics, his farfetched schemes, before he had tried to swindle her dying father out of thousands of pounds. That alone did not recommend him to her, particularly not as a potential husband.

Mortimer's eerie eyes narrowed ominously, but then he shrugged and adjusted the tails of his long green coat, arranging the folds to fit artfully over his partridge waistcoat and striped linen shirt of bright green and yellow stripes. His intricately tied cravat was so large as to limit the movement of his head. "I understand that felicitations are in order, Charlotte, my dear." A sharklike sneer crossed his features. "I did not quite know what to think when I heard the news. I was under the distinct impression that you were not entertaining offers of marriage."

She sat tensely, ignoring the lure. She had never done well when parrying with Mortimer; he was so double-tongued.

His face scrunched and his nose washed red with anger. "And how is my repulsive cousin?"

Charlotte clenched her hands.

"What? No sharp turn of phrase in defense of your beloved?" he mocked. "You were always so quick witted. Is my cousin's weak brain affecting you?"

She could not imagine how on earth one family could have produced such vastly different men. Where James was compact and lithe, Mortimer was tall and lanky. James moved with effortless grace; Mortimer's actions were jerky and erratic. Apparently the Spanish blood in their lineage had skipped past Mortimer, as he was pale, white-blond, and blue eyed. Charlotte was always amazed by his eye color. It was such a light blue as to make his eyes seem almost opaque.

"So what was it, Charlotte? What was it about my dear

cousin that gained him the coveted spot as your husband? Was it his charm?" He placed his hand under his chin, posing thoughtfully. "No. He is quite cross most of the time. Or his sense of humor? No, he has none. It cannot be his beauty, oh, no English beauty there. Could it quite possibly have been the threat of scandal?"

Her eyes narrowed.

"Going into your room not just once but twice really placed your reputation at risk, my dear. Cannot call the man honorable under those circumstances, can you? And if anyone found out about that brute Mr. Mason, well . . . I guess you had no choice."

Her faced flamed as the thrust hit home. How on earth did Mortimer Blanton know about the Beast who'd attacked her? Her eyes blazed like icicles in winter. "I do wonder where you come up with such nonsense, Mr. Blanton. Mayhap you would like to share your inspiration?"

His nostrils flared and anger burned brightly in his light eyes. "There is nothing that escapes my attention. For instance, I'll have you know that love has very little to do with your engagement. Your *beloved*," he spat the word as if it were a curse, "is the furthest thing from honorable. Do you believe he was saving your reputation by asking for your hand?" His ghostly laugh echoed in the small cabin. "More like saving his own hide. Precious diamonds look pretty good to a man outrunning the constable."

The pit in Charlotte's stomach suddenly swelled to a yawning chasm. "He seems perfectly well off," she countered hopefully.

"The man is wearing every penny he owns. Have you seen Montrose?" He did not wait for her answer. "Crumbling in on itself. No staff. Irate piss-poor tenants, it's a disgrace to the family name. My dear aunt has no idea. No one does. The bastard is wagering all his bets on you and your diamonds."

It was exactly what she had wanted to know, yet she had

not really wanted to face the ugly truth. Her hands clenched and she replied angrily, "Do you actually believe that smearing James will make any difference to me whatsoever? That it might somehow convince me to marry you instead? You are truly mad if you believe that I will ever, under any circumstances, consent to be your wife."

"You are mine, Charlotte, I set my sights on you long ago . . ."

"After realizing you lost an opportunity of a lifetime!"

Mortimer shook with unfettered rage. "I will have what is rightfully mine!" Madness clouded his eerie eyes as he waved his fisted hand. "And I swear by the gods that my mongrel cousin will never have the benefit of your hand." He leapt at Charlotte, grabbing her arms and pressing her back against the cushions. Charlotte kicked at him wildly and rammed her fist into his throat. His head flung back as he cried, "Oof!"

She booted him hard in his middle and he toppled against the far seat. She grabbed the door handle and practically fell out the door when it swung open. Lieutenant Freeman stood outside, holding the handle.

"Move aside, Lieutenant!" she yelled, as she scrambled onto the pavement.

The good lieutenant stepped back just as Mortimer crashed out of the carriage.

"Charlotte!" Mortimer screeched.

"Stay away from me, you bastard!"

"I would never hurt you!" The knife he brandished in his hand belied his words. Lieutenant Freeman instinctively swung his crutch down hard on Mortimer's arm. The blade clattered to the ground and Mortimer turned tail and pushed his way through the crowd. Lieutenant Freeman set down his crutch and moved to race after him.

"Lieutenant," Charlotte commanded, "stay here."

He reluctantly swung back on his crutch. "The bloody dastard's gone anyway."

Charlotte walked over and picked up Mortimer's knife. It was stained with old, dried blood. She shuddered. "And none too soon."

"Who was he?"

"Mr. Mortimer Blanton, James's cousin."

Lieutenant Freeman scowled. "Then why did he attack you?"

She gingerly handed him the knife. "Believe it or not, the madman wants to marry me."

"Not exactly the way to court a lady. Especially a lady betrothed to someone else."

"He was actually trying to warn me off of marrying James, among other things."

"I wouldn't listen to a word the rotter says."

She crossed her arms and hugged herself. "I wish that I could be so sure."

"You are not going to listen to a dog like him?"

"He is a scoundrel, but he is James's cousin and seems to know quite a bit about my situation." Her eyes narrowed. "More than he ought." She shuddered and looked around. Their presence on the street was drawing stares. "Come. Let us find John Driver."

Chapter 29

Back at Pennington House, Lieutenant Freeman was helping Charlotte pack her things, and he did not like it one bit. The duke was downstairs preparing for his travels and had no idea that Charlotte was leaving him.

"Like a thief in the night," the lieutenant stated, as he pushed a box into the corner by the door.

"If I have to hear that one more time from you I will scream." She glared, her hands fisting and unfisting as she scanned the open trunks scattered around the room. "If you cannot keep your opinions to yourself, you can leave."

"Fine." He spun on his crutch and loped out of the room. And headed straight for James's study.

He knocked on the door.

"Come," James called, looking up from his maps. "Yes, Lieutenant, what can I do for you?"

"I wish to speak with you privately. May I close the door, sir?"

"Certainly."

After securing the door, Lieutenant Freeman stood, military straight, before James's desk. "I need to speak with you man to man, sir. Is that possible?"

James straightened. "This sounds serious."

"Miss Charlotte's welfare is very serious business to me." He caught James's gaze. "I want you to look me squarely in the eye and swear to me that your intentions toward Miss Charlotte are right and honorable."

His eyes locked with the lieutenant's, James spoke quietly and solemnly. "On my honor, my intentions toward Charlotte are honorable and true. I wish to protect her, provide for her, and safeguard her well-being. She is to be my wife and the mother of my children."

They stood, rigidly erect, staring at each other as Lieutenant Freeman weighed the duke and his words. The lieutenant nodded slowly. "I expect you to fulfill that pledge."

"I will. Now what is this about?"

"Miss Charlotte is upstairs, getting ready to leave."

"Oh, has she left something at her brother's?"

"No, sir. Leaving for good."

"For good?" he growled. "I am about to set off on a possibly dangerous expedition, and now she decides to leave me? When was she planning on telling me?"

Lieutenant Freeman raised his hand. "Now, hold on a minute. Miss Charlotte has been through quite a lot today. Your dastard cousin tried to kill her this afternoon, and that was after planting some pretty hateful things about you in her head."

"Kill? Mortimer? Charlotte?" he choked. He sat down heavily in his chair. "But when? How?"

"In the carriage on the ride over here after leaving her brother's. He set up a trap, knocked John Driver but good on the head, and threw him into an alley. While I was off checking on the accident that stopped traffic, he jumped in the carriage. Luckily Miss Charlotte was quick on her feet. The dog didn't stand a chance."

He looked up warily. "She is all right?"

"Yes."

"What, what did he say about me to Charlotte?"

"I was not there, so I can't hardly say. But whatever he said, she seemed to take it pretty hard."

He blew out a gust of air.

The lieutenant's eyes narrowed. "Stuff and nonsense, right?"

James grimaced. "It is complicated. My intentions toward Charlotte are honorable now. But when I first asked her to marry me, well, that was before . . ." He looked up pleadingly. "Before I knew Charlotte."

The lieutenant nodded sagely, understanding all too well.

James stood and began pacing. "I cannot leave now, not like this."

He stepped over to the sofa, lay his crutch down by his side, and sank heavily into the plush fabric. "I do not think you have a choice. You need to collect that gold before it sets sail. We can protect Miss Charlotte well enough."

"You know I trust you with Charlotte's life. But it is my honor, my responsibility . . ." His voice trailed off.

"Protecting Miss Charlotte is a lifeline to me." He scratched his clean-shaven face, almost missing his beard. "I did some good things at the hospital, but it was not enough. No." He shook his head, smiling. "I have a purpose here. To help you recover that property and"—the taste of vengeance waxed his tongue—"to cur that scurrilous dog."

"I have to stop Charlotte from leaving." James looked toward the door. "But how can I? She thinks I am a monster. And," he frowned, "I cannot really blame her."

"Talk to her," he urged. "Make her understand."

James nodded absent-mindedly. After a moment, he stood. "Well, thank you for coming to me, Lieutenant. I am in your debt."

He swung his crutch up and stood. "Not mine, Miss Charlotte's."

Charlotte froze as she caught a glimpse of James, who stood tentatively on the threshold. With a sweep of his eyes, he could see that all her possessions were packed in boxes and trunks around the room.

Ignoring the initial stab of guilt, she clutched her skirts tensely while waiting for him to shout or rave.

Instead, he asked politely, "Charlotte? If we might have a word next door?"

She nodded stiffly and proceeded to the adjoining room. He gently closed the door behind them. Walking behind the large armchair as if it could shield her against anguish, Charlotte faced him warily.

Taut silence enveloped the small chamber.

He rubbed his hands over his mouth. "This is awkward."

She raised her brow.

"For you, as well, of course." He grimaced. "Granted, *much* worse for you. Which is why this is so difficult. I did not want to hurt you, Charlotte. I really meant well, only had the best intentions. Well, not all of them . . ." His voice trailed off.

"How about starting at the beginning?" she suggested softly, gripping the hard fabric of the chair, trying to buttress her already flagging spirit.

"I do not know when it really began. Maybe Mortimer and I hated each other from birth. We could certainly not be more different. He and I have always competed with each other. For Uncle's attention, for women, for everything. But I got the title and the lands. Granted, with the responsibility they entailed."

She stiffened. *Here it comes, his need for money to support the dukedom.*

"Mortimer always wanted more, needed more. Things got

much worse between us once Uncle died." He shuddered and paused. "Well, I guess I did not fully appreciate how depraved he really is. Or how his corruption could taint others."

"Are you suggesting that his immorality tainted you?"

James seemed to think about that for a long, hard moment. Slowly he nodded.

"How can you blame your cousin for your own duplicity?"

"In truth, I cannot."

Heavy silence transcended the room.

He extended his hand. "It is my burden, my fault, for dragging you into this horrid mess. I swear that if there were any way I could go back and do it all again . . ."

She crossed her arms, hugging herself, trying to keep from shattering. "What would you have done differently?"

"Well, for one, I never would have planted the map and keys in your room."

She started at the shift in topic. "Why *did* you do that?"

"Because I was made to understand that Mortimer fancied you. That he wanted to marry you."

"What does that have to do with anything?"

"Mortimer was always unbearably jealous of anything he supposed belonged to him. In this instance, you. I thought he would not allow anyone to enter your room or hurt you or your reputation in any way. Thus, your room was the perfect hiding place."

"You have lost me. Mortimer was not in Southbridge."

"But his lackeys were."

"Lackeys?"

"The ones after the map and keys."

She shook her head. "But what does Mortimer have to do with the map and keys?"

He dropped onto the sofa, pronouncing quietly, "Because he is the mastermind behind the thefts at the War Office."

Her mouth dropped open, she was so stunned. There was so much more to this crazed tangle than she had realized.

She had considered the investigation and her dowry distinct, but they were interwoven, with Mortimer interlacing the wretched pattern.

He shrugged. "I do not know if he orchestrated the thefts simply to embarrass me, support Napoleon, make himself rich, or maybe for all those reasons. But whatever his motivation, I know he is behind it all, and he likely killed Edgerton and set up the kidnapping attempt on you. I wanted to deal with him myself, to save my mother and sister from the scandal, the humiliation. I meant to handle him without anyone knowing his true colors."

She looked up quickly and saw the resolution in his dark eyes. So he meant to kill his cousin. She stepped from behind the chair and sank down wearily. She recognized that Mortimer was a devil-tongued snake, but to learn that he was a murderer and traitor, it was a bit much. She rubbed her hand over her eyes. But it made sense in the midst of this lunacy. Mortimer's thirst for power, prestige; the insidious scheme James described was a natural match for him.

"Say something, Charlotte," he begged.

She did not realize how long she had sat mulling over these revelations. "Strangely, it all rather makes sense. Mortimer's quest for, well, the whole lot has clouded every bit of reason he ever had."

"And I hate to say . . . some of mine as well. I am sorry to have brought you into this dreaded affair, Charlotte."

It was the final insult to injury. He regretted knowing her, the engagement . . . *everything*.

Her mouth was so dry; she was amazed the word was able to leave her lips. "Why?"

"It was not worth it all, using you so abominably . . ."

She was somewhat glad that he felt badly but he was not using the right words, saying the thing that would make it all end well. Her heart cried out, barely a whisper, she wanted him to confess his undying love and admiration, to say he had learned to care for her, for herself, and not her dowry or her bizarre place in Mortimer's machinations.

Instead, he only said, "I am so sorry for it all."

If she had any dignity, she would rant, admonish, slam the door in his face, but for her life she could barely move; her body felt shackled to the chair.

"Did he frighten you today?"

She blinked, trying to follow his train of thought.

"Before today, I did not really fear him."

"But now you do?"

"Yes."

"I hope you know that for all my horrific behavior, I never would have hurt you."

The searing pain piercing her heart belied his words.

He went on, "I pulled you into this madness to take you from him. To taunt him, to draw him out and make him come for you."

"You were using me as bait?"

"Yes." He grimaced. "And to hurt him. To plague him the way he has plagued me. To take what he wanted."

Her diamonds. She stared down at her hands, lying lifeless in her lap.

He leaned forward earnestly. "I am a dishonorable knave. I apologize for treating you so abominably. You deserve better."

Not looking up, she shook her head. "I do not know what to believe."

"I know I was not honest about my intentions at the beginning of our engagement, but I am quite sincere in my regard for you now. I, I would like to make it up to you."

She looked up slowly. "How?"

"By marrying. Give me a chance to make it up to you, and I swear on my honor I will make certain you never regret your choice."

The words tasted bitter on her tongue. "You mean, choosing you instead of your cousin?"

"This is not coming out right. I mean to say that I, I . . . have grown to care for you. I want to marry you."

For all the wrong reasons, her heart cried.

"I know this is a lot to ask of you. Just please consider the possibility of us marrying. I know that we could make a go of it."

Make a go of it. The words twisted in her gut. Charlotte needed more than a workable arrangement. She wanted, needed, so much more.

He crouched before her, taking her hand in his, pleading with those incredible midnight blue eyes. "Please, just think about it?"

Although she knew she should cry off immediately, she did not have the heart to say so. To tell him that she would never marry. Not him, not his foul cousin, no one. Instead, she nodded numbly, knowing she was going to think of little else.

"Thank you," he breathed.

Charlotte looked down at her pale hand in his larger olive-skinned one. His touch was at once comforting, and more: it was as if they had a connection, a warmth, a caring. But it was all a lie based upon *her* feelings, not *his.* She could read between the lines; he felt guilty, he felt obligated, perhaps he even cared for her somewhat, but it was all wrong. He still aimed to take what his cousin wanted and what he still needed: the diamonds.

He gently rubbed his finger across her hand. "I feel like I have let you down in so many ways." His dark hair gleamed with shiny blackness.

Knock.

His midnight gaze met hers. "Are we finished?"

"Yes," she whispered.

He looked over his shoulder. "Come."

Collin stepped into the room. "Everything is ready for your departure, your grace."

He let go of her hand and stood. He frowned and stated

apologetically, "I must go. I have made arrangements with Lieutenant Freeman for your protection."

"Do what you have to."

"Unless you want me to stay?"

"Go. Find that gold and bring it back." *And while you are there, please procure me another heart, for mine is shattered.*

He nodded, hesitating, and then leaned forward and brushed his velvety lips gently across hers. "Good-bye." He watched her a long moment. What did he want from her? A sign that all was forgiven, that the damage to her heart was just a rut in the road in his mission to stop a war and save his crumbling estates? Well, she could not give it.

He turned and strode out the door.

In her drawing room, the dowager dipped her quill once more and continued the missive to her cousin Audrey.

> . . . *Additionally, the Hastings girl has been quick to learn the little lessons I have been sharing on managing the households. All in all, she has intelligence, spirit, and keen wit. It took brains and pluck to turn the tables on Lady Carlton the other evening. Charlotte was sensible, perfectly proper in the affair, and deadly. I have to admire that in a person, particularly a duchess in training.*
>
> *I am beginning to believe that despite her unfortunate connections, she will make James an excellent match. Yet . . .*

Wavering over whether to share her misgivings, her pen paused on the paper. She dipped her quill, blotted it, and continued.

*Yet I am troubled by her seeming reluctance to set a date
for the wedding, to purchase a proper trousseau . . .*

James knocked once on the open door. She shuffled the
letter aside, set down her plume, and looked up at him expectantly.

He strode into the room; a frown marred his handsome
features, and lines etched his usually smooth brow.

"I need you to do something for me, Mother," he said
solemnly.

She straightened. She could not remember James needing
her assistance. Fear clutched at her heart. "I am at your service, James. Tell me what is wrong."

He rubbed his eyes. He was looking so tired, older somehow than his years. "I do not have time to explain everything
right now. I need to leave shortly."

"For the search."

"Yes. Well, I need your promise, Mother, that you will
help Charlotte."

She leaned forward. "What can I do?"

He ran his hand through his hair. It was a curly mess. The
dowager wished that he would push it back with that pomade
she'd bought him. He dropped his hand. "I do not know exactly what she will need, but there may be social repercus-
sions from this mess and I want you to promise to help
Charlotte in any way that you can."

"You mean to guide her?"

"It will probably be more like keeping the tigers at bay."
He looked up and her heart contracted at the pain she saw in
his dark blue eyes. The same eyes as his father's. "Just do
whatever you can not to let anyone hurt her."

She nodded solemnly. "I will do everything in my power
to protect her."

He met her gaze, and for a fleeting moment she thought

she saw a tear glisten in his eye. "Thank you," he replied gruffly. "I must go."

She stood and walked over to her son. "Farewell, James." And she squeezed his hand. He started at the gesture, then pressed her hand and left. She felt the powerful urge to call him back. To say something, anything, to erase the anguish from his countenance. He was her boy, after all.

Charlotte sat hunched over the edge of the big bed and looked around the room at the boxes and trunks, unable for the moment to rally her spirits to leave.

"Where do you think you are going?" the dowager asked from the threshold.

She looked up. The dowager's graying dark hair was pulled back severely in a bun, accenting her high cheekbones. She walked regally into the room, her dark green skirts swooshing around her legs. "I asked you a question."

"Home," she replied quietly.

The dowager crossed her arms. "This is your home."

She shrugged.

"I will not give anyone fodder with which to hurt my family, Charlotte. Our family."

She looked up, startled. The dowager had called her by her Christian name.

The dowager glided over to the bed. "James is gone," she pronounced. "He asked me to watch out for you."

She shifted her eyes and looked away.

The older woman stepped in front of her and with a single bony finger lifted Charlotte's chin. "What ails you, child?"

She pulled her head away. "Nothing."

"Poppycock."

Charlotte almost smiled. "Poppycock?"

"Yes. I have never heard such imprudence in all my life. You are meant to be here, to be the next Duchess of Girard. I cannot have you sulking about, creasing up your lovely face."

"You do not want me, remember?"

The matron waved her hand. "That was before, this is now."

"Why the sudden change of heart?"

"Can you not take the gift I am giving you graciously?"

"You are not giving me anything I want."

She huffed. "Of course you want it. You will be a wealthy, well connected duchess, for heaven's sake."

"I am already wealthy and well connected."

And you do not know the truth of the matter. Charlotte wondered how the dowager was going to respond when she learned that the dukedom was under the hatches. Probably with her usual hard-nosed flare.

The dowager crossed her arms and arched her brow, signaling her trump card. "Well, you can have James."

"James is not a gift to be given by you at will."

She frowned. This apparently was not going as she had planned. She shifted her stance, her silk skirts swooshing noisily. "Do you wish to marry your sister off this Season?"

Charlotte tilted her head, replying slowly, "Yes."

"Well then, you had best unpack your things, because no family of consequence will have her after the scandal erupts over your split with James. I do not believe your little sister will take too kindly to your ruining her chances at happiness, do you?" She pursed her lips and sauntered over to the dressing table. She carefully watched Charlotte's reflection in the mirror. "Stop chewing on your lip, child." She turned. "I do not know what is happening between you and my son. I only know this: if you leave, you are destroying your sister's chances for a future."

She shook her head, marveling. "And James thought I fought dirty."

"Stay until the end of the Season. See your sister well settled. Then you and James can make up."

"There is nothing to make up between James and me," she replied dourly. "We are . . . finished."

"Do not be ridiculous." The lady wagged her finger. "You young people can be so foolish. Whatever he has done, forgive him and get on with your lives, no use turning your days into a permanent row. Good relationships are few and far between. You need to cherish those who care for you and foster the connection. It takes work, and concessions and forgiveness. You will realize that as you mature."

Charlotte raised an eyebrow. "This from the lady who betrayed her best friend and spent thirty years punishing her for following her conscience and her heart?"

The dowager jerked her head as if slapped. "I did not betray Sylvie. She betrayed me."

"How?"

She sputtered. "How? How? Well, she . . . ran off."

"And how was that a betrayal of you?"

Furrowing her brow, the dowager crossed her arms tightly. "I do not have to answer to you . . . and I am not at fault."

"Oh, really? Do you not target Aunt Sylvie and her balls and events? Did you not support, albeit socially, that scoundrel Jeffries in his claim against the Jaspers? Did you not try to bar Aunt Sylvie from entering the house?" Charlotte stood, charging angrily, "You should be begging her for forgiveness, not barring her from your presence! You should be extending the olive branch instead of your barbed tongue. Do not deign to tell me how to keep my relationships, your grace." She crossed her arms. "I do not stab in the back those who love me most."

The matron stood frozen, transfixed by Charlotte's words. From the look on her face, the truth hit her hard. "Just tell me you will stay," she murmured.

Charlotte shook her head, her hands clenching her skirts. "I seem to have little choice in the matter without hurting my sister and turning her against me forever." She lifted her chin in the air. "Something I would never do."

"Fine," the older woman bit out. She thrust her hands into her pockets, turned, and rushed from the room.

Out in the hallway, the dowager pressed her fist to her belly, trying to stop the bile from rising to her throat. Charlotte's words hit her deep in the dark recesses of her conscience, where her guilt had burrowed for the last thirty years. Where the overwhelming blackness of shame and self-reproach had festered for decades. She had betrayed her best friend in the world and betrayed her still. It was too much for the matron to process.

She walked down the hallway without seeing and headed toward her rooms. Something inside her had broken, and the vile self-loathing and pain burned in her chest like a torrent.

Even the haven of her chamber did not settle her nerves as it usually did. She dismissed her maid and walked over to the mirror. An old, gray-haired bitter woman stood watching her. She wiped her hand over her eyes. Could she be the awful woman Charlotte had described? Could she have been so blind and self-absorbed to have repeatedly betrayed her closest friend, the only woman she felt was her true sister? She sat down heavily, overwhelmed by shame and a terrible sense of loss. If only she had someone to confer with! A lone tear trickled down her haggard cheek. If only she could talk to Sylvie.

Chapter 30

~~~OG~~~

Charlotte awoke in a cold sweat, her heart pounding as the memory of her nightmare hovered fresh in her mind, James's touch, his kisses, but never his love. Her damp chemise clung to her shivering body, making her feel soiled. Blackness enveloped the darkened room, the light from the dying fire the only illumination. The clock in the hallway struck three times, echoing loudly in the quiet. She got out of bed; her feet bit from the cold of the hardwood floor. She was freezing, but it was an inner chill, one that could find no relief from fire or creature comforts. She paced before the fire. What had happened to her grand plan, being an old maid and being happy with it?

She had fallen in love; that was what had happened to her great scheme. It was an insidious thing that had taken her unawares. James's charm, his aptitude, his quick wit, and yes, his heart-stopping beauty, had all conspired against her usually hearty armor, hammering at her resolve, causing her to fall victim to the most powerful challenger of all—love.

She grabbed the poker and stabbed at the fire as if to slaughter her demons. She threw down the metal instrument and huddled in front of the fire, hugging her knees to her chest, curled tight. She rocked from the balls of her feet to her heels and back, trying to settle her emotions. Trying to hide from the horrible truth that she had done the one thing that she had sworn never to do. She had fallen in love with a man who admitted to her face that he had been dishonest and had wronged her. And she still wanted him, even though he did not love her.

"Oh you fool, Charlotte," she whispered to the darkness. "You are the most irresponsible of fools. How I would not want to be in your shoes." From her throat a hoarse false laugh erupted, then immediately turned into a sob. She burrowed her face in her knees. Alone in the shadows, she faced the truth. She had not stayed at Pennington House solely to protect her sister. She had done so because she could not bear the thought of never seeing James again except at formal functions and the like. After being stoic and swearing off marriage, all she wanted was to be near the bloody knave.

She just wanted the precious little time together they might have after he returned from the Wash. It was folly, she knew, but there it was. She hugged herself close as she rocked, shaking before the fire. "Oh, you foolish girl," she cried. "What have you done?"

Someone was hammering at Charlotte's door, but she ignored them and burrowed deeper under the coverlet.

"Dear heavens, it is pitch black in here." Elizabeth bounded into the room. "I know it is fashionable to sleep in, Charlotte, but I am so excited I just had to show you." She leaned over Charlotte's sleeping form.

Charlotte peeped out from under her covers. Her eyes felt like glue and her head pounded. "What time is it?"

"Almost nine." Her pink lips pouted guiltily. "I am sorry.

You look so tired, but I have been waiting since eight-thirty and just could not wait another moment."

She slowly and laboriously sat up and pulled her covers up to her neck. "What is it?"

Elizabeth bubbled excitedly. "You made the Society column, Charlotte. And with much cachet, I do say." She held up the newspaper. "It is in the *Evening Gazette*. *'The Rout in the Retiring Room.'*" She grinned happily. "Is that not a wonderful title? It gets better." She danced from foot to foot with restrained enthusiasm and read:

The Rout in the Retiring Room

A certain recently engaged young lady of unquestionable moral character and virtue trounced an older widow who exhibited inexcusable, excessively vulgar behavior of an extremely improper sort in the ladies retiring room at the Cavendishes' ball the evening past. Despite the extreme provocation, the young lady maintained her dignity and comportment. We anticipate the older widow exiting Town shortly as her presence will be excused from all upcoming affairs.

Elizabeth poked her head from behind the paper. "They underlined all of the exes. How droll. Your idea, of course. That was so witty of you, Charlotte. However did you think of that?"

She opened her mouth, but Elizabeth interrupted, "This material is too good. I must write a song. Too bad you do not have a piano in here." She skipped with girlish enthusiasm toward the door. "Meet me in the green room and I will write something daringly wonderful for you." She exited but then poked her head back in. "I will order you some cucumbers for your eyes. And be sure to wear some rouge before we go out; you are looking a bit peaked." She smiled brightly. "We are certain to be busy after everyone reads the news accounts." And she was gone.

Charlotte groaned and buried her head under the covers, praying that everyone would just leave her alone and let her suffer in blessed silence.

Still in her dishabille, Sylvie was enjoying a solitary breakfast of eggs and ham, reading a letter from her cousin Elaine when Arthur, the butler, announced, "Her Grace, the Duchess of Girard, has come to call."

Sylvie's eyes widened with shock. "Here? Alone?"

"Yes, your grace. She is waiting in the front drawing room, unattended."

Sylvie stood, shaken, and dropped her letter. Something must be wrong, terribly wrong, for Katie to come.

"I will see her immediately, Arthur. Thank you."

She nervously adjusted her capote on her head as she rushed toward the front drawing room.

Sylvie stood rigidly across the room from her childhood friend, hands folded before her, prepared for the worst. The dowager turned from her inspection of the family portrait over the mantel.

Tense silence.

The dowager shifted her shoulders. She could not quite meet Sylvie's eyes.

Sylvie clenched her hands. "Where is Charlotte? Is she all right? Tell me."

She seemed relieved that Sylvie spoke first. "Nothing is amiss. Charlotte is safe back at Pennington House."

"Then why are you here? You do not speak to me for over thirty years and then you show up at an ungodly hour out of nowhere. What do you want?"

"There is no need to be belligerent," she admonished irritably.

"Just get to the point and then leave," Sylvie said, uncomfortable with facing her childhood friend and not knowing the cause of the visit.

"I can see that this was a mistake." The dowager began walking toward the door.

"Enough of your melodrama. Just tell me why you came."

The dowager looked torn. Finally she turned back to face Sylvie. "I, I just want you to know that . . . that . . . that I do not oppose the engagement." She admitted begrudgingly, "Charlotte is a fine girl."

She crossed her arms. "Let me understand this. You came here early this morning, after not speaking to me for thirty years, to tell me that you do not oppose Charlotte marrying your son?"

"Do you have a problem with that?"

Sylvie shook her head, still tense and wary. "Charlotte would make your son, or any man, for that matter, a wonderful wife and mother to his children. Along with being family, she is one of my dearest friends." The unspoken hurt hung heavily in the air.

The dowager bit her lip. Sylvie remembered the habit. She only did that when she was really nervous about something. Sylvie clasped her hands before her. "What else?"

The dowager looked up sharply. "I . . . I . . . ahem." She grimaced. "I . . . I owe you an apology."

Her eyes widened and she shook her head as if to clear it. "What?"

The dowager frowned and clutched her reticule closer to her stomach. "You heard me. Do not make me say it again."

Sylvie blew out a deep breath, then looked at the lady guardedly. "What are you apologizing for?"

"It seems like everything," she grumbled.

"Pardon?"

"I may have been a bit . . . rash about your nuptials."

"You just came to that conclusion?"

"You know that I was never one to do an *about-turn* easily."

The corners of Sylvie's lips almost lifted. It was a term they used when taking dancing instruction together from that awful Monsieur Merchund.

The dowager shrugged, not meeting her eyes. "Now that I think about it, I should not necessarily have set your parents on you, or . . . or turned you away that time you came to see me. Or . . . well, this is a blanket apology for all my transgressions."

She rubbed her hand over her mouth. "This certainly is unexpected." She looked up sharply. "You are not dying, are you?"

"No. But at this moment, the prospect is not unappealing."

Relief flooded through her. Yes, she was horrifically cross with her childhood friend. But if Katie had died without them making peace . . . *peace.* Sylvie was still mightily unsettled and angry, but the tempting olive branch Katie was extending could not be ignored.

Sylvie offered, "Have a seat."

The dowager nodded and sat on the edge of the sofa. She gripped her bag in her lap as if it was a shield of some sort. Sylvie slipped into one of the high-backed chairs across from her. She took a deep breath and let it out slowly. "I am glad that you do not oppose the marriage. I have been thinking about it and believe that there is a bond between them."

"The fools are in love," she pronounced, shaking her head.

"And what is so wrong with that?"

"It makes normally sane persons act irresponsibly."

Sylvie crossed her arms. "What could be irresponsible about falling in love, getting married, and making a family?"

"It should really be a more rational selection process."

"Some of us have the benefit of love to guide our way, while others must use more calculating methods."

The dowager sniffed.

She shifted in her seat. "Do you really believe that they are in love?"

"I do not know your Charlotte that well, but I'd guess she is in love. Meanwhile, my James, who keeps his feelings under lock and key, seems quite protective and fond of her. And if I can observe that, my boy must actually be head over heels in love. But they seem to be having difficulty figuring that out. The last time I saw James, he looked as if his heart was torn out of his chest, and Charlotte, well, she acts as if she has lost her dearest friend." A slight blush tinged her olive cheeks. "She is planning on leaving him, and he is set to let her go."

She shook her head. "We cannot let them."

"On this point you and I agree."

She tilted her head questioningly. "Why?"

"Because . . . well . . . because . . . I want more for him."

Sylvie nodded, understanding. Katie wanted more for her son than what she had, a business arrangement for a marriage.

"I will speak with Charlotte about it."

The dowager gracefully scooted back on the couch, setting her reticule down beside her. "You are welcome to come and go at Pennington House as you please." She patted her graying dark hair lightly and spoke casually, "You may even . . . visit me when you call."

She nodded guardedly. Katie was really making an effort. She was not quite ready to trust her former friend overmuch, but for the chance to have her Katie back, well, it was worth trying . . .

"Your Charlotte has quite a bit of pluck," the dowager offered.

"She always has. She was always the leader of the pack. I remember her father lamenting that she had been born a female. Then, after Jane died, well, Charlotte had to grow up fairly quickly."

"My James as well. After Arthur was gone, he had to assume responsibility for so much. James always was a bit . . . contained, but over the last few years he appears to be becoming much more like Arthur, quite . . . stoic." She looked down at her hands, as if fearing she had divulged too much.

"Well, we cannot have that," Sylvie commented wryly. "If he has any of you in him, he should be quite mischievous."

She looked up, her eyes twinkling. "I was quite a prankster, wasn't I?"

"Prankster? You were every governess's nightmare," Sylvie replied, grinning. "Remember what you did to poor Miss Davenport or Miss Fredrickson?"

"Do you recall that time I put that fish in your bonnet on the way to church?" asked the dowager, holding her hand to her mouth.

"Ohhh. I could have killed you. Mama would not let me go home and I smelled offensive," she replied, a broad, happy smile accompanying her words.

"Oh, but you got me back quite sufficiently with that trick you played in the boathouse . . ." And the ladies chatted on as if not a day had gone by in over thirty years.

Chapter 31

Charlotte found General Cumseby out in the gardens, enjoying a cigar as the patients inside took their midday meal. The cigar smoke could not quite eradicate the faint smell of sulfur and illness.

Beaming broadly, he stood. "Charlotte, my dear. The men have missed you. And so have I."

At the expression on her face, his brow furrowed worriedly. "Is everything all right? You look as if you've seen a ghost."

Surprising them both, she flew into his arms, relishing the comfort of his big bear hug.

He tossed his cigar away and rubbed her back gently. "Sit down and tell me, and we will make it right."

She was being melodramatic, and she hated it. She shuddered and pushed herself away. "I do not know if that is possible, General. But first tell me, is everyone here well? Mr. Vickers, Mr. Harteford?"

"The same."

They sat on the cold stone bench, and he implored, "Tell me what is bothering you, Charlotte."

She was not quite ready to confess her feelings for James, even to this man she admired most in the world. She took a deep breath and stated instead, "Mortimer Blanton paid me a visit yesterday."

"And what did the scoundrel have to say?"

"Before or after he tried to skewer me with a knife?"

"I knew that he was reprobate from what he tried to do to your father, but I really did not appreciate what a villain he had become." He shook his head. "I thank the good lord Richard is not here to see to what depths his son has sunk."

"James says his cousin is behind the thefts at the War Office."

"It is quite possible."

"Mortimer knew about the attack in my room at South-bridge. About James, everything; the only possible conclusion is that he is behind it all."

"That, my dear, is why Girard wants to deal with it quietly. No need to smear the entire family through the ugly business on Mortimer Blanton's account."

She picked at a ruffle on her pelisse.

"Somehow, I do not believe that you are so distressed over Mortimer Blanton?"

She shrugged.

"Is it Girard?" He took her hand in his. "Tell me, child."

A lone tear slipped down her cheek. "I am a fool, General," she whispered huskily.

The general wrapped his bullish arm around her shoulders and squeezed. "You are the farthest thing from a fool."

"Mortimer said that James . . . that James pressed for marriage to get at the diamonds. That his estate is in a shambles and he is mere footsteps ahead of the constable."

"And you believe the lying snake?"

"James admitted so himself. Well, about wanting me for my dowry and to take it from Mortimer."

He shook his head. "Now, that I find hard to believe. How would Girard even know about the diamond mines?"

"Maybe through his cousin or the War Office? The important thing is that he does know and . . . and he is all that is dishonorable."

"And this upsets you?"

Charlotte sniffed. "Of course it does."

"But the last time I saw you, you thought he was a fiend. What makes the difference now?"

She pulled her handkerchief out of her pocket and blew, pronouncing sardonically, "I fell in love with the bastard."

He smiled. "I've always liked Girard."

"You do not understand, General! I did the one thing I swore never to do again—I fell for a scoundrel. A foul, lying rogue who cares nothing for me. I am a fool."

"I have known Girard since he was a nursling. Despite his misguided notions concerning revenge on his cousin, he is a good man, or I never would have let him near you."

She sniffed. "Perhaps about some things, but not about me."

He scratched his nose and asked thoughtfully, "Has Girard ever discussed your dowry with Edward?"

"Well, he said we might put the dowry in a trust for the hospital."

"See?" he exclaimed. "He does not want or need your dowry."

She shook her head. "It makes no sense. He must have been lying."

"Unless there has been some sort of misinterpretation." He pursed his lips. "Charlotte, I would know if Girard were in financial straits. Moreover, I am quite certain that he is not pressing for marriage because of the diamonds."

She bowed her head. "I am just so disappointed in myself."

The general patted her back reassuringly. "Your instincts are sound. You would never have chosen an undeserving man for your love."

She raised her brow dubiously. "What about that scoundrel Myles Wilmington?"

"Did you really love him?"

"I thought I did."

"And now?"

She sighed, watching the little brown birds fly off. "Now I realize I did not truly understand the nature of love. And Myles Wilmington, well, blast, if I was half as daft then as Margaret is now, then I was not exactly the best judge of character."

"You were young. Then you were green, and now you are a lady of consequence. A young lady who has seen the worst despair." He gestured toward the wards of the hospital. "And shown grace and fortitude. Have faith in yourself and your choices. Your heart is not wrong about Girard."

"But what if I am wrong?"

He pushed his spectacles up his nose. "If you are wrong, then I will call Girard out and kill him."

Her eyes widened. "General Cumseby! You cannot!"

"I am willing to bet my life on Girard. Why can't you?"

Heavy silence. The muffled sounds of bedpans rumbling down a hallway on a metal tray resounded from inside.

"I will make you a pact," she replied sternly. "I will give James a chance to prove my fears wrong. But if I am right about his dishonorable intentions, I want to be the one to kill him. Then I can escape to the Continent and have myself a lovely tour."

He beamed. "Now, there is my Charlotte. Always taking on the next challenge! Truly, though, if I am mistaken about Girard, well, I will not allow you to be victimized by this mess."

"I fear it may be too late."

"No, my dear. It is only too late when you act rashly, not knowing if the man is true."

"Where in heaven's name are they?" a loud, commanding voice echoed from the hallway inside.

Charlotte straightened. "That sounds like the dowager."

Just then, a flustered Mr. Gladson led the dowager and Sylvie into the garden.

"There you are, my dear, we were wondering if we ever were going to find you in this horrid . . . ah place." The dowager swept into the small courtyard, her purple pelisse with matching hat and large swaying feathers dramatically announcing her formidable presence. She nodded to the general. "Ah, General Cumseby, so good to see you again."

He stood and bowed formally. "Your grace."

She waved her purple-gloved hand. "And you know Lady Jaspers."

Aunt Sylvie nodded regally, smiling.

Charlotte stood, asking uncertainly, "You, you are here . . . together?"

The dowager adjusted her bonnet. "Yes, well, Charlotte, my dear, it is all your doing. You got me all nostalgic, and I just decided to pay my old friend Sylvie a visit."

Her eyes widened. "Nostalgic? I insisted that you apologize."

She waved her hand airily. "Well that is behind us now, and we are friends again."

Sylvie nodded, beaming. "Yes, thank you, Charlotte, for setting the bee in Katie's bonnet, so to speak. We really have been having the most wonderful time catching up."

She shook her head as if to clear it. "This is so bizarre."

"We wanted to thank you, but you were not at Pennington House. Manton told us where to find you and, well," Sylvie smiled happily, "here we are."

"Shall I call for some refreshment?" the general asked, eyeing Gladson shifting uncomfortably from foot to foot.

"That would be lovely," Sylvie replied. "Oh, but wait, there was a letter at Pennington House for you, Charlotte, and it said 'urgent.' You may wish to read it first."

"Urgent?" Charlotte raised her hand to her mouth, fear clenching her stomach. *Dear heavens, let James be all right.* She took the missive from her aunt, tore it open, and quickly scanned the note. She frowned and handed it to Aunt Sylvie. She read it, frowned and handed it to the dowager.

"Something smells foul," Aunt Sylvie commented wryly.

The dowager shook her head, purple plumes bouncing. "I do not like this one bit."

"What is it?" the general asked.

The dowager held up the note. "Miss Constance Druthers wants to meet Charlotte at the pond at the park at five this afternoon. Prime time to see and be seen. She claims to have important information about my James relating to their impending marriage."

"What on earth could Constance Druthers know about your son?" Aunt Sylvie asked.

"I have no idea. Lies and innuendo, most likely. But whatever it is, the girl is up to no good." She straightened her pelisse. "I do not take kindly to some babbler trying to blacken my son's name. Let us pay a visit to the Druthers'."

"Shall I return home?" Aunt Sylvie offered uncertainly.

The dowager smiled. "And miss all the fun? She will likely run to you or any number of matrons of the *ton* to spread her venom. No, let us nip this in the bud. I would like your assistance, Sylvie."

"Gladly," she replied merrily.

"I would not want to be on the opposite side when you attack," the general added. "You are too crafty by far."

"There is no way Miss Druthers could ever anticipate our gambit. To her, you two are at war and I am the unwanted daughter-in-law to be." Charlotte smiled. "She will not know what hit her."

* * *

The dowager led Charlotte and her aunt into the salon where the Drutherses were having tea. Lady Druthers looked up at her friend and smiled in welcome.

"Your grace, what a pleasant surprise. And Miss Hastings . . . and . . . Lady Jaspers?" Lady Druthers' eyes widened. Miss Druthers looked up, panic lighting her gaze. She bit her lip and looked down quickly. Lady Druthers watched the ladies warily, obviously sensing that something was amiss. Smiling a tilted half-smile, she offered, "Please join us for some tea."

"Thank you, dear, but at the moment we have some pressing business with your daughter." The dowager glided to stand before Constance.

"Me?" Constance squeaked, all color washing out of her pale face. Suddenly her features took on a greenish cast.

Charlotte stepped in front of Constance. "We came as quickly as we could. We knew you would not have wanted to wait until this afternoon to share such important intelligence."

Lady Druthers adjusted her turban and asked nervously, "What news could you possibly need to discuss with Constance? She and I have been so busy preparing for our ball next week, we have barely had a moment to visit with anyone. Whatever you have heard must have come from another source."

With her eyes gleaming dangerously the dowager turned to Lady Druthers. "What do you believe I have heard, Druscilla? Do tell."

Lady Druthers blurted a rushed response. "Well, nothing, really. You know how some people will say just about anything. There's usually nothing to what one hears."

"We do so appreciate your loyalty," she answered cuttingly.

"Of course we are loyal. We would never do anything to hurt you or your family."

"Oh really? Then that must be why your daughter sent Charlotte a letter saying that she had critical information about James's character?" The dowager turned to Constance, who was trying to shrink into the couch.

Again Lady Druthers forged on, trying to remedy the situation before all was lost. "Constance would never do such a thing, would you, dear? Miss Hastings must be mistaken."

Charlotte took the note from her clutch. Lady Druthers recognized the writing and it was as if the wind was knocked from her sails. She sank down in the couch, her large green turban slipping over her eyes.

Constance's eyes darted about the room, searching for escape.

Charlotte hovered over the girl, asking sharply, "Who was supposed to meet me this afternoon?"

She sputtered, "It was a prank, merely a silly little jest. There is nothing to tell, no one to meet."

The dowager leaned in and stood over Constance, bearing her full impressive authority. "Constance Druthers, I will sue you for libel. I will see that your names are slashed from every invitation list in Town and that you never make a decent match. I will make it my purpose to torture you until the day I die if you so much as try to lay a rumor on my son or my daughter-in-law."

Constance blanched. Lady Druthers fell back on the couch and waved her hand frantically at her face, laboring for air. A sob burst from the young lady's throat as she looked around imploringly. "It was all Stuart's fault! He told me it would be the best way to take my revenge on Girard. He was supposed to marry me. *Me*. Not some unfashionable chit from the country. *I* was supposed to be the next Duchess of Girard."

Charlotte straightened. "Stuart? You mean Stuart Frickerby?"

"Yes," she sobbed. "He told me that James was under the hatches and had stolen some property from the government to cover his debts, that he was about to be exposed for a scoundrel. He swore that I was better off without him. That he found me far preferable to the dowdy Miss Hastings." She pulled a kerchief from her pocket and blew noisily.

"Was Mr. Frickerby supposed to meet Charlotte today at five?" Aunt Sylvie asked.

"Yes, he was going to cause a scandal—one from which she could never recover."

"Why, you evil little girl," the dowager charged softly. "You have no idea what trouble you have assumed." She turned to her friend. "Druscilla, I suggest that you and your daughter take off to the country. You are no longer welcome in Town."

"Oh, Katherine, is there nothing that I can say?" Lady Druthers whispered, begging.

"I know that it was not your idea, Druscilla. You are not that stupid. I do not envy you. I at least have decent level-headed children. You, on the other hand . . ." She turned to Aunt Sylvie and Charlotte. "Let's be off. There is little of interest to me here." And she swept out of the room in a blaze of justified anger.

"I have one more question for Constance." Charlotte turned back to the blubbering girl. "Did Mr. Frickerby say anything about having engaged in duels, or did he have any scars that you are aware of?"

She blushed crimson, her red-rimmed eyes darting to her mother. "How would I know any such things?"

"Just answer the question. Yes or no. It is important."

She replied vaguely, "He may have said something about a duel."

"And the scars?" Charlotte persisted.

Looking at her mother Constance whispered, "Yes."

"Thank you."

Once they were safely ensconced in the carriage, Sylvie asked, "What does Stuart Frickerby want with you?"

Charlotte grimaced angrily, her fisted hand clenching her reticule. "Oh, how Mr. Frickerby has been playing fast and loose with the various ladies. Mrs. Vane, Henrietta, Constance . . . oh no!" She turned to Sylvie and grabbed her arm. "Margaret fancies herself taken with the scoundrel. Sylvie, she would not listen to me. Maybe you can talk to her?"

"Certainly. She will hear from me immediately."

"Excellent. We will drop you off at Hanover Square. I want to go on to Pennington House and send James a message." She blushed and brushed at her skirts. "He should know what is happening here."

The matrons exchanged a telling glance.

The dowager gave her orders to the driver and subtly changed the topic, "That poor, foolish girl. What was she thinking?"

"My sense was that she was not thinking," replied Charlotte wryly. "That was why she was so easy to manipulate."

"Although I cannot condone them, at least I can understand Constance's motives, but what could Frickerby possibly gain by ruining your and James's reputations?" Aunt Sylvie asked.

Charlotte commented slowly, "There is more to this mystery than meets the eye. Let us leave it at that."

The ladies sat quietly. The muted sounds of the bustling streets were still loud, even in the enclosed cabin. Soon, the carriage slowed and stopped.

"Please send word, if you think that I should speak with Margaret myself," she requested worriedly as her aunt stood.

"I will send word regardless. Good-bye, my dear friends." Sylvie gave Charlotte a quick hug and then leaned over and kissed the dowager's cheek, apparently surprising them both.

After the door had slammed closed, Charlotte eyed the dowager.

The older lady glared. "So?"

She crossed her arms.

The matron huffed, "What is done is done. I have wasted thirty years on that row. I do not wish to discuss it further."

Charlotte smiled.

"Just know," she adjusted her skirts, "that I did not appreciate the things you said, and do not necessarily agree with all your charges."

"A wise lady once told me that good relationships are few and far between and that one must cherish those who care and foster the connection. If I remember the words correctly, she said something about work, concessions, and forgiveness."

She smiled haughtily. "A wise lady, indeed. I shall see that you follow that advice as well."

Charlotte's smile faded to a frown.

At White's, Mortimer was sitting up eagerly conferring with Lord Neberly, Sir Rickton, and Mr. Harraden. He leaned forward, his posture one of earnest appeal. "So, you see, gentlemen, for the sake of my father's friendship, I beg of you to stand by us during this difficult time."

"You say the thefts were from the War Office?" Mr. Harraden asked.

"Yes. Under my cousin James's branch. It was mere coincidence that the dukedom was in financial straits at the same time. You know how these investigations go. Superstition and conjecture, really. But we hope that for the sake of the family we can hold off the authorities. A terrible injustice can be avoided."

"Those investigations can be trying," commented Lord Neberly. "Nevertheless, where there is smoke . . ."

"You cannot believe that James had anything to do with

the thievery," cried Mortimer, his hand on his heart. A few heads turned in their direction at the commotion.

"No. No. Of course not."

"Of course not. One would never presume," Sir Rickton added, glad that he had not invested with James Morgan in the last venture overseas. Not that he had been invited to, of course.

"So glad we can count on you," Mortimer noted, all sincerity. "If you gentlemen will excuse me, I have an appointment with a lady at the Park."

"I did not know that you were courting," Lord Neberly commented. "Who is the lucky lady?"

He smiled mischievously. "I am not one to tell tales, gentlemen. *Adieu.*" He sauntered jerkily from the room, knowing that before he could step onto the pavement outside White's, the news would flash like wildfire around the club. Soon everyone would believe that James Morgan, Duke of Girard, was under the hatches and worse yet, the subject of a government investigation. The news would be greeted by some with disbelief, by others with confusion, and by still others with malicious glee. Mortimer was in the final category.

Chapter 32

As they entered Pennington House, Manton informed the ladies that James had come and gone and that Mr. Robert Jaspers, the Viscount Devane, was waiting for Charlotte in the garden.

"James is back?" Charlotte asked apprehensively, as she removed her pelisse. "If James is not here, I would speak with Collin."

"Mr. Collin did not return from the north with His Grace."

She frowned, concern gripping her. James rarely traveled without his man by his side. "Did His Grace say where he was headed?"

"No, my lady. He asked after you and then left, quite hurriedly, I might add." The usually stiff-back Manton was looking particularly stilted today, and a worried frown marred his habitually impassive features. Charlotte could only imagine the tongue-wagging going on belowstairs.

"The viscount is in the garden?" the dowager asked, surprised.

"He became tired of waiting in the drawing room and de-cided to 'stretch his legs,' he said," replied Manton, glower-ing disapprovingly. "He seems quite agitated."

"I had best see what he requires," Charlotte responded, as she headed toward the back gardens.

Stepping out the rear door, she spied Robert pacing along the walk. "Robert?"

He looked up at the sound of her voice and rushed to her, his arms outstretched. He grabbed her shoulders and squeezed, looking down at her upturned face. Deep lines of worry marred his usually handsome features and concern was reflected in his golden brown eyes.

"The most horrible rumors are circulating about Girard. They are saying that *he* stole the properties from the Crown to cover a mountainload of debt."

"Word certainly spreads quickly."

"So it is true?"

"About the thefts, stuff and nonsense. Stuart Frickerby is spreading tales. He is one of the scoundrels involved." It was too much to believe just yet about James's finances.

A deep resounding voice called from the house. "Char-lotte!"

She turned. James stood, angry and formidable in the doorway, his black coat wrinkled and his face unshaven. With his raven hair curling wildly about his head and the dark scowl on his handsome face, he looked more the en-dearing pirate than ever. Her heart leapt. He was safe; he was home. She had the overwhelming desire to race into his arms. For all her reservations, her fears, she could not imag-ine living a moment without him in her world. He flew down the few steps and grabbed Robert's hand, pulling it from her arm. "That is my betrothed you are manhandling," he charged fiercely.

Charlotte gasped, "Robert was doing no such thing!"

Robert stepped in front of her, his large bulk blocking her

from James. "You won't be marrying anyone if you are swinging from the gallows."

James's eyes narrowed and his chiseled face hardened. "I would be careful what slander you spread. I have no fear of meeting you on the field."

"It would be my privilege to kill the likes of you. You could at least have had the decency to break it off with Charlotte before the world learned of your misdeeds."

She stepped between the men, her hands pressing flat on Robert's broad chest. "Robert, please go inside. I wish to speak with James." It was like trying to push a mountain. "Robert, I *must* insist that you give us a moment."

"I am not leaving you alone with *him*."

"Lieutenant Freeman?" she called over her shoulder.

The lieutenant poked his head from the door. "Yes, my lady?"

"Robert, go inside. I will call you if I need you, and Lieutenant Freeman is right here."

He whispered, his eyes never leaving James's. "What good will that do you, Charlotte? The man is lame."

"He can certainly ride roughshod over you," James stated quietly, glaring.

"James, please contain yourself," she chided over her shoulder. She looked up at Robert. "I am fine, Robert. Please go inside. I will call you if I need you."

Robert glowered at James, his eyes never wavering. "Are you certain?"

"Absolutely."

Stiffly, he stepped back. "I will be within earshot."

Charlotte nodded and watched him walk inside. She turned to James. He looked so devilishly disheveled—dark, brooding, and masculine. Heat warmed her face and her palms grew damp. She opened her mouth to speak, but the moisture was gone from her mouth. She licked her lips, and eyeing him warily, asked, "Did you find the gold?"

"No." He expelled a gust of air. "Well, I don't know."

She looked up, confused.

"What I mean is that I set up the men and left Collin in charge."

"You did not stay to execute the search?"

"No."

Fear clutched at her gut. "Why not? What could possibly be so important as to call you back to Town?"

James squared his shoulders.

"I did not like leaving things the way they were here."

She crossed her arms, trying to understand and quell the rapid beating of her heart. "You mean, with your cousin?"

"Well, yes, with him—and with you."

Looking up, he caught her gaze. "With you. Things are too unsettled between us. I felt I needed to be here, with you."

Hope flared in her chest. She pushed it down; she could not trust this man. He did not care for her. Or did he? He came back for her, and left the gold, his long sought after treasure, to others. Hope, fear, and desperate longing clutched her heart. She shuddered and took a deep breath, clamping down on the hodgepodge of feelings threatening to overwhelm her. She turned away, stating quietly, "I have news to tell."

He blinked. "News?"

She faced him. "Frickerby is in league with your cousin. That is how Blanton knew what happened in Southbridge. He had someone on the inside." She clasped her hands tightly before her. "He is scandalmongering about you and he intended to humiliate me in the park."

"Humiliate you?" The muscle in his jaw clenched.

"Yes, Miss Druthers set it up, but we fouled the plan entirely. Me, your mother, and Sylvie Jaspers."

He shook his head as if to clear it. "You are all right?"

She would not look at him. "Fine."

He grabbed her hand and walked over to the bench, pulling her down beside him. He smelled of leather, horse, and male. Heat radiated off him, outstripping any chimney corner, and she had to withstand the urgent desire to warm herself in his flames. Tingles raced up her arm from the hand clutching hers; even through leather, his touch made her shiver.

Seemingly oblivious to the effect he had on her, he charged worriedly, "I have been frantically searching for you all over Town, and now that I've finally found you, you are here with Clark . . ."

"I am not *with* Robert," she countered, ignoring the deafening beat of her heart.

He went on as if she had not spoken, "—And blubbering about my mother."

She straightened, affronted. "I am *not blubbering*."

He clenched and unclenched his fisted hand on his thigh. "Please just explain to me what you and Clark were doing."

She took a deep breath and forced herself to address the facts at hand. "Robert and I were not *doing anything*. He came here today because he was concerned that you were the mastermind behind the thefts at the War Office. He feared for me. That is all." Charlotte grabbed his hand. "Stop doing that." She squeezed. "Did you not hear what I said? Frickerby is in league with your cousin. He and Miss Druthers tried to draw me into a trap with some nonsense about your character. Your mother, Aunt Sylvie, and I confronted the girl, and she confessed all. That was after your mother apologized to Aunt Sylvie, of course, and they are now reunited. Anyway, Frickerby fits to a tee the description of Mrs. Vane's seducer, and someone is spreading vile rumors about your financial circumstances and claiming that you masterminded the thefts at the War Office."

He looked up. "My mother apologized?"

She chuckled and pushed her favorite black curl from his forehead. She could not help herself. "Yes, I suppose to you that is the most unbelievable thing of all."

He froze.

She quickly removed her hand. "I, I apologize. I do not know what came over me." She stood awkwardly and stepped away.

He pushed himself off the bench, grabbed her shoulders, and spun her around. Hunger gleamed in his blue-black eyes. His lips claimed hers with crushing ferocity. Her senses thrilled with joy at the contact and at being enveloped in his strong arms. She threw her doubts to the wind. This was James. This was right; she knew it to the core of her being.

His rough face scratched her lips and cheeks, but she did not care as he kissed her deeply, longingly, with his open mouth. She wallowed in his passion, in his need, and in her own yearning for more of him. She wrapped her arms about his shoulders, pulling him closer, pressing against him, her breasts crushing against his chest. Heat infused every part of her skin. Fire coursed through her veins. She wanted him more than she had wanted anything in her whole life.

"James! James!" a female voice called from the doorway.

He blinked. He pulled his head up, holding her tightly in his strong arms. "Not now, Elizabeth."

Embarrassed, Charlotte tried to pull away, but he would not let her go.

"Your man Collin is back, and he found something."

He licked his lips; his eyes smoldered with fiery passion. Her face reddened, and she buried her head in his shoulder, praying that either she or Elizabeth would just disappear. She preferred it be Elizabeth.

"Well, are you coming in or not? We are all waiting for you to open the thing."

Over his shoulder, Charlotte watched as Elizabeth threw

her hands in the air. "You can kiss Charlotte later. You have your whole lives to kiss each other, but the chest is waiting, and so are we."

He slowly loosened his arms from around her.

Looking anywhere but at him, she shifted away. "We should go inside and see what Collin has brought back."

He lifted her chin with his fingers, forcing her to meet his gaze. She felt as if she could drown in the pools of his dark compelling eyes. "I don't want to go anywhere until you tell me that you will marry me. I do want to be able to kiss you for the rest of my life, Charlotte. Marry me."

Tears suddenly formed in her eyes. She spoke in barely a whisper, "I do not know, James. I just do not know."

He frowned. "Later, then."

He grabbed her hand and kissed it quickly, then tucked it into the crook of his arm. Together, they went inside.

A massive wooden sea chest bracketed with steel around the edges sat on top of James's large desk, dwarfing everything else in the room. The dowager and Elizabeth hovered nearby as James and Charlotte walked in with Lieutenant Freeman and Robert following close behind.

"Finally, James." The dowager turned to her son, waving her finger at Collin. "Your man brought in this monstrosity and will not tell us what it is or what is in it."

He nodded to Collin. "In the third cave?"

"Exactly where you said it would be, your grace."

"You have men posted outside?"

"Kent and Newson in front, Newbury and Warren out back. Jimmy and Richie are watching the side streets for warning."

James nodded. "Good."

"I am summoning the authorities," Robert declared. He turned to leave, but Lieutenant Freeman blocked him with his crutch. "How about finding out the facts before making a fool of yourself?"

He frowned and opened his mouth, but Charlotte moved next to him and rested her hand on his arm. "Robert. Trust me. James is not the villain in this piece. It will do no one any good except the true scoundrel if you summon the authorities too soon." He hesitated and then reluctantly nodded assent.

"What is in it, James?" the dowager demanded.

He ignored her and examined the intricate lock. "Do any of those keys work?"

Collin shook his head. "We were not able to open the bloo . . ." He cleared his throat. "Thing. So we brought it back for you."

Elizabeth jumped up and down. "What is inside?"

James looked at her, frowning. He had not wanted to have his sister involved in any of this dirty affair.

As if reading his mind, Charlotte walked to his side and prodded quietly, "She will likely hear the nasty rumors soon enough. Let her at least have the information with which to withstand the mudslinging."

He nodded and turned to his sister. "Elizabeth, if I can manage to find the key to open this chest, then I expect it to be filled with gold. Gold stolen from His Majesty's government." He glared at Robert. "Which I will place back in the Treasury where it belongs."

"How exciting!" Elizabeth raved, waving her hands. "Open it so I can see!"

"How are we supposed to know that it was not you who stole it in the first instance?" Robert charged.

He answered with indulgent patience, "If I stole it, why would I have been searching for it?"

"Devil take it!" Robert spat back, shaking his fist at James. "Who can know the goings on of you and your dastardly co-conspirators?"

"Will the two of you, please . . ."

A joyful shriek resounded from the desk and all eyes turned to see Elizabeth standing before the chest, her hand inserting a key in the lock.

"What the . . ." Collin stood with his mouth agape. "But we tried every blooming key on that thing!"

She grinned gleefully. "It was not one of the keys. It was like a puzzle of sorts, using . . ." She turned her hand in the lock and a loud *click* resonated through the quiet room. ". . . all of them!"

A hush of anticipation gripped the group. As one, they held their breath, everyone edging closer to see inside. Elizabeth unhooked the latch and lifted the heavy lid with both hands. "Dear heavens, this is heavy."

"Charlotte!" Edward came tearing into the room. "James! Robert, dear heavens! Someone has kidnapped Margaret!"

Chapter 33

The gold glittered brightly, blindingly, but all Charlotte could see was the image of her sister when she was barely out of the nursery. She had been a baby-faced, butter-toothed child; even then she looked like a girlish doll. Charlotte remembered clearly: she had fallen and skinned her knee and was crying pitifully and calling for her mama. Charlotte recalled the feel of her doughy little body racking with hysterical sobs and the echoing hiccups that followed. It was too much. "No," Charlotte whispered.

Edward held up the note with a shaky hand. "It says that Charlotte must give up the gold." His eyes were filled with fear and panic. "How can we give up something we do not have?"

"Who would do such a thing?" Robert asked, aghast.

James looked at Charlotte, pain etching his handsome features into a mask of anguish. "I am so sorry."

Edward looked up. "Is this your doing, Girard? Tell me!"

"No," Charlotte replied quietly, her eyes never leaving James's midnight blue ones. "It is not."

"Who is behind this treachery?" the dowager demanded. "We must deal with these scoundrels at once!"

Charlotte turned to Lieutenant Freeman. "Please, close the door." He shut the door and leaned warily against the wood grain, placing himself in front of the entry.

James rubbed his hand over his unshaven face. "I wanted this to be taken care of quietly. I, I did not want anyone else hurt, particularly not my family." He ran his hand over his eyes. "But because of my pride, my desire to salve off acrimony, Charlotte has suffered and Margaret may be . . ."

Seeing his pain tore at Charlotte's heart. Mortimer had been plaguing her family long before she met James, and she hated to see him shouldering all the blame for his cousin's villainy. She shook her head. "You can take blame for many things, James, but not for kidnapping my sister. We will get Margaret back, and then . . ." Bright hatred coursed through her being. She fisted her hands to stop them from shaking. "I want that bloody bastard to pay."

"What bast . . . I mean *who*?" the dowager demanded, flinging her arms in the air with frustration.

"Mortimer," James stated quietly.

"Who?" Robert asked.

"Mortimer Blanton," Edward echoed quietly. "The swigging dog."

"M . . . Mortimer?" the dowager raised her hand to her heart. "*Richard's* Mortimer?"

Grimacing, James nodded.

Charlotte charged bitterly, "He orchestrated the thefts at the War Office and is trying to set the blame on James. That"—she pointed at the sea chest—"is the fruit of those thefts. It was apparently intended for Mortimer Blanton's pockets, I am sure, and for Napoleon in Elba."

The dowager sat down heavily on the sofa, her eyes wide with shock. "Thievery, kidnapping? Richard's Mortimer?"

James squat down beside his mother and took her hand. "I was praying you would never find out."

She pressed her hand to her mouth, aghast. "Are you certain?"

He looked down at her hand in his and said quietly, "I was hoping no one would find out."

"A mountain of treasure, and now we have our troll," Elizabeth said quietly. All eyes turned toward the massive chest laden with gold on the desktop. "I have always despised Mortimer; he terrorized me since I was a child."

"Sheffield, what exactly does the demand letter say?" Lieutenant Freeman asked, leaning forward on his crutch.

Edward opened the paper with shaking hands. He read it aloud.

Charlotte will be at the pier at Longston Street on the Thames tonight at midnight, alone, with the gold. If anyone is seen with her or tries to interfere, then little Miss Margaret will wish she were dead.

Elizabeth shuddered. The dowager hung her head.

"Is he serious?" Robert asked.

Still crouching beside his mother, James stated grimly, "I wish that I could say otherwise."

"We will trap him. When we give him the gold, we will have witnesses, the magistrate. We can do it." Edward looked up hopefully. "Can't we?"

"If anyone interferes, he will hurt her," Charlotte stated. "I will not let that happen."

"But you will allow him to hurt you instead?" James demanded harshly.

"If necessary."

He shook his head. "I will not have it. I will not have you in his power. He is a madman. You said yourself that you fear him."

She pursed her lips. "I will do whatever is necessary to save my sister."

He stood. "I will not allow you to place yourself in jeopardy."

"You have little choice in the matter." She crossed her arms.

They stood glaring stubbornly, angry not with each other, but with the madman pulling the puppet strings.

"There may be another way," Lieutenant Freeman spoke quietly from the door.

James tore his gaze from Charlotte. "There must be."

The lieutenant leaned forward on his crutch. "It still is risky. And Charlotte will have to play a big part, but if I were a betting man, I'd lay my last farthing on Miss Charlotte."

"We are listening," Charlotte encouraged him, hugging her arms protectively about herself as she tried to stifle the frightful images of Margaret at Mortimer's mercy. "Whatever is necessary, so long as Margaret is safe."

"Well, it's a bit inventive, but I always say, feint, throw them off the scent. And when they least expect it, hit them hard!" And the good lieutenant proceeded to sketch out an idea so diabolical, they all agreed, although risky, it might actually work.

Chapter 34

E ven the darkness seemed cloaked in shadow as Charlotte heard the bells toll quarter past midnight while she waited at the pier on Longston Street. It seemed like ages ago since the men had dropped her off at the dock per Mortimer's instructions.

The waves lapped loudly against the wooden slates, echoing hauntingly in the gloom. The moon was shrouded by dark rolling clouds and the air smelled of storm. Despite the damp, she shivered and shifted her long woolen cloak tighter around her shoulders as she glanced down at the chest at her feet. She needed to be alert, prepared for any mishap. She had to get Margaret back. She just had to.

She squinted in the darkness, but the lantern beside her feet gave poor illumination to anything beyond three steps. This was a neighborhood she would not likely enter in broad daylight for fear of the seedier elements. She could hear stray dogs fighting and intermittently, drunken shouting and glass breaking. Her skin prickled with awareness that she was being watched. The rats were not her only companions along the river Thames that night.

It began to drizzle lightly. She licked her dry lips nervous-ly, tasting the moist air, and wrinkled her nose. The whole area smelled of refuse and human waste.

Finally, she heard the upsurge in the waves lapping to-ward the pier. A boat. She did not know whether she was relieved or frightened that the deadly game was finally en-gaged.

She watched as three men slipped from the shadows on the pier to greet the craft bouncing lazily in the water. One of the men from ashore called a gruff welcome and a line was thrown. The boat was secured and a cloaked figure alighted and conferred with the three men on shore. Charlotte did not move. She barely breathed, her heartbeat racing.

She took a deep breath and forced her body to relax, her mind to sharpen. She pressed her legs together, feeling the knife secured to her calf. James's knife. James's sheath. He was nearby. The prospect simultaneously comforted and alarmed her; he could be hurt or killed. She pushed away the reflection; the strategy was engaged and he would not want anything to lessen her resolve.

The cloaked figure walked toward her in the gloom. She could not make out his features but recognized the sensation she felt when Mortimer was near.

"Hello, my dear." His sharp white teeth gleamed in the darkness. "I am so pleased that you understood the gravity of the situation." He reached out to take her hand as if they were meeting at a party or a ball.

The man was truly round the bend. Charlotte wrapped her cloak more tightly around her body and drew herself up. "Where is Margaret?"

"All in due time, my dear. You did not think that I came only for the gold, did you?" He raised his eyebrow dramatically. "No. Of course not. You know I came for you as well. If you cooperate with me, then I will free your sister unharmed."

"She had best be unharmed or you will have hell to pay."

Mortimer's laugh was a grating high-pitched whine. "Just like you to be delivering threats when I hold all the cards." His face suddenly turned hard, malicious. "You are in no position to threaten anything. You are mine. It is better that you understand from the first." He turned and jerked his hand impatiently. "You, Jackson, you and your friends pick up this chest and put it in the boat." The three large and brutish men standing there turned and walked toward the chest.

She stepped in front of it as if to protect it. "You said I would get my sister back if I brought you the gold."

"Shhh!" Mortimer grabbed her arm roughly and hissed, "Would you like to have your throat cut?" Charlotte spun out of his grasp and watched the men warily. She could not make out their faces, but could smell the sour odors of sweat, grime, and unwashed bodies. They were ruffians, paid hands that Mortimer did not believe he could control. Her heart fluttered as the men lifted the heavy chest, carried it easily over to the boat, then handed it down. After a moment, they returned to Mortimer.

Stepping nearer, she watched as money changed hands. Apparently, Mortimer gave them more than they'd originally agreed upon.

"A bonus," he commented. The three men moved off, satisfied.

"Ladies first." Mortimer waved his hand and moved stiltedly toward the boat. Charlotte did not see many options before her but to follow the chest and wait for a lucky break. She walked guardedly toward the boat. Mortimer moved awkwardly to hand her down.

She shied away, deriding harshly, "I do not need your assistance." Leaning on one of the tall poles along the pier, she clutched her skirts and maneuvered herself down into the craft. The boat was stark. There was nowhere to sit, little equipment to speak of. A large brute of a man stood at the wheel, watching the happenings closely. He had a sidearm tucked into his belt and a knife in a scabbard at his waist. His square face was cold and impassive, like a block of granite.

Stuart Frickerby lowered his head while exiting the cabin. "What? She is not coming with us!"

"Clamp it, Frickerby."

"And who is he?" Frickerby pointed to the small, shrouded figure huddled at the edge of the pier. The little man visibly quaked at the reference. He nervously took a small flask from his cloak and swigged it, licking his lips.

Mortimer jumped inelegantly into the boat. "Mind your own business, Frickerby. I give the orders here, and I am telling you to keep your mouth shut! Jacques, get us out of here."

Jacques nodded, helped the little man aboard and untied the lines. Charlotte hid her distaste; the little man reeked of cheap spirits and onions.

Jacques used a long stick to push off from the pier.

Charlotte's stomach sank as she watched the land quickly move out of reach and disappear into the gloom as the boat bounced and drifted into the flowing river.

Stomping boot steps could be heard on the pier. Pistols were cocked and men grumbled.

"Where are they?" a man shouted.

"Where did they go?" A deep, cultured voice demanded, "Someone, get me a boat!"

Mortimer smiled wickedly. "Your duff-brained lover is a fool, Charlotte." He stroked his eyebrows lovingly. "The beastly mongrel." He jerked his hand and ordered, "Inside! All of you!" He nodded to Jacques.

Frickerby grumbled, but complied. Charlotte went quietly, hugging her black cloak closely around her. The nervous little man shuffled behind.

The cabin was completely barren except for the chest that sat in the center of the small space. A lamp hung on the wall, sending ghostly shadows dancing as the boat rocked and swayed.

"Give me the key," Mortimer demanded sharply.

She hesitated a moment and then reached into her cloak and threw it to him.

He grabbed for it but missed. "No games, you foolish girl, or your sister will suffer the consequences." He lifted the intricate keys off the wooden floor. "What the devil . . ." He walked over to the lamp and held up the complicated keys. "What kind of trick is this? Your sister's death will be on your hands because of your stupidity!"

"It is a trick, but not mine. Edgerton must have fashioned the key. It is a puzzle. I can show you how to use it. But first I want to see Margaret."

"Your sister is not here," Frickerby sneered. "She is indisposed." He turned to Mortimer. "I cannot understand why you took her with us. It is enough that we will have to switch crafts and cross the channel without having her to contend with. And I demand to know who *he* is." He pointed to the little man. "I will not be sharing my cut with anyone else."

"Ahem," the little man muttered nervously. "Father Whittney, at yer service. Rest assur'd I do not expect to cut or be cut anything."

"Shut up!" Mortimer lashed out, and the nervous little priest cowered back into the corner. Mortimer turned on Frickerby. "I am losing my patience with you. You will get exactly what you deserve. I will hear no more complaining or I will toss you overboard!"

Charlotte meanwhile had moved away from the men to

stand behind the chest. "So, Mr. Frickerby, he has not told you about the diamonds, then?"

"Shut up!" Mortimer hissed. "It has nothing to do with him."

Frickerby turned to him angrily. "What diamonds?"

"Why, the ones he will get when he marries me." She waved her hand toward the priest as she stepped farther from the men. "Thus the need for the priest. My dowry is diamonds. I own diamond mines, quite a number of them." She turned to Mortimer and shook her head dramatically. "Mortimer, how neglectful of you not to tell your partner. He *is* your partner, is he not?"

Frickerby's pale face flushed an angry red and his nose shone in the dim light as he puffed in outrage. "Diamonds? What about her sister? I never would have left her with my sister if she was worth anything. You were going to keep them for yourself! After everything I have done for you!"

"Done for *us*, you fool!" Mortimer jeered, his face distorting into a mad mask, an unholy light gleaming in his ghostly eyes. "And Napoleon, of course. You forget yourself, Frickerby. I am the one who brought you in and made you part of this glory. You will be a very rich man because of me." He stepped close and jammed his finger into Frickerby's chest. "You were a worthless country gentleman with no prospects and not even spit to your name when I met you. You were nothing. Now everything that you are is because of me. Do not tell me about what you have done for me!"

He swatted away Mortimer's hand angrily. "Worthless? How dare you!"

"I dare because I can!" Mortimer shouted mercilessly, spittle flying from his lips.

Shaking with rage, he stepped back, reached into his coat, and pulled out a revolver. He pointed it at Mortimer.

"You fool! Put that thing away," Mortimer demanded. Charlotte caught her breath. The moment suspended as

Frickerby stood there challenging his mentor. Shaking, his pistol wavering in his hand, he nervously wiped the sweat from his forehead. "I can have it all. I can take it all from you."

"You do not have the backbone," Mortimer jeered callously. Resolve lit Frickerby's features and his hand steadied. Suddenly, Mortimer whipped a knife from inside his coat and flung it, catching Frickerby full in the chest. Frickerby's shot was deafening as his gun discharged.

She jumped behind the sea chest, her ears ringing and the smoky odor of gunpowder filling her nostrils. The smoke cleared and peeking above the chest, she saw Frickerby's body flat on the floor, his hand clutching the knife protruding from his chest. Blood poured from his mouth as he gurgled and jerked, struggling to breathe. Mortimer kicked at Frickerby's struggling form. "I made you, I broke you! You are nothing!"

The priest whimpered from the corner where he had crawled. He sat hugging his knees, trembling. He was not going to be of any help.

Mortimer turned to Charlotte, holding out the keys. "Now, open that chest!"

She stood slowly, widening her stance to maintain her balance on the rolling boat. "Toss it."

He threw the key lightly to her. "Open it now."

She caught the key and walking around the chest, crouched before it. Outwardly calm and inwardly quaking, she asked in a matter-of-fact voice, "Now that Frickerby is no longer with us, are you actually going to take the gold to Napoleon, or just share with the man outside?"

He eyed her warily. "Some of the gold will go to Napoleon. There is my commission, of course. My now much larger commission."

She looked up at him, meeting that ghoulish gaze. "Tell me, Mortimer. Why did you do it? For the cause?"

He laughed, a harsh, bitter sound. "The only cause that drives me is the cause for Mortimer Blanton. In France, I will be a hero. I will be rich and powerful. Moreover, the ultimate delight for me is having that great fortune and prestige come at the expense of my mongrel cousin. Who," he playfully drummed his fingers on his cravat, smiling with wicked delight, "by all accounts, is now a desperately ruined thieving blackguard. It was one of my greatest pleasures in life to steal right from under his high and mighty nose. He is too trusting by far, believing in his men. Edgerton was the easiest of prey. He was just waiting for the right hunter. If only the fool had not had a fit of conscience. I blame it on that wife of his." He frowned with annoyance, as if realizing that he was rambling. "Hurry up, will you!" Charlotte fashioned the key into the proper shape and inserted it into the lock. She turned it and there was an audible *click*. She hesitated.

"Open it!" he barked.

She removed the latch and placed her hands on the lid. She pressed against it. "It is too heavy for me. I cannot do it."

"Move aside!" He pushed her away. Her gloved palms and gown-covered knees scraped across the hard wooden floor, saving her fall. She looked over her shoulder and watched anxiously as he placed his palms on the lid and heaved.

"What the . . . ?"

The top of the chest flew open and James jumped out, his hands reaching for Mortimer's throat. James's face was set in hard lines and sharp planes, fierce, determined, and angry as an inferno of wrath. As he throttled his cousin, through the linen of his shirt, the muscles of his arms stretched and knotted. Mortimer clawed at James, desperately trying to rip himself free.

"I will kill the sister," he shrieked hoarsely as he scratched and clawed at James's face.

"Not if I kill you first," James ground out.

Mortimer suddenly pulled a knife and slashed at James's chest. James jumped back, releasing Mortimer barely in time to avoid a death thrust. The knife had ripped through James's white shirt, exposing the olive flesh now stained red.

"James!" she cried out in horror as the blood oozed through the gash on his chest.

Mortimer slashed and cut wildly, viciously honing in.

"It's nothing! Get outside!" James yelled, pulling a knife from his boot and a pistol from his waistband. Charlotte stepped out of the way of the battling men in the small cabin, unable to reach the door. James cocked the firearm and aimed, but Mortimer jumped him, knocking the weapon from his grip and slashing the knife across his hand. The pistol slid noisily across the slanted cabin floor.

James's knuckles showed white as he gripped his knife. Resolution and hatred lit his dark eyes. The men circled each other cagily, balancing carefully as the boat rocked and swayed.

Mortimer whispered, "You are a fool." Abruptly he lunged at Charlotte and held the knife to her throat. "*Now* try your little games!"

James froze, his face paling, his jaw clenched in frustration and fear. He spoke softly, dangerously quiet, "*If you so much as harm a hair on her head . . .*"

Without warning the boat lurched violently, barreling Charlotte against Mortimer. She used the momentum to ram her back into his stomach and then, turning, swiped her elbow up under his chin. He released her, staggering back against the cabin wall.

She darted to the other side of the compartment beside James, her breast heaving from the effort. She leaned down and whipped out the knife from her boot, holding it skillfully, ready to strike. "Where is Margaret?" she demanded.

Again the boat pitched and then crashed into something hard across the bow, jolting them all. James grabbed Charlotte's hand to steady her, his eyes never leaving his prey. She felt a surge of confidence at his touch. James was with her; this could not end badly. A loud creaking sound reverberated in the tiny cabin. The bow cracked open a hand span and water began pouring into the small compartment.

Without taking his eyes off his cousin, James commanded, "Charlotte, go outside. See what is happening and call the others."

Watching Mortimer kill Frickerby had left her fearful for the man who had become so precious to her. She stood paralyzed.

He squeezed her hand. "I need you to call the others. Go, Charlotte!"

Pushing aside her misgivings, she turned and ran out into the now pouring rain. Jacques was hunched over the helm, unmoving. Stepping tentatively toward him, she poked him in the shoulder and pushed. His limp body fell to the floor of the boat and rolled over. A gaping hole marked where his left eye had been.

She covered her mouth, sickened.

"Frickerby's shot," she whispered to the black air.

Again the boat pitched and crashed. With her gloves, she swiped the rain from her eyes. She ran to the edge of the craft, and leaning out, looked toward the bow. The wind whipped her hood back and rain washed her face. Through the murky gloom she could see that the boat had run into the foundations of a bridge and the lapping water kept driving the craft into the stone wall again and again.

A gunshot roared on the far bank. Charlotte pulled the tiny pistol from her coat pocket, an undersized thing that Lieutenant Freeman said was more noise and smoke than accuracy. She raised it and fired. The odor of gunpowder filled her nostrils, overwhelming the stench of the grimy waters. She waited breathlessly and braced herself as the boat slammed into the stone wall once again.

"Charlotte!" She looked up into the dark rain, searching for the source of Edward's voice. "Charlotte!" She spotted him hanging over the top of the bridge.

She beckoned, yelling, "The boat is sinking!"

His head disappeared and returned a moment later. Robert was by his side and they began lowering a rope. "Take the rope! We will pull you up!"

"I must get James!" She turned to find the priest hovering behind her. She pushed the rope at him and yelled, "Go," then ran back into the cabin. James was pounding at his cousin's head, fists hammering. The water lapped about their calves as Mortimer fought back wildly, kicking and screaming. The knives were gone. Blood soaked James's torn shirt and his hand was covered with blood.

"James! The boat is sinking! We must go!"

He could not hear her through the wall of his rage. He smashed his fist into Mortimer's face as the boat pitched and crashed again. He used the force of the collision to slam his cousin's head into the wall of the cabin. Mortimer's eyes rolled back to the whites and he sank down, chest deep in water. She grabbed James's shoulder. He looked up, bloodied fist raised to confront another.

She shouted, "The boat is sinking! We must get off!" The craft heaved once again and crashed, throwing them off balance. James grabbed her shoulders and steadied her. The gash in the bow creaked open wider, now elbow-length. Water poured through the gap; the scent of refuse plagued the mucky waters.

James coiled his arm about her waist and pulled her with him toward the doorway. The boat pitched precariously and they had to fight the current and her dragging skirts. Her woolen cloak weighed heavily on her shoulders, but she was unwilling to cast it off; it was some protection against the rain.

Through the downpour, they saw two ropes and lanterns

hanging down from the bridge. Robert hung over the side, holding one of the lines. James seized the cord and roughly tied it around her waist. He stepped back and lifted her in the air, shouting, "Heave now!" She rested her hands on his broad shoulders, feeling the strong force of him against her chest.

The cord around her waist went taut, jerking her upward, but she clutched his shoulders. "You are coming too!"

He looked back at the cabin and Charlotte squeezed hard. "You are coming with me, James Morgan, or I will kill you myself!"

He held her close, unmoving, torn and indecisive, like a bear reluctant to leave his dinner. Fear bubbled in her chest; if he chose vengeance over her, lord help him, she *would* throttle him. She pressed her nose up close to his and stared him eye to eye. "I signed on for your wedding, James, not your funeral!"

She must have gotten through, for his eyes widened and cleared.

"I am with you," he said, just as she was lifted out of his arms.

She nodded grimly as she was lugged up the side of the bridge. He had better be.

He grabbed the second rope and wrapped it around his arm, using his legs to climb the stone-faced foundation as the men above heaved him up.

The ascent was painstakingly slow as the rain and wind pounded. Charlotte spun on the line and banged into the stone, scratching her face and bruising her wrist. She wondered if this was what a sack of grain felt like on a cold, rainy night right before it was slashed open and tossed to the chickens. She suppressed a burst of hysterical laughter, realizing that her nerves were frayed near end.

Suddenly Mortimer emerged shakily from the cabin, brandishing a pistol in his jerking hand. "James Morgan! You bloody spawn of the devil!" He swung the weapon wildly, aiming high.

She looked up to the rim of the bridge barely steps away, and saw Collin wielding a firearm over the side and aiming it down.

Dear God in heaven, this could not end well.

Two explosions erupted in quick succession, the loud booms piercing her already frazzled senses into a million pieces. Time suspended as she looked over at James and saw him screaming, frantically reaching for her, horror distorting his handsome face. The rope around her waist went slack and she dropped, floating free for one perilous moment, her long cloak hovering around her like black wings of death. Then she crashed down, hard, slamming into something jarringly solid.

Arms and legs entangled and her cloak and skirts tripped her legs as she and Mortimer submerged into the cold dark waters, each struggling to break free. Air vanished to be replaced by terrorizing blackness and rancid fear. The waters overwhelmed her.

She kicked and lashed, hammering at Mortimer's bony body, desperate to be released from the deadly tangle. The clasp of her cloak ripped at her throat, making the burning in her lungs all the more excruciating. She thrust Mortimer away, finally free, and desperately tugged at the clasp of the garment that was dragging her deeper under the murderous waters. But between the sodden leather of her gloves and her injured wrist, she could not manage the fastening. Frantically struggling to ascend, to her horror she continued to sink, slowly pulled downward in the dark depths.

In the murky dimness, hands clutched at her, yanking her near. Mortimer seized her throat. Dear God, he could not wait for the waters to finish the dastardly job. She lashed out but was perilously weak. His hand twisted at her neck while the other grasped her waist. Suddenly her weighty cloak fell away and he thrust her upward with a mighty shove. She almost flew aloft, quickly rising through the water with newfound buoyancy.

She broke the surface with a powerful wheeze, sucking in gulps of air. Her lungs burned and she felt sodden to the core, but blessed relief swelled in her chest, making tears pool in her already sopping eyes.

James swam just paces away, lashing his arms to reach her.

"Charlotte!" He grabbed her and lifted her in the water, helping her to float. She clutched at him, desperately happy he was all right. Despite the lapping water, she pressed her face to his soaked shirt, tasting the salty water mixed with her tears.

"Come," he urged gently, turning them toward the bridge.

She swallowed. "Mortimer?"

"Don't worry, he won't recover; Collin hit him in the chest."

Clarity sank in; Mortimer had used the last moments of his life to save her. Violent trembles shook her body and her teeth clattered noisily. "We must get you out of this freezing water," James insisted, tugging her toward the bridge. She wanted to help but could barely muster the strength to paddle along. The boat crashed into the stone foundations and a loud crack resounded, the craft crying a final salute as it sank below the murky depths to a watery grave.

Between James and the men above, Charlotte was maneuvered to safe ground. Warm blankets were swept around her drenched body.

"James?" Her teeth chattered.

Edward handed her a flask. "Coming over the edge now. Drink, Charlotte." His familiar face was lined with worry and strain. She gulped the liquid and it burned the whole way down. She sputtered and gasped, but warmth spread from her chest outward in welcome relief. She swigged another mouthful and shivered. Thank heaven at least the rain had stopped.

James slumped beside her. Pushing away the blanket someone thrust at him, he wrapped his arms around her. Edward took the flask from Charlotte and threw a blanket over James's shoulders, cloaking them both.

She pressed her hand on his chest and burrowed her face into his neck, blessedly thankful and relieved. She drank in the feel of him, the warmth of his flesh and blood. She breathed in the salty musky taste of him. The sounds of people walking, horses moving, carriage wheels rumbling all faded to the background as they held each other reverently, cherishing each other.

Slowly he pulled away from her and looked down at her upturned face. His lip was swollen, his eye blackened, and his nose bloodied. He had never looked dearer. He pushed her sodden hair away and looked into her eyes, lovingly, desperately. What she saw in them took her breath away. She raised her hand to his cheek, tracing the lines of tears. James's tears.

"I couldn't lose you," he choked.

"I am here," she whispered, stroking his face.

"I never would have forgiven myself." His body trembled. "If I had lost you in my daft quest—"

"Shhh," she whispered. "We are safe."

He pulled her close and pressed his lips to her hair. "It is almost over. This horrid nightmare is almost over." After a long moment, he insisted, "Look at me, Charlotte."

Slowly she raised her eyes.

"We will find her. *I promise you, we will find Margaret.*"

She merely nodded, focusing on the beating of the heart beneath her hand. Maybe if she pressed down hard enough her own heart would stop breaking.

"He saved me, James," she whispered.

His arms tensed around her.

She licked her lips and stared off into nothing, searching for answers she would not find. "I was drowning, my cloak was weighing me down . . ." The horror replayed in her mind. She shivered but pressed on, "I, I thought he was trying to kill me, but he saved me . . ."

"I cannot fathom Mortimer's having a valiant bone in his body, but perhaps at his end, he finally did something decent. Hell, not decent; bloody well splendid!" He squeezed her so tight she thought she might choke, but she did not protest. It felt too good.

He relaxed his hold and kissed her forehead, shaking his head disbelievingly. "Leave it to Mortimer to make me owe him a debt from the grave."

"I do not know about a debt, James; we would not be in this mess if it were not for him."

"Exactly. If it were not for him, I never would have kidnapped you and forced you into an engagement. I owe the man more than he could know." He swept her sodden hair from her neck and kissed her ear.

She wiped a tear from her eye. "Dear Lord, I never thought about it that way."

Edward hovered close. "I'm off to take Robert to the hospital. He would not go until you both were safe."

Anguish swept over her. "What happened to Robert?"

"Mortimer shot him, remember?"

"Dear lord," she whispered. "That was why I fell."

"Don't think he's not whipping himself about dropping you," Edward added.

"He is the one who got shot!"

"Do not worry, Charlotte; Lieutenant Freeman assures us that Robert was only grazed by the bullet and that it did not lodge."

But her training at the hospital and her need to do something kicked in. She gently unwound herself from James's arms and pushed up on legs that were as wobbly as jelly.

She would have fallen, but James caught her in his strong arms. "You, my dear, are going home to a hot bath and a warm bed."

"Margaret . . ." she murmured, her voice trailing off.

In response to the unspoken question James shook his head at Edward. "Go on, Edward, and send us word as soon as you are able. We will regroup at Pennington House."

A scowl marring his features, her brother trotted off to the waiting carriage.

She pushed James gently away. "Let me at least check your injuries."

"I am fine."

Ignoring him, she yanked off her sodden gloves and ripped open his shirt.

"Thank heavens," she breathed. It was a flesh wound. In the dim lantern light she pulled a soaking kerchief from her pocket and pressed it against the gash.

He lay his bloody hand over hers, whispering harshly, "Charlotte."

"Hold this down hard. Keep the pressure on to stop the bleeding." With a critical eye, she cleared the blood from his injured hand and examined it. Nothing serious at all; unlike the chest wound, it did not even require stitching. She trembled with relief.

"I need you more than I need this bloody handkerchief," he mumbled, enveloping her in his arms. "Come, let's go home."

Without warning, she burst into tears, bawling shamelessly into his broad shoulder. At least her frayed nerves had waited until now to erupt. She hiccupped, sobbing appallingly.

"We will find her, Charlotte. Frickerby said something

about leaving her with his sister. I promise you, we will find her." He hugged her close.

She sniffed, inhaling a shaky breath. "I am beginning to believe that you can do anything, James."

He gently wiped away her tears with his fingertips. "With you by my side I cannot fail, Charlotte."

Arm in arm, they staggered wearily toward the carriage, toward home.

Chapter 35

Hours later, they found Margaret tied up at Francesca Frickerby's boardinghouse, shaken and bruised, but none the worse for wear. Following many tears and recriminations, Edward took Margaret home, while James and Charlotte returned to Pennington House.

Charlotte's friend from the veterans' hospital, Dr. Marcus, was waiting to tell them about Robert and to see if he could be of any service. After stitching James's wound and cleaning him up, the good doctor wrapped Charlotte's wrist and washed out the scratches on her face. Aunt Sylvie and the dowager blessedly took charge of everything else.

Charlotte went through all this as if she were looking through a long glass tunnel. Everything seemed surreal. She knew what she was doing and all she was saying, but it seemed . . . off. Finally, snug in her bed, she sighed as Aunt Sylvie wrapped the covers around her and kissed her on her head. "Sleep now, darling. You certainly deserve it after all you've have been through."

She leaned back in the pillows but found it hard to rest her head, as her neck muscles were pulled so taut. Her body was like a whipcord, tense and wound. Everything hurt and she was afraid that if she finally let go, finally relaxed, she would just fall apart as she had for a few awful moments on the bridge. There, at least, she had James's broad shoulder to cry on.

For a moment Aunt Sylvie watched her trying to find a good position with her arm resting on the raised pillows beside her. Then she walked out the door with a frown.

Charlotte lay there listening to the sounds of the busy household. Servants stepped stridently about, murmured conversations buzzed down hallways. It was the middle of the day and everyone was hectic with his or her duties. Each sound jarred her and her skin prickled as if a knife stuck just below the surface.

The door opened and she started. Aunt Sylvie poked her head inside. "Charlotte, I was afraid you might not be sleeping. The general wanted to be certain you are all right. I assured him you were, but he wishes to see you with his own eyes."

"Of course." She scooted up and pulled the covers about her. Her aunt nodded, waved for him to come, then stepped inside and stood at the corner of her bed.

The general peeked in. "I do not remember the last time I was in a lady's room." He pushed his spectacles up his bulbous nose and stepped gingerly through the threshold. "How do you fare, my brave little soldier?"

She smiled. He had not called her that in a very long time. "Fine."

He clasped his hands and rested them on his large stomach. "Robert is resting comfortably at his home. The Earl of Swathmore was past all bearing with worry, but we finally got him settled when he realized his son had suffered merely a scratch. Then, after hearing the details, well, he was prancing around like a peacock, so proud of his boy's heroism." He nodded solemnly. "You did well, Charlotte. Everyone is safe due to your deeds."

"A group effort," she replied shakily.

He nodded. "Aren't all the good ones?" He sighed. "You just need to rest assured that for now, at least, your job is done. You, my dear, are simply in charge of one thing: to rest your weary body."

It was as if a weight lifted off her chest, suddenly allowing her to breathe. "You . . . you will stay here?" she asked tentatively.

He beamed his loving grandfatherly smile. "Right downstairs."

Smiling tremulously, she nodded. Her eyes suddenly felt leaden and her body sagged with fatigue. Aunt Sylvie and the general slipped silently out and she leaned back against the covers and collapsed. Her shoulders sank into the pillow, she snuggled her head in deeper, she closed her eyes, and blessed sleep wrapped her in its welcome arms.

A ghost with sharp white teeth was chasing her and Margaret. They ran through a meadow and into a forest. The trees and branches scraped at her face, her hands, and legs as she pulled her sister, desperately trying to get through the woods. Margaret kept stopping to check her bonnet. "Margaret!" Charlotte screamed. "You must move faster or he will get us!" She dragged Margaret through, but her skirts kept catching on the thistles. Her sister fell behind. The white-toothed monster charged closer, his gigantic jaws open and bearing down. "Margaret!" she screamed.

"Charlotte, wake up. It's only a dream."

She threw open her eyes and searched wildly for her sister. "Margaret?"

James said patiently, "Margaret is safe at home. Edward sent over a note that she is doing fine. Complaining, actually, about having to stay abed."

She let out the breath she was holding as her senses awakened and she came out from the dream. That sounded just like Margaret. She shuddered and looked around the room. The chamber was dark, except for the lines of light stretching across the floor from the open doorway to the adjacent room. The house was quiet. James sat on her bed, his hand resting lightly on her arm. His other hand lay in his lap, wrapped in a thick white bandage. He wore a burgundy dressing gown and smelled of soap, wine and . . . pie?

"What time is it?" she asked, suddenly nervous having him in her room, *on her bed*. Her face heated. She scooted up and he dropped his hand.

"About two in the morning."

She looked up at him but could not see his eyes for the shadows. "How are you feeling?"

"Sore, aching, hungry. You?"

She flexed her shoulders. "The same."

He nodded toward the open doorway. "I had a tray of food brought up to the sitting room. Care to join me?"

"Just give me a moment," she replied, not meeting his eyes.

He stood, and limping a little awkwardly, walked out the door, leaving it open. She grabbed her wrapper from the edge of the bed and pushed her long braid aside as she put it on. She walked into the cozy room and spied a large tray filled with cold meats, puddings, cakes, and pies on the table in front of the sofa.

She almost smiled. "Everything must be back to normal if I am hungry."

He stood next to the tray, pouring her a glass of wine. He held it out. She took it, sipped, and set it down. Awkward silence enveloped them, as if each did not know how to proceed after all they had been through.

"I smell pie," Charlotte noted, opting for the ordinary.

"Apple," he commented, a ghost of a smile lighting his swollen lips. "I misbehaved and went first for dessert."

She sat down and helped herself to a slice. She pierced a large piece, placed the fork in her mouth, and smiled. "Ummmm." She looked up at him, standing there watching her. "I imagine champagne is not exactly called for after this wild night."

He frowned, his face haunted. "Especially not after you kill your own flesh and blood."

"He may have saved me, James, but he was the only reason I was in peril in the first instance. The man was evil. Perhaps not to the core, but between the kidnappings and thefts and lord knows what else, well, Mortimer hated you with an unholy passion. He would never have let you rest."

He shrugged. "If anyone had to pay in this ghastly mess, it's best if it is him."

They sat quietly a moment. "Are you not going to join me?" she asked, licking a flake of crust from her lip.

He nodded and sat down, still not moving toward the food.

She looked up at him warily. "What is it?"

James looked down at his wrapped hand, playing with the bandage. "I just wanted to know . . . if you meant what you said."

"About what?" she asked guardedly.

"About marrying me. You said you signed on for my wedding . . ."

". . . Not your funeral," she finished. She took a deep breath and put the plate down on the table. Tense with apprehension, she bit her lip. "I just . . . just worry about our future."

He looked up, his dark eyes wary. "Why?"

"Because I always felt, believed, that the best marriages are based on mutual respect, admiration and . . . love."

He stiffened. "And that is why you think we will not do well together?"

"Yes."

"I see." He frowned.

The clock chimed half past the hour.

He stood and paced uncomfortably about the small chamber. "I, I meant what I said about being able to do anything if you are by my side, Charlotte. We respect each other and admire each other, I believe, and if you do not love me, then that may come in time. Or maybe my loving you is enough to sustain us. I don't know, but I really believe we have so much going for us, so much that we can be, that we can do together, that we should try."

She blinked. "W-what did you say?"

He stopped and stretched out his hand. "I think we should give it a try."

She shook her head impatiently. "No. The part about you loving me."

"What about it?"

She fisted her hands and took a deep breath. "Do you love me?"

"Of course. Did I not say that?"

She put her hand to her mouth and started to laugh, a low rumble deep in her belly. Tears formed in her eyes. "No, James. You skipped over that part."

He sat down beside her. "I thought it was understood."

She huffed, "That is *not* the kind of thing you leave unsaid."

"I am sorry. I thought it was clear."

"About as clear as the Thames." She wiped the tears springing from her eyes. "So I had better let you know in no uncertain terms that I love you deeply."

His eyes widened. "Really? You don't think I am a monster?"

She threw her arms around his neck. "Of course you are," she chided tenderly, her eyes watering uncontrollably. She gently kissed his swollen lips. "You are my monster, and I love you with all my heart."

He hugged her close, grimacing as she pressed against his chest wound. He held her anyway, shifting to his side.

She sighed happily. "I am just so relieved that you are not marrying me for the other reason."

He kissed her forehead and smiled. "I will have to confess all to the general. He was correct, as usual."

"The general? Was he the one who told you about the diamonds?"

"Diamonds? You mean the gold."

"You mean you truly don't know?"

"About what?"

She leaned against the back of the couch and laughed gleefully. "Now we *do* need that champagne."

"I will gladly get you some, Charlotte, as soon as you explain what you are talking about."

She held her hands to her mouth, beaming behind them. "I am an heiress, James. I own a fortune in South African diamond mines. I am as rich as Croesus!"

"Are you serious?"

"Yes. A few years ago Mortimer came to Papa trying to unload some land that he had won in a game of chance. Knowing Mortimer, he must have believed the land worthless. For the sake of your uncle, Papa took pity on Mortimer and executed the exchange. But Papa was curious about South Africa. He engaged a diamond mining firm to do some exploration. The mining was a great success. Papa formed a diamond mining company. My shares are my dowry."

He frowned. "I thought that was just a story to drive a wedge between Mortimer and Frickerby."

"It did that as well. But it was all true."

"Then that's why Mortimer wanted to marry you?"

"Why else would he want to marry me?" she asked, chagrined.

"I just assumed he had fallen in love with you." He shook his head, disbelievingly. "I found doing so easy enough myself."

"You are a silver-tongued devil." She leaned forward and snuggled closer, hugging him carefully.

"Only for you."

He pulled back, asking curiously, "But why didn't he try to marry Margaret? She must have the shares as her dowry as well. He had her in his power. It would have saved him quite a bit of trouble."

"Very amusing, James. First you tell me that you cannot imagine him not wanting me, and then you want to know why he did not want my sister," she teased. "Actually, Margaret does have some shares, but Papa knew me too well. He suspected that I was exceedingly particular about marrying, so he decided to make me so tempting a catch that I could not stay free for long."

He smiled. "He wanted you to be irresistible."

"Yes."

He brushed her hair from her face and curled it around her ear. "And he thought you needed diamond mines?"

She smiled, blushing at the compliment. "Sweet." She licked her lips and offered tentatively, "What is mine is yours, James. So if you are strapped for funds . . ."

"Strapped for funds!" He huffed, "Why, it is not puffing to say that I am one of the wealthiest men in England. What on earth ever gave you the idea that I was up the spout?"

"Oh, stuff and nonsense," she replied through her smile.

"Just so you know that I have much to offer you, Charlotte . . ."

"—You mean, besides your brave, strapping form?" she

teased, as she pressed butterfly kisses along his jaw. "So you are still willing to put my dowry in trust for charity?"

"It is completely up to you, Charlotte. I want you, only you." He squeezed her tightly.

A swell of gladness enveloped her, bringing fresh tears to her eyes. "I love you, James," she whispered.

"And I love you." He smiled down at her tenderly. "And I will love you forever and will never, ever let you go."

She beamed wickedly. "Is that a promise or a threat?"

"That depends."

"On what?"

"On whether you are going to finish that piece of pie."

**Don't Miss Any of the Fun and Sexy Novels
from Avon Trade Paperback**

Filthy Rich
by Dorothy Samuels
0-06-008638-6 • $13.95 US • $22.95 Can
"Frothy and good-natured . . .
it's part *Bridget Jones Diary*, part *Who Wants to Be a Millionaire*."
New York Times Book Review

Ain't Nobody's Business If I Do
by Valerie Wilson Wesley
0-06-051592-9 • $13.95 US • $20.95 Can
"Outstanding . . .[a] warm, witty comedy of midlife manners."
Boston Herald

The Boy Next Door
by Meggin Cabot
0-06-009619-5 • $13.95 US • $20.95 Can

A Promising Man (and About Time, Too)
by Elizabeth Young
0-06-050784-5 • $13.95 US

A Pair Like No Otha'
by Hunter Hayes
0-380-81485-4 • $13.95 US • $20.95 Can

And Coming Soon

A Little Help From Above
by Saralee Rosenberg
0-06-009620-9 • $13.95 US • $21.95 Can